Sonnedragon

A Novel by Kathryn L. Ramage

The Wapshott Press

Sonnedragon

Published by
The Wapshott Press
PO Box 31513
Los Angeles, CA 90031

The Wapshott Press

www.WapshottPress.com
www.KLR.WapshottPress.com

First printing September 2013

ISBN: 978-0-9848325-1-4

06 05 04 034 3 2 1

Wapshott Press logo by Molly Kiely
Maps and shields design by Molly Kiely and Kathryn L. Ramage
Cover design by Michelle Mauk
Dragon photograph by Pablo Debat

Also by Kathryn L. Ramage

The Wizard's Son

Maiden in Light

Sonnedragon Shield

Marchion Family Crest

UINLAND
(a Skandinavian colony)
Pendaunzel
Storm Port
New York
Guylliansburghe
Myame River
Micheline River
Eduardesmarch
PRINCELAND
Dennefort
Spainfort
Atlantic Ocean
TERROJOS
(The Redlands)
Iardinez
Tenochtitland Sea
N

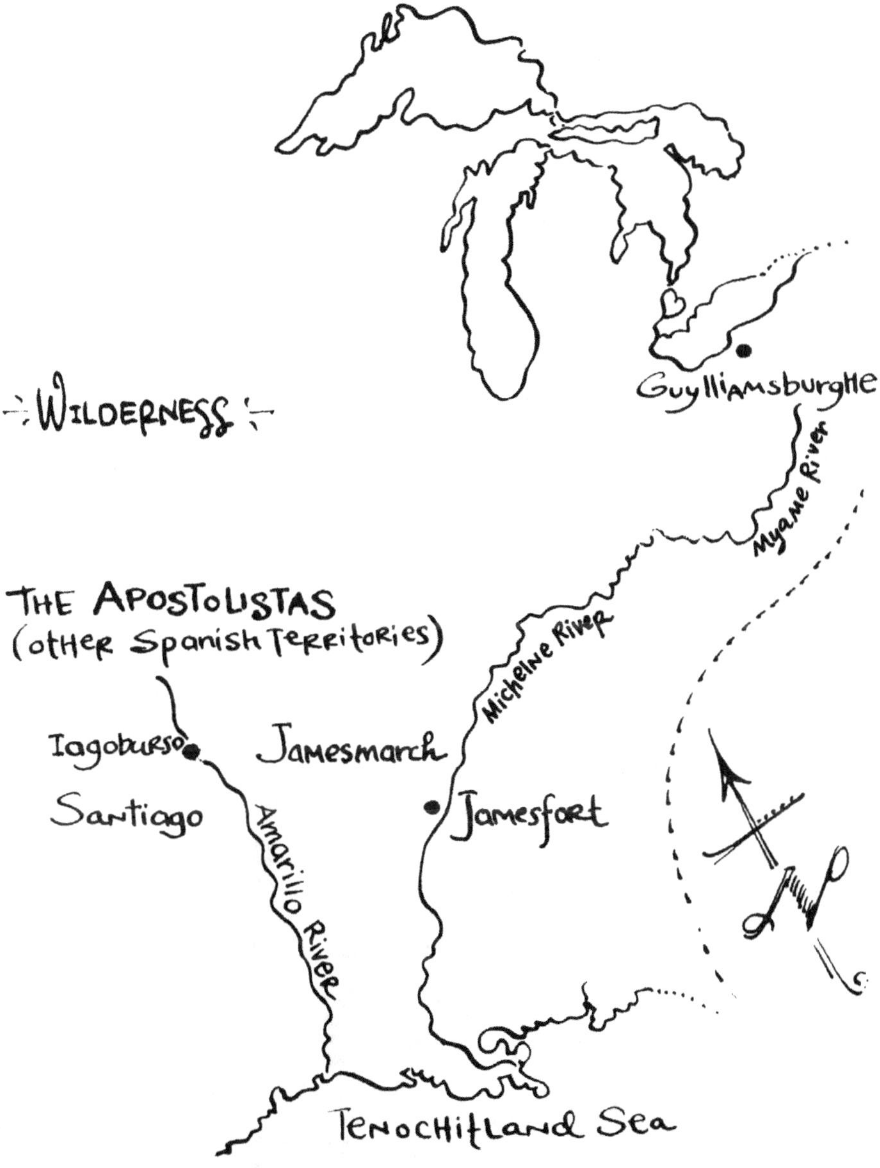

Wilderness
Guylliamsburghe
Myame River
The Apostolistas
(other Spanish Territories)
Micheine River
Iagoburso
Jamesmarch
Santiago
Jamesfort
Amarillo River
N
Tenochitland Sea

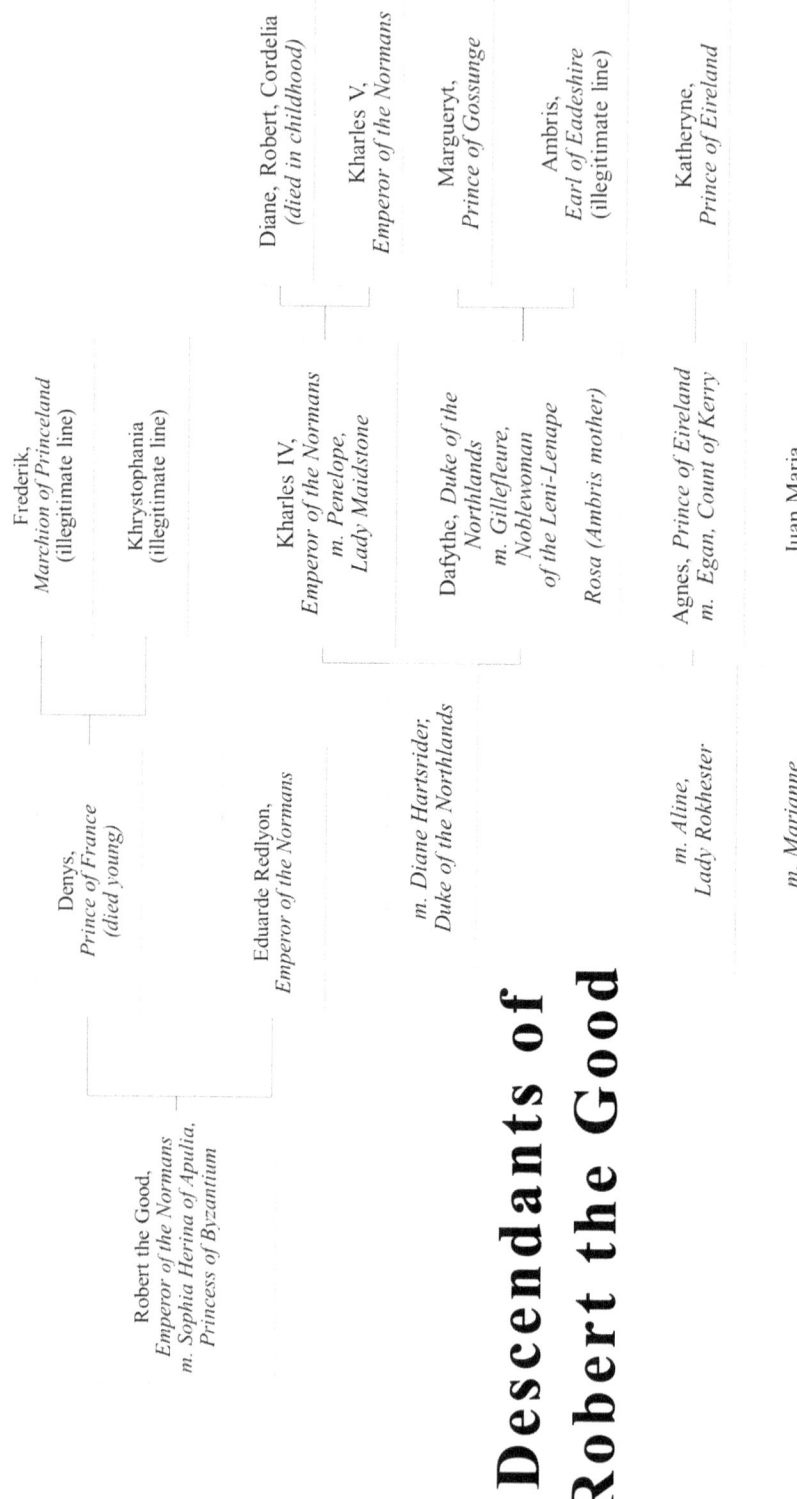

Descendants of Robert the Good

- Robert the Good, *Emperor of the Normans* *m. Sophia Herina of Apulia, Princess of Byzantium*
  - Denys, *Prince of France* *(died young)*
    - Frederik, *Marchion of Princeland* (illegitimate line)
    - Khrystophania (illegitimate line)
  - Eduarde Redlyon, *Emperor of the Normans*
    - *m. Diane Hartsrider, Duke of the Northlands*
      - Kharles IV, *Emperor of the Normans* *m. Penelope, Lady Maidstone*
        - Diane, Robert, Cordelia *(died in childhood)*
        - Kharles V, *Emperor of the Normans*
      - Dafythe, *Duke of the Northlands* *m. Gillefleure, Noblewoman of the Leni-Lenape*
        Rosa (Ambris mother)
        - Marguerylt, *Prince of Gossunge*
        - Ambris, *Earl of Eadeshire* (illegitimate line)
    - *m. Aline, Lady Rokhester*
      - Agnes, *Prince of Eireland* *m. Egan, Count of Kerry*
        - Katheryne, *Prince of Eireland*
    - *m. Marianne, Infanta of Naufarre*
      - Juan Maria, *Prince of Naufarre*

The Family of Dafythe, Duke of the Northlands

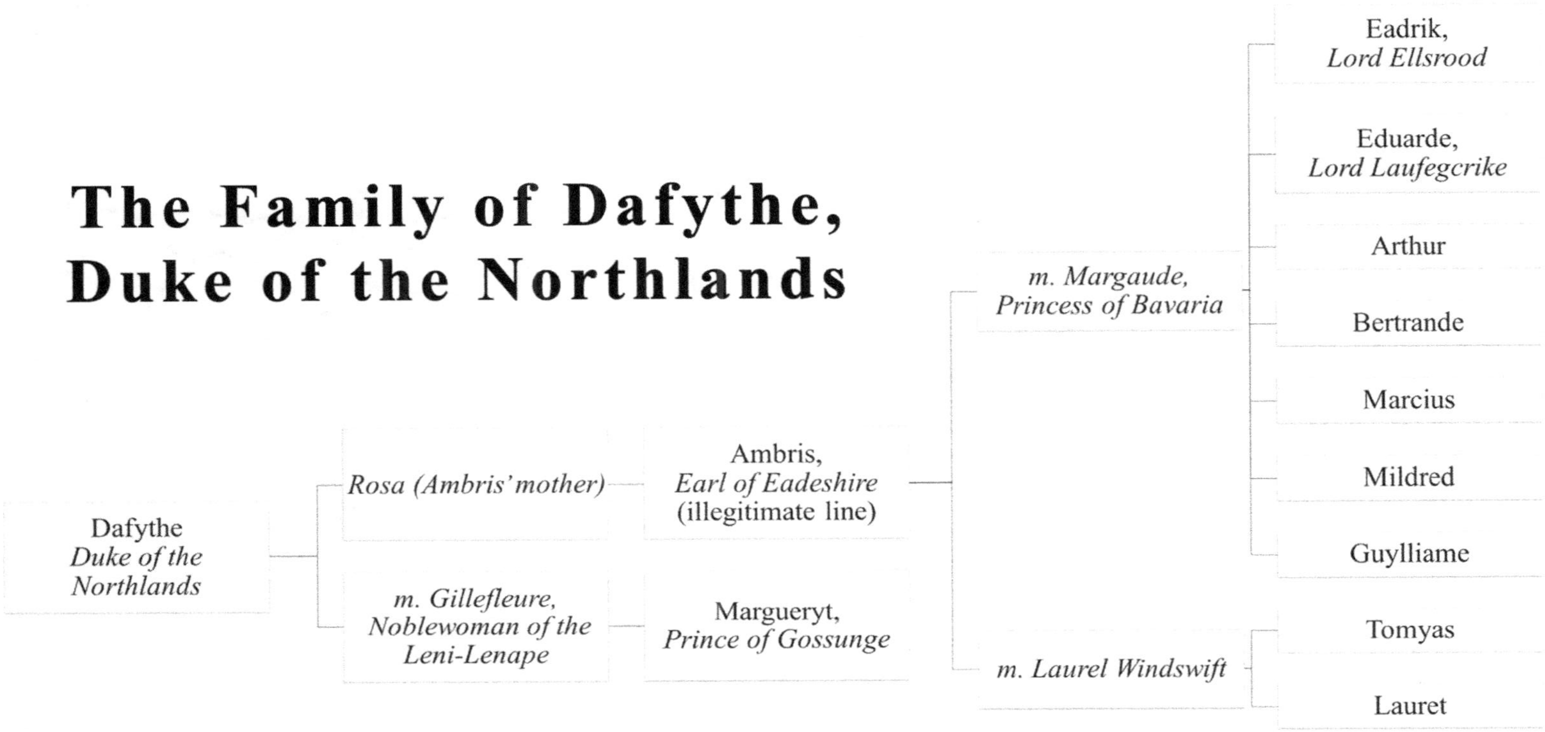

For Ginger.
If not for you, this book would never have been finished.

Sonnedragon

Table of Contents

Pendaunzel
1955

Santiago
1956

Pendaunzel
1957

Dramatis Personae

Dafythe: Duke of the Northlands, second son of the late Emperor Eduarde Redlyon.

Ambris: Duke Dafythe's illegitimate son, Earl of Eadeshire and Lord High Chancellor of the Northlands; later, Regent of the Northlands.

Marguerуt (Mara): Dafythe's legitimate daughter and heir; Prince of Gossunge; Ambris's half-sister.

Katheryne (Kat): Dafythe's niece and adopted daughter, nominally Prince of Eireland.

Laurel: niece to Lord Redmantyl, a lapsed magician and Ambris's second wife.

Eduarde Redlyon: the legendary 19th-century Norman Emperor; father to Kharles IV and Dafythe of the Northlands; died in 1901.

Denys: Prince of France, Eduarde Redlyon's elder brother, died in the 1840s.

Diane Hartsrider: former Duke of the Northlands; first wife to Eduarde Redlyon and mother of Kharles IV and Dafythe; died in 1881.

Marianne: Infanta of Naufarre, youngest daughter of the Emperor of Spain; third wife to Eduarde Redlyon and mother of Juan Maria.

Kharles IV, Emperor of the Normans, firstborn son of Eduarde

Redlyon and Diane; Dafythe's elder brother; died in 1939.

Kharles V, Emperor of the Normans, only surviving offspring of Kharles IV; Dafythe's nephew.

Juan Maria: Prince of Naufarre, youngest son of the late Eduarde Redlyon and half-brother to Kharles IV and Dafythe.

Frederik: Marchion of Princeland, on the southern border of the Northlands. Great-grandson of Prince Denys through an illegitimate line.

Khystophania, Frederik's younger sister.

Eadrik, Lord Ellsrood: Ambris's eldest son from his first marriage.

Eduarde, Lord Laufegcryke: Ambris's second son from his first marriage.

Arthur: Ambris's third son from his first marriage, Mara's squire.

Bertrande: Ambris's fourth son from his first marriage, one of the Dafythe's heralds.

Marcius, Mathilde, and Guylliame: younger children from Ambris's first marriage.

Tomyas and Lauret: Laurel's and Ambris's children.

Yryd, Lord Redmantyl: premiere wizard of the civilized world.

Orlan: Redmantyl's elder son.

Andemyon: Redmantyl's younger, adopted son; Dafythe's herald.

Othel, Lord Tuxsetau, Prime Minister of the Northlands.

Phyllida, Lady Peaque, Chief Justice of the Northlands.

Geoffrey, Lord Rafenshighte, Chief of the Duke's Diplomatic Office and a suitor for Margueryt.

Uismarde: Dafythe's Lieutenant of the armies of the Northlands.

Alyx, Belynde, Sautamie, and Martine: Friends and fellow Shieldmaids of Margueryt's.

Peter: Dafythe's court magician.

Delphyn: Dafythe's court bard.

Martleanne: Dafythe's secretary.

Rosandre, Lord Daubenai, a visiting dignitary from the court of Kharles V.

Forward

This is my third story set in the Northlands. It is not, however, a direct sequel to the first two—*The Wizard's Son* and *Maiden in Light*—but another part of an overarching storyline that involves the characters that appear in all three. *Sonnedragon* is the story of Prince Margueryt, heir to the Dukedom of the Northlands. It concerns the political, martial, and magical matters of Margueryt's life and times. *The Wizard's Son* and *Maiden in Light* have a more personal theme in common, concerning malevolent supernatural events that affect the main characters. How my characters react or fail to react to these events drives the narratives in those first two books.

The Wizard's Son introduces Orlan Lightesblood, a magically talented youth who is apprenticed to his father, the powerful wizard, Lord Redmantyl. After spending years in sheltered and rigorous training to become a wizard, Orlan travels beyond his father's castle to the city of Storm Port for the first time since childhood. During his visit to that city, his innocence is threatened by dark forces he doesn't understand or even recognize. These dark forces are only vaguely glimpsed in *The Wizard's Son,* but their intentions are revealed a little more clearly in *Maiden in Light*, the story of Laurel Windswift, Lord Redmantyl's niece. An extremely talented and promising young magician, Laurel is also apprenticed to Redmantyl. She is eager to learn all the secrets of wizardry, even those that are forbidden to her, and discovers the terrible duties wizards must perform to guard their world.

In *Sonnedragon*, the Norman Empire, which the Northlands is a part of, titles such as "prince" and "duke" are used by women who reign in their own right as well as by men. The usage would have begun centuries earlier when there were first ruling female emperors who were treated, and addressed, as if they were honorary men. This has some real historical precedence; Queen Elizabeth I sometimes referred to herself as a Prince of England, as for example in her famous speech at Tilbury. By the twentieth century, what were originally exclusively masculine titles have become commonplace regardless of gender.

I admit that I haven't provided much historical background for the Northlands or the Norman Empire in these novels. I've particularly avoided setting a definite point at which their world diverges from ours, but I have built my ideas for this alternate world on certain key changes during the Middle Ages. One difference is that the North American continent—here called Atlantea—was settled by Europeans much earlier, following the Viking colonization along the Newfoundland coast around 1000; I imagined that they kept these colonies up rather than abandoning them, and the Normans and Spanish sent out their own ships much earlier than Columbus's voyage to establish colonies of their own in the New World and, instead of eliminating the native population, absorbed them into their own cultures. A second difference is that the early Plantagenet rulers following the Norman Conquest held on to their territories in France, and the outcome of their version of the Hundred Years War was more successful, so that the British Isles and France have remained united as one empire for nearly seven centuries. There has been no Reformation. Another obvious change from the world that we know is that this alternate one has magic. But this is, after all, fantasy.

Unlike its European counterparts within the Norman Empire, the Northlands are a semi-autonomous dukedom. Located on the Atlantean continent, it covers approximately the area from the northern edge of Massachusetts, westward along the Appalachian mountains and south to Virginia. The Northlands are surrounded on the southern and western borders by sparsely populated marches to protect it from the neighboring Spanish territories. In the opening chapters of *Sonnedragon*, the Normans are not at war with Spain, but a long history of hostilities exists between the two great empires. Thus, the stage is set for Prince Margueryt of Northlands great adventure.

Sonnedragon

A Tale of The Northlands

Pendaunzel
1953

une

Whenever swords clanged against each other, Mara heard the ringing of the metal, clear and crystalline, urgent as a peal of church bells on a winter night calling the pure of heart from their warm beds to service. This was her service. She was guided by a higher power when she gave herself to swordfare. At this one moment, her mind was perfectly clear. She saw herself in motion. Her instinct never failed her if she acted instantly. Her faith was that of a knight in righteous cause. No candles, no chalice, no prayers save those she gave in the midst of battle—communion was achieved in the strike of blade against blade. The essence of life lay so near the danger.

Her opponent was her twin: the helm's curving cheek-guards bracketed a dash of grim mouth and square-set chin like her own. The eyes, watching her movements through the visor's grill, were blue while her own were hazel-flecked green, but the straight dark brows, drawn together in intense concentration, were nearly identical. The Shieldmaid's braids were like her own—two thin cords tucked in at the collar to protect the throat, two thicker ropes clasped back by a bronze clip—but a red-gold shade lighter than her own dark chestnut. They were dressed as twins: leathern arm-guard strapped to the shoulder of the sword-arm and fastened close at the wrist by a studded band; field gauntlets; light chain mail shirt under a short white tunic; scabbard belted at the waist; tall flat-heeled boots which covered the knee from the front; brief soldier's kirtle. Her opponent's shield bore the scarred image of a golden harp on field *azure*. Mara's own arms presented a hartshead *argent*, one star before its brow.

Left and right, left and right, Mara began to anticipate each stroke, to meet each blow before it fell. The dance was reflex. Abruptly, her foe swung left and left again lower, aiming at her knees. Mara leapt back to avoid the blade and swung at her opponent's head. The other ducked and came up at her from beneath. Mara had to jump again to deflect the blow on her shield rather than catch it in her ribs.

"Sweet Jesus!" she yelped as she skidded on the muddy grass. "You and your damnable traps!"

Her opponent laughed. At every match, she was more difficult to defeat.

"Ready, Mara?"

"When you are."

The assault resumed. Left and right, left and right, but Mara would not be lulled into the same trap. This time, she was prepared for the abrupt break in rhythm.

When her opponent's sword swung left and left again, Mara parried the second blow. The next feint came from the right in an undercut, then the blade arced to slice down from above. Mara swung up to meet it with her own sword. She was familiar with this tactic; her adversary meant to drive her back, to keep her maneuvers defensive. Each successive feint would draw her strokes broader, higher above, lower below, until she left her midsection vulnerable. She anticipated this too.

She broke the rhythm with a circular sweep. Her opponent's blade twisted to one side, and she swung down and thrust forward to the unguarded right flank. Her opponent, watching the blow fall and seeing that she could not dodge, responded with an unorthodox and completely unexpected defense. With a cry, she leapt forward, head down, shield advanced. Mara brought her own shield up. The flat of a blade slapped her helm. Their shields crashed against each other, the full weight of their bodies knocking them both down. A jarring jolt of pain shot up her left arm and Mara cried out as she fell to her knees.

"Mara, are you injured?"

Kat, her cousin and sparring partner, knelt over her.

Mara let her shield fall and cradled her throbbing arm. Tentatively, she moved the ends of her fingers then, encountering no fresh pain, wriggled her fingers more boldly, rotated her wrist, swung her arm at the elbow and shoulder. "No. Nothing's broken.

Let's go on. I'm ready."

"We ought to stop if you've been hurt–"

"I'm fine!"

But Kat had sheathed her sword. "You've said that before. Squire!" Their nephew Arthur, fifteen and bursting into ungainly adolescence, leapt down from the railings before the empty stadium seats. "Remember, you fell from your horse and broke an ankle at the tourney last winter, and got right back up and never said how it hurt until it swelled so great inside the boot they had to cut apart the leather to have a look at it."

"Honestly, I didn't feel it." Mara rose to her feet. It was spring; the playing field was slick with mud and wet grass from last night's rain. Her tunic and armor were spattered.

"You mean you wouldn't," Kat answered. "And only three months before that, you took a bad blow on that same arm. I won't match with you again `til you tend to it. You play too hard, Mara, for sport."

"Kat, understand this: in battle, we must overcome our physical discomforts and go on in spite of our injuries. Our lives depend upon it. A true foe would not be so merciful as you've been this day. For my weakness, I would've been cut down."

"But this was no true battle. Why risk increase to an injury in play and cripple yourself before you are called to fight?"

"All my injuries have been at your hands, Cousin," Mara answered, laughing. Young Arthur stood patiently at her side and she surrendered her shield to him. "In truth, I think you hold yourself back."

Kat shook her head in disbelief. "I'll never be so good as you, Mara."

She was Margueryt Cordelia Diane Sebastiane, Prince of Gossunge, Shieldmaid Commander, Chevalier Order St. Mykhael of the Holy Sword of Flame, the legitimate daughter and heir-apparent to Duke Dafythe of the Northlands. As first cousin to the Norman Emperor Kharles V, she was also next in line of succession to the imperial throne after her aged father so long as Kharles remained unmarried and fathered no licit child. At thirty-one, she was a vigorous woman in her prime, young enough to retain her ideals but old enough to strain impatiently at the bonds which kept her from achieving them.

Elsewhere in the world lived those who would think it odd that women of the highest birth should take up arms. Elsewhere, well-bred daughters were raised to perform domestic activities. Music, spinning, delicate needlecraft were appropriate; games with sword and shield were unseemly, unfeminine, immodest. Some would think Mara's pursuit of the warrior-life strange and remarkable—if they imagined it at all. Yet Mara and her cousin Katheryne took this vocation as their natural birthright, for this had been the way of Norman imperial daughters for centuries, since Eduarde Victor had named his firstborn Elizabeth heir before his infant son. A woman who would rule in this mighty Empire must be able to defend her given land and title. No one, not husband nor brother, could bear that responsibility for her; the earliest female Emperors—Elizabeth among them—had been betrayed by both.

Little princelings, boys and girls, were taught from childhood that battle waged for the sake of the Empire was their greatest service and highest honor. For an heir-apparent, this education was especially crucial. Younger sisters might have the luxury of dainty pursuits, but the firstborn couldn't afford to be demure.

Mara been born a Prince. From the cradle, she heard tales of her glorious ancestors: Kharlemagne, Rykharde Lyonheart, Robert the Bruce, Margueryt the Bold—how proud she had been at this legendary namesake! She was a daughter of ancient royal lines: Plantagenet, Stuart, Capet, a dozen others who had won their kingdoms through conquest. Their blood ran in her veins. Long before she understood its urgency, she felt the call to arms.

She hadn't forgotten the first exhilarating clash of tin when her elder and illegitimate brother Ambris had taught her the art of fencing. Norman princelings learned the rudiments of swordplay as soon as they were old enough to hold a hilt in their two small hands and Ambris, an excellent swordsman himself as a diplomat must be, was an adroit instructor. Even today, when he could be persuaded to spar with her for the sake of exercise, he moved with admirable elegance and dexterity, but he had no passion for the game. It didn't fire his blood as it did hers. From the moment she'd first held a sword as a little girl, she'd known that this wonderful sport was what she was meant for. Her first strokes and parries with the light foil seemed as natural as taking breath.

Her education had prepared her for a military life. She studied the Crusades with fervent interest and memorized the details of every campaign conducted against the Spanish by her illustrious grandparents, the Emperor Eduarde Redlyon and Duke Diana Hartsrider. She studied the most famous warrior women: Boudicca, the British matriarch who fought so fiercely against the Romans; Alys Ladyeknight, called the Last Holy Roman Emperor though her rightful legacy was never acknowledged by the Pope, for Sallic Law did not permit the title to descend through the female line; Elizabeth, the first Empress to rule both Angeland and France. Mara's father had instructed her tutors, the Brothers at Belminstre Abbey, to frame her lessons in terms which encompassed her interests. She learned Latin to read Caesar's campaigns in Gaul. Her mathematics excelled when she calculated the trajectories of rocks thrown from catapults, and she gave her most careful attention to budgets when she was asked to estimate the expense required to feed and equip armies of varying sizes. Heraldry taught her to recognize the arms of every noble line in Europe and the civilized parts of Atlantea.

Her knowledge of modern languages, however, was never more than rudimentary and she could never take an interest in law. Once she became Duke, she would have councilors and ministers to see to such dull things as trade agreements and civil contracts. Ambris, she trusted, would be as valued an advisor to her as he was to their father.

At sixteen, she entered the service of an ancient pensioned knight who held a small fief outside Pendaunzel. As squire, she learned to care for horses and gear and heard exhilarating stories of her master's campaigns with Eduarde Redlyon in the Northlands marches.

At eighteen, she entered the Shieldmaids. This elite regiment had been created in the sixteenth century by the Emperor Mildred Shieldmaid, who led a company of noblewomen on Crusade. Since that time, female Emperors and Princes traditionally appointed Shieldmaids to their personal honor guard, and young women of the royal family with an interest in the military invariably trained with them. Today, the Shieldmaids were a small force which conducted itself as a semi-religious order; their warrior spirituality fostered Mara's own.

On Mara's first day at the isolated woodland camp, the Captain told the new recruits: "Learn this, cadets—we do not train you as men. Do not compare yourselves with male warriors. Few women possess great strength in their arms as men do, and the rest of us can only feel ourselves weak and inadequate if we seek to compete on that masculine basis." Mara, accustomed from childhood to wield a sword, had well-developed arms and shoulders, but many of the girls with her were more sparely muscled. The Captain herself was slight and wiry. "You are women. Your strengths are elsewhere. Not upon the chest and arms, but in the leg. You have abilities men do not: your sense of balance is better, your endurance in physical hardships is greater, your reactions are quicker. These are the advantages you will learn to exploit to become the warrior-maids which are the pride of the Norman Empire."

The Shieldmaids taught young women defensive styles of hand-to-hand combat which emphasized strategy and ruthlessness before brute force. Even the most slender girls learned to use an opponent's own weight as a counterbalance and throw persons much larger than themselves over their shoulders, to escape a hold by breaking the grasping fingers or dislocating the restraining arm, to deliver powerful kicks. They learned to dodge and parry in dancing swordplay and to wield their blades with deadly dexterity. Some of the cadets had to overcome a certain squeamishness in carrying out violent assaults, but Mara did not.

In addition to these skills, the cadets learned medicine to employ emergency aid in dressing wounds and to locate the most vulnerable areas on an enemy body, pharmacology to recognize the plants and herbs which dulled pain or extended the stamina past the end of human endurance, metallurgy to recognize the qualities of the best swords and daggers.

The young Prince thrived under such rigorous training. Cadets spent long hours riding, tumbling, fencing, perfecting their archery, and more hours maintaining their equipment. No sword must become dull nor rusty, no leather gauntlet or hauberk stiff for lack of oiling, no bowstring frayed nor arrow unfletched. Every Shieldmaid bore this duty. The warriors, their horses, their gear must always be kept in peak condition; less was a disgrace upon the entire corps. Food was plain and filling and the cadets slept in cots placed row upon row in one long, low hall above the armory. They retired early and rose at dawn for prayers before their morning exercise. All the girls wore simple woolen garb which made their ranks indistinguishable.

It wasn't remarkable for a Prince, female or male, to receive intense military instruction; for most, it was the usual course. Mara had always expected to become a warrior, but the cadets she trained with—noble, merchant, and common-born—were for the most part misfits and outcasts. Muscular, vigorous, unusually tall or aggressive, many were considered too unattractive to marry well or too wild to take a productive place in their own social ranks. Norman citizens honored their warrior caste, but few wanted their daughters to join it. For many noble-born and merchant damosels, athletic interests were boyish and unseemly. For farm maids, physical strength was valued, but the peasant girls who came to the Shieldmaids were disinclined to spend all their energies working one plot of land for the rest of their lives. They were maids like Mara, but brought up to think differently of themselves and their prospects. They heard the call to arms too. They had their dreams of glory. They were a rowdy lot, freed for the first time in their lives from conventions and expectations which had repressed their natural spirits. They were full of noise and pranks and quarrels, but somehow the officers of the camp managed to guide that energy into useful channels. The officers understood; they had once been wild young girls themselves. Daughters of shopkeepers, millers, and rustic aristocrats, these incorrigible young hoydens became disciplined soldiers.

Shieldmaids were traditionally true maidens; the regiment had once demanded a vow of chastity throughout the years of service. These days, however, while cadets were cloistered as carefully as novice Sisters, older women were permitted to marry or to take lovers in discretion. Unlike the other maids, Mara meant to marry once a suitable bridegroom was discovered. That was also a Prince's duty.

It was unspoken regimental policy that a royal daughter rose to command eventually, but Mara needed no favoritism. She gave her training the same singlemindedness she'd given her schooling and her fellow Shieldmaids admired her greatly for her zeal and perseverance. Her superiors praised her. She rose through the ranks rapidly, from guardsmaid to captain to commander in three years. Any company she led was eager to follow her. Her cousin Kat had been among the first troop under her command.

Her reputation was born then; before she came of age, it was said that the Duke's daughter was a most remarkable young maid. Even now, the friendships and loyalties she'd formed with her sister-Shieldmaids were maintained. The small honor guard of Shieldmaids Mara kept at the Palace was led by one of her old companions, Captain Belinde of Storm Port. Even when Mara was not dressed for sparring or in the company of her guard, she wore the four long braids of a Shieldmaid with pride.

She was knighted at Belminstre on her twenty-first birthday. After she had confessed and received communion from the Archbishop himself, she'd spent the night in vigil in the Duke's Chapel at the cathedral, kneeling on the cold stones before the altar in a plain shift. A single candle glowed in the darkness. She'd expected to receive a vision from St. Mykhael the sword-bearer, patron of knights, or from St. Parsyfal, patron of the Holy Cause; they would sanction her knighthood by sending her a sign. This sign, the image of her talisman beast, would provide her with spiritual guidance. She would take it for a battle-name and bear its image on her personal arms.

Knees aching against the stone, fingers clumsy with cold as she told her rosary beads, she recited Aves through the night. She said the prayer of St. Mykhael, the prayer of the Sangrael, prayers that were vows of her devotion, prayers for the blessings of her namesakes Margueryt and Sebastian and for the blessing of St. Othelie, patron of the Northlands. She prayed for her mother, who had died that spring. She prayed for the intercession of her conquering ancestors who had surely gone to Heaven and she prayed for the souls of warriors who had died in righteous causes. She prayed that she would be made one of their worthy company, a true knight before the eyes of God. She thought once or twice that she dozed, but she received no vision.

At the time, girlish guilt had overwhelmed her. In spite of her efforts, had she been deemed unworthy? Was her knighting not blessed? Was she too base and vile in her sins to receive the most holy sanction? Her prayers became more simple and urgent: O

Lord, make me a knight. Grant me a holy cause in Your Service. She considered casting aside all worldly titles and possessions and joining the sisterhood of some strict and secluded order, or perhaps taking a pilgrimage to Rome or Jerusalem.

She had since learned that many knights received no vision on that night of vigil. The sign only came to them after they proved themselves in battle.

In the morning, her attendants entered the chapel. A cloak was thrown about her shoulders and she was led into a small private chamber where a copper tub was filled and waiting. Mara bathed, the warm water easing her stiff limbs and soothing her chilled skin, then she was dressed in robes of white samite spun with gold. She met her father in the nave of the cathedral. There, before a crowd of courtiers, clerics, and other witnesses, she vowed her undying loyalty to Christ and to her liege-lord and her vigilant service against the enemies of both. She promised unceasing generosity to the poor, protection of the weak and defenseless, a readiness to fight for justice whenever she might be called by any petitioner, noble or common, as befit the honor and dignity of her place as a knight. The famous Dentelyon, sword of her grandfather Redlyon, was laid upon one shoulder, then the other, and she rose Chevalier Layn Margueryt, Order of St Mykhael. The emblem of her order, a tiny sword, gold hilt studded with jewel chips, blade twisted like a flame and enameled red, was worn on her tunic breast.

As a Norman Prince, Mara believed she had a special relationship with God and her patron saints. By the divine right of royal birth, she was obliged to fulfill certain responsibilities. She was to govern the lands bestowed upon her—now the province of Gossunge, later the Dukedom and perhaps more—and to provide for and protect all citizens subject to her. From childhood, the duties of a prince were impressed upon her. There were things she must and mustn't do, things she must know, skills she must master in order to fulfill the obligations of her place. But, beyond these responsibilities of any other prince, she believed that she was also born to a solemn and holy purpose bestowed upon herself alone. She had a personal mission which would be gloriously revealed to her one day.

All her life had been spent in preparation for this purpose, yet

Mara had never once seen a battle.

The Norman kingdoms had known peace for nearly sixty years. The Redlyon's sons, Kharles IV and Dafythe of the Northlands, had established boundaries, alliances, trade agreements and safe routes, and lived on terms of truce and mutual respect with all nations since the old warrior had put up his sword. In Norman lands, a generation of citizens had been born and grown to maturity without knowing the threat of invasion, the destruction of a city, the famine of a burnt land, the bloodshed and sorrow and death which are inescapable in times of war.

In such moderate times, Mara had no hope of waging war, no matter how just and holy she considered her cause. Yet she was not the only one to yearn for the historic days of battle. The Empire was built on conquest. Angeland, Gallys, France, Skotsland, Eireland, the Northlands and Burgundy—each in turn had been overtaken by the noble family which had first called themselves Princes of Normandy. Through the intermarriage of royal houses and a series of bloody campaigns, the Norman Empire had grown to become the largest and most prosperous in the world. Its citizens took pride in their history. Elders recalled the days of Eduarde Redlyon with nostalgic fondness. Every little child could tell the sad tale of how Prince Denys, the Redlyon's brother, had been cut down so cruelly at Princemarch. Modern times were unexciting in comparison: people looked to the young Emperor Kharles V, the expatriate Irish Prince Kat, and especially the promising Mara for a return to the exciting days of old. She was the Empire's hope.

Pendaunzel Palace was no single castle, but a cluster of fourteen major buildings and a number of smaller houses within the shelter of ancient ramparts on the hilly parkland at the northern end of the city. The towers and spires of the great halls rose above the trees: Hartshall, the Hall of Record, the old castle keep, the stadium, the chapel of St. Othelie, and the Manor. This last, the Duke's residence, had been built from the stones of the original castle late in the last century and was commonly taken for all the palace by Pendaunzel visitors. The round keep on its mound remained intact behind the two wings of the modern building, though the moat had been filled in and a long, curved portico was set on the slope before it. Antiquated annexes and abutments joined the modern structure at odd angles and old towers rose at unexpected points, but trees grew close on all sides and an abundance of ivy concealed any awkward convergence of old and new.

The Duke's private apartments were on the ground floor of the east wing; his physician kept rooms nearby, for Dafythe of the Northlands was very old. Mara went to see the physician first. Dr. Dimitrios felt the bones of her injured arm, then flexed each joint for signs of pain before he affirmed her diagnosis: no bones were broken, but he predicted bruises and stiffness in the days to follow. The wrist was bandaged and the arm restrained by a linen sling. The Princes then sent their nephew Arthur to the wardroom upstairs with their gear and went down the lower corridor toward the entrance hall.

The Duke's Manor was built in the most modern style. Nothing was dim or dismal. No narrow, deep-set portals reminiscent of arrow slits here, but large multi-paned windows which let in light. Polished marble squares paved the floor at ground level; above, the floors were parquet. High arches along the length of the building supported the thin walls, and numerous sconces held candles for lighting the way at night. The intervening spaces were painted white and pale yellow and covered by decorative tapestries depicting great events in the Northlands' history: the brave little ships of Robert Gilthair sailing across the ocean to establish a Norman colony before the Scandinavians could lay claim to all the newly discovered continent; St. Othelie preaching to the pagans in the wilderness; Duke Maud's charging through the mountains in the battle of Bloodecrike; Prince Denys dying at Spanish hands.

As the Princes approached the entrance hall, they heard sounds of commotion ahead. Someone of importance had arrived. By the time Mara and Kat reached the open gallery above the hall, however, they found no more than the aftermath. The great door had shut. Grooms had taken the horses to the stables. Porters had carried away the visitors' baggage to the west wing. All that remained were two youths left alone, forgotten in the confusion. The elder, perhaps twenty with silver-white hair falling nearly to his waist in a froth of curls, was defiant in his uncertainty. The angelic-looking younger boy stood close beside his brother—surely, in identical traveling clothes of sooty gray, they must be brothers—and looked up and around the hall with undisguised wonder and bewilderment.

"Orlan! Demy!" A voice cried out from the opposite end of the gallery and the Lady Laurel rushed down. She embraced and kissed both boys in turn, which clearly embarrassed them even though they were relieved to see her. "I saw the bags go by. Are you come to stay long? Where's my uncle?"

The elder boy answered, "When he heard the Duke was at Council, he bid Andemyon and I find our rooms and he walked away."

Laurel was Ambris's wife. She was a young woman, twenty-six, and not gentle, soft, nor delicate enough to be considered a beauty by common standards, but her exotic appearance drew attention. Natives of the Northlands were usually more dark than their European cousins, but the Lady's complexion was ivory, her hair ash-white with a silvery sheen, and her eyes the palest shade of gray. She was also more than six feet tall, a height which Mara envied.

There'd been a mild scandal when Mara's brother had married this mysterious maid half his age. Niece to the wizard Lord Redmantyl, Laurel was the orphaned and illegitimate daughter of a garrisoned guardswoman and a magician herself though she had left her apprenticeship to marry. She had arrived at the Palace dressed like a traveling thespian in breeches and old-fashioned lace, and she handled a sword like a professional soldier—in fact, she had been briefly attached to the New York garrison where her mother once served. Mara had come to love her as a sister even before the wedding.

As the Princes stepped out along the gallery, Laurel looked up and said, "Why, Mara, what's happened to your arm?"

"I had a bad bang this morning on the playing field and the old fusspot healer will have it bound up all this week," Mara answered as she came down. "No riding, no fencing. You'll have to spar with Kat and keep her on her best. You need the exercise yourself, I daresay, after the baby."

Laurel laughed and turned to the boys. "You must come up

and see your nephew. Oh, Mara, Kat, may I present my cousin, Orlan Lightesblood, and this is Andemyon."

The boys were uncertain as to the correct behavior when meeting muddy and battle-geared royalty.

"What's this about a Council-meeting?" asked Mara once the appropriate courtesies had been exchanged.

"Hadn't you heard?"

"We were out all morning," said Kat. "What's happened?"

"`Tis said the Prince Juan Maria has betrothed himself to a Spanish princess."

"God's Body!" Mara cried. "Marry a Spaniard! It can't be! Kharles won't allow it. Juan daren't go against the Emperor."

"What does my uncle plan to do about it?" Kat asked.

"I don't know," Laurel answered. "Ambris went over to Hartshall immediately after breakfast and the Council's been talking it over since. I've heard nothing else." She took Andemyon by the hand and led both boys up to the nursery. Kat went with them.

"Are you coming, Mara?" the Irish Prince asked, turning back at the top of the stairs.

"No, I have to go and find Father. If this tale of Juan's treachery is true–"

Kat nodded. "There'll be hell to pay for it."

Mara left the Manor through the lowest level of the west wing and crossed to Hartshall, which was separated from the Manor by a statue-lined avenue. Hartshall was full of people; councilors, ministers, secretaries, clerks, pages, officers in the palace guard went up and down the corridors, all busy. All the branches of the government had their central offices here. Half a dozen courtiers stopped Mara in her search for her father to ask what she knew of the Naufarre situation, but the Prince could give no answer.

At last, she found her brother Ambris, Earl of Eadeshire and Lord High Chancellor, in the corridor outside the Advisory Chamber, where the Duke's Council met. Broad-browed and square-chinned, his resemblance to his younger sister was conspicuous, but he was forty-nine years old and half a head taller—as tall as his wife—and the features of his face more sharply defined. His hair was black and curly with glints of red where it caught the light and his complexion was Mediterranean; his mother had been a Spaniard. The thin, dark lines of short-clipped beard and mustache framed his mouth. He wore the gold-shot green robes of the Chief of Council and a heavy chain of office hung about his neck. The sash across his chest bore three golden lions, a token that he was recognized as a son of the imperial family even if illegitimate.

His face was drawn into a frown of great intensity, as he wore in times of crisis. When he saw his sister, he smiled, but the tense line between his brows did not relax. "Lord Redmantyl's come," he told her.

"Yes, we just met his sons," she answered.

"I wonder if they'll be here long. It's a most inconvenient time for guests."

Ambris's dismay wasn't for the boys, but for their father. Lord Redmantyl didn't approve of the marriage of his magical niece, even to the Duke's own son. A powerful wizard like Redmantyl wouldn't forgive the loss of so promising an apprentice easily; Ambris expected unpleasantness when courtesy obliged him to greet Redmantyl as a visitor to the Duke's household.

"Where's Father?" Mara asked.

"He left Council. At his age, he may take the privilege of calling for a recess whenever he chooses. We've been speaking together since, but can't come to a decision without him. I don't see a smooth way out of this difficulty if Juan can't be made to retract his position."

"We must stop him!"

"Yes," Ambris agreed, "or bind Juan's plans ineffective."

"What do you mean?"

"If Juan's betrothal to the Spanish Infanta indicates his intent to return Naufarre to Spanish hands," he explained, "he acts expressly against the terms of Grandfather Redlyon's marriage treaty."

"You aren't going to go on about treaties, are you?"

Ambris smiled. "Mara, the problem hangs upon that treaty."

To Mara, it seemed a waste of time to talk to Ambris in his legal moods. At heart, her brother was always a lawyer: if allowed, he would baffle her for the rest of the day with Latin phrases and obscure precedents of international agreement going back to the first days of the Empire. "What will Father do?" she asked before he could begin.

"I don't know. This situation may be too dangerous to be resolved peaceably."

Mara leapt upon this. "You mean, we may have war?"

Ambris's reply was cautious: "Feeling is high. Public sentiment against the Spanish hasn't changed one grainsweight since the last of the Redlyon's wars. Father can speak all he likes of sixty years of peace, but it doesn't put an end to hostile feelings. We Normans only want the opportunity to pick up where we left off, and Juan may give it to us whether he means to or not." His forefinger tapped her brow, a playful gesture. "Many are eager to see the old days come again, Sister."

"And you?" she asked.

"I hope it doesn't come to war, but it would be foolish not to foresee that probability."

"What would you have us do?"

"It's Father's choice, and Kharles's. We must follow the Emperor in this matter, if only we had a clear idea what he intends to do. We can't send out troops when they haven't been requested, nor send them to one location when they might be needed elsewhere." He sighed. "The difficulty is that this news is weeks old. Juan may have already sealed his betrothal in defiance, or Kharles sent troops to Naufarre to put the rebellion down, or the entire problem solved peaceably as Father would wish."

Mara found her father in the library. The Duke was in conversation with a lordling dressed in dusty, black riding clothes and the scarlet rune-woven mantle which gave him his title.

Pendaunzel had seen little of Lord Redmantyl's magic, but his power was undoubted. He'd defeated all other wizards to achieve his status as premiere wizard in the western world and he was therefore looked on as a sort of hero. No other Norman citizen had engaged in battle this century. And, more than that, Redmantyl was still a young man, not far past fifty, handsome and powerfully built, as strangely fair as his niece and elder son, white hair long and tarnished-silver beard close-clipped in the modern fashion of noblemen. His physical presence was vibrant; the aged Duke seated before him seemed fragile and insignificant.

Dafythe of the Northlands was near his century, but his bearing remained upright and dark strands of hair were still visible in the long gray mane pulled back from his austere face. The lines at the corners of his eyes and mouth and upon his brow were cut deep, and a fine net of wrinkles covered his skin. Yet these aged features—mouth a thin-lipped dash, jaw heavy, chin squared and cleft, cheekbones prominent, brow high and broad, eyebrows a straight, thick line broken briefly above a patrician nose—were unmistakably like those of Mara, Kat, Ambris, like the features stamped onto coins and carved onto statues commemorating the long line of Norman Emperors.

The royal face. Centuries of intermarriage had reproduced these same features on many faces with little variation. Royal and noble cousins throughout Europe bore the same distinctive cast: the Tsar of Russe, the Scandinavian King and the Grand Doge of Venice each looked more like the Norman Emperor than any resembled their own subjects. In an earlier, barbaric era, prime warriors governed by right of conquest. Today, a prince who carried the physical traits of these celebrated conquerors might stand six inches above the average height, large-boned, heavily muscled, and in relentless health. Royalty wasn't called to fight so often these days, but the physique remained and, with it, the implication that modern-day princes were able to hold the places their families had kept for so long.

Dafythe was the son of one Emperor, brother to another, uncle to a third, always a heartbeat from the throne. Duke of the Northlands for more than seventy years, for all the warrior-blood in his veins, he was a quiet man of education and civility. With his late brother, Kharles IV, he had shaped the *pax normania* of the twentieth century. The state of the modern world was in large part his own work, yet Dafythe wasn't spoken of with the great reverence bestowed upon his more flamboyant ancestors.

At Mara's entrance, Lord Redmantyl rose, and Dafythe brought the conversation to an end. "You haven't seen the baby yet?" he said to his guest. "You ought to. He's a fine little fellow. Nothing to shame any of his blood."

Lord Redmantyl seemed to take this as a command. "If I may do so now, My Liege."

"Yes, of course. I'll receive this boy of yours this afternoon.

Bring him to my chambers."

"Yes, My Liege. Gramercies. My Layn Prince." With a bow, the wizard went out.

The Duke took his daughter in at a glance—mud-spattered tunic, tall field boots, sling—but didn't ask, as if her condition were not remarkable. Why should he not receive wizards in riding leathers and princes in battle-gear? It was no day for formalities. He gestured to the empty seat before him. At his age, Dafythe wasn't willing to rise without good reason. "You have something to tell me, Mara?"

Her questions burst forth: "Father, what is this business? Juan's to marry again? What are we to do? She's a Spaniard!"

"Yes," Dafythe answered. "Serafina of Andalusia. She is young, I believe. The Infant Raimond's daughter and not long from the convent. We had the news this morning."

"You aren't distressed at it?"

"It seems extremely ill-advised for a Norman Prince to make such a choice. It is potentially treasonous. Kharles won't give his consent."

"Yes, but surely Juan will wed without it! It is in his blood, these sneaky Spanish ways."

"He is your uncle, Mara."

"I've never met him."

"Nevertheless, you must show some respect for his royal blood."

"Juan's blood is Spanish royal blood as well as Norman. He never forgets it. You know he's played this same sort of trick before."

Prince Juan Maria was Dafythe's half-brother, the child of Eduarde Redlyon's third marriage to the Infanta Marianne. The alliance with Spain was meant to establish peace between the warring nations. The Redlyon had been ninety-eight, and his bride twenty-five. Naufarre was her dowry; it became part of the Norman crown lands at the time of the marriage, but Marianne had resumed the governing of it after her elderly husband's death and it remained Spanish in all but taxation and garrisoned soldiery.

Juan was sixty now, but in his youth he'd been involved in a series of treacherous activities. He had incited the people of his mother's land to demand a release from Norman rule and, more provoking, had written letters to various rebel groups in the other Norman kingdoms encouraging them in their own subversive endeavors. This would have come to nothing, but Marianne seemed to give tacit approval to her son's schemes. Ambris, then a young diplomat in the late Emperor Kharles's service, traveled to Naufarre to conduct delicate negotiations with the Dowager Marianne and, in the end, Juan Maria was brought to Paris. The young man was kept under house arrest at the Louvre and met with his half-brother Kharles IV in private conferences. No one knew what was said between them, but after several months Juan returned to his homeland and married, at Kharles's direction, a Portuguese princess of reputed education and piety, and known Norman sympathies.

After the lady's death, fresh rumors of Juan's treachery reached the throne. It was said that Spanish mercenaries were established in Pamplona and war seemed imminent. Yet the young Emperor Kharles only sent a small compliment of soldiers into Naufarre as an auxiliary to the garrisons, and the uprising was quashed with little bloodshed. A state of tension had settled over Naufarre since. Relations between the Normans and Spanish were never more than coolly formal even in the best times, but all pretense of cordiality had disappeared. No one expected Juan to be inactive for long. Marianne was now an aged woman of eighty-six and much of her responsibilities were delegated to the renegade Prince. Naufarre was in his hands.

Mara had long ago grown accustomed to her uncle's sedition. Juan repeated his treason with such regularity that it was no surprise when the latest plot was revealed; like most Normans, she expected him to be put down quickly. Until today, she'd never imagined that actual war might be fought over Naufarre.

"Juan may marry without my nephew's approval," Dafythe agreed, "but I don't imagine he's foolish enough to take such an irretrievable step. It damages his own Spanish loyalties. Do you think he wishes to do that? If he weds this infanta, the alliance will be in direct contradiction with the accords of the Naufarre treaty."

It was as if shuttered windows in Mara's mind were suddenly flung open. Ambris had said this too, but Ambris was always on about one contract or another. "What are the terms of the treaty, Father, exactly?" She thought of all she had heard of it in her interminable lessons in legislative history. "Didn't you and my uncle Kharles draw them up?"

"Ah, that is precisely what I sought here." A loose scroll lay on the table at the Duke's elbow; he spread it flat and Mara twisted in her seat so that she could read with him.

As a border territory between France and Spain, Naufarre had been a source of contention for hundreds of years. Claimed by both empires, it had been the object of war after war. In the nineteenth century, the young Princes Denys and Eduarde had tried to take the long-disputed territory or, when that failed, another piece of Spanish land of equal importance. They fought furious battles in Naufarre, in the Madehef March in North Africa and, more successfully, in the Northlands' marches. Prince Denys had died young, but Eduarde fought on for over fifty years, his rage at his brother's death and his desire for revenge upon Spain unquenchable. In time, the lands now called Princeland, Eduardesmarch, Uolder, and Jamesmarch were his. His campaigns came to an end in 1892, when the unbending warrior-king had simply grown too old to wage one more war and at last heard the advice of his moderate sons.

The terms of the Treaty of Naufarre, signed by Eduarde Redlyon and Alamanzus the Great, were stated so simply that even one with no education in the law might understand: upon his marriage to the Spaniard Marianne and receipt of her dowry, Eduarde would remove his troops and cease all claims to the land between the Eduardesmarch and Iardinez, an area named Terrojos by the Spanish. So long as Naufarre remained Norman, this march would not be touched. A narrow barrier of neutral territory was established; this strip of land was termed the Shieldwall. Fortresses might be built on either side, but the encroachment of either Norman or Spanish troops would be considered an act of war.

"We meant to safeguard Norman interests in Naufarre," Dafythe explained. "You see, my father meant to have it at whatever cost. Kharles and I hoped to prevent the Spanish from reclaiming Naufarre as well as protect the Northlands' southern border by relinquishing all claims to lands beyond the current marches. Neither empire can hold both territories at once. It is a balance of rights and powers."

"But if Juan's marriage to the Spaniard takes place, then the treaty becomes void?" Mara asked.

"I fear it may be so."

Mara's thoughts were already turning upon the possibilities. Grandfather Redlyon and the Spaniard Alamanzus were long dead, their reasons for agreeing to the conditions of this treaty forgotten by their successors. The careful balance her father had achieved was already tipping dangerously. If Naufarre returned to Spain, the balance would fall.

Here at last was her opportunity! All those stories of brave warriors. All those mock-battles when she'd raised her sword against comrades and cadets, dreaming of the day when she would fight in earnest. All those years of waiting, wondering when her purpose would be revealed. Now was the time.

tu

Before dinner that evening the Duke received Lord Redmantyl in the private closet of his apartments.

“My Liege,” Lord Redmantyl introduced the young boy he had brought with him, “I present you my ward, Andemyon.”

Dafythe had assumed until this moment that the child must be Redmantyl’s unnamed son—Laurel often referred to both this boy and Redmantyl’s acknowledged son Orlan as her cousins—but he was now no longer certain. The silvery fairness of the wizard’s family was distinctive, and this boy nothing like them. Instead, he was gold-curled, rosy, blue-eyed and cherubic.

“Andemyon,” the Duke spoke directly to the boy, “welcome to my court. How old are you, lad?”

“Fourteen, My Gracious Lord Dafythe.” The child dropped to one knee and bowed his head with the practiced grace of a courtier or thespian. His voice, however, quavered.

“He was confirmed at Easter-week,” Redmantyl added.

“Indeed? What name did you take?”

The boy looked to Lord Redmantyl. “Tell him,” the wizard urged gently.

“`Twas Dafythe, My Lord.”

The Duke smiled. “An excellent choice. May I ask why?”

“My– My Lord Redmantyl suggested it, as you’ve been his most generous liege and he promised I would come here to your service,” the boy explained. “`Twas meant to honor you, My Lord Duke.”

“Well answered!” Dafythe had seen his share of unruly noble-born youths; he was able to appreciate well-mannered children when he met them. “You come to my service, lad? And how shall you serve me?”

“As you require me, My Lord.”

“Some of my heralds take up new responsibilities soon and

will need to be replaced," Dafythe told the wizard. "The child may be suitable. Andemyon, will you be a herald? It is an important first situation in my court. Your duties are simple: you'll accompany me at ceremonies, announce me, carry messages about the court and perhaps into the city, amuse me if you have any wit or talent, and occasionally sit up at night to attend me—my physician insists that I have someone nearby in case I fall ill. Are you willing?"

The boy was surprised to receive such an honor, but he answered modestly, "If you will."

"Does it please you as well, My Lord Redmantyl?"

"It does, My Liege."

"My own grandson has recently come from Samandra Abbey to begin his career at court. Andemyon, he's just your age." Dafythe turned to the open doorway and called out: "Bertie!"

A boy in heralds' garb—velvet knee-breeches and short tunic covered by a stiff tabard bearing the Dafythe's crest of three gold lions *passant* on a field of darkest blue—came in. A year younger than his brother Arthur, he was otherwise an identical sturdy and thick-set youth.

"My grandson Bertrande," Dafythe introduced the boy. "Bertie, I present you to My Lord Redmantyl, and this is Andemyon. Andemyon will join the heralds. Escort him to Old Toppet to have him fitted for livery. Introduce him to the other boys."

"Yes, Grandfather." Bertrande looked over the pretty, slight boy with curiosity and Andemyon stared back warily; they might be of an age, but the young lordling was much larger.

"Off you go." Dafythe dismissed them.

Once they had gone, the wizard said, "I'm grateful for your generosity, My Liege. I didn't expect so much for the boy."

"We are kinsmen now and it's time your family was brought forward. He's a handsome little lad, gentle, courteous," Dafythe replied, meaning to encourage a confidence. "I believe there was another matter concerning the boy which you wished to discuss?"

"I would request a second favor of you, My Liege. I wish to adopt Andemyon rightfully."

"Then he isn't...?"

"I cannot name him by Norman law," Redmantyl answered,

which was no true answer. "I don't make this request for reasons of inheritance—I have little beyond my title and Greenwaters Island, and those must go to my successor among the ranks of the magical unless you chose to alter that bequest. Orlan will be heir to anything else I have to leave. Andemyon may hope for little material wealth from me. I wish to call him my own son, no more."

Dafythe understood.

The love affairs of great wizards weren't usually a source of contemporary gossip, for it was assumed that wizards who reached the highest levels of power were beyond the baser passions. In his youth, Dafythe had met many wizards, including the three previous Redmantyls: Maxim Gnome, a tiny, wrinkled imp, no taller than Dafythe himself had been at fifteen; Moruen the Courtly—long before, as court magician to Duke Julia, Moruen had been a lively young woman who enjoyed a good dance and received and discarded lovers at a whim, but when Dafythe had met her, she was a chubby, merry, white-haired little creature very like the grandmotherly faeryes in folk tales; Dagobert the Paduan, a fierce-eyed, bald-pated Merlin with a snowy beard to his knees and a strict abstemiousness which suggested he'd forgotten such frivolous pastimes long ago. The great ones were wizened, austere ancients—so old, Dafythe reflected, as himself today. There were younger wizards too, wanderers of no remarkable powers and no established rank; their love-affairs passed without notice.

But *this* Redmantyl had come to his powers while still a youth less than forty. No gnarled little imp far past his prime, but a handsome, vital young man, powerful in physique as well as magic. If not for his red robes, he might be mistaken for a battle-weary knight.

The Duke bore a great admiration for Lord Redmantyl. The wizard was a prime example of what he believed to be the success of the modern Empire: the talented and intelligent were able to rise from low origins to positions of wealth and power. Redmantyl was common-born, a miller's son, but he conducted himself as elegantly as a nobleman of highest birth. He'd worked at it; the infamous boy-wizard Dafythe had first received at his court twenty years ago had spoken with conspicuous traces of a rural north-country accent. That provinciality had long since disappeared. The wizard's manners today were impeccable. He might be a son of one of the old families if his silver-fair appearance did not indicate some other more remarkable pedigree.

The more unsavory parts of the wizard's character Dafythe did not examine too closely. Redmantyl had killed fourteen wizards and destroyed the magic and minds of his remaining rivals, abruptly putting an end to the best of the last magical generation. All, of course, in his own defense—each had meant to kill him. Yet there was a touch of mystery about the death of the last Redmantyl, the reclusive Dagobert. Some said that his death had come later, not in the midst of battle with his former apprentice. Though the present Redmantyl always displayed perfect courtesy and deferential respect to his liege lord, no one could forget that he was a dangerous man. Dafythe felt as if he were master of a perhaps-tamed tiger; the beast had consented to be loyal to him and though he wasn't afraid for his own person, he sometimes imagined the damage it might cause if it capriciously chose to unsheath its claws or bare sharp fangs.

In spite of this implied danger, or because of it, and in spite of or because of the wizard's exotic appearance, women found Redmantyl attractive. There was always a flutter among the female courtiers whenever he visited.

Dafythe had heard stories of the wizard's dalliances. The mother of the little boy he'd just received was a wandering thespian, head of Redmantyl's patronized troupe, and a married woman. Andemyon might be her husband's child, but the wizard displayed astonishing affection for the boy. He'd taken him into his household at the thesper's death, had done all but name him. He proposed to do so now. Would he behave so if Andemyon weren't his own? The mother of Redmantyl's acknowledged son, it was whispered, had been a tavern drab. And the Lady Laurel was suspected to be his unclaimed firstborn, the daughter of an incestuous union with his own cousin.

"The papers might be drawn up during your stay here, My Lord. We can arrange a small ceremony—three persons to witness your claim of adoption." Three witnesses were required for any standard legal procedure. "Nothing extravagant. Much like that other claiming, if you recall."

Some years ago, the wizard had come to him with a similar

request for the sake of his elder son, Orlan. In that case, there had been no impediment; neither Redmantyl nor the boy's belated mother had ever married. The law required only that the young wizard declare his intention to marry the dead woman had she lived, since any children born to an unwed couple were automatically legitimate at the time of the marriage. This present adoption addressed a similar situation, if a slightly more delicate one.

Dafythe sympathized with Lord Redmantyl's efforts to name his sons. He was touched by the affection he observed; few men cared so much for their by-blows. Also, if he must be honest, he took some consolation in the ease with which he endorsed the rights of this other man's children. If only the situation with his own son Ambris could be resolved so easily.

Norman law permitted the acknowledgment of illegitimate children, but not to the disadvantage of the legitimate. History often recorded the monstrous results of such acts of generosity. Ambris wouldn't consider such treachery. Dafythe knew it. His brother Kharles, who had always had the power to name Ambris legitimate, knew it. The young Emperor knew it. Nevertheless, Ambris remained a bastard, a Prince in all but name.

The Emperor Redlyon had played his children as bargaining pieces, promising alliance through marriage to gain an advantage over the neighboring smaller countries and upstarts in his own kingdoms, yet withdrawing before the contracts were signed. In his youth, Dafythe had been betrothed to Leona of Napoli, Ysabella of Portugal, the Polish Prince Sarah, Katriana of Norway, Lorena of Hanover, and both the daughters of the Duke of Burgundy, sometimes two or three simultaneously. This political juggling had kept Dafythe and his brother Kharles in a bachelor state until they were both past fifty, but it didn't prevent them from taking occasional lovers.

These affairs could never last long; inevitably, the Redlyon would spoil his sons' romances once he discovered them. He wouldn't have objected, Dafythe believed, if they'd engaged in meaningless dalliances. But the Emperor's sons must be *serious* about women. Eduarde regarded such emotional attachments as weakness. Few things angered him more than the possibility of one of his princes falling in love. To Eduarde, women were creatures for pleasure. Wives were not fundamentally different from lovers, save that they were expected to provide their husbands with heirs. Diane, Aline, Marianne—none had had much power at court.

Dafythe's mother, Diane Hartsrider, had been Duke of the Northlands before him, though she lived in exile from her homeland after her marriage. As a child, Dafythe had heard tales of his mother's remarkable tactics when she'd led the Northlander troops in the first border wars. The skill of her riders was legendary. But she was long past those days of adventurous youth by the time he'd known her. He remembered her as a quiet woman who spent much of her time in her chambers, sipping wine and writing her memoirs. Eduarde often bragged of his wife's prowess in battle, but he wouldn't think of her riding out with him. A Lady's place was at her Lord's home. Dafythe guessed that there'd been a clash of great powers, and Diane had lost. He knew no more than this; the first years of his parents' marriage were obscure to him. He'd only learned recently from an unpublished history of the Redlyon's reign that Kharles hadn't been their firstborn. Two sons, both in turn christened Denys, had been born and died in the 1840's. Dafythe had never heard a word about their existence while his parents had lived.

When Diane had died in 1881, his father had summoned him to make a brief announcement: "Dafythe, you are now Duke. Arrange passage to Pendaunzel to assume your duties." Months had passed before he'd heard the details of his mother's illness and final days. His brother had written him, revealing what Dafythe had only suspected: Diane had been drinking heavily during the last years of her life.

Dafythe had been twenty-six and free of his father's forceful personality for the first time when he'd arrived at Pendaunzel and taken up residence in the ruins of the old castle. His mother's regent lived in a house in the city and the disused sections of the castle had been allowed to decay to an unbelievable state. It would be twenty years before he completed the construction of his new palace.

There were women during those early years, but young Dafythe dared not give his heart to anyone. He made no promises and when these lovers were sent away, he didn't miss them unbearably. Once he was past his first youth, Dafythe yearned more for a wife and children than another insignificant liaison. Then he had met Rosa.

My Lord's Love is a rose of Spain.
O where is she now? O where has she gone?
The path she leads down bears thorns of pain
O wither she? Wither she? Who?

My Lord's Love has raven hair
O where is she now? O where has she gone?
Dark as the nightsfall, this gypsy fair
O wither she? Wither she? Who?

My Lord's Love. Minstrels still sang of her.

Tradition recalled her as a sultry temptress, black-eyed and fiery-tempered, but Dafythe remembered a peasant girl with wild curls and a sharp, bird-beak nose. Not a beauty, but possessing a sulky sexual appeal. He'd first met her in Paris, when she'd been one of the maids in the Infanta Marianne's retinue. It was folly, he knew, to take as a lover a woman low-born, and Spanish besides. She couldn't be important to him. Yet she was. The depth of his emotions took him completely by surprise.

When duties recalled him to the Northlands, Rosa did not accompany him. She left the Emperor's court and Marianne's service soon after, but didn't return to Spain. Instead, she took up the life of a wanderer. Dafythe didn't know how she lived; from time to time, she arrived at Pendaunzel like a long-lost cat who returns safely home but remains coolly mysterious about its adventures. She offered no explanations, no promises, no more than her presence, and he was content with that. His desire for her was still strong, but he wasn't the sort of man to install a courtesan in his own household nor, of course, could he think of offering marriage to a peasant-maid even after the Redlyon's death. Always unimpressed by his exalted rank, she received his gifts, heard his loving words, and disappeared as abruptly as she had arrived.

My Lord's Love has gone again.
O where is she now? O where has she gone?
She's left my love heartsore and all forlorn.
O wither she? Wither she? Who?

My Lord's Love had gone again, but that was not the end of it. Some months after her last abrupt departure, she sent him a message from the almshouse at Belminstre: she'd given birth to a healthy boy. If Dafythe wished to claim his son, he would find him there.

His son. Dafythe's indiscretion wasn't that he'd made a fool of himself by loving an impossible woman nor that he'd fathered a bastard by her, but that he treated Ambris as he would a legitimate child. Eduarde Redlyon had fathered illegitimate children before Kharles and Dafythe and after them, but none were acknowledged as imperial offspring. They were cared for, educated, given positions befitting their mothers' stations, married well, but none were openly named as Eduarde's sons and daughters even if they appeared at court. Dafythe's secretary Martleanne was, in fact, the granddaughter of a child conceived during Eduarde's first visit to his son's dukedom. She didn't know it, but Dafythe advanced her career, as he'd promoted her father, now master-scribe in the Hall of Record, because they were his nephew and grand-niece.

After the bloody civil wars, royal bastards were an especially delicate matter. Provide for them, but do not know them—that was how a prince was expected to deal with his by-blows. Dafythe had been unable to do that. Once he'd gone to Belminstre, he couldn't have considered any other course except the one he had taken. Could a man of fifty look for the first time in his life upon his own child and refuse it? At the time, Dafythe believed he would never see another child of his. It was impossible to abandon that baby to namelessness.

Ambris had been baptized at Belminstre, then Dafythe had taken his son to Pendaunzel to present him to the court. The little boy was brought up as a rightborn princeling. This was considered outrageous behavior, more scandalous than any sexual impropriety.

Dafythe had long remained unmarried, but when he finally

took a wife, he chose a woman who would accept his child. Gillefleure was a noblewoman of ancient lineage, a descendant of one of the tribal chieftains who had ruled Atlantea long before any European had set foot on the continent and whose families, once they submitted to Norman rule, had been absorbed into the aristocracy. Since he hadn't been born in the Northlands, Dafythe thought it politically expedient to choose a wife from among the native nobility. But a greater point in Gillefleure's favor had been her treatment of his son. Ambris was a toddler when Gillefleure had first made her appearance at his court. A widow, childless, she seemed more at ease in Dafythe's presence when the little boy was there. Other women had fussed over Ambris, as if to convince Dafythe that they would be excellent mothers for his children, but Gillefleure was the first to win Ambris's affection. When the little boy first smiled at the sight of her and raised his arms to be lifted, Dafythe began to consider her seriously.

During the childless years at the beginning of their marriage, she treated Ambris as tenderly as if he were her own son. Ambris loved her as a mother and Dafythe had grown to love her himself though that had played no part in his decision to marry. After Rosa, he'd believed he could not feel such passions again. Nevertheless, he'd been broken-hearted at her death. Could it be ten years ago? He hadn't thought of another woman since.

At twelve, Ambris took a place in the court of Kharles IV, as Dafythe's heir would have done. Others might whisper of Dafythe's audacity but from the Emperor there was no rebuke. Frequent correspondence praised the boy's cleverness, his obedience, his courtesy and sweet temper, his honesty, his open affection to his imperial uncle and aunt and, because of these qualities, his popularity. Kharles understood his brother's intentions perfectly. Both of them knew what possibilities lay in Ambris's future: There was an unspoken understanding between Duke and Emperor that this boy, though illegitimate, was the only child of the Norman royal house besides Juan Maria. Their half-sister Agnes looked to be barren, and Dafythe and Gillefleure promised no better. Dafythe felt himself responsible: although he'd had many lovers in his youth, Ambris was his only child. Honesty forced him to acknowledge that their infertility might be his fault. It seemed unlikely that he would ever produce another heir. Kharles and his Empress Penelope had had three little princelings—Diane, Robert, and Cordelia. Dafythe had never met them, but he'd expected Cordelia, the youngest, to be educated at Pendaunzel and become his heir. He'd even hoped that she might marry Ambris when both were grown. But these plans were never fulfilled; a sudden fever in the nursery took all three princelings at once. The grieving imperial parents had embraced their nephew tenderly, and brought him forward.

The Norman people were more likely to accept Ambris than Juan. Kharles and Dafythe knew that they couldn't have a Spaniard ascend the Norman throne. Ambris might also be of Spanish blood, but he had grown up among Normans. No one looked on him with suspicion. The Emperor had considered naming Ambris Prince of France, the title of the imperial heir-apparent. The boy's virtues promised that he would be a good governor, perhaps even a good Emperor. But the unexpected late births of young Kharles, Mara, and Kat had put an end to these plans before Ambris could have realized the prospect existed.

A rightborn prince would have begun preparation for his eventual knighthood at seventeen, but Ambris was sent to Oxford to study law. After receiving his degree, he'd served in whatever official capacity Kharles required him, even to his first marriage to the Bavarian princess Margaude. He spent years away from the court on diplomatic missions, serving in the embassy at Venice, traveling to the Tsar's court at Russe, and achieving great success as emissary to Naufarre during the 1920's, when Juan first proved himself troublesome. He'd earned a reputation for fairness and honesty in negotiating difficult disputes.

Ambris didn't return to Pendaunzel until he brought the little Prince Kat from Eireland at Agnes's death. He met his six-year-old sister, the heir to the dukedom, for the first time. Dafythe had never properly explained the situation to his son, but Ambris seemed to understand.

Dafythe looked for signs of Rosa in their son. The dark complexion, the black curls, and the onyx eyes were hers. That hawk-beak nose had a certain elegance on the Plantagenet face. But there was nothing of her wayward personality. Ambris's temperament was calm and equitable, his sense of duty unwavering, his moral purpose and principles an echo of

Dafythe's own, if not more refined. The name of Ambris the Just was known and respected throughout the civilized world, and Dafythe was enormously proud, and often astonished, that he'd produced this remarkable young man.

Though he loved his daughter and niece and he had sworn allegiance to his nephew, Dafythe knew that Ambris would be a better ruler than any of these three. *He* was the proper one to carry on Dafythe's vision of a mighty and peaceable Northlands. He believed in it. He understood the importance of a secure kingdom in relation to its neighbors. The legitimate royal offspring were eager for excitement and would destroy the world's peace to have a taste of it. Young Kharles was self-indulgent, Mara impulsive, Kat impractical and too pliant before her cousin's stronger will; the *pax normania* which Dafythe and his brother had built so carefully would not survive them.

By acknowledging Ambris, Dafythe had assured his son a certain position in the Norman house, but the promising young man was out of the line of succession. Ambris was the Duke's son, the Emperor's cousin, yet forever misplaced. Ambris's understanding of this was apparent to Dafythe in his circumspect nature: he carried himself as one who has been granted every privilege, but knows that none of it is his by birthright. All was offered freely through the generosity of Dafythe and the elder Kharles, but Ambris was in no position to make demands.

When his sister Agnes had died and her little daughter was received into his household, Dafythe hoped again that he would one day see Ambris wed into the legitimate line. But, once again, these plans were not to be fulfilled. Ambris was so much older than the little Prince—Kat was just three years old when Ambris escorted her from Eireland. Years must pass before a formal betrothal; Norman law forbade the contracting of marriages for children less than sixteen. Ambris had married elsewhere long before Kat reached that age of consent. Meanwhile, Kat had grown up in the Northlands and, even if Ambris were free to marry now, Kat was entirely out of the question. A cousin grown up away from her betrothed might be considered a suitable bride, but a young woman who'd been brought up in the same household was too much like a sister.

It had been a mistake to bring her here, but what else could have been done? Dafythe's custody of his niece was originally meant to be a hostage fostering; Kharles had granted it in the hopes that Agnes's little daughter would insure her father's good behavior, but Count Egan turned this upon them. Kat meant more to them than she did to him. Kat was their sister's child. Dafythe had dearly loved Agnes, but she'd been no more than a means to power for Egan. Could he leave his sister's child in the care of a father who saw her only as his surest claim upon Eireland? Dafythe feared neglect: it was in Egan's interest that the little girl survived, but that didn't promise that she would be well cared for. Only after Ambris had spent weeks in negotiation did Egan agree to release the child. Once Kat had left Eireland, there was no opportunity to return her. Egan was firmly entrenched as its Regent and Kat was removed from her rightful inheritance. She was a stranger to Irish ways. Since she couldn't be restored to her homeland, Kat awaited another marriage, which would occur once a suitable bridegroom was found. But that would not be to Ambris.

Soon after his first wife's death, Ambris had met and married his second wife.

During the winter of 1947, Ambris had ridden between Pendaunzel and Eadeshire so frequently that the court began to jest that he traveled more than the most ambitious merchant. On each journey, he stopped at New York; it wasn't immediately apparent that he made these journeys primarily to pass through the town.

His first references to the object of his interest were casual. "The Mayor of New York is wed to a kinswoman of My Lord Redmantyl," he told his father. "The Lady has that same odd look to her. Silver-fair. Her daughters too. And there is a niece—*she* is a magician."

Then: "My Lord Redmantyl's niece is also his `prentice. She speaks to me of her education in the craft, yet she stays in New York. Why, I wonder. She isn't pleased to stay on there."

And, at last: "Father, do you believe in the Faerye? In truth, I begin to think myself spellbound. Such a thing has never happened to me before. There is a maiden—a magician..."

He confided his love. He described with great wonder how this young woman had captured his heart. He forgot his responsibilities for her. He thought of nothing save how to win her. He had even promised, defiantly, that if he didn't receive his father's consent, he would go to her without it.

Dafythe had wished him happiness. What else could he do? He'd never seen his son so impassioned. Ambris was the most dutiful of sons: his obedience had been tested in a thousand circumstances and he'd always been willing to act as his father wished. Certainly, if this girl meant so much to Ambris that he was ready to risk everything for her, Dafythe couldn't refuse him. He knew what it was to feel such love for a woman.

Laurel arrived at the court wild and mud-spattered in courier's garb, and Dafythe welcomed her as a noblewoman of highest birth though it meant that he must give over his plans for a more prestigious alliance for Ambris. He ceased to wonder that Ambris was entranced by her. He was enchanted by his son's beloved himself.

Dafythe had long been fascinated by Lord Redmantyl and had tried to cultivate a friendship with that remarkable young wizard since his introduction at court. His interest increased as he met others of that strange, upstart family: Laurel, the Lady Kaiese, her lovely daughter Igren. Even among the magical, they were singular. Dafythe was no traveler, but as Duke of the Northlands he received dignitaries from all parts of the world: Europeans, Africans, Asians, Incans. No one looked like this. Native Northlanders and citizens of the Spanish colonies to the south were usually much darker; the Uinlanders, their northern neighbors, were sometimes extremely fair due to their Scandanavian blood, but never so frosty haired and pale in complexion! This over-fair family wasn't even truly albino, for their eyes were clear, pale grey rather than pink. What were they then? Faerye, as Ambris had once suggested? Dafythe couldn't believe in that fantastic world of superstition and nursery-tales, but he had no better answer.

Magicians intrigued Dafythe. What were these beings who possessed powers that other humans did not? Where did their magic arise from? And for what purpose? Magicians were aware of things beyond the perception of ordinary folk, and their unearthly comprehension provided them with superior knowledge. It was their custom to suggest that they held great secrets, though they could never reveal these secrets to lesser mortals.

The look in Laurel's eyes that first summer after Ambris brought her to Pendaunzel was like that of a wounded creature, hunted, awaiting a doom which was inescapable. Dafythe had never observed such fear in any magician before. Though she quickly recovered her strength and lost the fragile, cautious quality of the gravely wounded, the Duke thought she was still frightened. He wondered what had shaken her so. She had abandoned her apprenticeship upon her marriage, though it was well-known that wizards were meant to hold their magic above all else.

Was she Lord Redmantyl's daughter? If the rumors were true, it was no shocking thing to Dafythe. Too many of his own relations were joined in such alliances for a first-cousin union to seem unnatural. It was a common source of jest; bards forever mocked the peculiar practice of the highest nobility and backwoods folk.

If Laurel knew the truth, she didn't reveal it. The wizard never spoke of it. Dafythe could only guess, but he couldn't resist seeing the results of a union between a royal son and wizardly daughter. His youngest grandchild had silvery curls. What talents might emerge once the child was grown?

"What's this?" asked Ambris as his sister dropped a rolled sheaf of parchment onto his desk.

"The Marriage Treaty of Naufarre. You spoke of it only this afternoon. Father bids you study it. It'll be the chief point of discussion at tomorrow's Council."

He unknotted the faded purple ribbon which bound the pages; Dafythe had opened it earlier in the day, and the fresh knot presented no difficulty. The ink, though old, was still dark. Ambris's eyes traveled over the written lines swiftly, taking in the pertinent phrases.

Mara turned to examine a large map on the wall depicting the eastern half of the continent Atlantea. "Where is this march, Terrojos?"

Ambris glanced up briefly. "Just above the southern peninsula."

"This thick, red line denotes the Shieldwall?"

"Yes."

"And there is Dennefort, not ten miles from it! An army might travel from here to there in less than a month. Ambris, what is Terrojos? Is it a swampy land?"

"No, the swamps are to the south and along the coast. Most of it is mountainous, with red clay. That is the name of the place—*red-earth* or *red-land.* By the way, the *j* is pronounced softly. Ro*h*os." Ambris spoke Spanish very well, though in Norman courts he kept that knowledge to himself. Mara's unskilled pronunciation, however, was too chafing to be ignored.

"Ro*h*os." With deliberate care, she reproduced her brother's trilling *r* and that unfathomable *j* which had turned out to be an *h*.

"Our grandfather calls it Redhills in his journals of the last campaign. There are pine forests. They grow cotton there, and tobacco."

"And oranges?" asked Mara.

"No, oranges grow in Iardinez."

"But it would be a good land to possess?"

"The mountains are an effective barrier against invasion—`tis why the Redlyon had so much difficulty in taking it. The Spanish might make a dozen strongholds in the hills south of the Shieldwall."

"So might we."

"You are determined to start a war, aren't you, Mara?"

"Juan's started it," she answered. "We'd be fools to ignore his challenge. Ambris, do you see the importance of this to us Northlanders? If Juan marries, his Spanish relations will lay claim to Naufarre and the treaty is broken. They forget we have claims to counter theirs! We may turn this treachery to our advantage."

"What does Father say to this?"

"He hopes that the threat of renewed warfare will force Juan to reconsider this alliance. But it won't! `Tis obvious that war is exactly what Juan and his Spanish kin desire. They want Naufarre. Juan will wed the Infanta regardless and Kharles will send his troops to put a stop to their plans."

"Yes," agreed Ambris cautiously.

"You know so well as I—it is inevitable. Juan has crossed into open treachery with his announcement of this betrothal. He can't retreat. Naufarre's forfeit if he does. He has no other choice but to fight for it. Whether or not Kharles takes back Naufarre, this Terrojos march is ours by rights as it was in the Redlyon's day. It will be as if the last sixty years had never existed. And we shall be ready. At the first word of war, we'll break the Shieldwall."

tre

"Won't you please speak for me, Ambris?" Mara asked her brother as they walked together from the Manor to Hartshall the next morning.

"Last night, you were eager to present your ideas about Terrojos to the Council yourself."

"So I was, but I've thought the matter over since then." Mara stopped at the entrance to the hall and caught Ambris by the sleeve of his robe. "I've decided that you are better suited to bring the matter to their attention. They call *you* a voice of reason. If you tell Father that we must claim Terrojos from the Spaniards, he'll give it serious consideration, and the others will too."

"I think you'd do better to speak for yourself, Mara," Ambris answered. "You've had that right since you reached the age of one-and-twenty. You can take your seat in the Advisory Chamber whenever you like."

"I do attend the Council whenever the matter at hand concerns me. I'll certainly join you today. But you know that I've never cared for all the politics involved in running this dukedom. It bores me—all those long-winded debates! If only they would speak to the point. Everything would be resolved much more quickly."

Ambris smiled. "You will speak to the point, and the arguments will carry more conviction if they come from you."

Mara knew that he was right. She *must* participate in the Council today. But she remained reluctant at the prospect of facing her father with her opinions. How would he receive them?

Her brother seemed to understand her fear, for he said, "You are bold enough to lead troops into battle, Mara. I do not doubt that. Arguing with Father before the Council will only be a small test of your courage."

"It seems a much greater one," Mara admitted.

Ambris laughed. "Stand your ground as you would if you faced an opponent with sword and shield. The worst Father can do is say No." Members of the Council were going into the hall, bowing their heads to the Prince and Chancellor and glancing at them with frank curiosity as they passed. "Come along now. The others are assembling and we don't want to be late in our seats."

The Advisory Chamber was a long, rectangular hall on the upper level of Hartshall. A double row of boxed benches like pews were set against the two longer walls. Above one were tall windows made up of many small panes, some faintly colored. Above the other hung painted wooden crests of the prominent noble houses of the Northlands, with the ducal hartshead on the largest crest in the center. A rectangular table spanned the length of the room; the Duke's seat was at the head.

The Council were all in attendance that day: Othel, Lord Tuxsetau, Prime Minister of the Council; Phyllida, Lady Peaque, Layn Chief Justice; Englebard, Lord Roodebroke, the Duke's Exchequer; Uismarde Striparroe, Layn Lieutenant; Geoffrey, the young Lord Rafenshighte, Chief of the Diplomatic Office; Kaeroth, Lord Chamberlain; Cherys, Layn Chief Constable; the Archbishop of Belminstre and the Bishop of Pendaunzel; Peter Scholar, Court Magician, and other persons of high office. All wore the distinctive gold-shot robes of state over their ordinary clothes. Elaborate devices upon their chains of office proclaimed the appointment of each minister.

Mara's Council attire was a semi-formal tunic of noble blue hemmed just above the knee, a white kirtle with a broad, embroidered border of gold, the blue and white robes of a prince, her chain and seal as governor of Gossunge and, like Ambris, a purple sash bearing the imperial lions. Her most formal wear was reserved for court ceremonies; the skirts, robes, and fur-trimmed cape dragged the ground. Her hair was unbound in the traditional noble-fashion, though she preferred her braids.

The Council sat in silence as Dafythe's secretary Martleanne read off her summary of the last Council meeting, concluding with the Duke' remarks on the significance of the marriage treaty of Eduarde Redlyon. Dafythe announced that the treaty was now at hand and Ambris began his presentation of its pertinent points.

"The treaty makes no mention of the future disposition of Naufarre?" asked Lady Peaque once he had finished.

"The firstborn issue of the union shall receive the title Prince of Naufarre in place of Prince of Gallys, as is usual for the fourth child of the Norman Emperor. The Prince will assume the governing of Naufarre upon the death of Marianne," said Ambris. "There is also a stipulation that the offspring of the Prince of Naufarre will continue the title."

"Alamanzus's advisors hoped that Naufarre would eventually be accorded the rights of a sovereign principality like Burgundy and the Northlands," Dafythe explained.

"*That* should never have been allowed, My Gracious Lord," said Lord Tuxsetau. "Naufarre would have been better kept directly under the Emperor's hand."

"Perhaps, but none of us expected a child to come of my father's last marriage. If Juan hadn't been born, Naufarre would've become Norman crown land."

"No conditions restrict the prospects of marriage for a Prince of Naufarre," Ambris added.

"So there is no express writ against Juan marrying a Spaniard?" asked Lady Peaque.

"No. Nor anyone he chooses."

"Then is the betrothal itself treasonous?"

"Surely Juan's betrothal to his Spaniard cousin declares his affiliation with Spain," said Uismarde.

"He's broken a solemn contract in order to favor a foreign and hostile nation," added Mara. "He means them to have Naufarre. Is that not treason enough?"

"We have begun with that presumption," answered Dafythe. "But can we be certain that my half-brother means to restore Naufarre to Spanish hands?"

"Juan's banns contain no political statement," Ambris said in agreement. "The published articles of handfast we received yesterday are blameless in themselves. No declaration of Spanish rights in Naufarre have yet been made by Juan."

"Has Spain made any claim?" asked Lord Roodebroke.

"Geoffrey?" Dafythe addressed his Diplomatic Chief.

"Don Peidro received me at the Spanish Embassy this morning," answered Lord Rafenshighte. "He expresses surprise at

Prince Juan's betrothal and avows that he heard nothing of it before yesterday. Indeed, he tells me that he hopes this marriage will not end the years of friendship between his homeland and this land he considers his second home." Rafenshighte repeated the Spanish Ambassador's assurances with a cynical note of his own; he didn't believe one word and didn't expect the rest of the Council to be deceived either. "I did ask, My Lord Duke, if his masters had designs upon Naufarre. He says not. Don Peidro also begs audience with you this afternoon."

"So Prince Juan hasn't declared his intentions," said Lieutenant Uismarde. "Nevertheless, there is treachery in this. We know the Prince's character too well. We are fools if we take his marriage to a Spanish Infanta as a love match and imagine it means nothing. Juan is a traitor. His previous actions have already declared him in this."

"It is a possibility," Dafythe replied. "We would be wise to prepare for the contingency if he makes such a claim, but it is folly to react impetuously."

"Even if this is a veiled declaration, can he be arrested?" asked Ambris. "We may assume that Kharles's councilors have also called this betrothal treasonous, yet Kharles has written no warrant—at least, no word of it has reached us. My imperial cousin would wish to make such a charge. If he hasn't, surely it's because he sees it is impossible to take Prince Juan into custody without sending an army to Naufarre to capture him. Juan wouldn't surrender himself."

"The Emperor will send troops to Naufarre if he must," Uismarde answered.

"The arrest of Prince Juan is advisable only if we wish to enter a war," Ambris replied. "He will take offense at a blatant accusation of treason, and he'll be that much more difficult to deal with in subsequent negotiations."

"Do we wish to prevent war, My Lord Duke?" one of the junior ministers asked, somewhat ingenuously.

"I do," Dafythe answered in a tone that would bear no argument. "'Tis too easy to fight great battles over little matters. As I am Sovereign Lord and Grand Duke of the Northlands, it is in my rights to declare war without the consent of my liege Emperor, or to refuse to fight if that is my will. I cannot consider the possibility of war until I've examined all other honorable options. A declaration of war is to be my last resort, not my first act. The point of this discussion should not be what Kharles ought to do, but what we as Northlanders can do. The question for us is how may we serve to support him or offer advice particular to our position."

"I repeat my advice of the last Council, Lord Duke," said Tuxsetau. "Offer to send My Lord Ambris to speak on the part of the Normans. All have heard my reasons for this course of action. I say again—My Lord Ambris has made his reputation as a man of justice among the Naufarrans. He's dealt with the Dowager Marianne and her son in previous difficulties. They like him. Prince Juan bears him special affection as the only other imperial son of both Spanish and Norman blood. They will hear his counsel as they would listen to no other emissary."

"I've thought a great deal on this matter, Othel," the Duke answered. "Though your advice is sound, my son is Chancellor now, no longer a young diplomat to be sent on distant errands. We have need of him here. He can't be spared."

"Then may I suggest Prince Kat as an alternative?" the Prime Minister continued.

This was a new proposal. "Prince Kat?" Layn Ystelake wondered aloud. "My Lord Tuxsetau, I pray you explain. What special qualifications does the Irish Prince offer?"

Tuxsetau smiled around the table. "You speak my reasons yourself. Prince Kat bears more than the title Prince of Eireland. She *is* Irish. Her father, the Lord Regent Egan, is one of the Irish separatists Juan so admires. He is sympathetic to rebels in other Norman lands. In particular, he wrote letters to the scoundrel Count when he worked his old espionage."

"'Tis fortunate that Count Egan's marriage to Prince Agnes and his present position as Regent have cured him of higher ambitions," said Lord Rafenshighte. "All rebels really want when they oppose their rightful ruler is to rule themselves."

Tuxsetau looked with disapproval upon the young cynic, and answered, "Yes, but Egan's reputation as an insurrectionist stands, and Prince Kat is his daughter. Mightn't Juan welcome her for that? She may gain his confidence more readily than another emissary. Also, she is a maiden of pleasing aspect and personality and I believe she will serve well in a mission of diplomacy. If you cannot send Ambris, My Lord Duke, I pray you are willing to send Prince Kat in his stead."

Dafythe looked to his son. "Do you think it will work?"

"I doubt Kharles will accept such an offer, but I believe it feasible," Ambris answered. "Count Egan is a hero to Juan. He sees him as a man who has stood against the Empire and gained from his rebellion. His admiration for Egan may give my cousin the opportunity to gain Juan's ear. Once there, much more may be gained. If it is required, I can instruct Kat myself in all that she needs to know of the Naufarrans and their ways."

"Very well then. Gramercies, Othel, for your proposal." Dafythe turned back to Ambris. "Whether or no we do this, Kat ought to be given proper warning. Will you speak with her this afternoon?"

"Yes, Father."

"Father," Mara spoke. "There's another point in the Naufarre treaty which hasn't been mentioned, yet it concerns us Northlanders more than all else." She glanced at Ambris across the table; her brother nodded slightly. Mara went on: "If the treaty is broken, Terrojos becomes Norman land by default."

The Council began to murmur. The voice of the Lieutenant rose above all others, "Lord Chancellor, is it so?"

"It is a licit claim," Ambris answered. "Our Emperor and the Spaniard Alamanzus were in conflict over the region at the time of truce. Father, I understand that the terms of the treaty drawn by yourself and the late Emperor Kharles were meant to hold both nations from claiming certain disputed territories, namely Terrojos and Naufarre?"

Dafythe was looking at Mara as he answered, "Yes."

"If those terms are made void by Juan's marriage, we may claim Terrojos if we choose."

"We must claim that march!" cried the Prince, encouraged by her brother's endorsement. "Naufarre is Kharles's concern, but what matter to us save as we are loyal subjects? It is thousands of miles away across the ocean. This land borders our own marches. With Juan working his treacheries for his Spaniard kin, we cannot hope Terrojos will remain quiet. I say we must assemble such troops as may be got together immediately and take action to secure our claims this summer. Kharles will agree that we are in the best position to take it! If I can have an army–"

"Don't call your troops up yet, Daughter," Dafythe interrupted. "The situation in Naufarre may come to nothing."

"The idea is precipitous," said Lady Peaque.

"Marching upon Spanish lands would distinctly be a hostile act," Tuxsetau added.

"Juan's betrothal is a hostile act," Mara answered.

"But it doesn't warrant the retaliation you propose, My Prince. Even so suspect an alliance may not be taken alone as a prelude to war."

"We have a right to compensation for my uncle's treachery. Juan begs for battle," she replied. This wasn't going as well as she'd hoped. One rousing speech ought to have brought half the Council to her side. Yet they sat still, complacently hearing her words. Didn't they understand? "We cannot let this insult pass. It is a matter of honor. Kharles will want us to fight for what's rightfully ours."

"Well, I hope yet we may avoid fighting altogether," said the Duke. "Rightful cause or no, war is nothing but misery."

"For the losers."

"No, for all concerned."

Mara blinked at this unnorman heresy. "It is all our history, our art, our pride. If `tis so horrible, why does everyone want it?"

"That, I have never understood. No, Mara, not yet."

That evening, a feast was set to welcome Lord Redmantyl and his sons to Pendaunzel. By proper custom, there should have been a banquet upon their arrival, but there was no time to prepare a great feast so quickly. The Palace had been in an uproar over the crisis in Naufarre and, these days, dinner in the banquet hall was a special occasion. Dafythe frequently dined alone in his apartments and the court only gathered together when they greeted important guests.

Tonight, the court bard Delphyn sang the ballad of Prince Denys for the court's amusement:

Attend ye, o nobles, for I sing ye a sad tale
Of the fall of Fair Denys, a brave prince in sooth.
As Saint Parsyfal of old, a most virtuous knight,

He came to Our Lord's arms yet a youth.

The sons of Good Robert were bold in those days,
Fit for battle and eager to face their foe.
On the sands of Madehef, they cast down all they met.
Down the mountains of Atlas blood flowed.

The firstborn Fair Denys, fleur-de-lys on his shield,
He was ever victorious, a most valiant knight.
The sword Dragonsfang he bore in his hands.
No Spaniard could withstand his might.

Prince Eduarde, the second, red lion of Skots,
Fierce, loyal he guarded his brave brother's side.
The youngest, Prince Margad, no more than a boy.
Squire to his elders he did ride.

Denys the Fair. Denys the Brave. Denys Spaniardslayer. Denys Charmgifted. Though the Emperor Redlyon's elder brother had died more than a century ago, his brief, sensational career was recalled vividly. The image of the blonde and handsome, white-robed Norman Prince was well-known and beloved throughout the Empire. Countless ballads praised Denys's valor and commemorated his astonishing victories in North Africa and in the Northlander marches.

It was sometimes said that Denys had a talisman that gave him surpassing strength. Many songs featured this charm, though none were accurate as to its shape or nature. In one tale, it might be a holy amulet containing fragments of a saint's bones; in another, it was a silver ring, a magician's or a lover's gift. The most popular talisman, however, was the sword Dragonsfang, in spite of the fact that Denys had died with this sword in his hands.

The ballad of Prince Denys was a favorite, but tonight the courtiers whispered as Delphyn sang. There was only one topic of conversation. The question passed over the table again and again—"Will there be a war?" "Do you think we'll go to war?" — sometimes with worry, sometimes with eagerness. The answer was long and involved, or short and comforting: "I hope not"; "Don't worry for it, my dear. My Lord Dafythe's kept us peaceable for years. I'll wager he see us through this crisis as well"; "I don't see a way out of it. Juan won't want to give over. His Spaniard's pride, you know"; "Are we ready to go to war over this? Naufarre's so far away and so small a part of the kingdom"; "Yes, but it is *our* land. We have our Norman pride as well."

Dafythe, in his seat at the head of the table, explained the situation to the Lady Laurel at his left and Lady Roodebroke at his right. Ambris spoke with Layn Pennykoke's daughter Ariane, recently returned from her studies at Paris. Lady Peaque, Lord Tuxsetau, Lord Roodebroke, and other members of the Council likewise explained recent events to their dinner companions. Lord Redmantyl, the honored guest, was in pleasant conversation with Martleanne. Dafythe's secretary gave her cautious opinion of the crisis, but the wizard's replies suggested that he had other things on his mind. Redmantyl had a reputation among the ladies of the court and the attractive yet reticent young woman was flustered by his attentions. Little Andemyon, seated on Martleanne's other side, listened with incomplete comprehension. Redmantyl's elder son Orlan, obviously self-conscious in his unfashionably long tunic, studied the short hemlines, the lace-trimmed shirts, the slashed sleeves, the braided and ribbon-bound plaits of the young nobles around him with envy, and he did not respond to the eager flirtations of the damosel at his right. Mara, at Orlan's left, was silent.

The Northlands were troubled, their borders imperiled,
Spanish foes in a rage at the Madehef assault.
Vengeance, they cried, for the Norman invasion.
Norman blood at the marches they sought.

Dear Cousin, Duke Julia wrote to Robert the Good King:
Succor, I pray thee. Send aid for our plight.
And so to the Northlands the brave princes did come.
Layn Diane did greet them, Gossunge's knight.

All Pendaunzel rejoiced with gay laughter and music.
In the feast-hall, Prince Eduarde paid Diane his court.
Their wooing, `tis said, was war counsel and love-talk
Diane pledged her horses with her heart.

The next stanzas were usually Mara's favorite. From childhood, she had thrilled to tales of her grandmother's exploits. Diane, like herself, had been a Shieldmaid as well as a master horsewoman. Niece and heir to the old Duke Julia, she had received command of the Duke's cavalry upon her knighting and it was said that Diane's riders were skilled as she was. All were practiced in amazing stunts. They stood balanced upon their saddles. They swung down with one hand upon the pommel and one foot in the stirrup to strike fallen foes. Such expert tumblers on horseback were rarely seen even in carnivals these days. But tonight, Mara had no heart to hear of another Shieldmaid's valor.

The Prince was mortified by her humiliation in the Council. She hadn't expected to encounter so much resistance. She knew herself to be right. Why could she not make the Council see the solution as clearly as she did? She half-listened to the remarks of those seated near her. Her heart thumped impatiently. Discussions, endless discussions! Should they? Ought they? A Mayor's Council? A Council of Nobles? A meeting with the Spanish Ambassador? An emissary to Naufarre. A message to Spain. So much talk! When would they act?

Spain had no match for Diane's fearless riders.
From Maudsland, from Princeland, in terror they flew.
In the heights of the Redhills they made fast their stronghold.
And there they waited for battle anew.

Ojos des Mantegnas, the Eyes of the Mountains,
The highest of passes the great fortress did crown.
A most tempting prize, Spain was loth to lose it.
Yet the Normans sought it for their own.

Three years passed at this sport, the princes triumphant.
The threat of the Spaniard was expelled from our land.
At the foot of the Redhills raised the bastion of Denys;
From plain and from peak, these great wards did stand.

The prince heard the familiar words with fresh agony. The Shieldwall lay between *Ojos des Mantegnas*—Spainfort, the

Normans called it these days—and Dennefort. Delphyn sang of the very lands Mara ached to see. This was unbearable! Diane had led her riders to the borders of the Redlands. Eduarde had conquered them. Denys had died there. Would she would never lead troops to the Shieldwall herself?

Old Julia departed at last for Christ's Kingdom.
The young Duke chose her consort at the dawn of her reign.
As Diane and Eduarde were bonded in handfast,
The Eyes of the Mountains was taken by Spain.

What Prince thinks of love when such danger arises?
They rode for the marches, the young husband and bride,
Brave Denys and Margad, to join in the battle,
And another, a maid, at their side.

The fair Khrystophania, she was Denys's beloved,
A warrior-maid of famed talents and grace.
Diane's lieutenant, yet she rode with the Bright Prince
She now rode in Eduarde's place.

She heard her father's voice: "It is a delicate situation, My Ladies. We don't know what Juan is up to with this intended marriage."

"Surely we can't think him innocently in love with this Infanta," Laurel said.

"To understand this problem, we must understand Juan. He is himself a product of the Treaty of Naufarre—the one child of both the Norman and Spanish houses. Naufarre is the one land he may claim by virtue of either parent. If it is Norman, he is its Prince. If it returns to Spain, he remains so. Only through an act of treason can it be taken from him. What does he gain by his treachery?"

"Then why does he do it?" asked Lady Roodebroke. "Does he hope for a reunion with Spain?"

"Perhaps," Dafythe answered. "Juan has been brought up a Spaniard, but his mother has had little communication with her family these fifty years. I don't believe she's ever forgiven them for her marriage to my father, but for that same reason she has no fondness for Normans either. You know, of course, that my father was so old as I am now at the time of his last marriage, and his bride no older than you, my dear Laurel."

"'Tisn't a fair comparison," Laurel replied playfully. "I'd wed you today if I weren't already married to that lout." She smiled across the table at her husband. "But you're nothing like the Redlyon, Father Dafythe. Poor Marianne. What a time she must have had!"

"She's had no more to do with her own family or ours than necessity and courtesy require. Naufarre is hers, Spanish as she is herself but for no more political reason. Merciful Lord Alone knows what she's taught her son to think of his relations in both nations. I think Juan has agreed to this marriage to make mischief and to play his Norman relations against his mother's family. He may promise Naufarre to Spain, but that doesn't mean he'll give it. He is at heart a separatist. He would like to see Naufarre an independent kingdom and himself its king, but he knows that so small a nation cannot survive long between two mighty empires which desire it. So he takes what revenge he may on both, stinging when he can."

"What will you do, My Lord?" asked Lady Roodebroke.

"I recommend that we do not respond overmuch to this threat of marriage, in the hope that Juan will abandon his plan for it. You see, Prince Juan means to provoke a response. He always has. He's like a naughty child who misbehaves to draw the attention of his elders—save that he is no child and his naughtiness no mere tantrum. He is far more dangerous if we take up his challenges. My brother Kharles knew how to restrain him. Juan respected our late Emperor, as an elder brother if not as his rightful sovereign. Kharles could always make him behave. Marianne also respected my brother's authority. Neither, I believe, cares for young Kharles. My nephew doesn't yet know how to command that same obedience from them. He has little experience of Juan's outbursts. He doesn't understand them and, if Juan is provocative, Kharles is certain to react precisely as Juan wishes."

"Will the Spanish try to take back Naufarre with this marriage?" asked Lady Roodebroke.

"If they do, Kharles will demand retaliation," said Laurel. "He must, as a point of honor."

"I wish it were not so, but I believe that Kharles desires this confrontation as much as Juan. They are both alike in that—they enjoy creating a grand explosion and never think of the injury they cause," Dafythe answered. "There are so few living who recall my father's wars over this same land."

On the plains of the Redlands the champions assembled.
Above in the stone heights awaited their prize.
Ten thousand encamped there, for dawns light they gathered.
They hoped to retrieve the lost Eyes.

Yet in that night was base treachery committed
Villains in the darkness the encampment alarmed
Denys leapt from his bed, but his foes were too many.
His young brother fell dead in his arms.

"Do you think there'll be a war over this Spanish business, Prince Margueryt?" Orlan asked.

"It is impossible for us to endure such insult and treachery," Mara answered. "If Juan persists in his games, we must certainly defend our Empire. It is our duty. The Spanish have always been our foes. It is an ancient rivalry between us though my father has kept things peaceable for so long. Peace cannot hold forever when we have such traitors as Prince Juan at our backs and his Spaniard kin at our borders."

"At our borders?" the boy asked. "Spain is half the world from the Northlands."

"Surely you know that there are Spanish colonies to our south." She waved in the minstrel's direction as Delphyn sung the ballad's most stirring verse:

The Bright Prince fell, not in battle, but murdered.
Heavens cry outrage! Lament at this blow!
Eduarde was wroth at the merciless slaying.
Revenge! cried the Prince for his foe.

"Only a narrow strip of neutral land separates us from them. The Spanish will not be slow to gather their garrisons because we are not yet at war."

Eduarde seized the blade his brother had let fall.
Limbs he hacked from the butchers in outrageous assault.
Unslaked by this bloodlet, he rode to the mountains
No Spaniard must live lest this crime be forgot.

"Do you think they'll invade?" the young damosel at Orlan's left wondered. "Surely they could never be so bold as to touch Norman lands."

"But they have already. The march they call Terrojos was once Norman. It is the Redlands of the old songs and stories. My grandfather Eduarde captured it. It would be ours now, save for this treaty that trades Terrojos for Naufarre."

At daybreak, Prince Eduarde saw the Mountain-Eyes besieged
He would tear stone from stone to force them to yield.
Fires burned at the walls. Rams battered the tall gate.
The cannons rolled up from the field.

"The marriage treaty," said Orlan, with a little gesture toward the Duke. He'd been listening to that conversation as attentively as Mara had.

"Exactly. My grandfather would have Naufarre instead. But the Spanish will claim Naufarre once Juan marries their Infanta. They can't have both!" Her voice was rising. "Can proper Normans endure such insult without demanding rightful recompense?"

Orlan and the damosel both shook their heads.

When the soldiers of Spain saw these weapons of terror,
They surrendered to Diane and pled pardon full thrice.
The Red Prince would not have spared them in mercy.
The Eyes were retaken, but at tragic price.

She heard the hoof-beats of the Duke's riders, the battle-cry of the Redlyon's men as they stormed up to the gates of Spainfort to have their vengeance. She heard the rumble of cannon like thunder. Eduarde's blood, Diane's blood, ran in her veins. She saw the mountains. Mara had never seen a mountain, but the image of the red peaks twisting up to spear the clouds was vivid in her mind. Cleft between the jagged heights, she saw the formidable stone walls of the Spanish fortress. It was in Spanish hands again these days.

"That land was once ours. We can have it again if we have the courage to claim it." She was suddenly aware that others around the table were listening to her, some with admiration, some in astonishment at her passionate words. Dafythe's eyes were upon her. He clearly did not approve. "It is ours," she finished defiantly.

"If the Redlyon had been so fierce upon it as you are, My Prince, we might have it *and* Naufarre," Lord Tuxsetau jested. "And all of Atlantea to the Orient Ocean as well."

Pardon, o nobles, for such sorrowful singing.
So ends my tale of Prince Denys the Brave.
At the chapel of Dennefort the princes lay sleeping.
The children of Khrysta weep over the grave.

As the court rose and left the dinner table, Mara stopped when a hand touched her shoulder.

"Prince Mara? May I offer advice? I am in agreement with you, and I hope to be of greater service in your cause."

Geoffrey, Lord Rafenshighte, was a handsome young man with sharp, elegant features and long, black hair braided in the latest, thesperish fashion. His ministerial robes were new; he'd been appointed to his office little more than a month ago.

Mara didn't refuse to hear him, and he went on in secretive tones. "If I may say so, My Prince, you are not subtle. Not knowledgeable in getting things done. 'Tis all very well if you have your faction with your swordsmaids, your cousin, My Lady Laurel, but these women have no power in political concerns—save what influence My Lady's faction may work upon her husband."

"I didn't know she had one."

"Perhaps she doesn't know it herself," Rafenshighte agreed, grinning. "Yet it exists. *That* family has risen much. It is impossible not to notice how My Lady's wizard-uncle is favored. And the wife of our Lord High Chancellor has her husband's ear.

You may be sure that others desire the opportunity to tell her what to whisper into it. *He* is highly sought."

Though he didn't say it, Mara understood: now that Dafythe was growing old, Ambris was considered the primary power in the Duke's Council. She was a little angry at the suggestion. *She* was the Prince, Dafythe's heir; why did the court not seek her favor? But, even as she felt the insult implied by Geoffrey's words, Mara knew that he had already provided the answer: she took no interest in court intrigues and political goings-on.

"What do you suggest?" she asked.

The young man smiled. "Power lies in the Council, My Prince. I've learned that at least since my appointment. It is there that significant alliances must be formed if you wish to carry your point. Many among the Council agree with you. We would see our Empire returned to its glory of old and we believe that you are the instrument of that rebirth. With our allegiance you'll have the opportunity you require to drive the threat of the traitor and his Spanish kin from our homeland."

"And what of my father? He will not give over so easily."

"No disrespect is intended to My Gracious Lord, you understand. But he is old. His judgment, I think, is not so reliable as it was and his will not so firm. If enough of the Council advises against his inclinations, he will sway."

"Ambris would speak to Father on my behalf..." Mara said thoughtfully.

"I would not dare suggest it, My Prince. I don't know My Lord Chancellor's sympathies in this. After all, he is the Duke your father's chief advisor and his first office must be to serve Dafythe's will. If I may say so, Prince Margueryt, you ought not turn to your brother as a mere courtier seeking our Chancellor's support. Step forward on your own. There are younger ministers whom I know to be your admirers and who will swear loyalty to you with only a little encouragement. The elders, Lady Peaque, Lord Tuxsetau, remain with the Duke even when they know him to be wrong, but Layn Lamsford, Lord Ayrton, Kaeroth, are sympathetic to your cause. They are my friends. They will be yours. Who would not wish to be called your friend?"

This was flattery in a form Mara was unused to. "Will you speak to them?" she asked.

"If you give me leave, My Prince, I would call it my highest honor." He bowed and left her.

"What did *he* want?" Kat asked. She had been waiting for her cousin at the banquet-hall doorway.

"He thinks I ought to court supporters among the Council."

"If any but Geoff offered his fellowship, I would call it sound," Kat answered grudgingly. "But you know him."

The Princes had known Lord Rafenshighte from childhood. His mother had been Layn Chancellor until her death last winter and he had grown up at the Palace. He was Kat's age, a few years younger than Mara; they had taken their first lessons with him, but had always thought him a little talebearer. He'd been the sort of boy who ran crying to his mother whenever he and his playmates got into some mischief and laid the blame on them although he was often the one to start it.

Even today, there was an obsequiousness in his manner which Mara didn't like, but he had given her useful advice. The Council might agree with her from time to time, but she didn't hold their allegiance. Though she was on good terms with most of them, she always chose her companions elsewhere. She'd never troubled to gain their friendship, but now she required a strong faction among the Council if her arguments were to carry any weight. She couldn't bear another defeat in the Advisory Chamber.

"You missed the first skirmish last night, Mara," said Kat. "Ambris and My Lord Redmantyl. `Tis a wonder he didn't explode on the spot."

"Ambris never loses his temper."

Kat laughed. "Not Ambris, simpleton. My Lord Wizard. They say he casts bolts of lightning to strike down his enemies. I thought we'd have a battle there in the nursery when *he* came in and Ambris was there. But do you know what came of it? He *froze*. I could feel the blast of cold when he made his greeting to Laurel. `Twas a fearsome thing to see. He didn't even give poor Ambris the courtesy of a glance. Of course, Ambris did the sensible thing and sounded retreat, took Laurel's cousins off to show them about the palace. I didn't stay long myself."

"I wonder why he's bothered to come at all," Mara said absently, her mind still on Rafenshighte's proposals. "He didn't attend the wedding."

"Well, he had to see her baby. You know why—you've heard the same stories I have. Besides, the little lad, the pretty one, is going to have a place here at court. Uncle Dafythe's made him a herald. I heard the talk around the table tonight. Is it true? Uncle Dafythe won't call for troops?"

"He won't hear of it."

"Surely he can't–"

"Oh, you know him. I've never met a Norman so reluctant to charge in where his sword was needed. Wait, he says."

"You won't."

"I must. He is my liege as well as father. When I took my oath as a knight, I didn't mean I would be loyal only when it suited me. You did the same."

"And so we must abide."

"Yes, but not for long. Even a peaceable man as Father is can't stand by and be seen as a coward when his nation is threatened. Did you hear him tonight? How can he speak of ignoring Juan? A naughty child, is he? Then the brat deserves a good smack. If Father and Uncle Kharles had put Juan in his proper place at his first tantrum, he wouldn't be playing these same tricks today. I pray young Kharles does strike back with all harshness. He has a heart like ours, my Cos. If *he* calls for the aid of our Northlander armies, Father must concede!"

Neither Prince had met their cousin Kharles. The young Emperor had been crowned at the age of twenty-one upon the death of his father in 1939; now, he was thirty-five and unmarried. Occasionally, they heard news of his life at Ouesteminstre and Paris. There had been a great scandal in his boyhood when he'd refused to wed the Bavarian princess chosen for him, and another scandal soon after his coronation when he'd become infatuated with a lady-in-waiting against the protests of his mother, the Dowager Penelope. The Princes knew that he had fathered two children by this favorite and rumors whispered of more shocking love-affairs since.

Kharles was reputed to be an expert hunter who rode to hounds frequently. He enjoyed all sports; travelers who came from his court carried tales of how the Emperor made them welcome by inviting them to match against him with swords or tennis rackets or the pieces of a chessboard—though he was happiest when he won. In his fourteen-year reign, he had shown a fondness for the trappings of soldiery: he'd created a dozen new regiments and two new orders of knighthood and he spent time drilling the honor guards at every castle he visited in his realm. It was said that he had battle-maps painted on the walls at Ouesteminstre Palace. Because of this, Mara believed that he was like her, keen for a warrior's life and impatient for his skills to be put to proper use. As a kinswomen, she gave him sympathy; as a vassal, she gave him ardent loyalty.

"Ambris has little compliment to give our cousin the Emperor," said Kat. "He calls Kharles an unprincipled youth."

"Yes, well, Ambris would call any man who lived more wildly than a cloistered Brother lax in his morals. You can't judge by that." Mara turned to her cousin and spoke with swift purpose, "We must make our strategy to win Father over. A battle of wits is like a battle of swords. We need a plan..."

cuar

"Magician, can you *see* for us?"

Mara had sought out her father's court magician, Peter Scholar. Ambris went with her. They had both been invited to witness Andemyon's adoption ceremony that evening in the Duke's apartments, but Mara thought that this was more important.

Peter was startled when the Duke's children entered the little library on the top floor of the Hall of Record, where generations of court magicians had formed their own collection. This was his favorite private place in all the palace, but he immediately set down his pipe and the book he'd chosen for his evening's study, and made them welcome as if he received guests in his own chambers.

He was a young man, slight, with a sandy beard and wispy fair hair that he grew long but bound back in an attempt to keep it from his eyes. English by birth, educated at the College of Magic at Uittenberg, he wore the voluminous moss-green robes of a university master, which in fact he was.

"I am no wizard, My Prince, but I can scry as well as any," Peter responded to Mara's request. "All human creatures possess a little of the prescient power. You may have heard tales yourself: one among the magicless suddenly feels overwhelming danger for no perceivable reason as he boards a ship. He refuses to sail—and the ship sinks. Another knows the tally of the next toss of dice, or senses that a loved one has died before the news arrives."

"But you possess more than the occasional accident of extrasensory knowledge," said Ambris.

Peter nodded. "It is so, My Lord. Mental magicians such as I am possess this ability more consistently than the average mortal. For the magicless, the incidents I have described are remarkable. For the mental magician, they occur daily."

"Yet you are not considered a true magician by the ranks of wizardry."

"No, I'm not," Peter confirmed modestly.

"What's the difference?" Mara wanted to know.

"You have acquaintance with wizards, My Prince. You see what they may do." He bowed slightly to Ambris. "The Lady Laurel is a magician of great power and might be a wizard of the highest rank if she chose. Witness her tricks for the amusement of this court—the fairylights, the sparkling orb balanced upon her fingertips. These are mild manifestations of the power she commands. She is a master of light. She casts spells. She has command of the material world."

"And you do not."

"My talents are in the psychical realm, My Prince. I command no earth, no fire, no wind nor water, only the essence of the mind. I may know the thoughts of those about me if they do not guard themselves, and I may read something of the character and actions of another if I touch their personal possessions. And, yes, I may glimpse the future, though you must understand that magicians do not value this talent highly."

"Why not?" Mara would have thought the ability to foresee the future to be extremely useful.

"It is an inexact ability beyond our command to refine. Little may be gained from what we see. Visions are vague. They may carry no import. Or, if they do, their significance is not perceived until after the fact. I can project your fate for you, My Prince, but an astrologer will do the same and may be as accurate."

"No, I want you. We trust the crafts of magic more than the calculations of fortune-tellers." Mara glanced back at her brother for confirmation. "I don't need you to cast my horoscope, Peter. Simply *see*. Will you?"

"As you wish, My Prince, My Lord Ambris."

At carnivals, seers used such devices as cards and crystal balls, chants and smoky incense to help them divine the future, but Ambris and Mara were sophisticated enough to know that this was simply a show for the ignorant and superstitious. They didn't require external signs of the magician's effort to believe that he worked his craft.

Peter bowed his head and long fingers gently stroked his

brow. His pale blue eyes gazed intensely at an undefined spot between himself and the eager Prince, then his sight grew unfocused. Mara felt an electric tingle in the air and she turned to Ambris, smiling in her excitement.

"Peter, what do you see?"

The magician didn't answer immediately. After a minute or so, he whispered, "A sword, its hilt damaged. The missing gem. The broken sword." Then, in a more clear voice, he went on: "The city burns. Not Pendaunzel. Tall towers. A fortress. The tower falls. The roof is in flames. The tower crashes through the roof. A broken wall. People push through the gaps."

"Many cities have walls about them and tall towers," Mara said. "Is it a Spanish city or Norman?"

"All is confusion. Turmoil." He paused. "There is a knight, a woman. Order of St. Mykhael. You, My Prince? No. Her shield is dark with mud, perhaps blood. Her device—what is it? Gold. The harp? Oh, `tis Prince Katheryne! She leads the crowd. She shouts, but I cannot hear her words. Her sword is upraised." Abruptly, Peter looked up. "It is gone. I see nothing more."

"What may we learn from this vision?" asked Ambris.

"Kat will be in battle," answered Mara promptly.

"Yes, but is it victory or defeat?" Ambris said. "Is the city ours or theirs? Does Kat defend the ruined wall or has she brought about its fall?" He looked to Peter.

"My Lord, I cannot say."

"If this vision is true..."

"It is. All visions reveal truly what will come."

"Where am I in this vision?" Mara wondered suddenly. "Kat is my lieutenant. Surely she would be at my side in battle."

"You were not there, My Prince." Peter's reply was apologetic. "I didn't see you."

"Does that mean I am dead?"

"I don't know. Perhaps. Perhaps not. Your absence may mean nothing. A vision, even so true, may reveal little of importance. Shall I go on?"

Ambris was willing to have the session end here, but his sister said, "Please, Peter, continue."

Peter resumed his seeing. "I see a dark-haired maid, not sixteen," he announced after a moment.

"I have a niece not sixteen," said Mara. "Mathilde."

"She is in commoner's garb."

"Who is she then? Of what importance will she be to me? Is she my squire?"

"You will meet her one day. Ah, she is gone now!"

Ambris laughed softly. "I begin to see the difficult nature of this *seeing*. The vision reveals what will be, yet we do not understand what it is we are shown."

The magician was silent for a long while. The Duke's children sat patiently, watching as Peter gazed toward events in the years ahead, until Mara could bear to wait no longer.

"Is there more?" she asked.

"I see a great celebration," Peter replied. "Here, in the Palace. In the old hall. It is a blaze of lights. People are cheering."

"Victory!" cried Mara.

"I see men in the Emperor's livery, courtiers I do not recognize. Fair-complected men, Europeans."

"Kharles' men? But what are they doing at Pendaunzel? Oh, I know, Peter, you cannot say. But you've told me enough. There will be a war, and we shall win. Kat leads a triumphant assault upon a Spanish city. Our cousin the Emperor sends troops to our aid, and we have victory at last!"

"There is little to indicate that any of this tale you tell is true," Ambris reminded her gently. "The images Magician Peter has seen may reveal another fate entirely."

But Mara wouldn't surrender her own interpretation. "You must agree that there will be battles ahead and a celebration?"

"Yes, battles," Ambris agreed. "But the celebration is apparently for Kharles. Peter hasn't seen you nor me, nor Father in his visions." The magician nodded confirmation.

"That doesn't mean we aren't there."

"True, but you mustn't allow your imagination to make more of the facts than may rightly be interpreted. You have your answer, Mara. War. This summer. Next summer. Ten years hence. Seek no more than that." Ambris rose from his seat. "Gramercies, Magician, for your services. I shall intrude on your studies no longer."

Peter smiled. "'Tis no intrusion, My Lord. I'm pleased to be of service to you both, even in so small a thing."

The Duke's son and daughter left the Hall of Record together, each lost in private thoughts. Mara was exultant, planning her first assaults. Ambris was more somber.

"Why do you suppose Laurel isn't the wizard she ought to be?" he asked as they crossed the dark lawns toward the Manor.

"You'd know that better than I," Mara answered. "I thought she left her magic to marry."

"I never asked her to. I imagined– I wondered how it would be to wed a wizard of power. Such a woman, so strange and dangerous. She ought to have been one of the great, a rival to her uncle. Yet she left it."

"Kat says she has the look of the haunted."

Ambris laughed softly. "Kat and her fancies. `Tis the Irish in her—leprechauns and banshees. Yet she may see something we don't. Laurel is not as she was when I met her. The girl I met was bold and bright with her magic. Like lightning. She was mysterious too—in New York on some sort of magician's errand she wouldn't speak of."

"They never will speak."

"There are such things out there beyond mortal understanding," Ambris said thoughtfully, gazing up at the night sky through the trees. "Perhaps it's best if we do not know too much. She has changed, Mara. On the day she came to me, she was so badly frightened. What could shake a brave woman down to her soul? Nothing on this earth. She is not the maiden I knew. If she were, she would never have consented to marry me. Oh, I knew that she came to me because she was frightened. I knew that it was not in her best interests to shelter her. I should've insisted she return to Wizardes Cliff—but of course I didn't. How could I? When all you desire is miraculously offered you, you cannot think of the right and wrong in taking it. A man in love is not sensible. I wanted to believe that she stayed here because of me."

Mara was surprised by this sudden confidence. Until this moment, she had assumed her brother and Laurel were perfectly happy in their marriage. Their match was so dramatic that it spoke of high romance. It disturbed her to think that it wasn't so.

She slipped an arm about his waist. Ambris briefly rested his cheek against her temple.

"Are there difficulties?" she asked.

"No," he said. "But I cannot help wondering.... You are her friend, Mara. Do you think she is happy here? Does she regret?"

"She's never spoken a word of complaint to me," Mara answered honestly. "She wouldn't abuse you to your own sister even if she did feel discontented. We hardly speak of such things. I would guess that she loves you, and she loves Tomyas dearly. If she regrets, she keeps it to herself."

He sighed. "Magicians keep their secrets."

They went into the Manor.

At the beginning of the Council meeting the next morning, Dafythe announced: "It is time that we form an answer to my nephew the Emperor. I've decided to send Kat as our courier. She will act as our representative and determine what services Kharles requires. My nephew shall know that the Northlands is prepared to support the Empire fully in this matter." Dafythe didn't appear pleased with his own decision, but loyalty to the Emperor was part of his duty as an imperial governor. He could not balk.

"Father, may I ask if my recommendation is included in our message?" Mara inquired.

"You wish to remind Kharles of the portion of the treaty which allows the Empire to claim Terrojos in the face of Naufarre's defection. Granted: it has been done." He gestured to Martleanne; the secretary lifted her notebook to show that Mara's suggestion was indeed included, although Mara sat across the table, too far away to read the minuscule writing. "I am aware that you wish to invade the Spanish territory to our south," Dafythe continued. "That, Daughter, I cannot support. It is an aggressive act of warfare, and I retain some hope of resolving this crisis, maintaining Naufarre as a Norman land, and keeping my wayward brother at least nominally a Norman governor, all without bloodshed. The threat of invasion must be sufficient to thwart Spain's allegiance with Juan at this time."

"Agreed."

Dafythe looked surprised at this apparent reversal. "Mara?"

"But we must be able to give credible weight to that threat," Mara continued. "I am not so impetuous as you believe, Father. If we can force Juan and his Spanish kin to concede without warfare, so much to the good. But can't we create a show of force to impress them of our ability and willingness to fight? Our present border guard is small. A threat of invasion now is as comical as the barking of an old hound. It has no teeth."

A chuckle rippled through the Counsel. The Prince smiled as she presented her argument: "Father, I propose that in addition to reminding my cousin Kharles of Terrojos, we make him aware of our exclusive power as Northlander to aid him. The Shieldwall is on *our* borders. We can have our troops at the marches more swiftly than Kharles's army can reach the Northlands."

"If we speak of invasion then," said Lieutenant Uismarde, "Spain will hear us."

"Exactly so," said Mara. "If Spain concedes, we will have won our war without striking a single blow—just as you would have it, Father. However, if they choose to ignore the threat and take arms against us, we are prepared to defend ourselves and protect our claims. Hear me on this, Father, Ministers, I pray. I do not believe the threat of invasion will be enough to stop whatever the Spanish intend with this marriage. I lay simple truth before this Council: there will be a war. I have evidence of its coming. Last night, I consulted Magician Peter. In a vision, he beheld a battle about a burning city." She turned to her brother. "You were there with me when he saw it, Ambris," Mara reminded him.

"I heard Peter describe a battle," Ambris confirmed.

The Duke turned to his magician. "Is it so, Peter?"

Peter was unaccustomed to speak at these meetings; the sudden shift of everyone's attention to him threw him into confusion. "It is exactly as Prince Margueryt says, My Lord. Such a battle will come one day in the future. A tower will fall amid a great fire. Prince Katheryne will be there. I saw her most distinctly."

The Council was generally doubtful and suspicious of all magical arts. "I understand that such visions are not completely reliable," said Lord Tuxsetau. "The magician *sees*, but does he understand what he perceives? Does he describe his impressions accurately to you, My Prince?"

Dafythe smiled. "I know you, Mara. When you heard Peter's words concerning a battle, you leapt upon them and construed them fit your own expectations. You believe he foretells the downfall of a Spanish city in Terrojos, but you know that when any city in all the world falls, there are fires. Towers collapse. Peter might've envisioned any one of a dozen cities you and your cousin will one day besiege or capture on some future campaign. I don't doubt this will happen one day."

"A magician's visions are subject to multiple interpretations, My Lord," Peter spoke carefully, "but their essential truth is unchanging. I saw what I saw."

"There will be a battle," Mara insisted. "Why and when and where—the rest is unimportant. It will come. I do not ask we take aggressive action if it is contrary to your principles, Father, but I must tell you that I think it is the highest folly to remain peaceable in the face of such danger as we face with the traitor Juan. Are we to be caught unprepared? I ask only that we establish our defenses. I request that you release troops in my name so that I can gather the city garrisons along the disputed border. I ask that this Council convey the message to my cousin the Emperor that we are ready to fight at the time when war is declared."

Dafythe answered, "The accumulation of armies at the marches invites such a declaration, Mara. Our border guards are ready. The forts along the Shieldwall are equipped and the regiments currently stand more than ten thousand strong. We need no more at present. It is unlikely that Spain will cross our borders first. They've made no declaration of war. They have no claim upon the Eduardesmarch or other marches in our possession. Our most recent intelligence from the marches reveals that the Spanish troops at the border are smaller than ours and there is no sign of an increase in past months."

Mara could not answer this. She was ready to think all the careful arguments she had constructed with Kat's assistance were ineffective, when other ministers suddenly came to her defense.

"My Lord Duke, you cannot mean to leave us unready."

"Prince Mara's advice is no act of impulse, My Gracious Lord. I call it a prudent move."

"There will be a war, My Duke. If it is so, surely it is in our best interests to make preparations."

"It is not an act of aggression to guard ourselves."

"My Lord, you cannot ignore our duty as proper Normans. We must not turn our backs blindly to an enemy!"

"Father, if we declare ourselves willing to carry out our claims in Terrojos, Spain may retreat. They will respect a show of strength even if it is not exercised."

"And if they don't, we will be ready to act!"

Dafythe saw the exultant light in Mara's eyes as she turned to find unexpected allies rising about the Advisory Hall, all shouting to make their voices heard. He held up his hand for silence. "Yes, this war will come. I do not doubt it. I trust Peter's visions. Yet I will not provoke it. I am old enough to remember what war was like in my father's time." He sighed. "However, I know the world too well to expect that my wishes are those of others—at this table or elsewhere. Ambris, begin your draft of the message to Kharles. Mara, I shall consider your requests and give you my answer before the letter is sent."

"Prince Margueryt!"

Mara had left the Council and was now on the lower level of Hartshall. The voice had called to her from the gallery above. She turned to look back; Geoffrey, Lord Rafenshighte leaned over the rail at the top of the stairway.

"I commend you, My Prince," he said. "You speak well to win the Council to your side. I pray you note who spoke first and most loudly."

Mara thought of those who had been first to support her today. She saw the faces accompanying the shouting voices: Lord Kaeroth, Layn Ayrton, Layn Lamsford. Not Geoffrey, but many of the ministers he had named as his friends.

He smiled down at her, seeing that she understood. "You see how it might be, My Prince. All are ardent now with the memory of your thrilling speeches, but their ardor will swiftly cool. Those who cheer you today may stand by your father at the next meeting. You may lose the very ground you've fought to gain. No good general would stand for that."

Mara nodded.

"Recall when you have your way, My Prince, who has been most loyal."

"I've always wanted to visit Europe," said Kat. "I was just a baby when I left." She paused, reliving old memories. "I remember how quiet it was when my mother died. My nurse hushed me and everyone whispered. I remember when Ambris came. The nursemaid picked me up and handed me to his arms, and my father told him to take me and be off. I remember the ocean. Ambris lifted me up to the ship's rail to show me the dolphins playing in the water. I think I was in London too, on the way from Eireland. There was a kindly old man who made a great fuss over me. I thought it was my grandfather."

"Grandfather was dead by then," Mara told her.

"Yes, of course. It must have been Uncle Kharles. I *was* in London once before, but I couldn't tell you a thing about it."

They sat in Mara's reception chamber. The room, with its flowery tapestries, velvet-cushioned chairs and tables with slender, ornately carved legs, had once been Gillefluere's. Mara had taken her mother's apartments after her knighting. Although she had altered the bedchamber and offices to suit her own tastes and converted the boudoir into a personal armory, she kept this room as her mother had left it. As children, she and Kat had attended reception teas for the Pendaunzel dames, conferences with courtiers, semi-private audiences with distinguished visitors in this same room. There were too many memories here.

The Irish Prince smiled. "Do you recall, Mara, how we used to gather news of where Ambris was in the world and find him on the maps in the schoolroom? We talked about all the cities with the wonderful names—Paris, Venice, Prague, Kiev. Now I'll have my chance to see a few grand cities for myself."

"It won't be a pleasure trip," said Mara. "Father's sending you on a most important errand to pledge fealty to our cousin the Emperor. You'll speak for us all."

"But that's the best of it. For the first time, I'm doing something of use. If you could know how delighted I was when Ambris brought the news of my mission to me. `Tis a magnificent honor. Uncle Dafythe has chosen me to represent him before the Emperor. Do you know, I think they still see me as a child? I have no duties in the Northlands. I'm too young in the Council's eyes. Too reckless. Too impulsive. Too excitable. Too much in–" she stopped.

"Too much in my influence," Mara finished for her. Since she spoken with Geoffrey, she had begun to suspect that the Council thought the same of her. She was beloved, no doubt, but Ambris's judgment was deemed more reliable. "I too feel as if this crisis has given me the opportunity to do something worthwhile. You haven't yet reached your thirtieth birthday, Kat, but I know you feel as I do. We are still young, but we are past our girlhood. When I look at my accomplishments so far, I feel that they are nothing. I've done nothing I've meant to do. Until we had this promise of war, the next ninety years seemed as dismal."

Kat nodded. "Ambris told me what went on in the Council today. Do you think our arguments will have any influence upon Uncle Dafythe's decision?"

"I don't know. He was about to reject my proposal, when some of the Council spoke in my support. He said..."

There was a knock at the chamber door and Mara cried, "Come!" Bel, the captain of the Prince's honor guard of Shieldmaids, entered.

Bel had been the smallest girl in Mara's cadet squad. During those first, brutal days of training, Mara's sympathies had gone out to the petite maid with a pert, little nose, doe-soft eyes, and brown curls that were tamed into the four traditional braids with difficulty, yet she had admired the pugnacity that repudiated this pixyish appearance. She'd taken the little maid into her protection and Bel's loyalty had been unwavering since.

"You sent for me, Prince Mara?" Bel's eyes darted from Mara to Kat and back. "Your arm's out of the sling."

"The healer said I might have it free if I did not abuse it. Light exercise only. No swordplay. Shall we test its fitness on the archery range?" Bel was famous for her deadly accuracy.

"I don't imagine any of the courtiers you match with give you a proper contest," Bel answered with a laugh. "No, that pretty, flattering lot deliberately shoots you worse."

Mara laughed with her. "'Tis true. All save Kat, and I must do without her for the next few months. But that's not the reason why I called you in." Although she intended to gain greater power in the court, Mara did not intend to overlook the influence of such friends as this. Her sister-Shieldmaids could do more to aid her than Rafenshighte would credit them with. "You've heard about the Council meeting?"

"I've heard little else this morning. Is it true? My Lord

Dafythe might release the garrisons to you?"

"He said he'll consider it and give me his answer. It's the first time he's shown signs of yielding. My request isn't unreasonable. It's a perfectly sound strategic move to impress Spain with our resolution. Surely, Father must concede to the sense of it. I'm not asking that he give me leave to overrun Terrojos with Northlander soldiers—not yet. Are you willing to ride with me, Captain?"

"You ask? Mara, my loyalty is yours. You know that. If war does come, we must be ready for it. No one can fault you for foresight."

"True." She gestured for Bel to sit down. "I know you keep up with our old company."

"Most of them. Alyx was commissioned Captain of the Guard at Storm Port this winter. And you know Martine is at the marches. Sataumie is at the camp in Ystelake, teaching little maids to become swordswomen. The others are too far scattered. Jeandanyel has gotten God-knows-where as a free agent. When I last heard from her two years ago, she was on her way to the Far East with a caravan of rich traveling merchants. Tessa's in France."

"We have three then, who can receive the news within days," Mara concluded. "Send messages to them—Alyx, Taumie, and Martine. I cannot write them myself—not `til Father gives me leave—but I think it best that we be prepared before the orders are given. Apprise them of the situation, of Prince Juan's latest treachery, of the treaty that allows us to claim Terrojos, of my request that my father allow me to lead an army to the marches. Tell them to keep the news to themselves for the present, but tell them: *Organize your troops. Be ready.* They are Shieldmaids. They'll know what to do."

"They'll be waiting for your word," Bel promised.

Mara smiled and turned to Kat. "There we are, Cos. If Father releases the garrisons, I am ready to march. If not, then nothing is lost. If I win Father over later on, then our friends are prepared to join me within days. I have covered all possibilities. We'll see the mountains of Terrojos yet!"

The Duke's court customarily celebrated Holy Week with somber ceremonies. This year, however, the possibility of war occupied everyone's thoughts and the nightly rituals recalling the sufferings of Christ were not the usual sorrowful enactments of ancient tradition. A restless energy, barely suppressed, enervated the court. The sobs, the torn shirts, the breast-beatings had a strange intensity. Prayers were especially passionate. Even on Holy Saturday, after the candles had been put out on Good Friday and the hours of silence began, urgent whispers could be heard in the dim corridors.

On Sunday, this hushed energy burst forth. The chapel bells pealed. Lights were lit again. The fast ended in feast and the court exploded in joyous laughter, not all for the sake of the Resurrection.

Mara hadn't pressed her father for his answer during Holy Week, but on Easter Sunday the Duke received petitions from Northlander citizens in the State Hall and she was resolved to address him then.

The State Hall was the oldest part of the Palace. Dafythe had taken care to have it repaired rather than demolished when he rebuilt his new manor from the old castle. Its stone faces were crumbling and its outer embellishments worn indistinguishable. The flagstones within were polished smooth and deep grooves had worn into the twin staircases to the galleries above by thousands of feet over the centuries. Here, the first Lord of the Northlands, Robert Gilthair, had held audience with his subjects on holidays and days of festival. His ancestors continued to carry on this tradition.

Commoners waited for the Duke on the Palace lawns, but members of the Council, merchant families of prominence and local nobility had gathered in the ancient Hall. The Layn Mayor was there with her husband and children. Bel and her Shieldmaids accompanied Mara in their best dress uniforms. The courtiers wore their finery; the elders were dressed in traditional, trailing formal robes while the younger folk had chosen more modern fashion.

The Lady Laurel had only recently thrown off the loose-fitting robes of pregnancy to put on clothes much like those she'd worn as a maiden. Her tunic of noble blue was cut several inches above the knee. Lace trimmed the front of her blouse and more lacy frills were sewn along the outer seam of each shirtsleeve to be pulled through gaps in the embroidered bands of her tunic sleeves. After years of more modest and austere tailoring, the Lady's wardrobe was unconventional and even somewhat shocking to the Pendaunzel court, but it was said that the courtiers of Paris dressed in similar fashion. Kat and others had already begun to copy her.

Lord Redmantyl's son Orlan had taken up the style of the court: a cluster of slender braids were woven into one plait of his long curls and tied with red ribbon; frills of lace were sewn onto his shirt-sleeves and pulled through the slashed sleeves of his tunic; the tunic's hemline had been taken up several inches above the knee. In sooty grey, scarlet and silver, he was striking figure even among the bright courtiers. He drew the giggling attention of young damosels as his father drew more discreet attention from older noblewomen.

"What a little peacock that boy is," Ambris murmured to Mara and Kat.

"He's a handsome lad and he knows it," Kat answered. Her costume was similarly brief and fashionable in princely white and blue. "But where did he find a tailor to make the alterations so swiftly?"

"He probably did it himself," Laurel said as she joined them.

"All that trimming and hemming?" asked Mara.

"All magicians are skilled in needlecraft," the Lady explained. "They have to embroider the spells they wear on their clothes."

This was a surprising piece of information. "You mean that My Lord Redmantyl did all that beautiful black and gold fancy-work on his robes himself?" said Kat.

"Every stitch is his own work," Laurel assured her. "The spells wouldn't be effective otherwise."

Kat smiled. "But, Laurel, you can't sew a straight seam to save your life."

"Exactly so. `Tis why I'm no longer a magician."

The Princes exchanged a glance. It was sometimes difficult to know when Laurel was joking.

While they had been speaking, Lord Rafenshighte approached Orlan. The nobleman spoke softly; the boy first appeared surprised at his words, then he smiled shyly.

"Oh, Christ," said Kat. "And him about to take his mage

vows!"

"I'll go put a stop to it before my cousin finds himself in trouble." Laurel crossed the room to distract Orlan with a playful remark. As she drew him away, Ambris stepped forward to intercept Rafenshighte. After a whispered warning, Rafenshighte laughed and retreated gracefully.

"A pretty lad isn't safe with that rakehell," Kat observed. "If My Lord Redmantyl should see..."

Lord Redmantyl was not in sight. Gossip this last week whispered that he'd been seen walking in the gardens with Martleanne, dancing with Damosel Ariane, speaking privately with Lady Kyntauke. Those who noticed his absence now casually scanned the crowd for missing ladies.

"Is Father down yet?" Mara asked when her brother returned. Laurel remained with her dandified cousin.

"Not yet," answered Ambris.

"Have you heard? Has he decided?"

"I don't know, Mara. He's been shut in his chambers since he returned from this morning's Mass. You've made him a request which he finds difficult to answer."

"The answer is obvious–"

Seven young boys in the Duke's dark blue and gold livery came through the open doors between the two stairways. On the little landing above the main floor, they fell into formation: three to the right, three to the left. Trumpets blared. The seventh boy, the new herald, stepped to the front. As he looked down at the crowd in the hall below him, his eyes grew wide and blank.

Laurel turned to Orlan with an anxious look; her cousin only lifted his eyebrows and shrugged.

Andemyon shut his eyes and squeaked out, "Gentle nobles, good citizens, all hail thee Dafythe Ambris Gabriel Lyonsbloode Plantagenet, Prince of the Norman Empire, Grand Duke, Sovereign Lord Governor and Protector of the Northlands by Grace of God!"

He'd gotten the Duke's name slightly wrong and had left out Dafythe's titles as Preserver of the Peace and Defender of the Faith, but it wasn't a bad first announcement. Some boys muddled it completely. Dafythe made his entrance to cheers and applause. Bertrande, at the Duke's right, gently took his grandfather's elbow and escorted him down the steps. The little procession made its way through the Hall to the Duke's Seat at the far end. Dafythe passed from one guest to the next, receiving hands, speaking with distracted courtesy. When he reached his children, Ambris, then Mara, then Kat each performed the ceremonial gesture of respect by offering him their hands and bowing their heads.

Mara whispered, "Father?"

"Ah, you have a petition for me?" the Duke replied, also in whisper.

"Only the request I made you at the Council Monday. Do you have an answer?"

"I've thought of little else. No, Mara, I will not grant your request."

"But–"

"Daughter, it is not proper that we speak of this now." Dafythe went on to take his seat and hear the petitions of his subjects before Mara could protest.

cinq

"Why not?" the Prince demanded the next morning.

Dafythe met his daughter's indignant gaze with his own more mild but indomitable one. "The time isn't right," he answered. "Wait 'til Kat has gone to London and brought back Kharles's response. If the Emperor calls to increase our troops at the border, I shall grant you command of the garrisons then. Not before. I won't be the one to provoke this war."

"Juan's started it! He's been straining toward this break for so long as I can recall. He invites war. He begs for it."

The Duke sighed. "Yes. If only you and Kharles weren't so eager for it yourselves."

"You don't understand. You have no warrior-heart. When you were knighted, Father, did you receive your vision?"

"No."

"Have you sought a talisman since?"

"I've never taken a battle-name, nor personal arms."

"You've never fought. Your heroes are scholars and Church Doctors." She was aware that she sounded improperly contemptuous and quickly amended her statements. "I do not fault you for it. You simply don't understand why such things are important to me. Kharles and I are not aggressive, though we ache to strike before we are first struck. It's impossible to remain meek before such antagonism! And what is wrong with an aggressive campaign? The Empire is built upon them. Do you think we would stand so strong as we do today if not for our ancestors' successful conquests?"

"This isn't the time to speculate upon whether or not our ancestors had rightful claim to Angeland or France or to our own Northlands," her father answered. "Those were barbaric days, when land was considered all. Many atrocities were committed in the name of God and Empire that I would not wish to see repeated. War unleashes a terrible cruelty in people. That darkness in the mortal soul compels us to such hatred and eagerness to see our foes suffer at our hands. Now I do not say this barbarian impulse is necessarily evil. The capacity for cruelty in conflict with our desire for civilization and peace is the root of our blessed free will. Without that struggle, we are not reasoning beings. However, since we are reasoning beings, we are responsible for our acts before the eyes of God. I wouldn't see such power released wantonly. It is to be reserved for the greatest emergencies. When we are called to defend home and family, it gives us the courage to face the danger and drive it away."

"But that is what we face now."

Dafythe smiled. "If that were so, I would agree that it is time to make a show of force. Yet our home is safe. The Northlands haven't been touched. No Norman soil has been invaded—not even Naufarre. Daughter, tell me: do you understand your own reasons for demanding aggressive action? Why is Naufarre important?"

"It is Norman crown land," Mara answered.

"It has been so for some sixty years," Dafythe agreed. "Before that, it was Spanish for more than two centuries, and before *that* Norman since we last captured it from Spain. Yet it holds nothing to make it so prized. `Tis not large enough to make a practical march, nor rich enough in its resources to increase the imperial income. In fact, it is expensive to maintain Norman garrisons to keep it ours against its Spanish traditions. We want it today because my father the Redlyon wanted it and *he* desired it only because his ancestors once lay claim to it. Kharles wants to keep it because he doesn't wish Spain to recover it. The Spanish want it because we have it."

This would have bordered on treason if any but Dafythe had said it. The belittling of the motives of at least two Emperors with one statement was suspect even so. Mara was shocked. "Do you suggest we surrender Naufarre without a fight?" she asked.

"I suggest we not be so eager to waste so much of the Empire's time, money, and energy as well as the lives of our soldiery over a worthless little strip of land that we keep only for our pride."

"Pride is not worthless," Mara answered. "We can't let this

challenge pass unanswered even if we have no use for Naufarre. Do you think of what will happen, Father, if we let it go? We will be seen as cowards and weaklings before all the world! Spain will demand Languedok next, or the Eduardesmarch. Will you surrender them as well? Will you see the Empire torn apart?"

"Of course not. But Naufarre is not the Empire."

"It is part of it. Spain wants it, and that's enough reason to keep it from them."

"I think it is not."

"Kharles will fight for it, no matter what you advise."

"I expect he will. With so many calling for it, I do not doubt we'll have war, but I will not be among those to shout of honor and glory when I mean to shed the blood of my subjects."

"But your subjects want war," Mara protested. "They cheer me on even more than the courtiers."

"They seek the memory of the Redlyon in you," answered Dafythe. "They are Norman and proud to give themselves in the service of their liege."

"If they are willing, then why should I not ask? You often say that you are guided by the will of your people, Father. They demand action against our enemy." She repeated her question of the Council meeting: "If war is so brutal and horrible and pointless, why do they clamor for it?"

The answer wasn't pleasant. Dafythe knew what Mara must also know, but wouldn't acknowledge: barbarity and bloodthirst were more in the nature of humanity than the desire for peace. In the soul's struggle between cruelty and civilization, cruelty usually won.

Dafythe placed one hand upon the table and rose stiffly. "You are no longer a willful girl, Mara. You will be Duke soon. It's time that you think of the people you are given to govern before your own desires. We are bound in covenant with our subjects. We protect them in times of danger, provide for them in scarcity, make their laws, answer their needs. In turn, they give us their loyalty, pay their taxes, serve their nation in our names. These obligations are mutual. So long as one is upheld, so is the other. I serve my people by seeing to their best interests. I hear their pleas and do all that is in my power to aid them. But I will not be guided by their whims and base demands. At times, a number of

Norman citizens have demanded the forced conversion of all Jews within our borders, the persecution of witches, pagans, and magicians, the expulsion of foreigners. Shall I give in to these mockeries of true Christian virtue? Would you? What sort of governor is led by the ignorant and superstitious on matters of state? Ridiculous! It is my business to guide my people. It will be yours as well."

He spoke with an intensity unexpected in so gentle and aged a man; Mara was taken aback. She had imagined Dafythe, a famous pacifist, to be weak-willed and vacillating. Yet she had underestimated him. For the moment, she was startled into inarticulacy.

"Mara, when you hear the common folk cry for the restoration of the old days of the Redlyon, ask yourself: is this war best for them? At your word, they will give their lives. But are you ready to ask for those lives? Can you look upon a battlefield red with blood and see the wounded and dead who wouldn't be there save that you sent them? Recall, you are sworn to protect them. Will you be the agency of their deaths?"

When Mara didn't answer, he added, "I've never been able to bear that weight upon my conscience. I wouldn't ask any subject to die in my name. I have always been able to find a peaceable and honorable alternative. It has served me well until now. I will not change."

Mara *was* like Eduarde Redlyon—that was the trouble. Dafythe had known it from his daughter's squalling infancy. "How like her grandfather she is!" He'd heard the words too often. "His very image! See how she holds her tin sword! See how she sits her pony. She has his skill! His courage! Brave child, she does not cry out even when she falls and scrapes her knees! What a warrior she will be!" Eloquence was predicted in every childish lisp, bravery in each toddling step.

Like her grandfather, Mara was short-tempered. She could get angry so fast when she didn't have her own way. Her voice rising—how like the Redlyon's roars! Like the Redlyon, she was impulsive. She had his confidence that whatever she wished to do was right. Mara possessed the bravery of one who does not imagine death. Her ferocity when the spirit was upon her was frightening. Dafythe had heard from various sparring partners that his daughter was insensate to her own injuries. She fought on wounded until her opponent called a stop to the game. It was not remarkable to see her in bandages. Mara seemed unaware of the hard facts of reality, but she ploughed on all the same and never ran against the truth. His daughter, like his father, ignored the obstacles before them and shaped the world to suit their liking. These were the qualities the Redlyon's subjects had most admired in their Emperor and sought among his descendants.

But those who worshiped the memory of the Redlyon hadn't truly known him. The common-folk, the soldiers, the rural nobility of Eduarde's day had had little opportunity to view their Emperor's private life: they saw him in public ceremonies and pageants, heard his commands on the battlefield, heard his proclamations read. They listened breathlessly to the news of his latest victory. They sang ballads to his memory even before his death. The Redlyon's legend grew swiftly beyond the living man.

Eduarde's closest friends and advisors were long dead now. Even so, none had known the late Emperor so well as his sons. From Ouestminstre to the Louvre to Holyrood to Fotheringhay, the court of the Redlyon traveled regularly from one royal residence to another, the Princes Kharles and Dafythe always in their imperious father's wake. Eduarde kept his sons with him from the time they were old enough to travel because he didn't trust nursery-maids and tutors to see them properly brought up. His sisters alone had his trust. Only Norman royal blood was fit to instruct and guide Norman princelings.

In spite of the efforts of Aunts Anne and Klarys, the little princes had been a disappointment to their fierce father. Eduarde's blustering, rough upbringing had made them timid children. Neither of them were much like him; neither possessed the warrior heart. They were not weaklings—his near-century and Kharles's eighty-nine years were proof of respectable health—but they were bookish, thoughtful, cautious. Their dispositions echoed the emperors who had preceded their father: Robert the Good, Elizabeth III, the Sainted Adalemarde, Cordelia Pax. These Norman rulers had valued peace above the glories of warfare. They had wrought a bright pinnacle of civilization from a collection of barbarian kingdoms. His father's reign was different.

Eduarde was not a ruler to delegate his duties. He wanted to see all the land that he'd been given by God's Grace. He liked to direct his regents personally and administer the business of every realm. He delighted in meeting his subjects, hearing their praise. And, if there was dissent, he must put it down by his own hand.

The Redlyon was a bully, an absolute ruler with no check upon his powers. Fearless of God and mortal-kind, he did whatever he wished. He waged his yearly wars because he enjoyed them; he always assumed that the money to fund his campaigns was there when he required it. He pursued any woman who caught his attention, certain that he wouldn't be refused. Humiliation came to any who hesitated in carrying out his commands. He spied on his courtiers and ruined the careers of the luckless who fell from his favor. He took what he desired and none dared oppose him. In Eduarde's day, opposition was taken as outright treason.

People didn't remember what it was like to live in a constant state of war, taxes high to support an enormous standing army, youths impressed into the Emperor's service, goods requisitioned, homes continually endangered by invasion. However, Dafythe recalled that the Norman citizens of his youth hadn't resented these hardships. They idolized Eduarde. When he was in their vicinity, they turned out by the thousands to cheer as he rode past, to glimpse him, to touch the hem of his cloak as if this simple contact conveyed some sort of blessing upon them. They believed their money, their children, their property well sacrificed in their beloved Redlyon's cause. As for Eduarde's intolerance of dissenting opinion, they firmly believed that those who dared disagree with the Emperor were traitors and deserved whatever punishment they received. In fact, Dafythe's leniency was seen as weakness; no imperial personage should endure the insult of opposition.

In his seventy years as Duke, Dafythe had never executed any subject for treason. He'd never been able to endure the sight of blood, not since he had witnessed his first execution at the age of thirteen. A man had been hung, drawn and quartered at Tyburn. A great crowd had gathered. Dafythe remembered how they'd shouted and pressed forward to get a better view. He had clung to his brother's cloak to avoid being lost in the milling as Kharles led him to the imperial dais where Eduarde stood. He didn't recall why they had gone on that occasion. Had they been summoned?

By the time they'd reached the platform, the prisoner was already hanging by his neck from the gallows. His wrists and ankles were bound but his limbs twitched as if he continued to struggle against the ropes. When the executioner cut him open, the prisoner gave out a shrill cry. He was still alive! Dafythe realized. Still alive! Blood flowed from the gash, turned the dirty-white hose of the prisoner red, spilled onto the straw beneath the gallows. The crowd moaned, a long, lowing sound as if they experienced the pain themselves.

The man was cut down, his arms still bound behind his back. Dafythe saw then that he held a small silver cross in his hands; it slipped from between them as he fell. The man's fingers moved, groped vaguely after it. It wasn't yet finished. The executioner cut the bonds and kicked the prisoner to turn him face up. Then he took up an axe. The limbs were severed with four neat chops. Red spread and spread. The lips of the limbless form moved. Still alive! Sweet Jesus, Dafythe wondered even to this day, how could a man endure such mutilation and live on?

He had prayed then, a boy at his brother's side. The world spun about him, red with living blood. The crowd murmured; the excited, pulsing rhythm of their mingling voices rose and fell in his ears like a heartbeat. Dafythe had wanted to hide his face against the folds of Kharles's cloak. He would have fainted, but Kharles slipped a steadying hand around his and squeezed gently.

"Father's looking this way, Davy," his elder brother had whispered. "Shut your eyes if you can't watch."

But Dafythe *had* to watch. It was impossible to look away until the axe fell a final time, beheading the prisoner and ending his agony.

Dafythe had never learned what the man's crime had been. Treason, he imagined. Perhaps the man had been a Spanish spy, or a Norman subject who had spoken out against the Emperor: Eduarde had executed others for that crime during the purges in the 1880's. Several prominent nobles had gone to the block and members of their households were hanged during that dark period.

How many times after that had Dafythe stood with Kharles

behind their father as bodies dangled from gallows or axes fell? How many decaying heads had he seen on the pikes at Traitors' Gate? Twice more, he knew, he'd been witness to the same abomination.

Whatever the man had done, Dafythe believed that no crime deserved such punishment. The thought of spilling blood sickened him—not with the queasiness of the faint-hearted, but with a moral repugnance that any human being could take delight in deliberately killing another. To him, this was the prime act of savagery. Nearly two thousand years had passed since the Crucifixion, and humanity had progressed no further than this? He was appalled by the ease with which his father slaughtered his enemies. Eduarde might call them God's foes, but Dafythe knew the difference. As a youth, however, Dafythe had kept his outrage silent. He was the Emperor's son, but that was no guarantee that his opinion would be more well-received than any other.

He was more fortunate than his brother, for he'd left his father's court at his mother's death. Eduarde rarely visited the Northlands and Dafythe was more or less an independent governor. He was free to exercise his own ideas in his state policies, although his father intervened from time to time. Dafythe returned to Europe only three times during Eduarde's reign.

He returned the first time for his father's second marriage. The bride, Aline, Lady Rokhester, was a cousin from the cadet Kent branch of the imperial family. Younger daughters and sons of the Dukes of Kent were brought up especially as prospective spouses for princes. In fact, Aline had been intended as a bride for Kharles, but at her presentation at Ouestminstre, Eduarde was so charmed by this pretty, timid maid that he decided to marry her himself. The marriage was brief; Aline died at the birth of her one child, Agnes.

The second time he'd returned had been after Aline's death. Dafythe had traveled to Paris for his sister's christening and, as it happened, arrived in time for his step-mother's funeral. After the two ceremonies, the Redlyon went to London to attend a trial. Dafythe remained with his brother. One night, they'd sat together in Kharles's apartments and spoke of their hopes to restore the Norman Empire to its glory of old. Father was completely mad,

Kharles told him in confidence. These recent purges of imagined traitors were evidence that he could no longer be trusted to govern responsibly. And if *that* were not enough, the Emperor planned to lead another campaign against Spain. Naufarre again. How many battles had been fought over that one little scrap of land? If Father could be persuaded to relinquish some of his powers...

They'd made plans that night. At the time, Dafythe hadn't truly believed that anything would come of it—not until after the Redlyon's death—but within a few months he began to hear that his father was indeed ceding responsibilities to Kharles. The trials for treason ended. Kharles reviewed the last cases personally and declared that there was insufficient evidence to support the charges; the prisoners were released. More astonishing, there was talk of establishing peaceful terms with Spain.

Dafythe was often credited with shaping the *pax normania* of this century, but in truth most of it had been Kharles's work. He had merely served as his brother's assistant. At Kharles's suggestion, he wrote their father letters that were a combination of flattery and his own long-concealed opinions. He urged Eduarde to heed Kharles's advice. A peaceful accord with their old enemy had economic and political advantages over perpetual war. The Norman Empire was the mightiest nation on Earth and Eduarde the greatest earthly ruler; was it not seemly that he be magnanimous? Dafythe proposed an exchange of disputed territories. The Treaty of Naufarre was the result. In this manner, perhaps, he was architect of the *pax normania*, but he would never have dared to write one word if Kharles hadn't asked him to.

He returned to his father's court one last time to aid Kharles in composing the historic treaty and to greet Eduarde's Spanish bride.

When Dafythe arrived in Paris, he was shocked at how his father had changed since his last visit five years before. The Redlyon who had left his wife's funeral to oversee the prosecution of dissenting nobles had been the same fearsome figure Dafythe had known from his childhood. This older Redlyon still roared. He burst into terrible rages. He made vicious threats, as gory and elaborate in their detail as ever to show that he remained the same bloody-minded bully at heart. But he was no longer dangerous. His rages were impotent, the squalls of a spoiled child who can't get his own way. When his commands were ignored, he fell into fits of weeping that were disturbing to see. He relied entirely on Kharles now, but his worst outbursts were directed at his son. From tractability, the Emperor leapt abruptly, unexpectedly to venom, cursing Kharles for a coward, a thief, a usurper. Kharles bore the old man's abuse with calm temper.

The Emperor was in his dotage, the Paris courtiers whispered. Brave Eduarde, brought so low! But how well Kharles managed the Empire during this troublesome time! How fortunate that the Prince of France, so long in his father's shadow, had emerged from obscurity and proved to be such a capable administrator. Many of them, like Dafythe, wondered how Kharles could hold so much influence over Eduarde, yet surrender on the important point of whether he or his father would marry the Spanish princess.

The first drafts of the Treaty of Naufarre had offered Kharles as bridegroom for Marianne but, as he had with Aline, Eduarde became enamored of the reputed beauty of the Infanta. The Redlyon saw his forty-two-year-old son as a mere boy. He, in his prime, would seal the alliance. This was the usual sort of outlandish declaration Eduarde made in his later days. The odd thing was that Kharles yielded to him.

Dafythe had his brother's confidence in most matters, but Kharles never discussed the subject of Marianne. When Dafythe arrived at Paris, the court was wild with rumor and speculation. Some said that Marianne's father, the Emperor Alamanzus, had insisted on the Redlyon making the match—though Dafythe found this implausible. Others said that Eduarde had retained some hold over Kharles. Kharles's most loyal adherents insisted that the Prince was too honorable to put himself forward as emperor while his father still lived, and therefore had conceded his intended bride to Eduarde as a gracious gesture. Peace between the empires was most important to the Prince, this last party insisted. It wasn't as if he loved the girl.

Marianne was now in her eighties, but Dafythe recalled her as the maid of five-and-twenty he'd met at Paris just before the wedding, rather pretty, tall, aloof, a princess bound by duties and, like himself, the child of an unbending ruler. She was furious that she was forced into so unequal a marriage. Dafythe had pitied her. He wasn't alone in this sentiment. The Emperor met his bride courteously—with only one or two offensive remarks of bawdry—and conducted himself quietly at the wedding, but everyone in attendance agreed that it was a shame to see any young maid, even a Spaniard, given to an aged madman.

Had Eduarde been mad? In the last years of his reign, when his bloodthirst had extended to his own subjects as well as to the Spanish, yes. Certainly, yes. But before that? The Emperor's closest advisors might have called him sane in his prime, but a strange darkness had lain over Eduarde's mind for as long as Dafythe could remember. His unceasing hatred of Spain, which he had engendered in the Norman people even to this day, was not rational. Eduarde might call the Spanish enemies of God. He might speak of borders threatened by the insidious foe. He might call for the restoration of stolen lands. But these were mere excuses. There was truly only one reason why the Redlyon waged war after war.

The memory of Denys, long dead, haunted Eduarde throughout his reign. One might think a man so brutal and ambitious as Eduarde Redlyon would welcome the death of the elder brother who stood between him and the Norman throne, but Dafythe believed his father's grief and desire for vengeance genuine. Denys had been the driving force in the late Emperor's life. All wars were fought for Denys's sake. Every campaign in the Northlands' marches, each attempt to claim Naufarre, was retaliation for the murder of the Bright Prince. As he had slain the actual assassins, so he desired the death of all Spaniards. He sought to eradicate the race from the face of the earth. *By the blood of Denys!* had been Eduarde's rallying cry. His prayers for victory invariably invoked his brother's name.

The sanctification of Denys had been Eduarde's doing. Dafythe and Kharles had been brought up to regard their uncle in the same light as the knights of legend, Launcelot and Parsyfal; lesser-born Norman children, raised on tales of Prince Denys's adventures, dreamed of great battles and magnificent deeds of bravery. Generations revered him as the warrior-prince exemplar. Denys the Bright Prince. Denys the Fair. Denys Spaniardslayer.

Would that cherished image exist if Eduarde hadn't taken such pains to keep the memory of his brother alive for his subjects as it remained vivid in his own mind?

The Emperor's unending grief had shaped his reign. Even when his actions seemed reasonable, his motives weren't those of a sane man. And there could never be a reasonable motive for the blood-letting Eduarde had loosed on his own people.

Eduarde lived for four years after his marriage to Marianne. Millions of Normans mourned his death, but Dafythe thought that if the Almighty had been more merciful, He would have taken the fierce, proud Redlyon before he'd decayed into a mewling, toothless old beast.

Eduarde's subjects didn't see this final degeneration. They knew of his illness, but Kharles had carefully concealed his true condition. The Emperor was only exposed to public gaze during his most lucid periods. No sight of their beloved Redlyon in a dotard's daze tarnished the common-folk's memories. In spite of their personal feelings, Dafythe and Kharles had maintained their father's exalted image. The old man was dead, they agreed, and his bloody reign ended. Why abuse his reputation? And so they'd raised statues in the city squares, commissioned historical plays, heard ballads praising the Redlyon's victories sung in their own halls, even while they revised every policy their father had decreed.

They restored the Empire to the laws and manners of its golden age. The Norman Empire was far richer today than it had ever been. Its citizens enjoyed a standard of living unsurpassed. Norman merchants traveled safely to every port in the world. The sons of Eduarde were well-respected, but none would glorify their administration. The citizens of the Empire were comfortable, prosperous and safe, but they were bored. They saw the Redlyon's violent but much more exciting reign as a glorious time, and they looked to Mara in hopes that she would bring those days back.

Mara didn't intend to repeat the Redlyon's brutal regime. Dafythe knew something of his daughter's character. She wasn't deliberately cruel. Her worst fault was that she was impetuous, preferring immediate action to solve any problem and giving no heed to the consequences. She thought only of the excitement of battle, not of the bloody deaths it would bring to her own soldiers as well as the Spanish troops. Mara wasn't heartless nor vindictive. Eduarde's colossal arrogance was not hers. While the Redlyon had approached God as a fellow king to be bargained with, cajoled, and cursed when He did not honor His pact, Mara's prayers were humble entreaties to be fit for holy service. Dafythe admired her solemn adherence to the chivalric code. Her idealism gave him hope. But she was yet Prince of Gossunge. Who today knew what Eduarde's intentions had been in his youth?

Given reliable advisors and a court atmosphere that did not feed her pride overmuch, Mara might become a capable governor. Dafythe hoped so. His own powers as Duke of the Northlands had always been limited by a higher authority: first his father, then his brother, and now his nephew. Each Emperor in his varied way had kept Dafythe from thinking too highly of himself. Despite his illustrious position, he'd never lost his sense of being a mere man with enormous responsibilities to those above and below him. It had kept him sane. But he couldn't assure himself that Mara would receive these same proofs against the applause of her subjects—already, they cheered at the sight of her. Who would restrain her once she was Duke?

Tuxsetau, Peaque, Roodebroke, his own most trusted ministers, might guide her for awhile if she retained them on the Council, but there was a faction of young courtiers who flattered Mara to win her favor. In the end, their influence would be greater. Kat, even if she were to remain in the Northlands, would follow Mara in whatever course she chose. Ambris? Dafythe had given his son as much power as he dared, in hopes that Ambris would aid Mara with his superior experience and judgment, but it seemed that even now Ambris hesitated to oppose her. He had learned his lesson too well; he refused to take a position that might appear to usurp his sister's authority. Instead, he aided her. Dafythe was well aware that Mara's understanding of the Treaty of Naufarre had been gained through her brother.

Once Duke, Mara would answer only to her liege lord Kharles and to God. Dafythe found no comfort here. Mara believed now that God meant her to kill Spaniards. She only awaited the call to perform that holy service. And Kharles? A better Emperor would encourage all that was noble and generous in Mara's nature, but

Dafythe had no illusions about his nephew. It was young Kharles who had inherited the Redlyon's supreme selfishness. Kharles was the sensualist. He placed his own pleasures before his duty to his subjects—a dangerous thing for any governor, and how much more so for one who wielded imperial powers! Dafythe's brother used to make excuses for the boy's conduct—young Kharles was only a child; he would learn temperance—but gossip from the imperial court confirmed Dafythe's suspicions that his nephew at five-and-thirty hadn't changed from the spoiled princeling of seventeen who had insulted the German princess meant for his bride. If there had been any change, it was for the worse now that Kharles had no one to check his profligate nature.

Young Kharles, like his grandfather, relished conquest but, unlike Eduarde, he didn't enjoy warfare. It was too risky; the young Emperor favored games he was certain to win. What if Kharles were to encourage the worst in Mara for his own ends?

If Kharles gave Mara commands that coincided with her own desires, she would obey him eagerly. She would lead campaigns in his name, take her victories for the glory of the Empire. With imperial sanction, proof against whatever counsel she received to the contrary, she would find no restraint. This, Dafythe feared above all. Kharles and Mara: one or the other was simply a self-indulgent ruler who needed firm counsel; together, they could restore the worst of the Redlyon's reign.

Mara slipped into the Othelie chapel at dusk. The little church was dark; the chaplain had gone for the night. She lit a spill from the sanctuary lamp and lit the candles by the door, then the candles at the altar. She dipped her fingers at the font, made the sign of the cross, and knelt.

"Holy Father, I plead you aid me. I present myself a humble disciple, troubled and seeking guidance. Is my cause just? I know that I am given to my nature for some service in Your purpose, but I do not know if this is truly the time You have chosen to call upon me."

Mara's instincts urged her to act upon her first impulse: if she had her way, the Northlands' troops would have been assembled and prepared to ride out when she'd first heard the news of Juan's latest treachery. She felt it was right to respond to this threat with immediate retaliation, yet her father obviously believed a different response was appropriate. Dafythe was a wise man, she knew, well-respected throughout the world. He had kept the Northlands peaceable for more years than she had been alive. And, while Mara itched with impatience in this undisturbed land, she could see that her father's *pax normania* hadn't undermined the might of the Norman Empire. They remained the most powerful realm on Earth. None would dare to call Dafythe a coward—well, Mara was forced to confess, she had thought him so but her better reason made her feel ashamed of giving her father and liege lord this insult.

No, Dafythe was not weak. She'd seen the strength of him today. She had seen it before, though she hadn't recognized the courage and determination implicit in her father's actions. When the Council shouted their support of her, he had cut them short with a word. A vacillating Duke would have been overwhelmed by dissent in that uproarious moment. He would have conceded to their demands. Dafythe had commanded them; he heard their opinions, but he kept his own. He had always been able to win people to his will by the force of his convictions. Could a weak man have shaped the world to his vision and maintained it for so many years?

Mara wasn't accustomed to feelings of doubt; if she wanted something, it must be the right thing to have. Now, she was uncertain. It disturbed her to think that all her dreams of glory might be nothing more than base bloodthirst.

"I know my father is a good and just ruler who has governed by Your Grace these many years. He wouldn't act against his conscience. None may speak greater evil of him than unwarrior-like gentleness. Is he wrong in this? Or am I guilty of disobedience and disloyalty if I try to sway him? As a Prince of Norman blood, I hold my honor above all. I have sworn to act as best befits my people, in my liege lord's interest, and as You will—not according to my own desires. I cannot be self-interested. Those I lead in battle may die in my name. Those I do battle against may die at my hand. Their blood is upon me if I act wrongly! Their souls will weigh upon mine. Heavenly Father, I do not know if this is what I am meant to do! I believe that I am given a divine destiny to fulfill in Your purpose. Is this it? I must know I am right! I pray You give me a sign."

What she hoped for was her vision, the holy blessing which she'd been denied on the night of vigil before her knighting. Nothing less would sanctify her goal.

"Guide me, Lord, please, to Your will."

She took up the rosary looped at her belt and kissed the cross. With her head bowed, she began to tell the beads, reciting formal prayers. The answer would come.

syx

Pendaunzel anxiously awaited news from Europe. In May, the Emperor summoned Juan Maria to London, where the renegade swore his fealty. Before Kharles's court, he declared himself a Norman Prince. Juan claimed that his betrothal to Serafina hadn't yet been formalized, but he felt unable to refuse her. His kinship to the Spanish imperial family was as strong to the Norman house. He hated to disappoint them, but he would do his liege's will. If Kharles insisted that the marriage-contract be dissolved...

Kharles insisted.

Juan returned to Naufarre still in possession of his lands and titles. Since he didn't retract his promises immediately upon his return, the tension between the two empires relaxed a little, but the situation remained unresolved throughout the summer.

That summer, the Dowager Penelope died and Kharles married before his court left off its formal mourning. His bride had been one of Penelope's ladies-in-waiting, a damosel of an obscure noble family. It was said that she had been Kharles's lover for some months and that the late Dowager had tried to discourage her son's attachment to this unimportant maid, as she'd discouraged all of the young Emperor's previous, ill-advised dalliances. It was also rumored that the bride was already pregnant and that Kharles had wed so swiftly in order to secure his heir; he didn't want the coming child to be removed from the line of succession as his children by the Lady Mellisaunte were.

Kat returned from London with a small delegation of the Emperor's advisors and spent several days in private conferences with Dafythe. When Mara asked about her travels, her cousin described games of chess and tennis with the Emperor, the memorial ceremonies for Penelope, the role she'd played as Guenithyre's kinswoman at the royal wedding, since Kharles's timid bride had no relations to stand with her, but she remained taciturn on political matters.

With the Emperor newly married and the rebellious Prince of Naufarre acquiescent after his broken betrothal, the situation was calm. Difficulties might arise again—indeed, no one expected things to remain quiet—but the crisis had been averted for a time.

Mara was disappointed.

Dafythe was relieved, though he knew that this late-summer lull was no more than a brief respite before the inevitable disaster. War was coming; he couldn't prevent it. It was only a matter of time before Juan and Kharles and Mara had their way, for time was the one thing he did not have.

Modern folk, he knew, lived longer and aged more slowly than those who had lived in the barbaric days of the early Empire. History revealed that girls of twelve and thirteen were considered marriageable—evidently, such young maids were ready for childbearing and boys of fifteen were capable of becoming fathers. Today, boys and girls of that age were undeveloped children and many youths were yet immature at eighteen and even twenty. In the barbaric days, a person in good health and good fortune might live to see fifty. Those who reached the age of sixty were wizened elders. Modern forty-year-olds were just past their youth. Sixty was the prime of middle-age. Many folk lived to see one hundred, and ancients of one hundred and twenty were not unknown.

Dafythe was ninety-eight. He had enjoyed a long life; nevertheless, he approached its end. A good Christian man, Dafythe knew he had sinned, but not so much that he feared the atonement which awaited him. He had few regrets.

True, he had made mistakes. It had been a mistake to honor Eduarde's memory. He and Kharles hadn't wished to denounce the Redlyon before his people. They had kept the legend alive when some part of the truth would have served them better. It had been a mistake to resolve Count Egan's rebellion by bringing him into the legitimate government structure, to marry him to Agnes, to take Kat away from Eireland. It had been a mistake to allow Mara to follow her own inclinations so often, but what father could refuse his only daughter?

There'd been great errors in the construction of this *pax normania.* The Treaty of Naufarre, which had established this peaceable era, also engendered its downfall. Dafythe wondered now that it had survived so long. They had granted Juan Maria Naufarre before his birth. Kharles had named Marianne Regent during her son's minority and left her largely unsupervised thereafter. Not perhaps the wisest decision, but Dafythe had never protested. He thought he understood his brother's generosity.

Kharles, Dafythe knew, had not only made the first overtures of peace to Spain, but had traveled to Toledo to meet with the Emperor Alamanzus. He'd made Marianne's acquaintance then. Had some feeling grown between them? Had he thought of what might have been? And what had Marianne felt, meeting the son but being given to the father?

It wasn't inconceivable that the lonely young wife of an elderly man might seek the friendship of a younger man whom she might have called husband. If the younger man had been any other but his brother, Dafythe wouldn't find the situation surprising. But it *was* Kharles; Dafythe's brother had held personal honor above all else. The adultery Dafythe contemplated ought to be unthinkable. Yet that little demon of speculation continued to dance about his thoughts, especially since Kharles had been so generous to her after the Redlyon's death.

Marianne and her small son had retreated to Naufarre. She was the most eligible young woman in Christendom at the time of her widowhood, but she had never chosen to remarry. For sixty years, she and Juan had governed their tiny kingdom almost as if it were an independent land, and the situation had been allowed to develop until it reached this present crisis. There had been problems before, but the elder Kharles had always been able to command Juan's respect and keep him from outright treason; the young Emperor excited the rebel Prince's open contempt. Marianne's influence over her son was weakening. Dafythe could only delay the explosion a little while longer.

The death of Penelope and the increasing infirmity of Marianne forced him to consider the end of his own existence. He might live a few years more, perhaps as many as ten, but he felt the impediments of a man at his century. He tired easily. He was long past the age when he could stay awake for days at a stretch. In his youth, an emergency such as the one he had faced this summer would have kept him at Council for twenty hours each day; now, he had to call for frequent recesses and he was often weary by midday. Though his physician promised that he was in excellent health, his joints ached, his sight deteriorated rapidly, his heart was not strong. Excellent health, perhaps, for a man of his age, but not the vigor he'd known all his life. He was not in his dotage, thank the Lord in Heaven, as his father had been in his last years. His mental faculties remained intact and his powers of concentration had not yet wavered, but Dafythe found himself thinking more and more of the past. Memories of his youth seemed more clear than recent events. The faces of people he hadn't seen for decades—Rosa, Agnes, Gillefluere, his brother Kharles, his mother and the roaring Redlyon—were vivid before him.

He was losing control of his Council. This too was due to his age—not because he had grown infirm and lost the will necessary to command, but because all his court knew as well as he did that he was near the end of his reign and his heir would not continue his policies. Already, they sought her favor.

Young Lord Rafenshighte, who lounged near him now in the Manor garden, had been courting Mara. They made a strange couple, the foppish courtier and the rough-and-tumble, all too frank Shieldmaid, yet they were seen together so often that there was gossip about their pending betrothal. Though Mara preferred the company of her cousin Kat and that pretty little Shieldmaid captain to the young noblemen of Pendaunzel, she didn't disdain them. She understood that marriage and the production of an heir were inevitable parts of her duty but, prior to this, no courtier had ever been so brave to dare make love to the stern Prince. Rafenshighte was more bold than most.

Dafythe might have been delighted in other circumstances to see his heir wed the son of Layn Rafenshighte, who had been his Chancellor for more than thirty years. In the abstract, Geoffrey was an excellent choice for Mara's consort: he was the right age, of a noble and prominent family, and possessed of sufficient courtly experience to be the helpmeet and advisor that a Duke's spouse must be. He was a handsome and well-mannered youth. If only he were not such a suspect character!

Young Rafenshighte's oily arts made him useful in the diplomatic office. The young man was well liked among the foreign ambassadors and could even win the stubborn Don Peidro D'Yzaguerre to his will, but the Duke didn't like to see these same sycophantic charms used to woo his daughter. Mara's mind was not subtle. She didn't possess the courtier's mastery of deceit; guilelessly honest, she presented herself as she was and took everyone else at face value. She could detect an outright lie, but how did she perceive Geoffrey's twisted truths?

Rafenshighte had been spending a great deal of time in Dafythe's company this summer as well. Not to petition—no, Dafythe didn't believe that this ambitious young man would bother to seek the favor of a dying lord while he anticipated the Duke's successor. Rafenshighte had other reasons for dancing attendance.

"Andemyon!"

While the rest of the heralds played a hide-and-tackle game of tag amidst the shrubbery, Andemyon walked alone on the shady garden paths. Whenever he joined the other boys' play, the boisterous games quickly became an excuse for all the heralds to trample him. He wasn't like them, and they knew it. The boy excluded himself rather than be subjected to this abuse. Dreamy-eyed, he seemed lost in thoughts far away from his duties and had stepped onto the circular path about the fountain, where Lord Rafenshighte sat, then drew closer to dabble his fingers in the water and scatter the goldfish. He looked up, startled, at Dafythe's abrupt summons.

Though he was concerned with the welfare of all his heralds, Dafythe took special interest in this boy. From Old Toppet, who had charge of the heralds, he learned that Andemyon was so quiet and sensitive that he was often teased and bullied by the larger boys. Toppet governed enough of the heralds' time to ensure that they couldn't cause much mischief, but even under his stern eyes the elder boys met the newcomer with snubs and slighting words. Bertie and Arthur both spoke of the boy with scornful disinterest; since Andemyon was a kinsman, they felt obligated to defend him from the bullies, but they didn't like this duty and they were contemptuous at his tears. From other sources, Dafythe heard that Andemyon spent his free hours alone in the libraries about the palace, favoring Magician Peter's hermetical texts. The magician, scribes and librarians of the court praised his manners and studious interests. Andemyon would take up a book and read for hours in a corner until they nearly forgot he was there. He was also a frequent companion to Laurel. Dafythe encouraged this, allowing the boy to spend as much time with her as she liked and duty allowed. A common jest was that Andemyon was the Lady's attendant, not the Duke's.

Andemyon came to stand before Dafythe's chair. "My Lord?"

"I have heard that you sing for the Lady Laurel's pleasure."

Andemyon nodded.

"Do you recall, my lad, that it is among your duties to amuse me? You've been in my service many months now and I've barely heard a word from you. Can it be you conceal this talent from me?"

"I didn't mean to, My Lord," the boy answered. "I didn't think you'd care to hear me."

"You are mistaken. If you amuse My Lady Laurel with your songs, you are fit to entertain me as well. Sing, Child. I would hear you."

The herald blinked in alarm and looked frantically about for a means of retreat, but Dafythe repeated his command and the boy didn't dare refuse. With a last glance at the shouting boys and strolling courtiers, he squeezed his eyes shut tightly and began to sing the hymn featured at the morning Mass, the ancient Song of Brother Caedmon, in a tremulous soprano trill:

Now sing we praise the Heavenly Lord,
His Might and His Creation,
His Wondrous Works—O Eternal Lord!
In the Beginning, He shaped for His children
The Heavens as a roof—O Holy Creator!
Afterwards He made for us,
A home to shelter us—O Mankind's Lord!
Middle-Earth He gave to us,
Our land for perpetuity—O Almighty King!

His voice rose as he gained confidence. Dafythe was astonished by the sound. He was accustomed to hearing professional sopranos—church choirs, female minstrels, *castrati*—but this sweet, bright chirrup, as unaffected as an outpouring of bird-song, was delightful. The boy's voice was untrained; his breath was shallow, his pitch wavered more than a singer in full control of his talent would allow, and the singing of both verse and counterpoint response by one person was strange to hear, but the overall effect was very pretty. The high notes were pure and clear once he found the courage to reach them. Andemyon rarely spoke. Who would suspect he sang so beautifully?

Andemyon opened his eyes to find he had drawn an audience. The boys had stopped their game to whisper and nudge each other. Courtiers had paused to listen. Lord Rafenshighte had drawn near.

"Was it not good?" the little herald asked.

"It was very good," Dafythe assured him.

"Lovely," Rafenshighte agreed. "'Tis a shame you've made laws to destroy such song, My Lord."

"The price required to maintain that beauty is too high," Dafythe answered.

The young nobleman's eyes traveled over the boy's blushing face. "No price is too dear to preserve beauty for the enjoyment of all."

Andemyon's remarkable beauty had already excited too much attention. Silent and solemn, blond and cherubic, he stood out among the other heralds—gangling, chubby, pre-adolescent lumps that boys of that age generally were. The heralds scorned him, the court ladies fussed over the pretty child and made a pet of him. People liked to see him at the forefront of processions, bearing Dafythe's standard. The more avuncular and auntish members of the Council rumpled his curls and spoke to him when they met him on errands about the palace. Pleasant jests were made on how he would break maidens' hearts in a few years. For a shy child, such attention was agonizing; Dafythe did not wonder why the boy hid away in the libraries and sought to go unnoticed whenever he could. And there were certain men...

Dafythe had seen the glances of some of his courtiers, ones he knew to be inclined toward Greekish tastes for youthful beauty. Most, he knew, were men of honor; they might gaze upon the lovely child, but they wouldn't dream of declared admiration. Dafythe, known for his broadminded policies in many matters, could be quite severe when concerned with his courtiers' personal conduct. The Duke was wont to overlook amorous intrigues among the nobility so long as they were seemly and discreet, but he would not allow open scandals. He was especially fierce in his protection of those in his service. No pages were buggered, no chambermaids accosted, no guards enticed into private chambers for noble sport. Dafythe meant his subjects to know that their sons and daughters could serve at the Palace without suffering corruption.

There were rumors of Rafenshighte's behavior in town, though no specific charges had been laid against him. Dafythe doubted that even if the gossip were true, Rafenshighte was fool enough to attempt the seduction of a boy less than sixteen under the Duke's eyes. Andemyon was, after all, Dafythe's young kinsman, wearing his livery and under his personal protection.

Andemyon was also guarded by another power. A silver talisman a little larger than a shilling hung about his throat, resting against the back of the uppermost lion on his tabard. Lord Redmantyl's mark was engraved upon it, declaring that this child was under the protection of a most powerful and vengeful wizard.

Rafenshighte had flirted with Redmantyl's elder son the previous spring. Laurel and Ambris had put a stop to it before Redmantyl noticed. The boy was apparently not of Greekish tastes himself, but vain enough to be flattered by the attention and silly enough to be offended that his father thought him capable of being so easily seduced. Of course, he had been seduced only a few months later in Storm Port and Redmantyl's revenge had been horrible.

All Pendaunzel had seen the dark storms which raged to south this summer. The full story hadn't yet reached the Duke's city; Dafythe only knew that Orlan had somehow been ensorcelled by the Mayor of Storm Port and Redmantyl had fought with her as he would a magical foe. The storm was only a fragment of the rage the wizard had loosed on Storm Port that day. The city had been flooded with rain, the Mayor's Hall had been burned to the ground and the Mayor's husband killed. Some more terrible punishment had been visited upon the Mayor, a magical blasting that even the closest witnesses could not adequately describe. It was said that both the woman's mind and soul had been destroyed.

This was the first exercise of Lord Redmantyl's vast power any had witnessed since the wizard-battles which had established him supreme. It was the first time he'd exercised his powers against the non-magical and had killed a man who couldn't harm him.

There had been some discussion in Pendaunzel about charging the wizard with murder and the wanton destruction of property, but Ambris had pointed out that the incident in Storm Port was within the long-standing traditions of wizard-battle, which all earthly governors had determined were beyond their jurisdiction. The death of the Mayor's husband was said to be an accident. No one in Storm Port demanded recompense except for the damage to the Mayor's Hall. After this dry summer, they welcomed the rain. Even if the wizard were summoned to account for his misconduct, who would dare to carry the warrant?

Dafythe's tiger had unsheathed its claws, and he was unable to check the damage done. Lord Redmantyl was beyond his control if the wizard chose to step outside Norman law and act as a law onto himself. Yet this episode served to remind mere mortals how dangerous a wizard truly was. They had all seen what little Andemyon's father was capable of when his child was threatened. Unless Geoffrey was a great fool—and Dafythe knew he was not—he must realize that Lord Redmantyl's sons were not to be toyed with.

Another young nobleman had stopped to hear Andemyon's song as well.

The elegant Rosandre of Daubenai was one of the small group of advisors who had accompanied Kat from London. Dafythe thought him astonishingly young for the responsibilities he bore, but his personal charm and exquisite courtesy made him a promising negotiator in spite of the fact that he was still in his middle twenties. He spoke as the Emperor's representative; he'd been Kharles's aide during Juan Maria's recent visit and he would travel to Naufarre as soon as his business here was finished. Some whispered of how this young man had risen so rapidly in the Emperor's favor, but what successful courtier was not whispered about?

"Beauty is more valued when it is brief and elusive, My Lord Rafenshighte," said Daubenai. "Would you have been willing to make such sacrifice yourself for beauty's sake?"

Rafenshighte laughed. "Me? I could never carry a tune. More would've been lost than preserved. But I think that if I'd been so lovely a lad with such a voice..."

"It is likely that it would've been done before you were of an age to decide such things for yourself. A grown man may choose to mutilate himself so, but of course the operation is not performed upon grown men."

"I think it is. Is it not, My Lord?" Rafenshighte addressed Dafythe.

"The penalty is reserved for repeated and unrepentant defilers of the innocent," replied Dafythe. "It is not done lightly. The punishment is far too cruel—the loss of life's greatest gift, the ability to procreate and see life continued in one's children. I would not suffer it on a free-born Norman child for the sake of a pretty song."

"Yet it is committed by Normans, My Lord. Ambitious parents sometimes give their sons over to choirmasters to extend their soprano talents."

"And such parents and choirmasters are arrested and punished for criminal mutilation."

"But what of the boys?" asked Rafenshighte. "If the cuts have already been made, can else be done but allow them to continue their musical careers? They are fit for nothing else. We have often received such creatures to sing at court once they are grown."

"To see them remain singers condones the crime against them," said Daubenai. "But what else can be done?"

"Some do travel to foreign nations when they are grown men," Dafythe said darkly, for he did not like it when he could do nothing to repair an injustice against one of his subjects. "And some return as professional sopranos. Regardless of–" he became aware that Andemyon was listening to the conversation with incomplete comprehension but intense interest. "You may go now, Lad. Gramercies for your delightful song.

"Regardless of the subsequent public success of those unfortunates," the Duke continued once Andemyon had moved some distance away, "it remains a barbarous act. What has been done is done. But I will not allow it to be performed on a young boy in my protection while it is in my power to prevent it."

But Rafenshighte had lost interest in the argument. "I didn't dream of suggesting it as a national policy, My Gracious Lord." He bowed slightly and walked away.

Rosandre remained. "A charming child," he said after watching Andemyon for a few minutes. Rafenshighte had not followed the boy. "I see him often with my dearest friend, the Lady Laurel. It is good that he has so devoted a kinswoman to watch over him. Such beauty is dangerous to one so young. Pray God he will grow past it before it brings him to harm."

Dafythe studied the courtier's face, now turned in profile. The nose was delicate and the chin was well-modeled. The eyelashes were the same ginger shade as his fashionably braided and beribbonned curls. He was a very handsome youth himself and, in the aged Duke's eyes, not much older than little Andemyon. Did he speak from experience? Dafythe thought again of the odd rumors he'd heard concerning this pretty and personable young man, but he wouldn't dream of inquiring into so private a matter.

Rosandre turned back to Dafythe. "My Gracious Lord, may I speak with you?"

"Certainly."

"My Lord Dafythe, we depart in the morning. I wish to bid you farewell and offer gramercies for your hospitality. You must know we have hopes that the unpleasant Juan will behave himself for a time."

"As do I," answered Dafythe.

"However," Rosandre sat down and lowered his voice, "My Lord, I must suggest that you will be wiser if you permit your daughter the Prince to prepare. My Lord the Emperor thinks of the Terrojos march. He intends to claim it as soon as Prince Juan has been made peaceable."

"If Juan is peaceable–?"

Rosandre nodded. "Exactly so, My Lord Duke. The Imperial Council has given him to understand that the treaty has already been broken and he may act as he chooses."

Dafythe might have known. He'd had no control over his nephew since the youth had ascended his throne. With Penelope's death, no one could restrain him. He would fight against this for as long as he could, but he was old now and they very young—they would win out in time. This *pax normania* was at an end.

The young Frenchman rose. "I comprehend that you do not think of war yourself, My Gracious Lord. I promise you it will not come for a year, perhaps two. And now, I must make my farewells to My Lady Laurel." He bowed and left the garden.

After the tumultuous summer of 1953, autumn began placidly. Rumors proved themselves true when Guenithyre gave birth to a son; the infant was christened Lyonel Eduarde Pendragon. Mara was listed as a godmother to the newborn princeling and sent him twelve silver apostle spoons as a christening gift.

Juan Maria was well-behaved, so quiet in fact that the Pendaunzel court was certain he must be up to something. Everyone knew the rebel Prince wouldn't acquiesce to the Emperor's demands so easily. Dafythe himself said that his half-brother's pride would never allow him to surrender. And so they waited.

The news came at All Hallows.

"Juan's wed!" The cry went up about the court. "The Spanish Infanta! They were wed this summer, secretly, in spite of his promises!"

"It is a characteristic act of defiance," Ambris said at the Council which followed. "He might be persuaded to turn away from his plans if he believes it's to his advantage to do so, but Kharles made demands without condition. To Juan, that is sufficient incentive to act. He would marry against our Emperor's wishes even if he sets two great nations at war with each other and imperils his own little land—even if he dies for it."

"It is an act of war!" cried Mara. "You see his sneaky Spanish ways! He can't be trusted! Father, we must respond now!"

Every day, the Northlanders expected their Emperor to call them to war, but no message came. The situation remained at an infuriating standstill. Prince Juan had taken his defiant stand and seemed satisfied. He had married and his bride had come to Naufarre, but Naufarre remained Norman. The Spanish did not claim it. Juan did not declare his allegiance to his bride's family. Kharles sent reinforcements to the Naufarre garrisons, but Serafina brought no troops with her beyond her personal honor guard, a compliment of six women more ornamental than experienced soldiers.

Mara was especially baffled by her cousin's complacency. Kharles ought to have declared war. Juan should have been arrested for treason. He ought to be imprisoned with his Spanish-Infanta wife right now. Yet they lived unhindered in Naufarre, free to work whatever sedition they chose. Why did Kharles allow it? He was no pacifist, reluctant to join in conflict against an open foe. He wouldn't dawdle over a difficult situation when the solution was so obvious. He had only to command, and his will would be done. Juan would be removed from his given fief and the problem in Naufarre ended. Instead, it was said that Kharles intended to receive Juan and his bride at the Paris court at Christmastide.

What could the Emperor be thinking? Surely Juan had announced his intentions with his marriage. It didn't matter that he hadn't acted yet; he would in time. He only waited until the Normans had relaxed their watch upon him. It would be prudent to strike first, to thwart Juan's treachery before he could initiate his plans. Delay only gave him more time.

Kharles must mean to do something.

At the beginning of December, Kat was called to an audience with the Duke.

"I'm to be sent to Naufarre," she announced to Mara after this private conference. "Kharles proposes a marriage contract for me."

"To whom?" Mara considered the possibilities. Juan had a son. "Not little Eduarde? He can't be more than twelve."

"No, not Eduarde. Serafina has a brother, Iosephus. He isn't the Infant Raimond's heir-apparent, but a younger son of the house. I'm to take a place in Juan's household, in order that I learn something of Spanish ways. My betrothed and I might eventually meet there, but the contract will not be signed—may never be."

"Did you know of this?"

"The possibility of a match with a Spanish Prince was discussed when I was in London last spring, so I can't say it's a full surprise."

"It is to me! You never said a word!"

"I hoped nothing would come of it. `Tisn't what I wanted at

all. Kharles calls me a bride, but in truth I'm to be his spy. I'm to keep our relations in Naufarre well-behaved with my presence so long as it's deemed necessary. I've seen the private missive Kharles sent Uncle Dafythe about it, so I can't mistake the purpose of my mission. I'm authorized to take command of the garrisons and direct a coup if I see that Juan and his bride are treacherous to Norman interests. I may become Regent of Naufarre, if it comes to that."

"A Prince cannot have her choice of duties," said Mara. "Our marriages are a matter of politics." But she knew as well as Kat that this betrothal was nothing like the usual sort of marital alliance.

"I've always understood it to be the fate of the third Prince to marry as the Empire requires," said Kat. "`Tis why Eireland makes such riot—its princes are betrothed to Russians or Danes or Italians and the Irish are forever slighted in their loyalties. So, they would have my natural father before me and I've no right place. I do not mind being commissioned as an agent in my Emperor's name, but this– *this* infuriates me! Yet what else is there for me? I might as well be Naufarre's governor as Eireland's."

"You'll always have a place with me, Kat."

Her cousin smiled softly. "A place in your heart, I know. But I am no Prince in the Northlands."

"Then I shall make you a proper place once I am Duke. Layn Lieutenant of the Armies, Chamberlain, Chief of Council—whatever you like." Mara had always known that Kat would leave the Northlands one day, but now that she was faced with the very real possibility of it happening, it was impossible for her to let Kat go. Kat was as dear to her as a sister. "You shan't go to godforsaken Naufarre if I can prevent it."

"You don't have that kind of authority," Kat answered. "But Uncle Dafythe doesn't approve Kharles's proposal either. He intends to delay my departure."

"Ah, Kat," said Mara, "the whole problem hangs on a scarcity of eligible men. I too have a duty to wed—but who is worthy to become my consort? I cannot choose a man of higher rank than myself, and I have no equals. If Kharles had a younger brother, or Alex of Russe, *he* might suit. Honestly, Kat, I feel no urgency to birth my own heir. Ambris has done enough duty for all the Norman house. When I am Duke, I shall name Eadrik my Prince of Gossunge. He's a good lad and he's had the governing of Eadeshire since Ambris came back to Pendaunzel."

"It's different for you, Mara. You know it is."

"True," Mara admitted. "Whether I wed or no, I shall be Duke of the Northlands for all the days God in His Ultimate Mercy allows me. What matter if my consort is a German or even a Spaniard? He must come to my household and make himself pleasing to me for duty's sake. Of course," she added, grinning, "I might marry Geoffrey."

The words were spoken on impulse. She'd spent a good deal of time with Geoffrey in Kat's absence. She hadn't meant to, but he always seemed to be there, ready to escort her to the theatre in the city, to dance with her at balls, to ride at her side on hunts, even to watch her sparring matches though he declined to compete with her himself. Mara first thought that he'd only sought to retain her favor now that she held a little power in the Council, but he was so attentive, respectful, flattering that she began to imagine that he desired something more.

Kat exploded with astonishment. "That predatory sod?"

"Only a rumor, Cos," Mara answered lightly. "He exaggerates his vices, I think. He likes to make a show of admiring pretty lads and behaving as if no youth's virtue was safe from his voracious appetites. True, he flirts shamelessly with the young lads around the court, but he can't have taken very many of them to his bed. Surely there'd be daily scandals if he were the wicked seducer he presents himself to be. No boy's ever made a charge against him, and no outraged parent has come to Father for justice for their disgraced son. No one's taken a horsewhip to him. Even if it were all true, I imagine he'd give over his fancies long enough to sire the next Prince of Gossunge. I don't need him for more than that. In truth, I'd rather not have a lovesome husband hanging about me."

"You're joking," said Kat. "But I pray you never let *him* hear you say such things. He'll do it. You know he couldn't hope to climb higher. He's ambitious, that lad."

"Yes, but he declares it quite openly. His ambitions are so plain `tis impossible to be misled."

"Marry Geoffrey," Kat said scornfully. "Naufarre would be a pleasure by comparison! Uncle Juan has not so bad a character. He was most courteous when we met at London. He spoke his highest admiration to me of my father."

"Begin by thinking so well of him, Kat, and he'll bring you around to his traitorous opinions before the end of a fortnight."

Kat laughed. "I think not. `Tis true, I didn't expect to find him so well-mannered and well-spoken. His claims are modest for a revolutionary. He doesn't seek to overtake the Empire—he only wants to remove Naufarre from it. I can respect his desire to see Naufarre an independent state, but I can't forget that it must be either Norman or Spanish and we cannot let it fall to their hands. No, I like him but I am in no danger of taking up his cause. Besides, My Lord Rosandre will be there. He will meet me at the port and escort me to Pamplona. I can't imagine a more delightful companion."

"There are rumors about that young man as well."

"Yes," Kat answered after a pause. "The advisors we traveled with from London were full of stories."

"Repulsive stories! My Lord Rosandre is supposed to have told Laurel tales in confidence while he was here this summer. `Tis said he claims to be a victim of our cousin Kharles's abuse of imperial privilege—or a beneficiary, depending on how one views it."

"You don't believe it."

"How can I? `Tis nothing to banter gossip on the conduct of one courtly dandy or another. But to carry tales of our Emperor! The suggestion is nearly blasphemous."

If she expected Kat to agree with this, she was disappointed. Her cousin only replied quietly: "Kharles is not as you imagine him, Mara."

But Mara refused to hear her. "You're mistaken. Of course, everyone knows of Lady Mellisaunte's children and we can all count the months between the Emperor's wedding and the birth of the little princeling, but Kharles's misbehavior with court ladies gives no one an excuse to whisper worse about him. One tale doesn't prove the other. Rather, it refutes it. No, Kat, your imagination has run riot with this vile slander. I will have no more of it." And, as abruptly as Mara's indignation has arisen over the insult to her liege lord, it abated. "When must you leave for Naufarre?"

"Kharles asks that I be prepared to travel as soon as the weather permits."

"Why then there is plenty of time to act! You cannot think of travel when the roads are deep with snow and mud and there is ice in the harbor. February, at the soonest. March, more likely. If Father chooses to hinder your departure, you may remain here `til summer. Six months, Kat! In six months, everything may change again. This spy-match may be all but forgotten. You won't go. I can almost promise it."

Prince Juan and his bride went to Paris at Christmas and, in January, Juan's son Eduarde was sent to serve as a page in Kharles' court. Pendaunzel didn't know how to interpret this gesture. Was the boy taken as a hostage? Or had Juan offered him as a token of his loyalty? It seemed to indicate only one thing certainly: the war had been averted. Kat's betrothal was not mentioned again.

Then, as the winter melted away, Mara was called to her father's chambers. Dafythe dismissed Martleanne and his attending heralds before he told her, "There was a courier from Paris this morning. A message from Kharles, for you." Dafythe gave her the folded vellum square bearing the imperial seal.

Mara had never received a personal missive from her cousin before and, given the current, peaceable political situation, she couldn't imagine what Kharles had to tell her.

The language of the message astonished her. Kharles's address lacked all protocols. And, more strange still, he referred to himself in the first-person singular. Dafythe rarely used the royal plural, but who would expect the same informality from the young emperor? Mara was certain he had written this with his own hand. How unlike the impersonal phrases and neat, scribe's pencraft of his imperial decrees! And the message itself was completely unexpected:

My dearest Cousin Margueryt,

It has long been my disappointment to hear exemplary accounts from all sources with regard to a relation removed one degree from that of a sister, yet never to meet this veritable paragon of the traditional Norman virtues in her person. It is you I speak of, Dearest Cousin. Know that I have followed your career with great interest for many years. Your reputation is known: that you are courageous, possessed of remarkable fortitude, piety, and unwavering loyalty. Our mutual cousin Katheryne speaks of you with unfeigned pride and affection. So warm a praise from an intimate companion also marks you well. Indeed, I am proud to call you kinswoman. May all you do resound in greater glory for your homeland and your Empire. No Prince can hope to attain higher honor.

As I have heard so much in your favor, therefore, I am certain I have chosen you well to perform a momentous act in my service. Admired Cousin, know that my feelings toward our Uncle the Prince Juan Maria of Naufarre are in accord with yours. Your opinions have been conveyed to me: I trust that such expressions of hatred for this betrayer of all Norman honor are not misrepresented. I too sicken of Naufarre's treacherous games and long to put an end to this intolerable state of uncertainty which threatens our peace.

It is my intention to lead the armies of Britain and France against Naufarre this summer and give the traitor a taste of the chaos he courts so wantonly. Should this campaign prove successful, the Prince Juan will be taken captive and his lands restored to a proper semblance of Norman order. Cousin, may I depend upon your support in this endeavor? It is my will that the territory stolen from us in our Grandfather Redlyon's last days and now called Terrojos by its invaders likewise be restored to Norman hands. To accomplish this, I require that you lead a counterpart assault on the land presently called Terrojos in my name. It is my hope that all Northlander armies as you are able to gather will be ready to march to Princeland at the beginning of May.

I send further instructions to your father, my devoted Uncle the Duke, in which I make formal requests that he release the Northlander garrisons to your command in this time of great emergency. A separate courier travels to Dennefort. Marchion Frederik of Princeland and the

Eduardesmarch has been apprised of my purposes and will be prepared to receive you at Dennefort at the end of your journey.

Know, Cousin Marguerytt, that you have my fullest confidence.

The bottom margin bore the simple signature, *Kharles.*

Mara gave the letter to her father. "Will you tell me not to?" she asked while he read.

"I cannot. If Kharles declares war and requires our aid as his kindred and confederates, it is my duty to support him."

"I'm surprised that this announcement comes now. Juan has been quiet for months," said Mara. "Perhaps Kharles's spies in Naufarre have uncovered some new treachery that makes it prudent to act immediately."

"Perhaps," said Dafythe.

Mara didn't understand his tone. "You cannot fault Kharles, Father. He's been as patient with Juan as anyone could wish. There was nothing else to be done."

"No, I suppose not. And so you will go. This evening, I shall call a special meeting of the Council to announce our Emperor's decision. You will be named General of the Northlands' armies and the city garrisons will be released to your command. Lieutenant Uismarde will assist you in the organization of the march to Dennefort." Dafythe had paced to the end of the room while he spoke and he paused now beneath a sword which hung in its jeweled scabbard on a prominent place on the wall. Abruptly, he reached up toward it. "Here, Mara. Help me take this down."

Once she had helped her father remove the scabbard from the wall, Dafythe presented the golden hilt with a ruby set into the pommel and the face of a snarling beast in relief at the crossbar to her. "This is your sword, Mara. "

"Dentelyon?" The lion's tooth. The elder Kharles had sent it to Dafythe after the Redlyon's death, and Mara had not seen it taken down from its place since her knighting. She was astonished at the casual manner in which her father offered this family treasure. "You give me Grandfather's sword?"

"Many will die in the battle to come. I do not wish to see you among them."

Mara took the hilt between her hands and pulled gently, unsheathing the steel. The sword was heavy; her grip tightened and her wrists stiffened to keep the tip of the blade from striking the floor. Then she found the balance and lifted it clear. The blade, she saw, had been recently honed; the edges were sharp and the flat above the hilt polished so that the spider-leg tracings she'd taken for decorative etching were revealed as glinting runes. This wasn't an impulsive decision on Dafythe's part, she realized now; he'd prepared for this day.

"'Tis magical?" she asked.

"The spells were crafted by Maxim Gnome, who was Redmantyl when I was a boy, but I doubt they hold any virtue today. Spells fade. Nevertheless, it is a good sword. My father never knew defeat with this in his hands."

Mara lowered the sword. "Father, gramercies." Her eyes suddenly filled with tears, so deeply was she touched by this magnificent gift. Her father did not wish her to go to war, but he'd taken care to ensure that she went well armed. It spite of his opposition, he would support her.

And, at last—at last!—she was going to go!

"I know you didn't want this war," she said in a rush of gratitude. "I'm sorry that it must pain you."

Dafythe placed one hand on her shoulder and kissed her cheek. "It is the way of things, Mara. The peace had to end one day. In truth, I wonder now that it lasted so long."

sen

War! Dafythe made his announcement that evening and the court hummed with the news by late morning. From Pendaunzel, word spread quickly to the neighboring cities and countryside. By the end of March, all the Northlands was in an uproar. No one could talk of anything else. It seemed too wonderful. Could it be true? The Duke had released troops to Prince Marguerуt. The armies of the Northlands were to march to the southern border. At last, they would give Spain a taste of what they deserved and Norman honor would be avenged!

For sixty years, there had been no standing army in the Northlands proper, and only a few thousands stationed with the border guards in the marches. Retired soldiers from the frontiers and youths who would train for soldiery served as auxiliaries to the city constabulary. Through these garrisons, elite corps such as the Shieldmaids, and the various orders of knights, the arts of warfare were passed on through the peaceful generations. Young guards learned their profession from their elders. Archery, fencing, and jousting were encouraged as sport, so that these skills would not be lost, but none had practiced them in earnest for decades.

In the months since Juan's betrothal, however, the city garrisons had swollen to twice and thrice their normal complement and adventurous youths traveled to join the guard at the Eduardesmarch and Uoldor. Scores of knights had been newly consecrated. This spring, hundreds more—retired soldiers, young hopefuls, and many who had no martial training—swarmed to enlist. Overwhelmed captains absorbed as many of the most promising applicants as they could into their companies; others were given non-combatant positions in transportation or requisition or the courier relays. The rest were sent home to their shops and farms. But for every one turned away, another arrived with the same aspirations to serve the Prince. Their eagerness astonished Mara. Had they waited so long for her?

Mara wanted to think of her responsibility to these people, as Dafythe had entreated, but it was difficult not to respond to that adoration. How could she refuse when their hopes fit so well with her own desires? She meant no disrespect to her father and his principles, but it seemed obvious to her that the signs were clear: this was the destiny she was meant to fulfill. Everything urged her forward.

The Exchequer had levied a tax to equip and support her army, and the Treasury had provided her with generous amounts of immediate gold, including the funds set aside for her coronation and her wedding; Mara had argued that one was, Merciful Lord permitting, many years off and the other might be even more distant. Over 70,000 gold crowns were placed in her hands to finance her expedition.

Once the Council approved her plans, Mara enacted them eagerly. She began by drilling the Palace guard and Pendaunzel garrison, testing her strategies in the hills above the city and making practical improvements. She sent messages to her Shieldmaid friends; with the exception of Martine, who was already stationed at Dennefort, they would rendezvous in Storm Port. It was understood that her old companions would serve as her personal honor guard and her lieutenants. Mara also wrote to the Marchion of the Eduardesmarch and Princeland to let him know when she and her armies were to be expected. She spent her days marching and riding in the muddy woods, and stayed up late at night studying maps of the borderlands with Lieutenant Uismarde, Kat, Bel, and Ambris. She authorized the commissioning of supplies to ensure that all troops would be fed throughout each stage of their long journey. She established campsites. These were swift preparations, given the short weeks since Kharles's message had arrived, but in truth they were the culmination of ideas which Mara had formed over many weeks. By April, she was ready. The weather was good, the road was clear.

The Coast Road was the pride of Dafythe's reign. Over one thousand miles long, it ran from Heofon at the northern border to Dennefort in the south, a stone-paved line that cut through forests, bridged rivers, and curved about the walls of every major coastal city to link them all. A merchant could cart wares from farm to town market without danger of damage; a courier could ride through the night without his horse stumbling. Dafythe often told the story of how his father had scoffed at the idea of a smooth, straight road for improved commerce and mail services, until Eduarde realized that he could run an army down the paved surface in half the time it would have taken to travel the muddy, wheel-rutted path that had lain there before.

Mara would take this same road to Dennefort.

On May Day, Ambris brought a half-dozen copies of the official declaration of war to his father's private closet.

"One for the archives, to be read aloud at the ceremony, one to be sent to the Spanish Ambassador, one to Spain, one to our Emperor, one to the Governor of Terrojos," he counted them off, shifting each scroll in turn from the cradle of his left arm to place on the table before Dafythe. "And one to be sent to the engravers to be copied for posted proclamations."

"The timing is appropriate," said Dafythe. He smoothed down the blue ribbons dangling from the bottom of each curling parchment sheet. "Let's have this done with quickly. We have a parade to attend and Mara will be disappointed if we are late for her triumphal moment. Martley! Are the witnesses assembled?"

"They await in the State Hall, My Lord," replied Martleanne.

"Bring them in."

If time had allowed, Dafythe would have signed the declaration before all the Council instead of a handful of selected members, but Mara was leading the Pendaunzel garrison and local corps out of the city today and it was more fitting that she march under official endorsement. Also, Dafythe wished no further delay. He had contrived to pass this day as it if were no different from any other, in spite of the loud music of celebration in the city and the merry courtiers in the garden outside his windows, but the worst had come. Procrastination would accomplish nothing.

The designated witnesses—Tuxsetau, Peaque, Roodebroke, Lieutenant Uismarde, Rafenshighte—filed in and gathered in a semi-circle about the table where Dafythe had spread the parchment copies.

"You know why you've been summoned," said the Duke. "I hold here the fair copies of our declaration against Spain. You have all had a part in its composition and you are familiar with its contents, so I shall dispense with the reading." Dafythe dipped his quill and shook away the excess ink. "As we are Dafythe Gabriel Holyrood Ambris Lyonsbloode Plantagenet, Prince of the Norman Empire, Preserver of the Peace, Defender of the Christian Faith, Grand Duke, Sovereign Lord Governor and Protector of the Northlands by Grace of God, it is our intent and pleasure to make this declaration of war against our foe, Ignatius, Emperor of Spain and all citizens and soldiers of that empire who hold themselves in allegiance to his name. Before this company we here affix the sign and seal of the Northlands as tokens of our sanction to all conditions writ here.

"Witness our hand!" Dafythe had already written his name out twice while he made his formal recitation; now, he placed his signature across the bottom of the remaining four documents. "Witness our device!" Six times, Martleanne splashed wax across the slips of ribbon and Dafythe pressed his signet ring into the cooling pools. Silently, Ambris added the seal of the Chancellor. "So it is done. Let none contest its verity."

The rite was ended. "Gramercies, Ministers," the Duke said. "Layn Lieutenant, you may go to join my daughter now."

Martleanne sprinkled sand onto the damp ink and gathered up the copies, leaving one for Dafythe to read at the ceremonies. Ambris remained after the ministers had departed.

"It confounds me," Dafythe said once they were alone. "'Our intent and pleasure,' indeed! It was the worst piece of work I've ever done. There ought to have been some way to avoid this madness."

"You did all you could, Father," Ambris answered gently. "I don't like it either, but don't see how it could have been avoided. Everyone is so keen upon it. Juan is what he is, and Kharles..."

Dafythe looked up. "You knew?"

"Lord Rosandre suggested the possibility, in confidence. I know Kharles. It was no disillusion."

"Have you told Mara?"

"She wouldn't believe it. When the delegates were here, they were full of rumors, but Mara wouldn't hear a word spoken against the Emperor."

"In some respects, she is a remarkably naive young woman. She cannot see ignominy when it stands before her, much less when it sits in London." Dafythe sighed. "You will aid her, won't you, Ambris?" They had never discussed his fears for Mara, but his son seemed to understand.

"I'll do what I can," Ambris answered, "but I will not be Duke for her. If you had meant me to be so, you should have done something about it years ago."

"I did think of it," Dafythe admitted. "But once Mara was born, I couldn't set her aside for your sake." Ambris nodded; he knew the law. "And yet, I have allowed Mara too much her own way. I let her play her war games with the Shieldmaids when she ought to have been learning to bear the responsibilities of government because I knew that I could rely on you to take those burdens from her. It was wrong of me, I know. Unfair. Well, I pay for it now."

"It wouldn't have made a difference, Father. We would still be here. You mustn't worry for Mara. She'll do well enough. She is not like Kharles. There is nothing base nor dishonorable in her. The people already love her. The littlest children and oldest gran'thers would take up arms to march with her if they could. My sons–" Ambris paused. "Eadrik was so proud at his knighting. I can't forget the look on his face when he made his vows. He's dreamed of it since he was a boy. And Arthur taunts Bertrande with his place as Mara's squire. Bertie's so jealous that he won't be able to go too."

"He may have the opportunity if this goes on long enough." Dafythe took up the single remaining copy of the proclamation. "Well, shall we go?"

Ambris took his father's arm and helped him to his feet. "Why can't we behave like rational creatures?"

"Ah, but are we creatures of reason? Sometimes, my son, I seriously question that definition of humanity."

They went out together.

The heralds milled about the state hall, waiting for Dafythe to emerge. The eldest boys diced against the wall. Others were engaged in some childish boasting contest. A few conversed with the courtiers who had remained to accompany the Duke. At Dafythe's entrance, they all drew to attention. Andemyon had been seated at the window with Lord Rafenshighte; when he rose to take his place, the Diplomatic Officer detained him and spoke urgent words too soft for anyone else to hear. Andemyon whispered a reply, and Rafenshighte released his arm.

As Dafythe ascended the curving stairway to the rostrum atop the palace gates, Ambris at one elbow and Martleanne at the other, he wondered why he'd ever thought it a good idea to address his subjects from a position so far above the ground. Each time he made this climb, the stairs grew steeper and there seemed to be more of them. Seventy years ago, when the platform had been newly built according to his own design, he'd leapt up these same steps two at a time without a thought. At least, he'd had the foresight to keep his new palace on the hill and set the gates at the foot of the slope; from the inner side, the climb was much shorter than it might have been if the stairs had begun on level ground. Once atop, he stood thirty feet above the crowd.

The streets of Pendaunzel thronged with people. Townsfolk hung dangerously out of upper-floor windows and leaned over the rails of the shop porches in hopes of seeing the young general lead her troops out. The Processional directly below had been cleared by those constables who remained in the city; the Prince could ride unhindered from the palace gates down the Avenue of Heroes, where her glorious ancestors were commemorated in marble, and pass under the stony gaze of the enormous monument to Eduarde Redlyon in the square.

At the appearance of the Duke in his blue robes, the uproar redoubled with cries of "Hail, Lord Dafythe!" and "Blessings on yer Grace!" The heralds blasted their trumpets to add to the din. The Lords and Layns of the Council gathered behind Dafythe, as if to present themselves as a solid phalanx in support of whatever decree their liege might pronounce. Martleanne offered him a cup of honeyed wine to ease his breathless thirst and clear his throat. One of the heralds, an older boy with a booming voice, shouted out, "Harken ye! Harken ye all, gentle-born and common citizens of the Northlands! Dafythe, our Gracious Lord Duke, addresses this assembly on a matter of great importance!" and the roar of the crowd fell to an expectant murmur.

With few preliminaries, Dafythe introduced the declaration of war. His audience hung upon his words, for the Duke's eloquence was long famed. He spoke phrases to stir the Norman heart: "Our foes beset us"; "The peace and prosperity of our beloved nation is endangered"; "We are left with no honorable solution save to claim what is ours by right through conquest"; "As our ancestors emerged valiant, so shall we!" Though his speech followed a formula which had been employed for centuries, the crowd assumed the words were Dafythe's own. They drank them up eagerly, heartened that their peaceable lord had at last come to his senses.

Yet Dafythe heard his own words with less jubilant emotions. The phrases he spoke were painfully familiar. How often had he heard his father employ these same words before adoring subjects?

When he was done, Dafythe made a small gesture to signal the waiting companies in the palace yard. The trumpets blared a second time and the great gates swung open beneath him. A deafening cry of delight rose from the crowd.

Mara rode out first in polished armor and mail under the white singlet of a Prince. A golden circlet encompassed her brow. Her plumed helm and shield were strapped to her saddle at the horse's flank. Kat rode beside her in similar garb; her dangling shield announced her identity to those too far away to see her face. The Palace Shieldmaids followed, led by Bel, each in dress uniform. Behind them walked the standard bearers, the trumpeters and drummers, then the captains each leading a column of footsoldiers. The pikers were next, then the archers, longbows to the right and crossbows to the left. Then the knights rode by in formation, all in polished armor and bearing their shields before them. Most were of local noble families and many were known in the city. Fresh cheers and encouraging shouts rose at the familiar crests, and extra hails and blessings were given to one youth bearing the crest of Eadeshire, Ambris's eldest son Eadrik. The squires and baggage passed last. It made a splendid parade.

More people had gathered outside the city, crowding the slopes on either side of the road. Flags and banners waved wildly. Farm folk stood in their carts and wagons. Three and four children sat on the backs of plough horses. Mothers and fathers lifted the smallest up onto their shoulders in hopes that the little ones might catch a glimpse of Prince Margueryt—a memory to last a lifetime.

They shouted and cheered and waved as Mara rode out of the city, and even after she had passed from their sight through the rolling hills. They were still cheering after the last baggage cart had gone by.

That night, Dafythe turned restlessly in a dream. Images jumbled and fused: Mara's knights rode past the palace gates, then became his father's troops. Nearly one hundred years ago, he'd been so small that he couldn't see over the parapet of the nursery balcony. It was the first time he'd seen his father go to war. The Empire's finest knights rode out in full battle dress, the crests of their demesnes painted in bright colors on their shields. Kharles had lifted him up to watch them ride by.

"Where are they going?"

"To Naufarre," Kharles answered. "Juan Maria's playing his pranks again. Father's determined to put him in his place for once and all."

Eduarde was going to fight his upstart son. The war had been going on for one hundred years and there was no hope it would ever cease.

"Can't we stop it?" he asked.

"Father never listens," said Kharles. "When has he ever heard any opinion but his own? I envy the way you govern the Northlands, Davy. I've wished for years that I could do the same here, but Father always overrides my endeavors to make changes. He prefers to keep things just as they are."

But of course Kharles had said that many years later when they were grown men. On the day of that long-ago parade—at Roquefort?—when the Redlyon had ridden for Naufarre, they couldn't have been more than five and ten.

In the room behind them, young Kharles played chess with Ambris. Abruptly, the Prince leapt up and kicked over the chessboard. Ambris was winning, had just captured his queen.

"I never wanted it! I have other pieces!" cried Prince Kharles.

"You only want to play if you win," Ambris replied calmly.

"Better to have someone play for you and take the risks."

Knights scattered on the floor, tiny warrior-maids with bronze-bound braids. There seemed to be dozens of them.

"Knights?" Dafythe wondered.

"Knights, queens, princes—we're all pawns in this, Davy," said his brother. "Except for Father and he's quite mad. It's never been our game." Kharles smiled suddenly. "However, I think I have found a way to play."

Dafythe tossed and turned in his bed. It was impossible find rest in this troubled sleep.

His bedchamber was dark; only a faint red glow came from the dying fire. He could hear the sounds of continued merry-making outside. His subjects were not yet abed. There were dances and bonfires in the city tonight and a banquet had been held at the Palace. Everyone at court knew that the Duke disapproved of this war but he wouldn't spoil their pleasure by making a churlish display of his remarkable opinions. Dafythe had maintained his usual graciousness throughout the evening, but he excused himself soon after dinner, citing his age as the reason for foregoing the entertainments.

"Boy?" He peered down at the little lump on the cushioned bench at the foot of his bed, the herald in attendance. "Boy?"

The boy stirred. "M'Lord?"

"Which one are you?"

"Andemyon, if it please you." The boy sat up, rubbing his eyes with the back of his hand. "Are you ill, My Lord Duke? Shall I fetch the `pothecary?"

"No, I'm not ill. The room is chilly."

Andemyon went to the hearth to toss a few sticks of kindling onto the glowing embers and poke the dying fire into renewed life. The firelight limned the boy's delicate profile and shone red-gold through his rumpled hair. When he blinked, silvery glints flickered on his eyelashes.

"Will that be all, Your Grace?"

"Talk with me awhile, Lad. I cannot sleep." The boy smoothed down his crushed tunic and sat at the foot of the bed with one foot tucked beneath him. "Tell me, do you wish you were going off to war with Prince Marguerყt tonight?"

"No, My Lord. Father wouldn't allow it."

"You've no thought of being a squire or knight? Most boys your age dream of it, you know."

"I know," said Andemyon. "No." He offered no further explanation.

How many little heralds had there been during his reign? Dafythe wondered. Hundreds. The first boys were now gray-bearded grandfathers. Some he recalled very well: Tuxsetau as an earnest, chubby child; Roodebroke's youngest son, who was never where he ought to be; Rafenshighte, as sycophantic at fifteen as he was today. Others he couldn't remember at all. For two years or three, they served him, then they passed on to other responsibilities. It was Dafythe's duty to determine what position each was most suited for. He conversed with them whenever he found an opportunity, struggling through the mumbled *Yes, M'Lord's* that came in response to his questions to learn what he could about each boy before starting them on their careers. The mind of the average young boy was by this time tediously familiar to Dafythe, and its potential easily divined.

Andemyon, however, remained a mystery. Dafythe suspected that a remarkable intelligence lay behind the child's silence, but his efforts to draw the boy out brought few satisfying results. The little he did know intrigued him. This quiet boy who didn't fit in with his fellows, the wizard's ward, the astonishing soprano, the voracious reader—What could be made of him? Was there any place at court that could exercise his unusual talents?

"Andemyon, what am I do with you?"

"My Lord?"

"You know that you'll be leaving me in another year or so, don't you?" said Dafythe. "It is in my power to set you upon the path to your future. Have you given any thought to what you would like to be when you are grown?"

Andemyon blinked shyly, then leaned forward as if to impart a secret. "A wizard," he confided. "But that's impossible. I'm not magical." Then he added helpfully: "You mustn't worry for my future, My Lord Duke. My Lord Rafenshighte said that I might join the diplomatic office when I am no longer your herald."

"Did he?" cried Dafythe. "Is that what he was speaking of so urgently to you this afternoon?"

"Just before the parade? Yes. He's spoken of it before. I told him I would consider it."

The Duke didn't like this at all. "Do you wish to enter the diplomatic service?"

"I don't know. What is it they do?"

"Rafenshighte and his staff are my liaison with the foreign ambassadors here in Pendaunzel and they represent the Dukedom in foreign courts. They work to establish harmony between nations and ensure that our interests are being served. They must make themselves pleasing to foreign dignitaries. It is a profession where personal charm and a gift for pretty speech are most useful."

"I don't think I can do that," the boy answered. "But My Lord Rafenshighte promises–"

"Never mind Rafenshighte's promises."

"I am meant to get on at court, My Lord."

"Is it what you wish, Andemyon, to be a successful courtier?"

"Father thinks it best. I'm not of an age to judge for myself and so I must trust the judgment of my elders, who are wise and know what is best for me."

Dafythe nearly laughed aloud in surprise at this extremely proper sentiment. It was the sort of morally improving platitude young Normans were always taught, but he'd never before met any child who seemed to take it to heart.

"You do as you are instructed by your elders?" he asked. "My boy, at your age, that's the majority of the population!"

"No, My Lord," Andemyon replied in all seriousness. "Not all my elders are wise."

"Then how do you choose?"

"I know."

"You consult your own judgment?" Dafythe pursued, still amused.

"I obey those who act for my good. If someone means me harm, I won't do as they ask."

It was a simple, innocent view of life. The boy was as guileless as a kitten, trusting caresses and kind words as if they were true signs of an honest character. He could wander so easily into danger. "And what," asked Dafythe, "do you imagine My Lord Rafenshighte means for you?"

"I don't know," the boy answered thoughtfully. "He is kind to me. His words are sweet. He says that he wishes to help me, and yet..." Andemyon sat upright. "My Lord, do you think Lord Rafenshighte isn't honorable? You speak as if I ought not trust him."

Dafythe was astonished by this sudden show of penetration so soon after he'd decided that the boy must be a complete naif. Innocent Andemyon was, but not a fool.

"I think Geoffrey means to serve himself," the Duke replied with less condescension. "A youth might find Lord Rafenshighte's patronage beneficial—a young man of his own sort, who is eloquent, ambitious, and self-interested. My lad, that is not you. I'm afraid you're more likely to become a dupe in the plots of such a mercenary creature. You are not ambitious enough to promote yourself and I think you must be willing to sacrifice much to have another promote you. Even if you are prepared to do that, I cannot recommend you sacrifice anything to Rafenshighte."

Andemyon nodded solemnly. "Then what shall I do, Your Grace?"

It was an honest appeal; Dafythe found himself on the side of Andemyon's angels. He took up a weighty responsibility.

"I cannot see you as a court functionary," he said after giving the matter some consideration. He could keep the boy under his personal protection for another year or so, but what then? "No, I think you would do best to seek a position of the court, yet not courtly. The Chancellor's office. What do you think of that? Service as a clerk can be boring, I know, but Ambris will have your best interests at heart and he can put you in the way of many great opportunities. If you show an aptitude for legislative work, you might read law at a university. Maryesfont, perhaps?" This university, the only one in the Northlands, was run by the Sisters of the Holy Font of Wisdom.

"I'd like to go to Maryesfont," Andemyon confessed. "My grandfather is Dean of St. Anne's College and my great-aunt is prior at the Abbey."

"Indeed!" said Dafythe. He hadn't known that the boy's family was so well-placed. The thesper's family, he wondered, or Redmantyl's?

Dafythe had initially proposed the university as a haven to

keep the child safe until he outgrew his present unworldliness, but now he began to consider the idea more seriously. A university education would increase Andemyon's capacities. He *was* intelligent—Dafythe was certain of that. The Sisters at Maryesfont would do more than guard his innocence; they would shape the unformed material of his mind, develop his critical judgment, sharpen his intellectual skills, and provide him with the knowledge he would need to make his way in the world. They would arm him for greater battles than any the boys who dreamed of knighthood would ever face.

This morning, Dafythe had questioned the definition of Man as a creature of reason. He'd spoken with bitterness then, with no hope that anything sane or rational in humanity would survive this absurd war, but now he began to hope for this young boy who sat watching him expectantly. Here was promise. Here were so many possibilities. He was sorry he wouldn't live to see them fulfilled.

"Shall I write your father and see if this course is agreeable to him?" he asked. "Is it agreeable to you?"

"If it please Your Grace," Andemyon answered properly. "I am meant to serve you."

"And so you shall, Lad," the Duke replied.

The War in the Marches
1954

heyghte

"It's her! That's the Prince!"

The crowd in the Huitelm murmured excitedly as Mara and her Shieldmaid companions descended into the cool relief of the basement tavern. They'd been eagerly awaiting their first glimpse of her for days, since the first soldiers' encampments had appeared in the fallow fields, pastures, and woodlands beyond the city walls. Thousands of soldiers were camped around the city now, for Mara's army had increased three-fold since they'd begun the long march from Pendaunzel. Though they were prepared to march again at a day's notice, they waited here for the Guylleshire troops to join them before they continued their journey south.

The Prince had arrived at Storm Port that morning. Alyx, Captain of the Storm Port garrison, had gone out to greet her sister-Shieldmaids and escort Mara, Bel, and Kat into her city.

Though they were not in full armor, they were a stunning quartet: long braids bound in bronze, brief soldiers' kirtles covered by studded leather tuilles, boots tall and swords agirt. To the common folk of Storm Port who had awaited Mara's coming, they seemed more than mortal women. History walked before them. These were warriors out of legend—Mildred and the first band of Shieldmaidens, Hippolyta's Amazons, Brunhilde's Valkyrie—or at least their daughters incarnate.

This meeting was meant to be a reunion as much as a council, for these women were Mara's dearest friends: dependable Bel, wry and wiry Alyx, and pensive Sataumie who traveled with the Guylleshires and would join them shortly. They were more than sisters of her order—hundreds among her troops and officers might make that claim—but the women she had trained with. If Mara had met them in other circumstances, she would've considered them her natural inferiors and treated them with the courteous grace a Prince must use toward her subjects. But because they'd been Shieldmaids with her, they were her intimates. Their bond was so close as true kinswomen. They were nearly so beloved as Kat.

With the exception of Kat, they had all begun as cadets together. As young girls, they'd suffered pangs of homesickness from adjoining cots. They'd wept in frustration and exhaustion at the seemingly impossible drills their demanding captain had set for them, and had celebrated when these difficult exercises were mastered. They had conspired in a dozen childish pranks, and suffered the punishment for one and all rather than lay blame on each other. They had developed their sword skills against each other's blades, suffered bruises in mock combat, crawled through mud and underbrush in battle-games—and together they had captured more enemy flags than any other squadron in the camp's history. When Mara received her first command, Alyx had been her lieutenant. Long ago, they had learned to act as a unit.

It might seem like favoritism that the Prince appointed her old friends to her personal entourage, but it was not unexpected. She knew how to rely on their particular strengths. She knew their abilities. She knew their loyalty; she trusted them more than she trusted anyone. It was fitting that they should be at Mara's side for this magnificent adventure.

The tavern patrons made way for them. As the Prince and her companions took their seats at an open table, a little alemaid approached.

"Rennie, honeymead, for us all," Alyx ordered. Then she turned to business: "I received a message from Sataumie this morning. She is our liaison to Commander Arnauld Hardmarch in command of the Guylleshire legions. They will reach Storm Port tomorrow."

"The Guylleshires must be traveling swiftly," said Bel. "If our information is correct, Old Arnauld left Guylliamesburghe only two days before we rode from Pendaunzel. `Tis twice the distance."

"Commander Arnauld is famous for his swift marches," Mara

answered. "When he commanded the Border Guard under the old Marchion, it was said he could run fresh recruits from Dennefort to the Jamesmarch in a fortnight and have seasoned guards at the end of it."

"Besides," Alyx added, "it's a safe wager he's anxious to prove he's as fit to serve the Redlyon's granddaughter in his aging years as he was to serve the Redlyon himself as a boy. `Tis a shame he never saw battle in his prime."

"That might be said of many," said Kat.

"I thank the Almighty that it won't be said of *us*," Bel replied. Ren, the alemaid, returned with their mead. "Oh, Mara, remember when we were girls at the camp? We were to be your honor guard and ride at your side into the heart of a dozen glorious battles. None would stand against us. We knew we would see days such as Diana's riders knew in her company."

"The finest Shields to ride in any Layn Prince's name," said Alyx, raising her mug. "I pity those who are not able to join us. Your sister, My Lady Laurel—I'm sorry she didn't come with you. I've long wanted to meet this swordsmaster magician who served in the New-York guard."

"It wasn't possible," Mara answered. "Laurel has a little child and she expects another this summer. I would not ask a trained Shieldmaid to march under such circumstances."

"We could use a wizard. What about Lord Redmantyl? After such storms as he conjured here last summer, Terrojos would surrender at the first threat of a dark cloud."

"He might be prevailed upon to aid us if Father requests it as his liege—but Father won't."

"It'd take all the fun out of this war to have it won with bolts of lightning," Bel said peevishly. "If we can send a wizard to do our fighting for us, why go ourselves? What glory is there in a battle gained by magic?"

"It would give us a strategic advantage to have a magician in our company," Kat answered. "But there simply aren't enough to go around these days."

"Who commands the other legions?" asked Alyx. "Arnauld, My Layn Lieutenant Uismarde, my commander Tortos of the Oerykeshires if the Earl doesn't take command himself..."

"Urthor is in command of the Maudeslande Guards," Mara

supplied the rest of the names. "The Earl Brachise has the Eadeshire and Frankeshire garrisons. They will both join us between New York and the Northlands border. The Marchion Frederik commands the Border Guard himself."

"What do you know of Frederik?" asked Alyx.

"He is young," the Prince answered. "He came to his title a few years ago upon the death of his mother, and he was commander of the Guard under her. He has the reputation of a capable military leader. We've corresponded these past weeks. He writes that he looks forward to welcoming us to Dennefort. Courtesy demands he say such things, but I believe he means it."

"He is great-grandson to that Khrystophania of legend," Kat added.

"Khrystophania's heir," Alyx began tentatively. "I have sometimes wondered. `Tis said the first Marchion's son was born before her marriage, and not so many months after the death of Prince Denys."

"Hush," said Bel, with a glance toward the Princes.

"No, she may wonder," Mara answered. "We wonder too."

"Of course, it isn't fit to discuss in public," Kat said, "but we are among friends here." She looked at the others about the table, and continued in a voice barely above a whisper. "Are the descendants of Marchion Khrystophania our cousins? Norman Emperors have always taken an interest in the family at Dennefort as if they were a cadet branch of the imperial house."

"But they aren't a cadet line if they are akin," said Alyx, also in low voice. "Prince Denys–"

"True," Mara admitted. "`Tis why we don't speak of them." She was aware of the common-folk seated so near them. It wasn't fit to speak of this matter here, even among her friends.

Ren returned to their table to refill Alyx's mug. The alemaid served Bel, then Kat, then paused when she came to Mara. "More ale, My Prince?"

"No, gramercies. Not yet."

But the girl remained beside her chair until Alyx waved her away. "Rennie, leave us."

"Will there be sufficient quarters for all the troops?" Kat changed the subject, seeing that her cousin was uncomfortable. "The legions will number twelve thousand by the time we reach

Dennefort. `Tis more than twice the normal complement of the Border Guard in Eduardesmarch now."

"The Marchion promises that there will be. Dennefort, fortress and town, is set on uncluttered land and there is plenty of room for our encampments. I've been thinking of settling our troops in over the course of several days to avoid unnecessary complication. This march will be difficult enough before we reach the end of it."

"I can't wait `til we reach the frontier," said Bel. "This campaign is going to be wonderful. Just like the Redlyon and Denys and Diane."

"We've waited so long," Alyx agreed. "Everyone." She gestured at the tavern patrons, who were keeping a respectful distance, but most eyes were on the Prince's table. "This war has made every one of us heroes and we haven't yet faced the Spanish. *My* popularity has increased enormously—not simply because I'm taking the garrison to the frontier, but because I am your friend, Mara. They ask me—'Captain, when will the Prince come? When will Prince Margueryt be here?' Your mother, Bel, stopped me in the street last week. No, truly, she did! Dame Prenelda, who hasn't spoken two courteous words to me in my life. She asked after you. 'Have you news of my daughter, the Prince's captain?' she said."

Bel laughed. "For once, she is proud of me. What a turn-about! When I left for the camp, Mama told me that daughters of the great merchant-houses had no place playing at soldiers. Nobles were meant to lead and commoners to march, but I would only expose myself to contempt and ridicule if I were foolish enough to join the Shieldmaids. And yet where would I be without the Shieldmaids?"

"No doubt you would have the life set out for Damosel Belinde Chisdaughter," Alyx told her.

"I used to see Alyx about the city," Bel announced. "Mama wouldn't allow me to associate with the common children, but I knew who you were, Alyx, and I envied that you played on the wharfs and spoke with the garrison guards."

"I served them in my mother's inn," Alyx answered. She looked to the little alemaid who was busy with customers at another table. "Not so enviable a task." Ren glanced their way, met the Captain's eyes, and smiled shyly before a shout from another table drew her away.

"Yes, but you befriended them. While you were squire to Captain Kerrith, I sat in the parlor in velvet skirts and silk ribbons, waiting for suitors. From my sixteenth birthday, my family planned my marriage as if they were a little kingdom seeking alliance with another nation. Yet my sisters and brothers and all my girlhood friends seemed to think this matchmaking perfectly appropriate. They all married happily. Until I went to the Shieldmaid camp, I was made to feel that there was something wrong with me because I didn't share their ambitions."

Alyx replied softly: "*We are not ordinary women, nor are we meant to be. That which contents lesser folk drives us mad.*" This quotation was attributed to the founder of their order. Its authenticity was questioned, but they all took its essential truth to heart.

Bel patted her comrade's arm. "Precisely so, Alyx. We aren't suited to the ordinary ways at all."

"My Layn Prince?"

"What is it, Maiden?" Mara looked up at the little alemaid who stood again beside the table.

"My Prince, I have a boon to beg of you."

This was not unusual. Mara didn't have the authority to grant most requests asked of her: in Gossunge, she had the magisterial power to dispense pardons for minor transgressions, and of course she gifted those who asked for trinkets or small amounts of money, but long-standing tradition obliged her to hear all petitions no matter how unreasonable. What sort of noblewoman held herself unapproachable to her subjects?

"Speak," she responded. "If it is in my power, I shall grant it."

Encouraged, Ren blurted her request: "My Layn, may I come with you?"

Around the table, the Shieldmaids chuckled. Mara ignored them. "What can you do in my service, little maid?" she asked with gentle courtesy. This tiny chit—smaller even than Bel, dark hair tucked modestly beneath a servant's kerchief, large brown eyes full of hope beyond reason, slender arms that could never lift a sword—truly, it was absurd that *she* should make such a request, but Mara couldn't laugh. The desire to follow one's liege into battle was in the heart of all good Norman citizens. It would be cruel to mock a child who shared that sensibility but didn't have the physical strength to fulfill it.

"I'll do whatever you will, My Prince," the girl promised earnestly. "I can sew. I can polish. I do all the pewter work here."

"Yes, it's very nice." Mara turned the mug in her hand to examine it.

"I can polish armor as well. I can care for your clothes and such."

"A gentyl-maid in a soldier's camp!" said Kat, grinning.

"Please, My Layn?" Ren pursued. "I've always wished to see a battle. I'll do whatever you ask if you let me go with you."

"It shows proper virtue that you choose to go among Shieldmaids," said Mara. "But you know you are no soldier yourself, Lass."

"I can learn. Orlan once told me he would speak to you, Captain Alyx, and I might be your squire."

"And who is this Orlan?" asked Bel. "A sweetheart?"

The little maid touched the tarnished gilt pomander tied to her skirt. "A nobleman. He is called Orlan Lightesblood."

Kat burst into fresh laughter. "Lord Redmantyl's son?"

Ren nodded.

"How in seven raging hells does a child like you know Redmantyl's son?"

"The tavern keeper, her mother, was once My Lord Redmantyl's chatelaine," Alyx explained. "At any rate, `twas impossible to miss Chyelde Orlan's antics here last summer."

"But this lass is barely sixteen," Kat frowned. "Do you suggest–?"

"Oh, hush. You'll make the poor little thing blush more than her blood can bear," Bel said in a motherly manner. "She's not used to the rough jests of coarse soldiers. Mara, if you can't make them conduct themselves like well-born women in a tavern, we'll all soon have the reputation of marauding crusaders."

But Mara was staring at the little alemaid. Ren blushed at the teasing, but her eyes remained hopefully on her Prince as if Mara were the only one who truly mattered to her. A small maid, dark and common-born, not sixteen—or just upon it. Was this Ren the fulfillment of Magician Peter's vision? She fit his description perfectly. Was she the one?

Mara rose from the table. "Lass, I shall speak to your mother."

Kat made a surprised sound. "Oh, Mara, `tis only in jest! I never meant a thing. What, will you have the good alekeep take a horsewhip to me for questioning her daughter's virtue?"

"Don't be stupid. The girl's coming with us."

Adyna Alekeep consented reluctantly. She didn't wish her young daughter to go so far away with the armies, but she acknowledged that Ren was growing into a pretty maiden; some of her customers had begun to pay too much attention to the girl. If the Prince herself should take a kindly interest in Ren's future, who was *she* to spoil the opportunity? Both Mara and Captain Alyx promised that Ren would not come to harm. Ren was to be the Prince's gentyl-maid and page. She wouldn't see battle.

Though she had no official duties yet, Ren accompanied Mara while the army remained in Storm Port. When Mara went out to greet the officers of the Guylleshire troops, Ren stood unobtrusively at her side. She attended Mara during the long conferences that weekend in which the Prince and her commanders planned the next phase of their journey.

The army's departure required painstaking effort. Its size, which would be its strength in battle, was a handicap while it traveled. The transportation of so many at once demanded the careful organization of all components, and the problems wouldn't end once they left Storm Port. When the army began to move, it must fragment. The entire force would not camp together again until they reached Dennefort. Storm Port was the only city in the Northlands capable of supporting the extra thousands; hereafter, the troops must play a sort of leap-frog, overtaking each other to stagger their campsites so that no more than a few hundred burdened any one town or village. At least three thousand more, soldiers and non-combatants, were expected to join them as they moved south.

As Mara struggled with these complexities and argued with her commanders over the future placement of their troops, she often thought of the enormous puppets of dragons and other fabulous monsters which thespians used in their productions. These complex mechanisms of painted cloth and slender poles were operated from within by skilled puppeteers working in careful synchronization. If their efforts were successfully coordinated, the great puppets rose and moved with astonishing grace and what looked like fearsome life. Without that coordination, the poor dragon suffered a muddle of conflicting motions and looked as if it writhed helplessly in fits. The movement of the legions must be orchestrated with the same skill: each division must move in its turn for the army to travel as one graceful, powerful beast.

On Saturday, the officers received their instructions. Lieutenant Uismarde acted as chief coordinator. Prior to this time, her duty as Layn Lieutenant of the Northlander armies consisted primarily of knowing where the garrisons were stationed, who captained and commanded them, and how many soldiers made up each battalion. Now, that knowledge was put to practical use. The Lieutenant's information became vitally important, for the smaller companies were to move first and give the larger corps more time. The confusion resulting from troops marching out through fields still occupied by unprepared battalions might delay the departure of both for hours. Commanders were responsible for briefing their captains and overseeing the orderly movement of all troops under their command. Commander Arnauld was especially zealous; in order to impress Mara with his efficiency and earnestness, he had given orders that his newly arrived troops were not to open their packs so that they wouldn't waste time repacking the next day. When Sataumie related her commander's great show of effort, Alyx laughed and said that she would have won her wager.

Sataumie joined the circle of friends about Mara upon her arrival and was assigned as liaison officer between all the legions. Messengers flew from campsite to campsite. Each captain received an assigned hour of departure and a route out of Storm Port's environs. The great clock in the belltower of the cathedral of St. Khrystopher was the signal; its hourly peals could be heard for miles around the city.

One by one, the camps were disbanded, the soldiers' packs stuffed, and the carts loaded. When the bells rang prime at dawn Monday, the first troops marched without incident. Others followed swiftly, efficiently. By Wednesday, the last of the armies were gone from Storm Port. The dragon began to move.

In the one hundred and thirty years since Denys had raised its first walls, Dennefort had grown to enormous proportions. The outermost walls encompassed miles of hilly countryside. Concentric rings of stone walls and earthen works circled the town, and the town itself was built below the original fortress on its rocky abutment.

As Mara and Kat rode across the outer fields and through the town gates behind the Marchion's herald, both were impressed by the impregnability of the place. Dennefort had stood as the first line of Norman defense for many years; even today, with nearly ten miles between it and the Shieldwall, it remained the keystone of the border defenses. Where the northern cities supported garrisons of a standard complement of one hundred each, Dennefort was capable of providing for thousands of soldiers. The Border Guard received their orders here. As they rode through the streets of Dennefort-town, both Princes observed that there were no luxury shops common to ports or mercantile cities—no crystalware, no exotic spices, no silks. Blacksmiths, armorers, swordmakers were abundant. And every tavern they passed bore a military name.

They had arrived with the first troops the evening before, but messages had come to them while they were still *en route*. The Marchion Frederik planned a formal feast of greeting for all the Northlands officers once the last of them had arrived, but he invited the Princes into Dennefort as soon as they were able. His herald had arrived for them this morning.

Frederik was not Dafythe's vassal, for the marches were not part of the Northlands. Princeland and the Eduardesmarch were separate imperial territories, of lesser importance than the dukedom with their governor of a lower rank than the Duke, but the Marchion swore fealty only to the Emperor. Frederik had received his instructions directly from Kharles; he knew to expect Mara and her legions even before she had left Pendaunzel.

They approached the old fortress. The walls were thirty feet tall, huge piles of mortared stone, enormously thick to support their own weight and capable of withstanding the full battery of an invasion. Nearly so broad at the base as they were tall, no catapult nor cannon could knock them down. Though they loomed too near for Mara to examine their configuration and, at any rate, were obscured by the buildings crowded about their base, she thought that the fortress must be star-shaped; each massive wall lay at an acute angle to its neighbors. The entrance lay between two of these jutting points. Squat pennant-capped towers stood atop each point, and two more towers flanked the great, oaken door.

The herald shouted up, "I escort the Princes of the Northlands to audience with My Lord Marchion!"

The great doors swung open. The herald turned his horse and bowed slightly from the saddle as he gestured for the Princes to enter before him.

Ramparts rose immediately behind the wall with only a narrow road between the foot of one and the other. Again, the first impression of Dennefort was its massiveness. It seemed to be a pile of rocks, solid, enormous, seated low on its natural pedestal.

Kat leaned toward Mara to whisper: "Pendaunzel might be stormed more easily than *this*."

The herald led them along the narrow road to the western side of the fortress, then up a path carved into the steep, rocky face. At the top was a gate that opened onto a courtyard, the entrance to the Marchion's private residence. Dennefort Manor was small by Pendaunzel standards, but three levels of tall and slender shuttered windows set close against each other faced the courtyard. The crest of the Marchion's family was displayed above the door: a broken sword as a *bend sinistre* across a field *gules*.

Groomsmen took their horses and the herald escorted them in.

"Layn Princes, My Lord awaits you in his reception chamber," the herald told them with a full bow. "Pray accompany me." He led them through the large entrance hall and up a flight of stairs to the room directly above.

As they entered the chamber, a dark room of oak paneling and battle tapestries, the young man seated at the far end in excited, whispered conversation with a young woman started up and came toward them even before the herald announced his guests.

The Marchion Frederik was indeed young, not yet thirty by Mara's guess. In honor of the occasion, he wore a semi-formal costume: a natural leather tunic with a frogged front and an elaborate pattern of beaded embroidery and a noble-blue robe trimmed with the Border Guards' signal color of dark green. A gold-edged purple sash lay across his chest, marking him as the Emperor's designated governor. A heavy gold chain of office hung about his neck and a plain gold circlet restrained his long hair. The badge of a Chevalier, Order of the Holy Cross was pinned to the right breast of his coat.

"Prince Marguerytl! Prince Katheryne! I welcome you to Dennefort. It is my honor to receive you both. If you could know how I've looked forward to this day!"

Kat smiled at his unaffected enthusiasm, but Mara only stared.

By all historical accounts, Prince Denys had been blond. But, with the exception of Frederik's dark brown hair—obviously the consequence of three generations of the darker, native Atlantean stock—he was the image of that late Norman Prince. The broad brow, prominent cheekbones and square jaw of the Plantagenet face were unmistakable. His eyes were a clear, astonishing bright blue—rare in Northlanders, and more so in the marches. The tales were true: this was Denys's great-grandson. If Denys had lived, this young man might well have been Emperor instead of Kharles.

The thought seemed somehow treacherous, and Mara abandoned it.

"My Lord Marchion," she reached out to take his offered hand. "I am honored to call you my host."

"And I to call you my guest," he made the polite response and let her place his hand against the circlet on her brow. "Oh, and I wish to present you my sister, Khrystophania. She is one of your order."

The young woman he had been speaking with stepped forward shyly. She was perhaps twenty-five, her long braids bound in the Shieldmaid style though she wore her long, formal robes. Like her brother, she was dark-haired and blue-eyed, but the lines of her cheekbones and jaw were more delicate, and her nose was an extremely un-Plantagenet snub.

"It is an honor, Princes," she said. "I too have looked forward to this meeting."

"We've heard about you—you both—from one of our patrol officers," added Frederik. "Martine of the Senneoke demesne. Do you recall her, Prince Marguerytt? She says that she served with you as a cadet."

"She did," Mara answered.

"Her patrol has been out since Midwinter, but I called for her especially when My Lord's messages arrived from London. We took great interest in the troubles with Prince Juan Maria last summer—as you may imagine—but we didn't dream it would come to this." He looked to his sister for confirmation; Khrystophania nodded. "Have you broken fast yet? I worried that I'd sent Ardis out for you too early." The abrupt invitation of refreshment wasn't couched in the elaborate phrases and humble apologies for the meager fare which the Princes were accustomed to at court.

"No, we were up at dawn," Mara answered. "It was not inconvenient."

"But we haven't had a respectable breakfast," Kat added, evidently ready to match her host's informality. "I'd be glad of a cup of tea."

"Ardis, tea for our guests, if you please." He sent the herald out. "Come into the sitting room. We'll be more comfortable there." He opened the door to a smaller chamber. The chairs and tables here looked older and well used, unlike the polished and pristine furniture of the reception chamber. A low fire burned in the grate and the draperies, which had been drawn over the windows in the other room, were here thrown back to display the view.

Kat paused to gaze out at the courtyard, the battlements, and the gray-green mountain to the south.

"Shall I show you about the castle, Prince Katheryne?" Frederik asked. "There are excellent views of our march on every side. You can see Spainfort from the central tower. And of course there's the chapel–" he hesitated, slightly embarrassed. Mara understood; Frederik knew very well who he was in relation to the famous Princes buried there, and he felt perhaps the allusion had been insinuating.

Kat rescued him. “Yes, I’d love to see it. But you promised us breakfast first.”

Breakfast was brought in and laid out on a little table near the fire. As they drank the hot, bitter Indian tea and ate the fresh rolls with apple and peach preserves and heavy cream, the Princes described their journey, making light of the difficulties of traveling with so large an army. They asked after Martine—Khrystophania knew the Shieldmaid better than her brother did—and relayed news from the north.

Then they toured Dennefort. While they were indoors, the morning mists had dissipated and the early summer day had become bright and brisk. The pennants on the towers, each bearing the family emblem of the broken sword, snapped in the breeze as they walked the encircling battlements and took in the spectacular view in every direction.

Frederik led them around the ramparts personally. An informative host, he drew their attention to every item of interest and answered every question. “The star-shape of the lower ramparts? Why, `tis the most progressive form of military architecture. No blind spots between those sharp angles! My grandfather raised them at the Redlyon’s behest”; “There you see the jousting yards behind the barracks where we lodge the guards currently serving at the fortress. You may exercise there, if you like”; “Yes, those are our orchards—the jam you had at breakfast was made from fruit plucked off those very trees. There are also gardens around the town, and the small farms in the open fields keep poultry, sheep, and even cattle. Dennefort can endure a siege for years.” In the distant north, white patches of tents on the enclosed fields and infinitesimal dots moving on the narrow band of the Coast Road were discernible. To the east and south, the mountains sloped down toward the coastal plains and thin silver rivers cut through the craggy green.

“That’s the Shieldwall.” Frederik said as they stood atop the central tower. “`Tis too far away to see the walls from here, but they border that river, and another, beyond it but hidden in the hills. Spainfort is between those two peaks.”

“Where?” asked Kat, who stood near him. “Beneath that jagged crest?”

“No, the one beside it, to the right.” He pointed. “Can you see it? That large blot like an enormous rock."

Kat inched closer and placed a hand on his shoulder as she tried to set her line of sight directly down his extended arm. "No, I see nothing."

Her hair brushed his cheek; the young man blushed and stepped away quickly.

Kat's smile flashed again. "Your eyes must be remarkable, Marchion."

"'Tis more easy to see the Shieldwall on the plains," Frederik replied. Abruptly, he began to describe the little forts that ranged along the rivers. These were not fortified towns like his Dennefort, but outposts established with their own garrisons and regular patrols.

"I've ridden on patrol myself," he added. "I served as a squire to one of the Border commanders, and eventually captained my own squad. We rode the riverside nightly. I know my marches, every ford and pass."

"You were brought up to it," said Kat.

"A Marchion must be qualified to command the Empire's frontiers," Frederik answered. "Our title and rights are not inherited without reason. No Marchion's firstborn can receive the Emperor's appointment unless he is trained and proven capable of defending so important a bastion as Dennefort." He spoke with humility, honored that he'd been chosen by his Emperor to carry on his family's position, and yet proud that he was worthy of the appointment. "It was made certain when I was a boy that I was fit to take my place. My sister was trained as well. Mother impressed me from the cradle with the danger we faced here. We live at the very edge of Norman civilization, and any moment the Spanish might take it into their heads to lay siege to our home. When Khrysta and I were mere babies, we were taught to run and hide in the storerooms if Dennefort were invaded. When I was so small that I must cling to my mother's hand and ride on her saddle before her, she took me about to see every line of defense within a day's ride. Every new commander and captain was presented to me, and I must learn their names and know where they were to be stationed. I attended the counsels whenever she met with her officers. I was hand-fasted to the Border Guard, you might say, as some are betrothed in infancy."

"It sounds rather grim."

"Not at all. In truth, Prince Kat," he added, smiling. "I'd grown rather cynical about my duties. In all my years on patrol, I never met with one skirmish. Indeed, we were on good terms with Don Francisco, the Terrojos governor. We rode out to *Ojos des Mantegnas* to greet the new Teniente Don Miguel—*he* is one of the Andalusians. Until last year, Spanish merchants were permitted to bring their wares into our markets. Most of us speak their language, and our neighbors speak the Norman tongue."

They descended from the battlements to the artillery yard, where the catapults and cannons stood. The former were enormously tall machines of wood, their great leather slings thrust skyward, empty; the latter were like huge iron churchbells upturned between two cartwheels.

"You've heard the tale of Eduarde's siege of Spainfort," said Frederik. "Duke Diane brought these same cannons up the mountainside. But do you know that they never once fired the monsters? Simply the sight of the cannon coming up the pass caused the Spanish to surrender. And lucky too for Diane's soldiers. `Tis a dangerous weapon, as much so for the wielder as for the target. Playing with that Chinese rocket-powder is a fool's game. The blast can fling the cannon itself back into your own troops if it isn't pegged down tightly, or it may explode and scatter iron fragments to kill everyone who stands near it. They make a dreadful noise."

"Have you fired them yourself?" Mara asked. She had read about the fearsome cannons and had heard tales of how dangerous they were, but these were the first she'd ever seen.

"Not these, Prince Mara. I confess it—I am too much a coward to risk my life for such an experiment. There are smaller cannon at the Delta fortress, where I was stationed as a young officer shortly before my knighting." He grinned elfishly. "My staff and I drank far more than was good for us one night and touched them off for sport. It seemed enormous fun when we began, and incredible folly only minutes later. My ears rang for days and my lieutenant's beard was singed on one side. I pray we are never called to use these demons, though we try to keep them ready for service." He patted the nearest iron muzzle. "The cats will be much more efficient if we must batter down Spainfort's wall. `Tis an enormous effort to drag them out, but at least you might hit what you aim at and there's little chance your own artillery will be killed."

The Marchion's frontier manners were more direct than Mara and Kat were used to, but neither took the young man for an ill-bred rustic. Mara quickly grew to like him; the fact that he was a cousin, though this could not be acknowledged, gave him a higher standing in her eyes. It was impossible to think the great-grandson of Denys any less refined than his venerated ancestor. Frederik was open, affable, eager to please. His unguarded remarks were refreshingly different from the obsequies of the men they knew at court. Frederik was no flatterer. He recognized their superior rank and extended the requisite courtesies, but he wasn't afraid of them. He meant to be friends and, receiving no immediate rebuff, assumed that they were.

He was not the image of Denys, Mara decided. No, he was more like her father had been in his youth. She'd seen portraits of Dafythe in his twenties and thirties; Frederik might easily be taken for a son of that young Duke. He might be taken for her own younger brother. Though Frederik didn't possess Dafythe's courtly sophistication, he had the same affection, sense of responsibility, and concern for his subjects' well-being that Mara had only recently learned to appreciate in her father. He carried himself with the graciousness of one well-born and the confidence of one brought up to command and defend. He was as much the proud master of Dennefort as Dafythe was master of Pendaunzel.

She was impressed by his competence. He did know his marches, more well than she knew Gossunge. He spoke in friendly terms with every guard they met on their way, and the guards, in turn, seemed fond of him. They responded to his familiar jests with equal retorts. None seemed awed or intimidated by their commander, nor were they contemptuous at his informality. Mara had this sort of friendship with her Shieldmaids, but she was surprised to see it shared between a noble lord and common soldiers. The Dennefort guards considered Frederik one of them. He had served in the patrols; he knew their business as well as they did, and they respected him all the more for it.

Kat was clearly amused by his enthusiasm, Mara observed, yet she saw nothing condescending in her cousin's banter. For Kat, too, Frederik's provincial charm was a delightful change from the polished manners of the Pendaunzel courtiers, and she responded to him playfully.

At the end of the tour, they visited the chapel. The tombs of Denys and his youngest brother Margad were not gravesites in the chapel grounds, as Mara had always imagined, but elevated mausoleums of native stone at the mouth of the family crypt; Frederik explained that the earth beneath the chapel was too rocky for burial. Each tomb was topped by an effigy of the dead Prince within—the knight and his squire, both clad in armor, their stone faces solemn and sleeping. The image of Denys held a sword to its breast; Margad embraced a shield. In the excavated crypt beyond them, Frederik's ancestors lay in sealed vaults.

Here, Frederik's mood changed. He grew more sober as he genuflected at the crucifix above the doorway, then approached Denys's tomb.

"Mother brought me here too," he told them. "She never fought a battle in her life, but she meant me to know that war was no thing of play. Even the boldest and bravest warriors can fall. Her grandmother–" he paused. "The first Marchion. She told her that fortunes might be changed in one night."

He knew; Mara was certain. It was the one point on which his frankness failed.

Kat, on the other side of Denys's tomb, smiled softly. "One might be nearly Empress, and then as abruptly left alone on the battlefield," she said.

Frederik blinked at this allusion, more bold than he would dare to make himself. "I didn't wish to be pushing, Prince Katheryne."

"You aren't. Did you think we hadn't guessed for ourselves? `Tis nothing to be ashamed of, Cousin." She reached across the effigy to take his hand. "Rather, be proud."

The armies of the Northlands were still moving into campsites about Dennefort that Sunday, but Mara and Kat were well settled by then. They had located their friends and, on Sunday afternoon, they gathered to spar on the jousting yards by the barracks.

Frederik had been most generous, reserving one field exclusively for their use and providing a private room where the Shieldmaids could store their armor and weaponry. Off-duty Border Guards watched the fencing match from the edge of the yard, but none interrupted the Princes' exercise.

Since there were five of them, they exercised in the interchange formation they had learned as cadets: Mara sparred with Alyx, Bel with Sataumie; Kat assumed the role of swordsmaster and circled the matched pairs, pointing out flaws in their form. Partners changed frequently. When Mara's saber tip darted under Alyx's shield to prick her unguarded flank, Kat took the Captain's place. Alyx soon replaced Bel, and Bel rejoined the action when Kat tagged Mara. They spun in a furious minuet, flailing extravagantly to drive each other back, leaping boldly into an undefended spot. The dance was intense, but lively, and playful taunts and shrieking laughter rose above the rhythmic clash of steel. Their swords never struck except to graze mail or leather lightly. Yet their grace and merriment barely disguised the ferocity of their game. In a few weeks, they would meet other swordsmasters with deadly intent and today's practice made them all the more eager for it.

After an hour or so, all were bright with perspiration and their strikes and steps grew more slow. There were fewer bold leaps and dramatic flails. The steps of the dance became more deliberate.

"Stop," Mara commanded. "Taumie's holding her point low and you're too weary, Alyx, to take advantage of it. Besides, we've only got an hour before Evensong and I'd like to bathe and have dinner before Mass."

They went to the wardroom, where Ren sat with the two young girls who served as squires to Bel and Alyx; the little maids had been watching the swordplay wistfully.

"Where's Arthur?" asked Kat as she tossed her gauntlets on the bench inside the door.

"M'Layn, with his brother Chevalier Eadrik."

"And left knowing we were out on the playing field, careless brat! Rennie, can you serve as squire?"

"If you like, My Prince," Ren answered tentatively. "I haven't learnt how to care for soldiers' gear."

"'Tisn't difficult," Mara assured her. "We all began our careers in such service. First, take this–" she handed the girl her scabbard. "Hang it on the rack in the wall behind you. Kat's goes below it. Place the shields against the wall beneath. Watch Marisel and Tenna and do as they do. Now for my gloves..." She extended her hands for the girl to pull off the leather fencing gauntlets.

As the Shieldmaids shed their battle gear, Ren received each piece and stored it with great care. Mara offered directions whenever the girl hesitated and Bel's and Alyx's squires made helpful suggestions. While the officers bathed, the girl turned to the more comfortable chores of a gentyl-maid and laid out fresh linen shirts, silk hose to replace the discarded woolens, and tunics and kirtles appropriate for Mass.

"Shall I carry your arms, My Prince?" Ren offered once Mara had dressed. "Chyelde Arthur would."

"Arthur can carry my gear with ease," Mara answered. "It's too heavy for you." But at the girl's crestfallen expression, she reconsidered. "Very well, take the shield. Leave the armor here, and I'll take my fencing saber."

The sword Dentelyon hung above the rest of the gear. On an impulse, she took it down as well. An idea had come to her. Why shouldn't she teach Ren something of the Shieldmaid arts? The girl took such interest in the equipment and practices of battle-play that it seemed a shame not to teach her a little.

"Rennie, have you ever handled a sword?"

"No, Prince Mara."

"Would you like to?"

The girl's eyes shone at the suggestion. "May I?"

Mara unsheathed Dentelyon. Gold-hilted and more than a yard long, the sword was too heavy for ordinary use; Mara felt the weight of it at her hip when she wore it. She didn't fence with it, but saved it for the saddle, when it was more easily handled.

She gave it to the girl; Ren took the hilt in both hands and the point dropped instantly. Kat and the Shieldmaids ducked their heads to conceal their amusement. One of the squires giggled.

"Give it up, Mara," Bel said. "That's too much for her."

"No, I can–" Ren insisted, though she obviously struggled to keep her balance.

"Nonsense. You're too small."

"You're not so much larger than she is, Bel," Mara answered.

"True," said Sataumie, "but Bel didn't begin to train with a sword made for a grown man."

"I doubt even the Redlyon could lift *that* when he was a lad her age," Bel added. "It's easier for you big women. You've got shoulders like a man, Mara. The Shieldmaids taught us to use our skills as women, but the truth of it is that you could fight as well on masculine terms. I couldn't. I don't have the arms for it. Oh, you might make a swordsmaid out of that little girl if she trained long enough, but she'll never be able to wield that thing any more than I can."

Reluctantly, Mara returned Dentelyon to its place and followed her Shieldmaids out, the disappointed Ren bearing her shield. The Prince could never surrender anything easily.

She stopped on the field. "Then we'll have to start with something lighter. Here," she held out her free hand. The Shieldmaids were always ready to obey her commands; Alyx drew her fencing saber, a foot shorter than the famous broadsword, and gave it to her. Alyx received Mara's shield and Mara gave the saber to Ren.

She took the girl's arm gently between her hands and steadied her grip. "The wrist must be straight, Rennie. Not so rigid that it cannot bear a blow, but firm. Move by bending the elbow. Gauntlets will brace your wrists, but `tis best to strengthen the muscles.

"Now–" Mara stepped back and drew her own saber. "The object of swordplay is simple: never let your opponent's sword touch you. In fencing, this means the game is lost. In battle, it may be your death." Ambris had taught her this when she was six, and she repeated it to every squire and cadet she ever instructed. "Keep your eyes upon your foe's swordpoint."

Ren did so with unwavering intensity.

"To deflect the blade, you block and parry. Block–" She demonstrated by lifting her sword against Ren's unsteady blade, "And parry." With a smooth, slow, downward motion, she swept the blade aside. "Do you see?"

Ren nodded, her eyes still on the tip of Mara's sword.

"When your opponent is unguarded, you make your own

strike." Gently, she extended the saber to touch the breast of Ren's jerkin; the girl recoiled. "Good! Will you try?" Mara brought her sword up again. "Block, Ren."

The girl danced back and knocked the sword aside with a jerk.

Ren leaned into the swing, Mara noted, throwing herself off balance and leaving her lower body vulnerable, but Mara spoke encouragingly, "Not too badly done. Your stance can be improved. You must learn to brace yourself for the counterstroke. Even in a friendly match, the blows will be hard. You can be knocked off your feet. Place one leg behind the other–"

"Mara," Alyx reminded her. "Mass? Dinner? It will not be seemly if My Layn Prince's entourage is tardy."

She was right, of course. Mara sheathed her sword. "We'll continue your lessons later, Rennie."

They walked toward the fortress, Shieldmaids ahead and squires behind. Kat whispered to her cousin: "The girl can't become your squire, Mara. You promised her mother."

"I promised that Ren wouldn't see battle and she shan't. The maid is small, but that's all the more reason for her to learn to defend herself."

"I don't understand why you've taken her on," said Kat. "She's a well-behaved child, but there must be hundreds of little alemaids exactly like her. Why pick her out?"

"Because she asked."

"And will you grant that same boon to all who ask? Mara, I know how you return their affection, but you cannot take every subject into your personal protection."

"No, this is different. I knew there would be a little maid. Magician Peter *saw* her. She is going to be important to me somehow."

"'Tisn't like you to be so superstitious."

"It's not superstition. Our Heavenly Father bestows the gift of foresight to magicians. He gave these visions to Peter for a reason. Peter saw this war, Kat, and here we are! He saw our victory celebration at the Palace."

"The Emperor's men," said Kat, who had heard all of this many times before.

"But do you understand what this means? Peter saw three things—the battle, the young maid not sixteen, and our victory. If he has been right twice, then his visions are true and divinely inspired. Victory too will come to pass!"

It was difficult for Kat to remain skeptical before the force of her cousin's conviction. Indeed, it was difficult for her to doubt any cause of Mara's for very long. "It may be so," she conceded, and glanced over her shoulder at the determined girl who bore Mara's shield even though it was too heavy for her. "But how do you know that she's the right one?"

"She suits Peter's description," Mara answered, "and she's the only one who's come to me with a request to enter my personal service." They stopped at the gate. "Ren, is that too much for you? I can take it–"

"No, My Layn!"

As they entered Dennefort, the little maid trailing after them, Kat looked up at the fortress and said, "Wasn't there a fourth vision? I recall you mentioned it once. Peter spoke of a sword."

"A broken sword," Mara answered, and followed her cousin's gaze up to the tower-tops. Each bore the pennant of the Marchion's family. "The broken sword."

"You may be right, Mara. There may be something to this." Kat was smiling. "Look, there's Frederik!"

nyne

Six weeks later, the armies of the Northlands began to cross the Shieldwall. They had mobilized with astonishing swiftness; Mara had deployed cohorts of one hundred each at intervals along the border with Arnauld commanding a legion at Delta fortress on the coast and Brachis in command of another in the western mountains, but the main Northlands' force crossed at the vulnerable point where the Shieldwall was narrowest. Spainfort lay directly south. The invasion of Terrojos would commence at dawn.

So enormous an undertaking was impossible to overlook. Spanish troops had taken up defensive positions along the southern boundary of the Shieldwall; flickering orange pinpoints of campfires were visible in the darkness. Messages had thrice been sent to Spainfort, demanding surrender and promising peaceable passage to any who disdained Norman rule. This gesture was required by long-established codes of conduct between civilized nations, but it was understood that Spanish honor would never allow these terms to be accepted. Terrojos meant to hold back the invasion for as long as they were able. Their numbers were much smaller than the combined might of the Normans but, while they couldn't hope to prevent the onslaught, they could hinder the progress of the invading army. Crags and outcroppings in the river-cut hills provided a hundred strong strategic points for barricades and ambushes. The most recent intelligence reports revealed that reinforcements had been sent for from Spain and would reach Terrojos within the week. Mara knew that she must strike now.

In preparation for the coming battle, she had spent the afternoon in prayer. Her chaplain heard her confession and she received communion. Then, her soul in order, she had attended to certain practical matters which must be addressed. Though she would rather not think of them, she knew they were necessary.

She made out her will. She had also written a letter to her father, to be delivered only if she died; in it, she told him of her love, apologized for any act he might disapprove of, and urged him to consider naming Eadrik his heir-apparent—or, if Eadrik died too, Ambris's second son Eduarde. In a similar letter to the Emperor, she wrote that she was proud to give her life in his cause. These personal papers would go in Ren's care when the little maid and the other non-combatants retreated to the safety of Dennefort.

In addition, Mara had issued general instructions regarding ransom for herself as well as her cousin and Shieldmaids in the contingency of capture by the Spanish. She demanded retribution against every Spaniard if she or any of her companions were treated brutally while in captivity. Mara hoped it wouldn't come to that; the threat of bloody revenge was meant to be preventative, not punitive. She would rather keep her person safe than see any mistreatment avenged by the wholesale slaughter and mutilation of Spanish prisoners, but she had this means to protect herself. Spainfort had likewise received word of her orders. In kind, she also forbade atrocities against the enemy. Offenses committed by any of her soldiers would be punished as if they were crimes committed on Norman soil against Norman citizens. Cruelty to the captured and fallen was not only abhorrent to Mara's own principles; she also hoped that mercy to the conquered Terrojos natives would facilitate their subjugation and she wished to impress her father with her civilized conduct. This battle would not become an excuse for barbarian bloodletting.

Some soldiers slept that night. Others were worried and restless. Knowing her own uneasiness, the Prince called her friends together. After this afternoon's grim business, she needed light-hearted company. While her Shieldmaids gathered about the campfire, their squires sat drowsily in attendance and Arthur sprawled on the grass nearby. Bard Delphyn told heart-stirring tales and sang the odd conceits of *The Hart and the Lion*:

The swift hart of the Northlands,
Its brow bears the star.
Its horns sharp as green-thorn,
Let none dare it spar!

The lion of Skotsland,
Fierce lord of the wood.
Its roar foments terror,
Its mane red as blood.

The hart and the lion
O how can it be?
What strange love lies between
Such antipathies?

The hart and the lion
O how can it be?
Can the fallow lie down
With the king of all beasts?

"I never understood that," said Bel as she tossed a handful of popcorn kernels onto the hot, flat rocks surrounding the fire. "Why an Emperor married a Duke of the Northlands. Do you know, when I was a little girl and first learnt my histories, I was forever baffled by the Redlyon's Princes. Who was meant by Gossunge? It ought to have been the Duke's firstborn."

"No," Mara answered. "Father was Prince of Gossunge, and Skotsland too."

"Old Kharles couldn't have been heir to the Empire and Dukedom both, Bel," Alyx added. "The Northlands is meant to be autonomous, not an imperial fief like the European kingdoms. The title of Gossunge, and afterwards, Duke of the Northlands, was given My Lord Dafythe so that the Northland's line remained separate from the imperial house. Didn't your history lessons teach you that?"

"But that's my point exactly!" Bel insisted. "Why create so much confusion between which of two sons was heir to what, when more prudent matches might've avoided the problem from the start? What if the marriage had produced only one child? I wonder that it was ever allowed."

"They weren't Emperor and Duke when they met," Sataumie reminded her. "No one could've known that Prince Denys would die young. If he'd lived, the Redlyon would've been Diane's consort."

Bel laughed. "Imagine the Redlyon as a mere consort! He was hardly the sort to stand in support of another."

"He stood in support of Denys," said Alyx. "He was his brother's left-arm ward, remember. If you can't trust the soldier who shields your weaker side, who on this earth can you trust?" The kernels of popcorn began to burst. Some leapt into the fire; others scattered across the hot rocks and the Shieldmaids and squires scrambled to catch them before they burned. "Eduarde and Diane—" Alyx continued once she had gathered her handful. "Did they have visions?"

"Of course," Mara answered. "The Redlyon and the Hart."

"But did they truly see their talisman-beasts? They aren't visionary—rather, prosaic. Redlyon is an obvious battle-name for a red-haired prince, especially so for a Prince of Skots. Skotsland's crest has been a lion on field *gules* for centuries. And the hart has been the crest of the Northlands for nearly as long."

"Visions are a divine grant," Mara insisted. "If they saw the lion and the hart, it merely confirmed their right to rule under those ancient and traditional devices. Delphyn," she appealed to the minstrel, "is it not so?"

"Captain Alyx is right, My Prince," Delphyn answered apologetically. "Many tales speak of Eduarde's glory in battle, but none describe a vision of a lion, red or otherwise."

Martine of Senneoke, who was a dark-skinned, black-haired woman with the strong-boned features of an aboriginal Atlantean, asked, "Have any of you received your vision yet?"

Bel shook her head slightly and Alyx said, "Surely *you* have, Mara."

Mara looked around at the faces bright in the firelight and noted immediately that one familiar face was missing. "No, I haven't," she answered. "Not at my knighting nor in the ten years since."

"It'll come," Alyx assured her, "once you dispatch your first Spaniard."

"I've had a vision," Sataumie said quietly, and found herself the focus of attention.

"Well?" Bel demanded.

"It's your turn to tell a tale, Shieldmaid," Delphyn prompted.

With these appeals, Sataumie consented reluctantly. "It

happened before I took my assignment at the Ystelake camp," she began. "I went back to my home village in the Allegheny hills. `Tis a peaceful place. I wondered if I should stay. For the first time, I doubted my chosen path. I mean no slight to you, Mara, but I didn't believe I would ever use my battle-skills. It seemed hopeless. I had worked so hard and dreamed so of being a Shieldmaid in battle at my Prince's side, and it might come to nothing. I thought: was it better that I stay with my family and return to their way of life even though I didn't choose that same way in the beginning? Its people live by customs so old that even the village elders cannot tell you their true meanings. Most of the people there are content with the old ways."

"And you received your vision then?" Martine urged.

Sataumie nodded. "On the night before I meant to go to Ystelake, I walked up into the hills above the village. I went to the top of the Mystery Hill. You may have heard of it or another place like it, for such hills are common in the Northlander wilderness where the Old Folk lived. It is an ancient, holy place—they say ceremonies were held there long before the first Normans set foot on this land. There is a ring of standing stones, each no more than a yard high and some of them fallen. A little chapel of St. Othelie stands at the edge of the glade with a stone angel at the door. I didn't pray in the old way or the new, but lay down at the center of the ring and watched the moon rise over the trees. I lay there all night. In the late hours, I sensed something near me. I opened my eyes, but didn't move, for I thought it must be a deer or fox and I didn't wish to frighten it away."

"Was it a fox?" asked Ren in a hushed voice.

"No," Sataumie answered, "a wolf. A bitch, I think. Its fur was gray and white—in the moonlight, it looked silver. Its eyes caught the moon and shone like embers. Now, I had never seen a wild wolf before and I thought suddenly that I had done a very foolish thing to come into the woods at night alone. No one knew where I was. I had no weapon with me but a little knife. Yet the she-wolf did not pounce. It sat beneath the wide wings of Othelie's angel and stared at me with its gleaming eyes. My heart was pounding and the palm of my hand was slick with moisture as I gripped my little knife. I was ready to defend myself against this beast, and yet when our eyes met I was taken by a strange calm. I saw how my truest nature had urged me to lay hands on a weapon rather than shriek and flee as another might've done. I had met a great danger boldly. I felt my own bravery and I knew certainly that I was a warrior born. I had chosen my right course.

"The wolf rose and bowed its head as if to acknowledge the truth of this discovery. Then it vanished. It was no dream, for I saw the clearing and the chapel, the angel and the wolf, so clearly as I see you all about this fire tonight. I tell you the wolf dissolved like so much mist. I knew then that I'd seen my talisman beast."

Alyx smiled. "You haven't taken it for a battle-name."

Sataumie grinned in return. "The silver she-wolf beneath the angel's wings in the moonlight? If I should declare myself by that name tomorrow on the battlefield, my foes would have plenty of time to flee. Yet I do bear it as my sign." She reached into her jerkin and brought out a small silver amulet on a leather tether. She held it up for her friends to see: a wolfs-head with tiny chips of red stone set for eyes between a spreading pair of white feathers to represent wings; a sliver of crescent-shaped moonstone hung a half-inch above. "This was made for me at Guylliamesburghe."

The other Shieldmaids were awed, and a little envious, of their friend's good fortune. Sataumie's certainty was something every warrior desired. Because one of their number had received this holy sign, they all had reason to hope that their purpose here was sanctioned too.

"What of Prince Denys?" Bel wondered. "Did he have his vision?"

"Surely he–" Martine began, then paused. "I've never heard such a tale. Did he?"

"Delphyn–"

"Where's Kat got to?" Alyx asked suddenly, breaking Mara from thoughts that had little to do with visions. She had barely listened to Sataumie's tale.

"I don't know," Bel looked around. "She was here when we met, but I don't think I've seen her since before Taumie told us about her wolf."

"Mara, did you send her off on an errand?" Alyx pursued. "I don't mean to pry if you did—only that we are so near the Spanish and she *is* a prime target for their malice. Anything might happen to her alone in the night."

"I know," Mara answered. "I haven't sent her anywhere."

"Perhaps she accompanied Khrystophania to the Marchion's camp?" Sataumie suggested.

"No, I'm here," said a quiet voice from the darkness. Khrystophania served as a liaison between Mara and her brother. She had spent a great deal of her time with the Prince and her friends these past weeks, but was too overwhelmed by them to join in their conversations and was sometimes forgotten.

"She seems taken with him," said Bel, smiling.

Alyx turned to her. "Marchion Frederik?"

"I wouldn't mind being `taken' with him myself," Martine chuckled. "My Lord Marchion's quite fancied by many of the Border Guardswomen—by your pardon, Damosel," she bowed her head to the Marchion's sister. "He is the sort of man we most admire."

Khrystophania nodded shyly. "You are noble-born yourself, Patrol Leader," she answered. "But `tisn't respectful for the common soldiers in my brother's command to look on him so. I'm sure he means nothing more than friendliness towards them."

"As do I, Damosel," Martine replied. "But it does My Lord Marchion no harm. It's not as if he'd notice one of our lot—I include myself, for the Emperor's own man is too far above the youngest daughter of a backwoods Earl's vassal for *me* to have a hope of catching his eye. Now, Prince Kat..."

"Kat? She's been positively kittenish," Bel laughed.

"Enough," Mara cut this giggling conversation short. She couldn't bear another word. "You sound like gossipy old merchant-dames at a bathhouse. I regret I called you here tonight. I would've been better left alone!"

Her companions were stunned by this outburst. Martine blinked in astonishment; Bel was abashed and Khrysta looked as if she had been slapped. Even little Ren, who hadn't spoken once, sat open-mouthed.

"I apologize if we've offended you or your kinswoman," Alyx ventured into the silence. "`Twas only meant in jest."

"I know," Mara answered, ashamed of herself. "I'm not offended. I'm simply too wrought up to listen to such nonsense tonight."

Her Shieldmaids nodded; they thought they understood.

"Perhaps we ought to go now," said Sataumie. "You may find more comfort in peace."

"Yes, perhaps."

With some murmurs of farewell and further apologies, the Shieldmaids gathered their belongings and respective squires and slipped quietly back to their own camps.

"Arthur, gather up the rest of the popcorn. We'll have it cold as we march tomorrow. Delphyn, you may return to Dennefort," Mara dismissed the minstrel who remained by the fire. "Rennie, you too. You'll be protected there. Khrysta, I pray you accompany them." As Alyx had suggested, Spanish spies might plan to assassinate or kidnap one of her retinue. Even her minstrel and her gentyl-maid were not safe. Khrysta would provide Delphyn and Ren with safe escort to the Marchion's manor within the fortress, where they would wait out the battle as Frederik's guests.

Mara wasn't worried for Kat's safety, however. She knew no such danger had befallen her cousin.

After the last of her party had gone, Mara kicked out her bedroll by the dying fire. She didn't expect to sleep. How could she with the dawn only a few hours away and Kat still absent?

Oh, she knew where Kat had gone. It wasn't difficult to see; even the Shieldmaids had guessed. They might laugh, but Mara was troubled. Kat had been out with Frederik before, but never so late.

These past six weeks, the relationship between Kat and Frederik had grown alarmingly intimate. Though they must work together in coordinating the Border Guard with the Norman troops, Mara observed that they quickly passed from professional courtesy to casual friendliness—and perhaps to more?

From the day of their arrival, Kat had responded playfully to Frederik's warm and open manner. She was the one to speak indiscreetly of his ancestry when Mara had understood the delicacy of the situation and Frederik had been embarrassed to allude to it. Once this barrier had been breached, all traditional conduct crumbled. Kat let Frederik consider himself her kinsman and equal. She addressed him as *Cousin*. And, more provoking still, Kat seemed indifferent to the importance of their mission here, and persuaded Frederik to disregard it as well. They attended to their duties efficiently, but they were too merry in the face of imminent battle for Mara's liking. At the welcoming banquet, Kat had sat beside their host and teased him until he laughed out loud. At strategic conferences, they whispered together over the maps spread on the wardroom tables. They rode slowly behind the other officers when they reviewed the troops. More than once, Mara caught them smiling at each other over a chance word and knew that she had stumbled into some private joke. This was infuriating: war was grave business, and two of her most important subordinates gamboled like nursery playmates!

It was all Kat's doing. Frederik, for all his frontier informality, would never abuse the proprieties if he were not encouraged. Nor would he dare to court an imperial prince unless that prince had made it plain that his advances were welcome. Though she was no delicate beauty, Kat was attractive. They looked much alike, but Mara saw that her cousin was more fair than she: her nose was pleasantly pert; her blue eyes were full of good humor; her figure was slender, for her training as a Shieldmaid had toned her body but not made it boyish. Plus, the reckless Irish spirit she had inherited from her rebellious father gave her a fey boldness that was strange, yet heartening, to the grim Northlanders. Frederik must have admired her from the first. And Kat flung herself at him. What could he do, surprised, smitten man, but reciprocate?

Mara didn't have the time to act as chaperon, but she tried to keep an eye on her cousin. She had overheard a dozen personal conversations between Kat and Frederik, each more disturbing than the last. The young man grew less reticent. Where he had first blushed at the name of his celebrated great-grandfather, he now spoke freely

"`Tis no secret to us," he said once. "The first Khrystophania told her heir and her granddaughter whose blood they bore in their veins. Mother made me know it too. `Twasn't shame that kept me silent, Prince Kat. You must understand that. We know we have no rights in the imperial house, and we've always believed that we behave ourselves better to keep silent on it rather than seem pushing."

"It isn't right that your family is ignored," said Kat.

"Not ignored," Frederik answered. "The Emperors have always been generous to us. We have been raised to the highest ranks. We've been given this land to protect in our Emperor's name—and we bear that duty with pride, since our exalted ancestor fought to claim it and died here. Prince Denys's sword has hung in Dennefort Manor from the day Eduarde Redlyon left it to my great-grandmother. What more honor can we expect?"

On another day, he showed Kat and Mara this family treasure. The sword hung on the wall of the gallery between two long murals, one depicting Denys on horseback amidst a throng of victorious Norman soldiers, the other showing the Prince standing bravely against the Spanish assassins minutes before his death.

Kat took down the ancient steel. "So this is Dragonsfang," she said. "The sword of legend. When the bards sing of Denys's talisman, I often think that this must have been it."

Frederik grinned. "If it is, it can't have done him much good. He had it at his side to the last. We keep it as a showpiece, polished but not sharpened. I won't take it to battle."

"It's so old. I thought it'd be a twin to Dentelyon."

"No, our swordcrafters place it at the twelfth century, Moorish Spain. Denys won it in his first campaigns in North Africa. See the swirls of interworked metal? Two ores are hammered together to give the steel a wonderful strength. 'Tis a craft that none employ today and few know of."

"What do these mean?" asked Kat, her fingertips tracing the finely etched markings just below the hilt. "Are they Arabic?"

"I've no idea. It looks to be some sort of spellcraft."

"As Maxim Gnome cast runes upon Dentelyon. There's a jewel missing here."

"The Black Ruby," Frederik answered. "A rather famous gem. It is described in the old tales. 'Tis said that it was knocked loose while Prince Denys fought his assassins. Look to the hangings." Taking Kat's hand, he led her across the gallery so that the tapestries on either side were in full view. "Do you see? There's a red stone on the hilt in that one, yet it is missing in the other. For all I know, it lies still in the dust of the old battlefield."

"When these campaigns have ended, we ought to look for it." She smiled at him. "It belongs to you."

Frederik squeezed her hand, then released it with sudden shyness. “Will you be able before you return to Pendaunzel?”

“Oh, there’s no reason for me to hurry back,” Kat laughed. “I’m not needed. With so much to be done once we’ve retaken Terrojos, I’m certain I can be of more use if I remain here—if you will have me stay.”

Mara had heard Kat say such things several times, and these remarks alarmed her. So much of what she observed between Kat and the young Marchion suggested an improper intimacy. Though she never heard them exchange the pretty love-talk she imagined sweethearts shared, nor even once caught them in a kiss, she knew that they were entangled in a romance that was both imprudent and dangerous. They had gone too far. What else could she think after this night?

It wasn’t that she disliked Frederik. On the contrary, Mara’s first impressions of him hadn’t changed. As Marchion of Princeland and the Eduardesmarch, he was admirable. As commander of the Border Guard, he was more than capable. As a young man, he was handsome, earnest and charming. Mara would’ve been pleased to see him win another woman’s heart—but not Kat’s. This love affair was insupportable. In spite of his finer points, Frederik was not an appropriate suitor for Prince Katheryne of Eireland.

Mara remembered when the little Irish Prince had come to Pendaunzel. Even in the earliest days of her childhood, her father had read aloud to her from Ambris’s letters, for she was fascinated by this grown-up brother she’d never seen. Whenever a packet arrived from remote parts of the world, she always asked if he mentioned her, if he had sent her any gifts, if he was coming to see her. And then, when she was six, a great many letters had come at once. There was trouble in Eireland, which she didn’t understand. From the passages her father read to her mother in private chambers, she knew that Ambris was arguing with some nasty man who refused to yield on a number of baffling points. At last, this man seemed to surrender, and Father had made a wonderful announcement: Ambris was coming home! More wonderful still, he would bring a little sister for her.

At that age, Mara had known nothing of how babies were born and she imagined that this was how they were normally delivered, brought from across the sea with great fanfare. At least, that was how a little Prince arrived. She recalled it vividly: the stiff velvet of Mother's long, ceremonial skirts, which she stood against, the trumpets' blast, the herald's cry of "My Lord Duke, My Lady, Ambris of the Northlands presents the princeling Katheryne!" A strange, dark young man clutching a bundle to his chest had entered the Duke's chambers and bowed before her father, then rose to kiss him. Father had smiled and embraced him; until that moment, Mara hadn't truly realized that this was the Ambris she'd waited so long to see. Then Ambris pulled back the bundle of blankets concealing the child he carried in his arms. A head of curly, fair hair emerged; wide blue eyes blinked at the courtiers who pressed forward to see, then stared directly at her. Then Kat had howled.

In the hours that followed, Mara had offered this strange, noisy little creature sugar-plums, her favorite toys, and a multitude of pats and kisses, none of which had stopped Kat's wails. The little girl shrieked whenever Ambris set her down and struggled when Mother or her ladies tried to take her from his arms. She was only quiet when she fell asleep. They put her to bed in the old cradle in Mara's nursery. After the nurse had put out the light, Mara stood watching the sleeping child with fearful wonder, for who could say when she might wake and begin screaming again?

Mara hadn't understood at the time that her Aunt Agnes in Eireland had recently died and this toddler was her cousin. So far as Mara was concerned, Kat was her sister. Even today, she considered her no less.

Dafythe and Gillefleure had never treated Kat differently than Mara, save for those natural distinctions between a firstborn and younger daughter, but they couldn't make Kat a Northlander Prince. Eireland was her place of birth and her land by rights, though she hadn't seen it since infancy. She couldn't return to it now; her father, Count Egan, wouldn't relinquish his regency and the Irish threatened rebellion if he were removed. Eireland's standards for good governors were precise and unyielding. No foreign regents were tolerated. Norman Princes were accepted, for the blood of Irish kings ran in the imperial veins, but the governing Prince must first prove to be one of their own, placing the welfare of Eireland before the rest of the Empire. Long ago, Emperors had found it easier to accede to these demands than to suppress every uprising caused by an unsuitable administrator. Eireland was peaceable under Egan's authority. They might be persuaded to accept his daughter at his death but, once Kat went to Eireland, she must stay there. A temporary governor would not be received. The Irish felt it was an insult to lose their Princes in marriages to foreigners and both the elder and younger Kharles had decided that it wouldn't be prudent to install Kat as governor until all possibilities for her marriage were exhausted. The possibility of a foreign marriage remained likely and so, for the present, Kat remained in the Northlands.

From the first, Kat's marriage had been a topic of discussion at Pendaunzel. It had seemed inexplicable to Mara when her mother and father told her that this three-year-old was meant to marry grown-up Ambris. What could it mean? Surely her sister must be his sister and if that were so, why couldn't she marry him herself? She saw even then that her father wanted Ambris to marry into what he called the "rightborn" line, and to her this seemed the most sensible solution. When she had a better grasp of the situation, Mara fully supported the betrothal of her brother and cousin; the two little maids had followed Ambris's career in their uncle Emperor Kharles's service with great interest. Kat, caught up in the tales of fairytale princes, endowed Ambris with similar heroic virtues. Yet when Ambris returned to Pendaunzel four years later with his German bride, the little girl was able to meet him without disappointment. She explained to Mara afterward: he wasn't at all as she had imagined her betrothed.

After Ambris had married, Dafythe contemplated a series of tentative betrothals for his niece—young Kharles, various German and Italian princes, even the Tsar of Russe—but each in turn came to nothing. Kat took an interest in each prospective bridegroom. As a child, she had gathered whatever news she could of Ambris's career and prattled endlessly about her handsome prince who traveled everywhere. After Ambris, Kat looked to each new betrothed with the same romantic optimism. She spoke their names aloud. What must her future husband be like? Her fancy ran wild, and the qualities she had bestowed on the last prince were quickly retailored for the new. As she grew from a little girl to a young woman, the image grew more elaborate and eventually took up a life of its own.

Mara knew this imagined prince quite well. His physical form was never described—for it might not match the figure of her future husband—but his character was well-defined. He was bold and brave, perhaps reckless, but good-hearted; he was honest in his desire to act for the good of his homeland and his subjects; his people loved him; he was a knight; he was a skilled horsemaster and rode to the hunt with dogs and falcons; he was generous; he was a better swordsman and archer than she, but she would be able to beat him from time to time; he didn't care for high ceremonies and fancy dress; he was plain in his tastes and simple in his piety, but by no means slow witted! Mara knew the catalog of virtues well, and knew that they applied to no one.

While she waited for a husband, Kat conducted little romances with young noblemen of the court, officers of the Pendaunzel guard, and once a thespian from the Duke's Theatre. None of these men, however, had distressed Mara as Frederik did. Even the most handsome and most pleasantly mannered among them had meant little to Kat. She flirted with them, danced at court festivals, rode the countryside, and perhaps kissed the ones she liked best, but she'd never taken one of these transient suitors to her bed. Mara was certain of that. No, Frederik wasn't like Kat's Pendaunzel romances. Kat had never spoken of leaving all her responsibilities to remain with a lover before. She'd never been out so late as this.

Mara was still awake when the sound of soft-stepping boots cautiously approached her campsite. She opened her eyes as Kat reached the circle of firelight.

Mara leaned up on one elbow. "It's long past midnight," she hissed.

Kat spread her cloak on the grass on the opposite side of the fire and sat down to unlace her boots.

"Have you been with him?"

"What if I have? I'm nearly thirty years old. Maids of sixteen may choose their own suitors."

"Not you. You are meant for another match."

"To whom?" Kat demanded, flinging one boot aside

petulantly. "Tsar Alexandre? Little Robert of Champagne? Infant Iosephus? I have been half-promised to one man or another since I was too small to understand what that meant, and yet I remained a maiden. No spectacular match awaits me. Can't I be permitted to choose for myself who I will have?"

"*Have?*" Mara sprang upon the word. "You fly off to meet him in the night like a common soldier's drab!"

Kat flinched and Mara immediately regretted the accusation. Before she could speak, Kat answered, "It isn't so disgraceful as you imagine. Frederik's asked me to stay as his wife. I shall marry him once this campaign has ended."

"You cannot do it," Mara protested. "Leave the Northlands!"

"I would've gone eventually, either to Eireland or as a bride to a foreign land."

"Yes, but those are matters of duty. I would have hated it, but I couldn't speak against your obligations to the imperial good. I cannot let you go for a pleasure-romp. This is nothing but folly! You forget every duty in some base passion for a man you've only known a few weeks."

"I might've been married blind to any one of a dozen men," Kat replied. "I've been in Frederik's company enough these days to form a reasonable opinion of his character. I see how his sister admires him. The Dennefort guard adore him. They would follow him to the Four Corners, and even to Hell's gate to do battle with the Devil's Legion."

Mara laughed. "A fine recommendation if you wish to join the Border Guard."

"It shows what sort of man he is," Kat retorted. "If Khrysta went in fear of him or if those in his command mistrusted his judgment, I would know him for a coward and a bully. If the guardswomen whispered tales rather than wishes, I would see him as wanton. But he is not! Frederik's lived as we always wanted to. Mara, imagine—While you and I have been playing our battle-games these ten years, he's been riding the borders in his Emperor's service. Granted, he's never fought Spaniards more than we have, but he's worked for the safety of the Empire. I envy him that. I want to be with him while he does so. I would wish to stay here even if I didn't love him."

"You admire him as a captain admires a good commander."

"I love him," Kat insisted. "He is brave, honest, kind–"

"Do you think him your fancied prince?"

This was perhaps the cruelest taunt Mara could make, but her cousin didn't reproach her. Kat appeared to consider the suggestion seriously for a moment, then she shook her head. "No," she answered, "but he's as close as I can expect any living man to be. You know Frederik nearly so well as I do. He is no inferior man. On your honesty, Mara, can you speak ill of him?"

"No, Kat," Mara replied honestly. "You know I'm fond of him myself. But–"

"Frederik's blood is as good as ours," Kat went on before she could finish. "I should think Uncle Dafythe would welcome the opportunity to restore the descendants of Denys to the legitimate line. We cannot continue to treat Frederik and his sister as outcasts. Even if he were not our kinsman, he is Marchion in his own right. He is eligible. Extremely eligible," she smiled a little to herself. "`Tis criminal to let so extraordinary a young man go unnoticed!"

"Is that why you do this?" Mara asked. "You wish to redress the wrong done to him? Then take it to Father and you'll see justice done without marrying yourself into it."

Kat frowned suddenly. "Cousin," she said in her most serious tones, "it isn't outrage over the injustice. Nor is it envy of his place, nor admiration for his skill as a commander. You mislead yourself. You can't know—you've never felt as I do. `Tis true I want to see him acknowledged as one of our family. I want to ride these marches at his side and act as his lieutenant as I have been yours. I want to fight for him. I also want to hold him down and cover him with kisses and tear the leathers from his chest with my bare hands." This was meant to shock, and it did. "These are all in me and I feel them, but there's more than that. I can think of nothing to make me happier than staying with him. I see the rest of my life here."

"That's not my concern," Mara answered. It frightened her a little to hear Kat speak this way. "Love as you will, but Father will insist upon his choice above yours."

But Kat refused to be reasonable. "You don't understand, Mara. I will have Frederik, or no one. We pledged our troth tonight."

"Not in public."

"No," Kat conceded. "Privately. Our promise was not witnessed, but it binds us. We sealed our troth in the flesh."

This confirmation that her worst suspicions were correct was more than Mara's sensibilities could bear. "You abandon chastity–!" she sputtered.

"Deliberately," Kat explained. "I didn't forget myself in passion. I meant to do it. I may die this day and I wouldn't lose my one chance at love if it were all I ever had, but I thought of tomorrow too. Do you see? No other contract can be legal. Uncle Dafythe must let us wed."

"What of Frederik's allegiance to Kharles? What if *he* refuses?"

"Kharles has made his own marriage of choice. He'll understand. If he doesn't, I'll marry Frederik without his approval. Hang it, they can't have me brought back to Pendaunzel under guard."

"I can."

"You wouldn't," Kat answered with a touch of her old playfulness. "You have too much need of me tomorrow and you can't spare the guards. Will the Shieldmaids keep watch over me during the battle?" She tried to smile, but her eyes were sad. "You can't stop me, Mara. But you might make it easier for me to leave you and my home if you can say you're glad for me. Wish me happiness, even if you don't mean it now."

Mara couldn't give her blessing. How could she condone this? Kat had always been light-hearted and fanciful, but tonight she passed from simple folly into wild indecency. And without a sign of remorse! Rather, she flaunted her new-found licentiousness—tear away his leathers!—and delighted in her calculated loss of virginity. Dafythe might well be forced to give his consent rather than see his niece disgraced. Mara was lost before this strange young woman who stood in the place of her beloved Kat. Never had she seen her cousin so defiant. What further argument could she make to bring Kat back to her senses? Duty, virtue, the consent of Dafythe and Frederik's liege—each of these arrows struck their mark and fell away useless. Kat wouldn't listen. She was ready to abandon everything for her love. Mara was used to bending Kat to her own will, but for once Kat refused to bend.

Kat waited awhile for an answer, then drew her feet up, hugging her knees to her breast. She sighed once or twice. Mara turned her back and lay awake knowing that her cousin was watching her, but neither spoke.

ten

Mara lay awake through the night, furious and heartsick. The words she and Kat had spoken to each other tumbled thorough her head. She reviewed them countless times. Where had her arguments failed? What might've been said instead to sway Kat? Could she still turn her cousin from this folly even now?

As the sky grew grey in the hour before daybreak, she rose to put on her battle-gear. Kat awoke and, untangling herself from the cloak she had wrapped around her in the night, rose too. Side by side, they armored themselves. The breach between them wasn't healed, but had instead grown during the hours of silence. Neither was yet willing to break it. Both were cool, formal, and distant. This coming battle with the Spanish took precedence over the argument between them; private differences must be suppressed. And what could be said before Arthur? The sleepy squire assisted with the most difficult straps, catches, and buckles, but even after he left them to fit up the horses, they didn't speak.

Mara imagined bitter and spiteful retorts she might say, but she knew that insults would accomplish nothing. She saw no point in reproaching Kat for her unchaste behavior. Kat was no frivolous wanton and, with regards to Frederik, was impervious to shame. Kat believed that she'd done nothing wrong, but she was certain to remember any harsh words whether they were deserved or not. Nor could Mara claim that Frederik had wooed her cousin with mercenary aims, hoping to wed his way into the imperial legitimate line. She didn't believe it herself, and Kat would never forgive the insinuation.

As much as she wanted to place Kat and Frederik under guard far apart from each other, Mara couldn't afford to alienate two of her most important aides. The Border Guard would take it ill to see their Marchion insulted, and Mara knew that their loyalties lay with Frederik more than herself. Rage as she might, it wasn't in her power to stop this folly.

She told herself that it wasn't her concern if Kat and Frederik chose to make fools of themselves. Whatever promises they made to each other, they must face Dafythe and the Emperor—and see what their respective liege lords thought of this self-made match!

"Aunt Mara?" Arthur asked as he struggled to fasten the girth of her horse's saddle beneath the heavy mailcoat which covered the animal from breastbone to tail and hung to its knees. "Which sword will you carry?"

"Grandfather's," she answered. Dentelyon's scabbard was already belted at her side. "The saber can go on the saddle, beside the flails."

Arthur strapped the smaller scabbard to the forepart of the saddle, so that it dangled at the horse's mail-draped right shoulder. Her shield hung on the left side.

"And bring my daggers!" Mara called to the boy. She glanced at Kat. "Have you got one?"

Kat patted the sheathed dirk at her belt. "I've carried it with me since we left Dennefort," she answered impersonally.

"Take another," Mara said in the same frosty tone. Arthur unrolled the soft cloth parcel marked with Mara's crest. The daggers were a matched set, a gift from Ambris on her knighting; the blades were from four to seven inches long and each hilt was topped with a garnet, her birthstone. Mara selected two for herself and tucked one into each boot. The hilts glinted at her knees, ready to hand while she rode. She chose a third for Kat, who received it wordlessly and tucked it into her own boot-top. A fourth, Mara tucked into Arthur's belt.

"You may have need of it, Nephew." Her squire would remain here until he was called to join them once Spainfort was secured, but who could say what tricks Fate might play before this victory was obtained? The Spanish might creep so far north.

In the campsites all around them, soldiers were also arming themselves. As the Princes ate a quick, light breakfast in the waning darkness, Bel, Sataumie, and Alyx arrived. All three were clad in similar mailshirts and armor, their forebraids tucked into their tunic collars.

"Good morrow, Princes!" Bel greeted them cheerfully as she climbed down from her horse. "We couldn't have wished for a clearer day—not a rain cloud in the sky and barely a hint of mist."

"That'll burn off once the sun touches it," Sataumie added.

"We'll see the bastard Spaniards coming from miles away!"

"I'm glad to see you are unharmed, Kat," said Alyx. "We missed you last night."

"We also missed our assignments," Sataumie reminded Mara gently.

Mara felt the reproach. She'd meant to do this before they'd parted last night, but her worry over Kat had driven her plans from her mind and she'd sent her companions away in anger. It was beneath her dignity to apologize; instead, she amended the error by giving her assignments immediately. "Martine leads her old patrol. She's rejoined Marchion Frederik's troops and I do not command her. Bel, you'll captain the archers."

"On foot?" the captain asked, reluctant to leave her horse behind.

"You won't be so tempting a target," laughed Alyx.

"You may ride to lead the archers to battle, but I expect you'll wish to drop from the saddle when the arrows begin to fly," said Mara. "You're the best of the lot." Bel's dead-on accuracy had guaranteed her position at the head of the archers.

"Diane's riders could shoot longbows from the saddle," Bel said wistfully. "'Tis a shame the skill hasn't survived."

"The archers will advance first on my mark and lay out a thick spread of arrows once we sight the Spanish. You'll shoot from the higher and lower phalanx at once." It was said that bowmaids couldn't shoot so far as their men-fellows, but their aim was more true. Mara saw no difference—the best always struck their mark—but she used the traditional formation: tall, standing archers, mostly male, shot high and long into the air, and smaller, kneeling archers, usually female, aimed at closer targets. "Cry clear when you've spread your cover, and hold your fire. The footsoldiers will come behind and make short work of whatever's been missed. Lieutenant Uismarde leads the infantry. She is with a squad of Shieldmaids just down the hill, there. Sataumie, you will march with them. The knights, I have divided into companies. The Chevalier Lord Khrespian of Frankeshire has command of the cavalry to our north—Eadrik is with him. Marchion Frederik rides with his knights of the borderlands south of us. The knights here shall ride in two flanks, one to each side of the archers. The smaller company to the left acts as vanguard. The larger, to the right, supports the footsoldiers. I'll lead this second group. Alyx, you'll be my left-arm ward."

There followed an awkward silence. Even Alyx, who was gratified by this unexpected honor, knew that at Mara's side was where Kat ought to be.

"Do I ride with you, Cousin?" Kat asked coolly.

"I thought you meant to relinquish your place at my left and ride in another company."

Kat bit her lip, stung at the deliberate insult. The Shieldmaids glanced from one to the other, wondering at Mara's strange mood.

"You may captain the vanguard if you like, Cousin," Mara offered.

"As you will it, My Prince." Kat rose to help Arthur, who had apparently caught her horse's mail on the woolen pad beneath and was in danger of dragging both from the animal's back in his effort to detach them. All the camp was active now. Captains gathered their troops; sergeants shouted orders to assemble. Gear was gathered and campfires were kicked out. Thousands of shadow-shapes moved through the faint light, hurrying to complete their tasks.

Bel and Sataumie dispersed to attend to their duties—one to convey instructions to her archers, the other down the hillside to find Lieutenant Uismarde's camp. Alyx, who had no obligations save to remain at Mara's side, loitered nearby; as she casually inspected her gear and tugged to test the straps and buckles on her horse's fittings, she glanced now and again at Mara, who sat brooding by the fire. She was one of Mara's closest friends, trusted and beloved even among the Shieldmaids, but she was close enough to know that Kat was dearer still. This was a dangerous ground to tread upon uninvited. All she could do was wait until Mara desired to confide in her, but her Prince only tossed the crusts and rinds of breakfast into the fire and put away the kits.

Sataumie returned from her conference with Uismarde and joined Alyx; Mara heard them whispering together.

"I've never seen her so before, Taumie. She won't speak."

"You know what it is."

"I can guess. I dare not ask, not after last night. And now this unlooked-for honor. You know I expected to lead the vanguard myself, or perhaps have your place among Uismarde's Shields. Never left-arm ward!"

"'Tis unconventional, certainly, to place one hart-shield against another before the enemy."

"It's done to spite Kat."

Mara's three friends bore the Northlands hartshead freshly painted on their shields. They were meant to act as decoys to baffle the foe on the field, though Mara thought it unlikely that any but the most near-sighted Spaniard could be deceived by the ruse. None were physically like her: petite, curly-headed Bel, lean and fair-haired Alyx, black-haired, lithe Sataumie. Yet it was the traditional role of a Shieldmaid; when the first of their order had numbered less than one dozen, all had bravely borne the arms of their royal founder. Today, lesser Shieldmaids bore the devices of their squadrons and a few carried the arms of the noblewomen they served—Khrystophania's honor guard bore the broken sword of the Marchion's family. These three alone were chosen for the proud office of standing in place of the Prince. Kat, who did look like her, bore the Irish harp. No one would stand in her place.

"If Kat has," Sataumie whispered, "it's not so unpardonable a crime that she must be set aside. Shieldmaids aren't bound by the old vows these days."

"But she's a Prince," Alyx hissed back. "Their cares are different from yours and mine."

"Even a Prince may take the opportunity for love, especially when she rides to battle the next day."

I may die this day. A casual remark, spoken to defend an impulsive, foolish act—but Mara now recalled Kat's words with superstitious dread. She knew Kat's fey spirit. Was it a premonition? Peter's vision had placed Kat in battle about a burning city, but that omen of fortune might not be the end of the tale. Kat might be killed today, and Mara found that more difficult to bear than the possibility of her own death. The sensation of pending danger was impossible to disregard.

She was suddenly contrite. Kat's behavior didn't excuse her own. Though Alyx and Sataumie were impertinent to discuss her private business, their opinions were justified: casting her cousin from her side was petty; her words were spiteful and her sulkiness was unseemly. While Mara believed she had good reasons to be angry, her actions were beneath her dignity as General of these armies. They marred the solemnity of this great day. In a moment, once the troops were in order, she would offer the ritual prayer for victory. How could she ask God's favor with such errors fresh on her soul? The presumption was almost blasphemous. Kat might be struck down, if not for her own sins, then for Mara's. She could not in her conscience let her cousin ride to battle unreconciled.

She turned to find Kat, face stony and eyes flashing, holding her horse's bridle while Arthur fixed the tester over its head. "Kat–"

The sound of two more horses approaching stopped her.

"Who is it?" Sataumie called as the dark shapes rode toward them through the camp, silhouettes among the bustling soldiers.

The horses pulled up near the fire. The riders were Frederik and Khrystophania, in mail covered by tunics of natural buckskin. Frederik had two thin stripes of blue diagonally down his left cheek. His sister bore a single stripe and a penny-sized circle at her temple.

"Warriors' paint?" asked Alyx.

"It is our custom, to bring luck in battle," the younger Shieldmaid explained.

"It is a custom in the north as well," said Sataumie, "but not `til you've shed the blood of your foe and can rightly be called a warrior."

"And so none of you wear it?" Frederik grinned.

"No, My Lord, but we hope to after this day."

"My Lord Marchion," Mara asked, rising. "What brings you here?"

"Our troops are assembled, Prince Margueryt. We've come to ask if there are any last orders before we march."

Mara found this explanation implausible. All her plans had been discussed thoroughly in the past weeks at Dennefort. From the commander of the Montegnecrest fortress that guarded the mountain passes to Arnault who awaited the Spanish reinforcements at the coast, her generals knew their business—and Frederik especially so, for he'd been her chief source of information and advice as she formed her strategies. No, there was only one reason for this visit: he wanted to see Kat once again.

Frederik ducked his head at her cutting stare, nonplussed that his motives should be so easily exposed, and by one who clearly disapproved. It was obvious to Mara that he believed Kat had confided in her. But when Kat stepped forward, smiling, he forgot his embarrassment. Before his beloved, the young Marchion sat taller in his saddle. His heart could be read plainly in his expression: the feelings Kat had described last night were completely mutual. The intimacy revealed in that brief moment when their eyes met was nearly indecent. When Frederik turned back to Mara, he no longer looked abashed. He regretted that his love must displease her, but he was no more willing to retract than Kat was.

"Last orders, Marchion? There is nothing new," Mara answered tersely. "We march as soon as the sun rises—My troops here first, and the flanks to follow in spearhead formation. We aim at the Spainfort gate. Once the Shieldwall is breached, all will converge upon that point."

"We were about to pray Our Highest Lord's blessing," Kat added. "Will you join us?" The invitation sounded like simple courtesy, but Mara saw it as an act of mischief. Kat knew perfectly well that she couldn't turn anyone away from this Christian service.

She shot a furious look at Kat, who continued to smile in guileless welcome to her lover. "Will you?" Mara offered grudgingly.

Frederik swung down from his horse and offered a hand to help Khrystophania. "Prince Marguerryt, we are delighted."

Mara stuck Dentelyon's point into the earth. Her captains knelt in a semi-circle about this impromptu cross; beyond them, the assembled soldiers bowed their heads. The chaplain had returned to Dennefort with the other non-combatants. Mara spoke a prayer of her own composition, a variation of the traditional plea for divine intercession:

"O Heavenly Father, grant Thy humble servants victory this day,
As our venerable ancestors were blessed in Thy sight

And did service against Thine enemies on this same field.
We pray this same boon from Thy Divine Grace,
For our cause is just and our faith in Thy Will strong.
O Lord, guide us to victory in Thy name,
Else receive our souls in Heaven if we should fall."

"Grant us victory, O Lord," the captains murmured as they crossed themselves; the response rippled through the crowd. "Soothly."

As the company rose, Frederik took Kat by the arm and drew her close for a quick, whispered conference. Mara didn't hear most of what was said, but Kat's last words—"It doesn't matter"—were quite clear, for her cousin glanced at her as she spoke. They kissed once, quickly. The Shieldmaids averted their gaze. Mara turned her back to them and plucked up Dentelyon.

This was intolerable. By making a public show of her affection, Kat flaunted all propriety. Forcing Mara to acknowledge her lover was plainly contentious. Mara had meant to apologize for her conduct, if not her opinion; evidently, no such consciousness of error occurred to Kat. She deliberately provoked further dissention, and took perverse delight in doing so. *It doesn't matter.* The words burned in Mara's mind; they'd been meant for her to hear. What didn't matter? Her presence? Her disapproval? How dare they dismiss her! The brazenness of it was infuriating, and unforgivable. She couldn't think of reconciliation.

At any rate, it was too late now. The sky was light with the approach of dawn. She must march with this rage as a blot upon her soul, and hope that God might forgive it in the greater justice of her cause.

"Be ready!" she shouted. "Captains, to your places! Frederik, Khrysta, I bid you go and godspeed you in your errand." The eastern horizon glowed red. The light was yet dim, but the landscape lay clear before them. The low mist that curled through the clefts and valleys did not obscure their way.

She mounted her horse and rode out ahead of the first line of archers, then turned. "On my mark!"

As she raised her sword, the upper rim of the rising sun appeared above the eastward hills. The first rays caught the flat of the blade and the steel flashed, casting brilliant, blinding glints of orange and gold as if by divine portent. A thrill ran through the waiting soldiers.

"Archers advance!"

The first charge marched down, knights riding on either side and infantry behind. Some gave battle-cry; a few were laughing with eagerness; others were grim. Once they reached the southern border of the Shieldwall, all the Spanish troops that had gathered since the Normans began their journey from Dennefort awaited them—not enough to deflect the force of Mara's army, but enough to be a difficulty. It was to be expected that the majority defended the border, but advance troops might hide themselves anywhere behind the hills, in the wooded dells or creek-cut ravines. This route was most perilous. The main gate in the southern wall lay on the road between Dennefort and Spainfort. The road had been frequently traveled in more peaceful days and the gate was designed for times of peace; it was no wider than necessary to admit a cart or a few travelers walking abreast. Yet it was the vulnerable point. The Norman army had entered the Shieldwall through its northern counterpart and now followed the road. Though they moved more swiftly in a straight line, they kept this thin, dusty-grey trace winding through the green hills in sight. Their primary goal was to breach the gate. Once that was accomplished, they would storm the mountains and lay siege upon Spainfort.

Spainfort, the Eyes of the Mountains. Twenty miles away, it was the most prominent feature in the range of mountains ahead, a great stone bastion wedged into its pass like an enormous boulder amid the green peaks.

The vanguard, a dozen of Mara's best knights, spread out ahead of the archers. At Kat's command, they divided into four trios: one to guard the road, two to explore the clefts and copses the army must pass, and the last to race on and spy out what lay beyond the next hill. A warning yip went up when the first Spaniards were spotted. Advance troops had come out to meet them and make a stand at a deep gully below the road. It was the first time the Normans faced their enemy, but they were well drilled and prepared for this moment.

"Second phalanx down!" Bel dropped from her saddle, bow

drawn and quiver at hand, as the front line of archers knelt. "Ready on my mark!" The Spanish marched toward them. The swift knights darted out of the way before the arrows began to fly. "Fire!" A rain of arrows fell, thick and fast. The archers fired in swift rotation, shooting and drawing fresh arrows in turn, so that there should be no cease to the onslaught until Bel cried, "Hold!" The Spanish were greatly outnumbered and devastated by the first volleys. Scores lay pierced even before the Norman knights thundered in among them. The skirmish concluded swiftly. In accordance with Mara's directives, mercy was shown to the wounded and to those who surrendered. The rest were cut down. Prisoners were relieved of all weapons; Spanish knights and captains were separated from the rank and file and held under guard by a small company left behind. A second advance, which surprised them in a wooded gully, was dispatched as easily.

Casualties were light in these first encounters; none were killed and the injured were able to retreat with their wounds. The Norman ranks closed swiftly to fill the gaps and they marched on without breaking formation.

As the sun climbed into the clear sky, spirits were high. Bel led her archers in a merry battle song from the days of the Redlyon. The tune soon spread through the ranks:

We'll spear `em right through to the liver,
Then toss `em clear up to the sky!
Let bloody Spain run to the Devil
When they hear us make this cry:
One Norman's worth ten of the others, my lad!
O, one Norman's worth ten of the others!

They shouted the grisly chorus gleefully as they marched. Mara, though she had yet had little taste of battle herself, exulted in these early triumphs. Worse lay ahead, to be sure, but she was eager to meet it. Her troops had proved themselves. She never doubted her eventual victory, but now it was surely in her grasp. The Spanish dare not stand before them.

On the slope below the Terrojos wall, the orderly progression burst apart. As the first archers approached the wall, scores of arrows showered down upon them from the other side. The

Spanish archers shot high and blind; their arrows fell amid the advancing army but were aimed at no precise target. None struck true, but their purpose was accomplished. With no one to return volleys against, the Norman archers were forced to scatter.

As they sought cover, a multitude of Spanish footsoldiers appeared and charged down toward the baffled Normans below. The archers directed their attention to this oncoming assault. Bows twanged and arrows hissed; Spaniards fell, but more poured down into the dell. There were too many, too close for the archers to wield their best weapon. Then the Spaniards were upon them. Each archer carried a short sword or dagger for hand-to-hand combat. Blades were drawn as the two forces clashed. The footsoldiers at the eastern end of the dell charged down to join the fight. Shrieks rose from both sides, shouts of command and curses in both Norman and Spanish. Horses screamed. All was turmoil.

Mara's knights had stopped on a rise above the battle.

"Hundreds of them!" Alyx shouted to her. "It must be their main force. Christ's mercy, Mara, Bel's down there." They had looked after Bel since their cadet days. In spite of the hundreds in danger now, it was impossible not to think foremost of their friend.

Mara was about to give the command to send her knights down, when Kat came tearing at them over the hills. She had ridden off to scout the area with a trio of her knights just before the Spanish assault. She sped back now, bursting through the company and forcing them to scatter, then pulled her horse up abruptly before she ran onto the downward slope.

"The gate is atop the next hill," she reported, breathless from her hard ride. "There, where the bastards burst forth. Nobody defends it now. A few score knights. Pike squares." She spoke in short bursts, with no tone of sarcasm nor bitterness. In the crisis, all conflict was laid aside; she was a captain in the service of her prince, no more.

"'Tis impossible to break a pike square from horseback," Mara answered, "but they move so slowly. A rider might sweep around them while the rest of our knights keep theirs from the gate. Their knights are no match for ours!" The knights gathered about this conference heartily shouted agreement. "Did you sight Khrespian's company?"

"They aren't very far north, beyond the next ridge and riding in this direction."

"Send a messenger to call them to the gate. Our company will meet him there." Mara glanced anxiously at the conflict below.

"Shall I lead the charge?" Kat offered.

Mara nodded. "Take these knights, all who will go. The rest may ride with me to the aid of my archers. Godspeed you in your errand, Cousin."

Kat smiled. "And you, My Prince." She wheeled her horse around and shouted commands. Alyx remained at Mara's side, eyes on the battle.

"Can you see Bel?" asked Mara.

"I lost sight of her shield when the arrows began to fly. That's her horse, without rider."

"She's such a little thing. Perhaps they've missed her." Mara tried to smile, but she was worried too. "Let's go." Dentelyon upraised, Mara spurred her horse and rode down into the melee, Alyx beside her. The knights who hadn't followed Kat charged after them.

Footsoldiers yielded before the oncoming riders; they must, or be trampled. The ones who weren't quick enough were knocked down. Mara herself rode over the shield of one luckless man—whether he was her own soldier or a Spaniard, she didn't know. In the gory mix of blood and mud amidst this screaming confusion, it was difficult to distinguish between the two. Uniforms were ragged, shields spattered, and faces stained. The Spanish helms were shaped differently, with pointed crests rather than the rounded tops of her own troops, and they wore molded bronze cuirasses rather than the circular breastplates favored by the Normans, but these distinctions were difficult to perceive accurately from the back of a charging horse. Soldiers rolled in the crushed grass, wrestling with their foes. Even the archers fought hand to hand. The battle resembled nothing so much as a deadly alehouse brawl.

She spotted a small woman very like Bel fighting viciously in the underbrush and shouted to Alyx. They spurred their horses in that direction.

A hearty cheer went up as Mara rode past. The Normans were heartened by her appearance. The Spanish, too, knew who she was. "La Infanta!" Their name for a female prince was murmured with an excitement Mara could not misinterpret. A captured general was a magnificent prize.

One eager Spaniard reached for her; her sword darted out and struck his shoulder. He fell away and she rode on without pausing to see how deeply she had cut. They would drag her down from her saddle if they were able to lay hands on her—she mustn't allow that! A second stepped into her path, then faltered to one side when he saw she didn't intend to stop. Alyx cut down a third who came at her from the left. Another leapt out to grasp her reins. Mara swung at his exposed neck, feeling the hitch and hesitation as her sword met bone. Blood sprayed over her leg, up to her knee. Dentelyon was nearly torn from her hand.

She put her foot on the armor-plated chest to kick the dying man away and, inadvertently, looked into his face. It was said to be dangerous to gaze into the eyes of the dead, especially of those you had killed. Your soul would be drawn down with theirs. The Spaniard's eyes were wide and black like a rabbit's freshly strung in a hunting snare. She recoiled in revulsion, and kicked as hard as she could. The blade pulled free, but she was thrown off her balance and forced to jump from her saddle to avoid falling more dangerously. Fatal folly to break a leg or accidentally impale herself!

She landed on her knees. With zealous cries, a score of Spaniards flew at her. Mara swung her sword, slicing back the pressing mob, and regained her feet as they retreated. The horse nickered and tossed its head, but it stood its ground at her back. Her own soldiers rushed to her aid. They'd seen her fall and the idea of the filthy Spaniards daring to touch their Prince was more than the most loyal could bear. With a low, growling sound of outrage, they pushed forward to seize their foe. Their brutality was astonishing: punches were aimed at kidneys; ears were boxed; knees thrust up into groins. Three and four set themselves against one. Some clubbed their opponents with branches torn from the trees. A bowmaid yanked one Spaniard backwards by the shoulder and drove her helmed brow into his face. Mara had expected these sorts of dirty tricks from the Spanish, but it was a surprise to see them employed so effectively by her own troops. She wasn't certain she liked to see them abandon the codes of civilized conduct in warfare but, since they acted for her deliverance, she couldn't complain.

Though this battle raged at the same intensity through the length of the dell and on the hills above, it seemed to Mara as if everyone had converged upon this spot before her. All around were glinting steel, thrashing, leather-clad arms and legs, and more blood than she had ever seen. The grass was red with it. Half a dozen Spaniards were stabbed through the back; Mara cut down another three while they were distracted by Norman arms about their throats. The fight was reflex—strike and strike again, then dodge the counterstrike. She was at her best when she let her instincts guide her and didn't trouble herself with thoughts of death and pain. Later, there would be time to reflect on the first foes to die at her hands. Now, she simply fought. She didn't act with deliberate cruelty; this was a matter of killing those she faced before they killed her. It was what she'd trained for, what she was prepared to do to accomplish her victory. In this, her first battle, she acquitted herself bravely. She gave a clean death wherever she could.

Her blade clove deep beneath an upraised arm, and the Spanish soldier fell at her feet with Dentelyon wedged into the earth under him. If she stooped to retrieve it, they would be on her like ravenous wolves. She drew the dagger from her right boot. The short blade wasn't as effective as Dentelyon for keeping her foes at a distance, but it was sufficient to hold them back while she reached up with her left hand, groped along the rim of the saddle behind her head, and found the flails. She snatched one down to crack a few helms. The dagger flashed in, finding vulnerable points. A Spanish soldier swung at her head; she ducked as if flinching from the blow, then stabbed upward under his cuirass. The soldier stepped back, clutching his chest, and fell, the blade still in him. Mara tossed her flail to her right hand, and drew the second dagger with her left. She hadn't meant to use them at all—at least, not under such conditions. But Dentelyon lay trapped, its hilt just visible beneath the body at her feet, and her fencing saber was out of reach behind her. She would have to turn her back to her foes to extract it from the scabbard. Until she was given that opportunity, she must do her best with the weapons at hand.

"Mara!"

Alyx had ridden around from Mara's left and fought to reach her. Her horse reared up, unable to ride through the swarms of footsoldiers. She was beset on all sides, slashing left and right and kicking angrily at any who tried to lay hands on her. Blood spattered over her from head to horse's hooves. There was now some confusion among the Spanish. Mara didn't know their language, but she understood their bafflement: this terrifying warrior-maid who bore the Northlands' arms, screamed like a Valkyrie, and dripped blood from her sword and her blonde braids—Was *she* the fearsome granddaughter of the Redlyon? Had they sought the wrong prize?

"Mara!" Alyx shouted. "Do you hear it?"

Yes, there *was* a strange sound, faint amid the uproar—a distant chant, one word repeated that she couldn't quite discern. A triumphal cry? Spanish or Norman? Had her knights taken the gate?

As she strained to make sense of the repeated word, she left herself unguarded for an instant. A body struck her. She fell back against the curtain of the horse's mail, raked against it, and crashed to the ground beneath the animal. The blade of a dagger grazed the skin beneath her ear. A red garnet flashed at the corner of her eye—her own dagger! The bastard must have plucked it from the corpse of his comrade! This was more outrageous than the assault.

She clouted the side of her opponent's head with her flail and shoved him back. His head struck the horse's belly. The horse danced fretfully—its hind hooves stamped dangerously near Mara's head and the heavy mail-curtain swung to knock the Spanish soldier down upon her—then it bolted, leaving her exposed in the midst of chaos and wrestling with a man who meant to kill her.

A second stab. Pain shot from her right shoulder. Mara shrieked, more in rage than pain, and grabbed his wrist. She yanked his hand away from her, but the dagger remained wedged in the rings of her mailshirt.

Fury gave her strength. Mindless of her injury, she pulled the dagger free and thrust upward viciously. Her first strike drove deep into the Spaniard's throat; his hands went to her upraised arm, but the struggle was short. Mara twisted the blade sharply, slicing back to his ear.

The eyes of the dead still looked surprised.

The body fell forward on top of her. She lay beneath it, breathing hard through clenched teeth. Her white tunic was now stained deepest red—and not all the blood was Spanish. Her own blood soaked the leather lining beneath the mail and seeped through the metal rings. Her left arm was pinned across her breast beneath her shield. Her right arm was on fire. The dagger slipped from her fingers. If she must die, she thought, at least she had brought her murderer to the Afterlife with her. He wouldn't be able to boast of how he'd killed a Norman Prince.

Someone screamed her name. Alyx, probably. Or perhaps one of the soldiers who fought to reach her. How distant they all seemed now! She could barely hear the roar of the battle. Yet one thing emerged quite clearly: far away, the chant of a single word rose exuberantly to the heavens.

"Kat! Kat! Kat!"

Kat? Then everything faded.

elfen

Red.

All was a haze of red. Red enshrouded her. Red filled her. She swam in it.

Was this death?

There was no pain. Silence pressed against her. She was calm. Comfortable. She ought to worry for her friends. She ought to wonder who had won the battle. But these questions didn't interest her. She *ought* to care. She did not. Once she'd passed through the veil, the red mists of blood, all earthly matters were forgotten.

Holy Marye, Mother of God, pray for this sinner, now, at the hour of my death.

A light shone through the blood-red mist. White light. A blazing disk.

She was unafraid. She'd made her last confession and offered prayers for divine intercession on behalf of her soul before the battle. If she and Kat were not reconciled before they marched, then surely they'd come to some sort of unspoken understanding while they fought. She didn't feel that blot upon her now. Her life had not been stainless, but she'd lived it as a proper Christian—honest, just, chaste, faithful. She departed in a state of Grace.

Holy Marye, Mother of God, pray for this sinner, now, at the hour of my death.

A dark shape passed before the light.

This was not Heaven.

The sun blazed into her eyes, dappled her vision with red. Hundreds of fallen soldiers, Norman and Spanish, some dead and others dying, lay around her. The battlefield was quiet except for the buzz of flies. Gnats swarmed like small patches of haze. The stink of the bodies in the heat was overpowering. The grass was shredded and muddied with blood. Her tunic was dark and stiff with blood. Not all her own. A great weight pinned her down. The assassin lay across her. The face that pressed against her shield had become blotched and purple.

She was alive.

She moved her free arm slightly; little jolts of pain shot from her shoulder. It wasn't over. She might yet die here.

Holy Marye, Mother of God...

Her arm throbbed dully now. She would've made the sign of the cross, but once she moved her arm, fresh blood began to seep through her mail.

A dark shape crossed the bright disk of the sun. A carrion crow. Or, so high up, perhaps a hawk or eagle. Were buzzards found so far south? A large, winged creature, swooping. No, not a crow. The neck was too long. A crane? A wild swan?

What was it? Mara squinted to focus through the burnt-blind spots dappling her sight. What was it? Its movements were wonderfully graceful. It swooped and darted so high that her dazzled eyes lost it. It looked as if flew simply for the joy of it. A dance in the sunlight.

The jointure of the wings was wrong. The forewing bent toward the head rather than back against the lithesome body. Did light shine through them? The tail was whip-thin—a few long feathers? Its flexibility made her doubt that it had plumage at all. Its skin glittered. Scales? This was no bird. Sweet Jesus, could it be?

It couldn't be! If such creatures had ever existed, the last had died centuries ago. Yet there it was. Diving to land on the hilltop above her, enormous, terrible, glorious in the sunlight...

The dragon landed.

It stretched and uncoiled, delighting in the warmth with delicious abandon like a huge, dazzling lizard basking. Iridescent scales glittered like a million beetles' wings. Wings spread. Delicate, thin-as-vellum webbing blocked the sun. The light behind the wings made them bright with myriad colors like the stained glass of cathedral windows—ten times larger than any window. Colors played on the grass.

It threw back its head and let out a screeching cry that made the earth tremble. Then it descended into the dell.

Mara watched, horrified, fascinated as it picked its way

through the fallen. Gently, it prodded corpses with its muzzle. Long claws sifted through the bodies. Now and again, it paused to turn one face-up with exquisite care. It snuffled at them; its red-ribbon tongue, forked like a serpent's, darted out to taste the bloody limbs. It ate a few. Mara couldn't guess how it chose its meal: human, animal, Norman, Spanish, dead, living. She heard a few faint cries and saw arms and legs twitch feebly in the reptilian grasp. It tossed its selections up and devoured them with a snap of its vast jaws. Discarded helms and weapons fell clattering to the earth. Armor crunched between its teeth.

Was this a prelude to Divine Judgment? A gathering up of the wicked? What more fitting end for the Devil's own than the belly of the Beast! No. That wasn't right. Mara could conceive of malignant souls among her own troops as well as the Spanish, but... evil horses? Did mute beasts have souls? Nothing in Christian theology allowed for that absurdity.

The dragon had another purpose as it moved through the field, snapping trees effortlessly, rumbling its thunderous purr, examining the dead and wounded with careful deliberation. It searched, she realized, for one particular person.

It found her.

The long neck bent in a sinuous curve. Hot breath blasted upon her face. The tips of fangs protruded from the long slit of a mouth; it might swallow her in one bite.

Mara pushed up against her shield as hard as she could with the arm trapped beneath and shoved at the body of her attempted assassin with her free hand. Her shoulder flared with pain and her head spun sickeningly. It was useless. Even if she freed herself, where would she run to? How could she fight? She didn't have a sword. The dagger that lay near her right hand was no weapon to wield against this fabulous monster.

Three wickedly clawed fingers—each as thick as a child's arm—slipped about the body that pinned her and moved it aside. The ribbon of tongue shot out to caress her bloodied tunic front. Mara held her breath. She was prepared to die, but not to be eaten alive. In spite of the stabs of pain, she sought her dagger. It would give the dragon no more than a pin-prick, but at least she wouldn't go down its gullet helplessly. She would stab its innards.

Ancient eyes gazed deeply into hers. *Fear not, O Prince.*

The dragon spoke. Or, rather, as she looked into those dark gold, black-streaked eyes, wise beyond mortal knowing, she heard a deep, melodious voice. It spoke the language of Old High Norman. Such polite, second-person pronouns and archaic verb tenses were reserved today for the highest of antique ceremonies and most formal modes of address, but Mara found them appropriate for this beast. This seemed the proper tone for a dragon to take.

Thou shalt not die here, brave Prince. Such courage and fortitude as art thine will be rewarded tenfold. Thou shalt receive a sign of thy fortune, a talisman of kings. See it here revealed unto thee. The dragon betokens thy royal lineage, older than the lion, the hart, the unicorn, and the eagle, for the dragon is eldest of all beasts that walketh the Earth or spanneth the Heavens. Its body possesseth great magics: The Dragon's Tooth is a weapon surpassing all others, even the tooth of the lion. The Dragon's Eye is prized beyond all gems. No steel may pierce the scales of its hide. No terror may quail the courage of its heart. Its blood healeth all wounds.

The dragon lifted one talon to its mouth and, with the same deliberate precision it had shown in all its motions, punctured one finger with a tooth in its lower jaw. A single droplet of blood, bright as a ruby, suspended from the tip of an arced claw like a polished steel hook.

Receivest thou these gifts, O Prince, for thy power lieth in their virtues. This token shalt thou bear upon thy shield. Thy foes shall flee in terror at its sight. All shall honor thy name, which hereafter shall be known as Sonnedragon. Takest thou the might of the dragon. It is thine.

The droplet fell.

Mara drank. The ichor coursed down her throat, hot, sweet, exhilarating as the finest spiced wine. A flush of warmth ran through her. She felt strong again—indeed, stronger than she'd ever felt before. She might take on army single-handed. Such was the power of the Sonnedragon.

This was her vision, all she had hoped for, more than she had imagined. Sonnedragon. What better talisman for a warrior-prince? It stood as her guardian and guide. It offered its healing blood. She received the sacrament. Here was the most holy communion.

The warm breath and rumbling purr were comforting. All would be well. Mara shut her eyes.

"Here she is! Alyx, I've found her! Merciful Christ, she's alive!"

She woke to great pain. Her fingertips throbbed with her heartbeat. Her chest ached when she drew deep breath. The wound in her shoulder had grown to a blazing mountain. Impossible to get around, impossible to ignore, it loomed over her consciousness. She turned restlessly beneath it. Yet she must have slept; each time she opened her eyes the scene was changed. She lay on a stretcher in an open field, then on a cot in a wardroom; later, it was a strange, large bed with a feather mattress and netted curtains. The orange light of late afternoon became midnight in a blink, and then bold sunlight shot in through the small panes of a window on the wall above her. A cup was pressed to her lips and she drank cool water. Damp cloths bathed her brow and strips of bandages were wrapped about her shoulder. She thought Sataumie tended her—all Shieldmaids were trained in field medicine—but when she cried out Sataumie's name, Alyx was there. She heard Spanish spoken and wondered if she'd only dreamed that her friends were with her. Was she a prisoner? Once, Kat knelt beside her, weeping. She looked more angry than sorrowful and Mara felt immense sympathy for her. She wanted to tell her cousin not to worry, that everything would be fine, but as she lifted her hand to Kat's tear-streaked cheek, Kat disappeared.

The dragon was always nearby. It hadn't abandoned her to her torment; its shadow lurked at the edge of her sight. Its rumbling purr sounded like distant thunder. It flew through the night skies, a dark shape with wings that blotted the stars. Its long flexible talons, iron claws, scraped stone. Scales scraped stone as it wound its way through corridors. A wooden door splintered. It pressed its muzzle against barrels and crates. With a blast of its hot breath, sparks flew. She felt the heat of its breath upon her—too hot now and she demanded cool water to soothe her scorched flesh.

Her whispering attendants took no notice of the huge creature.

Did they not see it? Was the dragon visible only to her, or did those who nursed her accept that this remarkable beast belonged here at her side? Mara wondered if she ought to warn them of the dragon's indiscriminate appetite; it had feasted well at the battle, but a beast so large must surely hunger again before long. It seemed cruelly unjust that her friends and servants be placed in such danger unawares.

Then she woke. Her head was clear and the pain in her shoulder abated. She lay in a large bed canopied with gauzy mosquito nets in a strange, richly furnished room. Kat sat in a chair at her side.

"Did we win?" she asked.

Kat looked plainly relieved at this simple question. "Of course."

"What is this place?"

"The bedchamber of Don Miguel D'Andaluz, Teniente of Spainfort. We sent him to less well-appointed apartments for your sake, so you needn't lie at hospital with the rest of the wounded. A victorious general deserves better." She smiled. "How do you feel?"

"Thirsty."

Kat filled a cup with water from a pitcher on a small table beside the bed and offered it to her. Mara took the cup in her left hand, surprised at how heavy it felt. Her fingers slipped uncertainly over the curved porcelain, as if they were unused to handling such a familiar object. She must be very weak.

"Spainfort," Mara looked about the chamber as she sipped. "How long have I slept?"

"It's been five days since the battle." Kat took the empty cup. "Your wound is not so bad. The lung was not pierced, nor the bone." Mara tugged open the lacings of her nightshirt to bare her wounded shoulder; a thick pad of faintly stained dressing was bound over it by thin linen strips tied about her upper arm and across her chest and back. "There was some infection. You've been in a fever since we brought you here. The healer applied a poultice and it seems to have performed marvels."

"A Spanish healer?" asked Mara, thinking of the Spanish she had heard spoken during her illness.

Kat nodded. "She was the only one available. Don Miguel

brought her in. We didn't trust her, but we put her under threat of sword and I think she did her best for you. We've taken turns sitting up with you ourselves, Alyx most often, for she doesn't have so much to do as the rest of us. You couldn't have chosen a better left-arm ward, Mara. You must tell her so when she comes in, for I think she blames herself for losing you in the battle. She fought to draw them from you, you know, and tried to reach you `til she fell herself."

"Is she badly injured?"

"She took a blow on her shield arm, but it isn't broken. Her thigh was cut and her face, here–" Kat drew a finger along the edge of her chin. "Yet Sataumie says that when she found her, Alyx was still on her feet, wandering about in search of you. She wouldn't rest `til you were found and brought to the field hospital."

"She deserves commendation," said Mara, touched by this show of loyalty, though it was no more than she expected of her companions. "What of Bel?" she asked.

"Bel is unharmed," Kat assured her. "She led the archers through the gate herself to have revenge on the Spanish bows. Sataumie is also well."

"And you?"

"I'm not injured, " Kat said quietly.

"Not a bruise!" Mara said with appreciation. "Tell me of the battle, how it ended."

"We met Khrespian's knights at the rise at the western end of the dell," Kat began after a moment. "At the spot where the Spanish footsoldiers first lay in wait for us. The pikers stood three squares in a row before the gate and the Spanish knights behind them. I gave Khrespian command of the main flank and I led the other, six of our most swift knights. We swept wide around the pike squares from either side and charged the gate. The Spanish knights rode to block us, but Khrespian engaged them and they were forced to defend themselves rather than chase after my little band. They numbered less than one hundred and we had thrice that. It was nothing to breach the gate. It was a single wooden door exactly like the gate we entered the Shieldwall through. Only one knight could pass at a time. I went in first. Archers waited within. They fired on us as we came through the little door, but I couldn't think of retreat, not with the pikes at our backs. We couldn't go back and we couldn't ride around. So we advanced."

Mara chuckled at the familiar tactic. "You rode through them?"

"I rode straight at the archers as fast as I could," Kat answered as if it were a sensible thing to do. "They weren't expecting that. Their arrows glanced off my armor and stuck in the mail so thick I felt like a hedgehog, but I didn't stop. My company rode after me, hooting and shouting for blood. `Twas terrifying to hear. I wouldn't have been a Spaniard to see a band of Norman knights flying at me giving such fierce battle-cry."

"I heard them shout your name."

"The Spaniards mistook me for you, but our knights would have none of it. They must let it be known that I was the hero of the Shieldwall. I'm sure they meant no disrespect."

"Of course not," Mara answered. Such petty jealousy was beneath her. Kat's actions had been marvelously brave and, so she inferred from this room at captured Spainfort, extremely successful. "The honor is yours, and fairly won. What happened after you rode into the Spanish archers?"

"We were among them," her cousin said. "Khrespian's knights began to come through. They all screamed my name as if they fought for my sake. Then someone shouted 'Clear the field!' just as Bel had when we first engaged the Spanish vanguard. It was Bel, of course. Frederik," Kat paused. "I learned later that Frederik's guards had come to the aid of our soldiers in the dell and made short work of the Spaniards. Even before the battle ended, Bel gathered together all the archers who were able to fight and came up to the gate. You know how Bel can be when her blood's up. She told me afterwards—she was furious that she'd led her bowmen and maids into such a scurvy trap. She saw you fall from your horse and she was afraid you were killed. She wanted the Spanish archers to have a taste of Norman arrows. She meant to kill every one of them she caught in her sites. When she gave the cry to clear, I called the knights to stand away, and the arrows began to fly. The battle in the dell had ended and more of our soldiers pushed through the gate every minute. They knocked the door off its hinges and tore down the posts. They battered at the stones to widen the way. God Alone knows what they did with the pikes. We cut the archers to ribbons."

Her eyes were glittering and there was a slight tremor to her voice as she recalled her first slaughter. Mara did not press her. Kat had always been sensitive, and the brutality of battle must have disturbed her deeply. It was a shock to drive your sword into human flesh for the first time, to see your comrades fall, to stand covered in blood and know what barbaric acts you were capable of committing; Mara had learned this for herself, and she knew these same grisly experiences would have a profound effect on Kat. In the small hesitations between Kat's slightly disjointed sentences, Mara heard all that her cousin remembered but wasn't willing to speak of.

"We held council at the guardhouse," Kat continued. "There were a dozen reports that you had fallen. No one could say you were dead, but you were missing and we must go on. Frederik said I was the one to take command of the armies. Lieutenant Uismarde would support me. The soldiers were for it. After the Shieldwall had broken, they were ready to follow me. It is–" Kat paused. "`Tis a fearful responsibility to have thousands of soldiers cry out for you to lead them—but you know that, Mara. I couldn't think what to do. I wasn't prepared to take your place, but I did my best, as I imagined you would've done. I decided we must move swiftly into the mountains before the enemy had time to regroup. We all agreed that you would wish us to carry on and seize the fortress."

"Yes," Mara agreed.

"I sent Sataumie with a squadron of Shieldmaids to search for you and Alyx, and we set up a field hospital for the wounded. Those of us who were fit for the march advanced up the mountain road. Sataumie rode up after us with the news that you were found alive and had been taken to the hospital. It heartened us all. We marched through the night and surrounded Spainfort at dawn. We demanded their surrender. The Teniente refused us, but that was expected. They were prepared for a siege. They had stores inside to last `til the autumn if necessary. There were cannons on the rampart below the curtain wall and more of their bloody archers. They need only wait `til reinforcements arrived."

"And how did you take them?" asked Mara, growing more

proud of her cousin as Kat's tale unfolded.

"It wasn't my doing," Kat replied. "Rather, God's Grace. They held us at bay for two days. Our armies crowded the pass. We battered the gates to no avail. They are barred with iron poles. Our one hope of ending the siege was to break through the curtain wall. This fortress is built into a cleft in the mountainside above the pass—impregnable on three sides. The wall protected the forward side. Frederik sent Khrysta to fetch the catapults from Dennefort. Then it began to rain and the road was slick and muddy. Our supplies were slow in coming. It might be a full sennight or more before the catapults reached us. I was in despair. The troops' spirits were still high from our first victory, but that wouldn't last long if they were wet and miserable and on short rations for many more days. I prayed to Heaven for aid.

"Then there came an explosion like a thunderclap. The ground shook with it. The poor soldiers were howling in terror. Some threw themselves flat to the ground. I covered my ears against the noise. Black smoke blasted from Spainfort, and when it cleared there was a huge gap in the curtain wall and rubble piled beneath."

Mara laughed in surprise. "They brought down their own wall?"

Kat nodded.

"Was it the cannon?"

"I thought so. They'd touched them off once or twice to frighten us. We stood amazed at our luck. `Twas very early in the morning and none of us were prepared to lead an assault, but this was too much like a divine grant to spurn the opportunity. I jumped up and rallied the troops. We took what arms were at hand and charged in over the ruined rampart. There was a fire in the yard below. It wasn't the cannon that had exploded, but that Devil's own black powder they use to fire them. They had stored the barrels in a little shack beneath the wall, and there'd been some horrible accident. One of the towers had fallen through the armory roof."

Mara started upright at this description, despite a sudden twinge of pain. She had heard this before. "Just as Peter saw it, Kat—the breached wall, the burning city, the fallen tower. He saw your triumph at Spainfort months ago! He knew that I wouldn't be there."

The corners of Kat's mouth twitched slightly. "Peter's visions."

"Do you refuse to credit the truth of these portents?" asked Mara.

"No, I believe they are true. `Tis pity the magician couldn't foresee something more important."

Mara didn't know how to answer this last, bitter remark.

Kat went on as if she hadn't been interrupted. "The Spainfort guard was all in confusion when we came upon them. We captured them with ease. Don Miguel ordered his guards to be peaceable and he surrendered Spainfort to me. He is well behaved for a hostage. You will find him a nobleman of honor—certainly, more courteous than I expected him to be. He was quite generous with these rooms when you were brought up yesterday morning. He recommended the healer. And he brought you these." Mara's shield and Dentelyon sheathed lay against the wall behind her.

"I thought the sword was lost."

"It was retrieved when the Spanish cleared their dead away for burial. We recovered one of your daggers too. The other wasn't found, I'm afraid."

Mara was baffled. Kat remained remote. Though she spoke freely, her tale of the battle sounded impersonal; it was the detailed account of a conscientious officer reporting to her superior, and not an adventure in which she had played the hero. It might have happened to someone else. Was Kat so horrified at the bloodletting? Had the burden of command been too heavy? No, Mara knew her cousin; Kat, although gentle and unassuming, was the daughter of conquerors. They were not a fragile race; they didn't break easily. Kat had the strength to endure whatever hardship she faced.

What was wrong then? Mara had never seen her cousin so cold. Kat was glad to see her recovered—Mara couldn't mistake that—but the affectionate, impulsive cousin she'd known from childhood wouldn't be so restrained. That familiar Kat would have thanked the Heavens aloud and thrown herself on the bed to take Mara in a hearty embrace. She would've grasped Mara's hands and wept. She would have told her tale, the good and the ill, as if it were a secret to share between them. They would've laughed together and made light of Kat's difficulties at the siege of Spainfort. And, in turn, Mara would've spoken of the Sonnedragon—but how could she reveal that wondrous vision to this detached and ironic young woman?

She thought of the images she'd seen in her delirium: the dragon's lithe and scaly body slipping through narrow corridors, its sharp claws scraping rock, its muzzle snuffling at the crates and barrels. She had imagined the dragon sought her in this Spanish fortress, but what if it had been seeking something else? The Spanish storage room? The volatile cannon-powder? But that was impossible. The dragon was only a creature of vision. It could guide her, but it couldn't work miracles for her.

She and Kat had always understood each other perfectly. Grown together as sisters, born of the same ancient blood, their minds traveled the same paths and arrived at same destinations. Their opinions so often coincided that each knew what the other thought without the necessity of speech. That intimacy was missing now. For the first time, Mara didn't know what Kat was thinking: all her playful feints, her laughing questions, her enthusiasm met with strange, unexpected, and disheartening responses. She couldn't reach Kat. The barrier remained between them.

Was Kat still angry? Mara couldn't believe that, not after all that had passed since their quarrel. If Kat was not warm, neither was she defiant, nor sullen, nor spiteful. Kat had wept in outrage at her injury. Mara's memories of the past days were muddled, but *that* had been no illusion. Kat had tended her through her fever, in spite of her pressing duties as provisional general of the armies and commander of this captured fortress. She'd been here when Mara awoke; indeed, she must have sat for hours, waiting. These were acts of devotion. Injury and illness had made her forget her anger.

But they hadn't made her forget Frederik. With this sudden realization, Mara's mind leapt on toward understanding. Yes, Kat had had time to regret her behavior before the battle, but she wasn't sorry for her love. Her worry for Mara hadn't displaced her determination to marry Frederik. Was she afraid too? Their argument had been set aside by necessity during the fighting and through the days of her fever, but now that these emergencies had passed, they might easily find themselves in exactly the same situation they'd been on that night if both refused to yield. Surely, Kat recalled every harsh word Mara had spoken and she expected more of the same. Unwilling to retreat, she steeled herself for fresh battle and guarded her heart against further insult.

Well, Kat might be ready to continue the fight, but Mara was determined not to reenact that ugly scene. She disapproved Kat's choice of Frederik. She thought her cousin foolish and obstinate and she was heartsick at the shameless way Kat had abandoned all moral sense for passion's sake. But, in spite of this, she loved Kat dearly and this chilly reserve was more than she could bear. She wanted her old, familiar Kat restored to her. If they were ever to be reconciled, she must concede.

"You're not angry with me, are you, Cos?" she began. "Very well, if it must be said, I shall say it: Marry Frederik if you will. I wish you all happiness. I'll offer my blessing to you both if he's here." She struggled to sit up, but stopped suddenly at her cousin's expression. She'd seen it before: Kat had looked so as she'd knelt beside her weeping. It had moved her to pity—that face stricken by inconceivable tragedy, heartbroken, tear-streaked but enraged. Her indomitable Kat, who had the strength to survive any disaster. Mara understood at last. Kat had wept, but not for her. "Oh, Kat. Frederik?"

Kat answered dispassionately, "Frederik is dead," and she rose abruptly and left the room.

tuelfe

During her recovery, Mara sat with Alyx, also in bandages, on the terrace below her apartment. Together, they observed the restoration of the fallen curtain wall. From the morning after their triumph, soldiers had been laboring to restore it as swiftly as possible.

"I pray they'll have it in place before the first Spanish reinforcements try to recapture Spainfort from us," said Mara. "Is there any news of Spanish movements? Do we know where they are?"

"We've no better news than we had yesterday, Prince Mara," Alyx reported. "Our scouts haven't sighted them yet. They might be a day or two away, or not come for a week or more. But you may rest assured that the wall will be raised before they come."

Although Mara issued no orders to undermine Kat's authority, she received reports every day in order to keep herself informed of all preparations for Spainfort's defense. She knew scouting parties had ventured into the unconquered territory; while they had exacted tribute in the form of supplies from farms and villages, they'd found no fortified towns or castles, nor any place where a stronghold might be established within twenty miles. She'd been told that Kat had placed troops on the southward slopes of the mountain and sentinels to keep watch at the southern end of the pass, which afforded a view of Terrojos's rugged hills. An advancing army might be seen and met long before they threatened the Norman-held fortress. She knew that several pieces of Spanish artillery had been recovered from the ruins in working condition, but that no one wanted to touch the remaining cannon. She also knew that most of the Spanish prisoners had been transported to Dennefort along with the seriously injured at the field hospital. Only Don Miguel and a few of his officers remained here at Spainfort.

"It'll be an ugly lump," said Alyx, referring to the squat, tumulus-like barricade that rose from the pile of rubble where the forty-foot curtain wall had been. "Not so formidable a barrier as it once was."

"No," Mara had to agree, "but it will serve as well—Perhaps better. It can't be knocked down."

Don Miguel, the former Teniente of the captured fortress, stepped onto the terrace and bowed tentatively to Mara.

"I think he wants you, My Prince," Alys murmured.

"I sent for him." Mara turned to Don Miguel and nodded to him, not only to acknowledge his presence, but to indicate that he could approach.

In spite of Kat's description of the captured Teniente's civility, Mara had been surprised by Miguel's personable demeanor when they'd first been introduced. She'd imagined that this Spanish noble must be extremely proud, swarthy, and black-haired, with piercing eyes and a fixed sneer of ill-disguised contempt as he uttered veiled insults in halting Norman—exactly like the Ambassador Don Peidro. But Don Miguel spoke excellent Norman and presented himself with impeccable manners, even if they were Spanish manners. He had tawny hair, green eyes, and a fairer complexion than her brother's. Although he'd been appointed commander of this remote colonial fortress, Miguel was the youngest son of the Duq D'Andaluz, a nobleman born of a powerful and ancient family; he'd been schooled with his cousins Serafina and that Infant Iosephus who had once been proposed as a suitor for Kat.

From their first meeting, Miguel had treated Mara as an honored guest, as if he didn't truly detest the invasion of his post and even his rooms. He expressed relief at her recovery and hoped that she found the apartment comfortable. He willingly answered her questions regarding *Los Ojos*, as he called the fortress, and had offered to escort her on a tour once she regained her strength. Mara was amazed at his cooperation and determination to uphold the fiction that she and her people were welcome here. She knew she couldn't have behaved so well if she'd been taken prisoner. But she had also noticed how nervous he was around Kat.

At first, Mara had imagined that he was ill at ease with this bold young woman. Although there were common guardsmaids among the Spanish soldiery, their codes of conduct for noblewomen were quite different from the Normans. Spanish *Donas* were brought up to be as modest and retiring as Holy Sisters; no well-bred maiden ventured out without her duenna. A few famous queens had taken up swords in defense of their land or their faith, but a warrior-maid in the Norman style was a rare and remarkable thing. How odd she and her Shieldmaids must seem to him. How terrifying it must've been to see Kat charge over the ruined wall, the full force of an army in her wake! It must have astonished Miguel to be conquered by such a woman.

But there was more to it than that. Whenever Kat joined them on the terrace, Mara observed that Don Miguel lost his well-mannered composure; he averted his eyes as he replied to Kat's questions and, unable to retreat, he placed himself at Mara's side as if he sought her protection. His agitation was unmistakable. Kat frightened him.

Mara meant to discover why. She'd already begun to guess the cause.

Kat had never disclosed the full facts of Frederik's death; Mara learned them from Sataumie, who had climbed over the ruined wall at Kat's side. Frederik's troops had swarmed into the fortress yard behind them. They'd been taken by surprise when the wall fell and most were geared and armed lightly with whatever weapons were at hand. Frederik had gone without his mailshirt, and that had been his doom. An arrow caught him in the back—shot, Sataumie said, by an archer high on the battlements of the remaining gate tower.

Sataumie didn't speak of what followed. She seemed reluctant to describe the battle and in questioning her other officers, Mara found a similar reticence. All gave full accounts of the breaching of the Shieldwall, the days of the siege, the disposition of the fortress. Some had seen Frederik fall; others had learned of it only after victory had been achieved. On the battle itself, all were equally vague. Mara recalled that Kat had omitted this part of her tale as well, moving swiftly from the explosion to Don Miguel's surrender.

If none of her own people would tell her what lay at the heart of this mystery, then she must turn to a Spaniard for the truth.

"Don Miguel," she began once Alyx had been dismissed, "I have a special request to ask of you. I pray you tell me about the death of Marchion Frederik."

"Surely that is the place of your kinswoman and officers, Prince Marguerkyt," Miguel replied with another courteous bow.

"I've asked them. Now I ask you to tell me what they will not. What followed the Marchion's death?" Miguel remained reluctant, and Mara pressed him further. "You know that he and my cousin Katheryne considered themselves betrothed to each other, and she grieves for him still. Did she *do* something after his death that makes you dread the sight of her? I see it is so. Did she not behave as a proper soldier during her capture of this fortress?"

Persuaded by these pointed questions for which Mara already knew the answer, Miguel told her, "She passed into madness, Prince Marguerkyt." He crossed himself as he spoke. "She would have cut down every one of my soldiers, even those who put away their swords, if your captains had not restrained her."

Mara saw it all now. After Frederik fell, Kat would have transformed sorrow into fury and spent it against those who had wronged her. She would fly at her foes in bloodthirsty, shrieking rage and kill every Spaniard she met, cutting them down without mercy. Had she continued her vengeance even after the surrender? Mara was shocked at the idea, yet she knew her cousin was capable of dark, dangerous moods. Kat had a quickness and depth of emotion Mara didn't possess herself; anger burst from her abruptly, passionately and powerfully. Mara had seen the force of her love for Frederik. She couldn't forget the look on Kat's face—tear-streaked and furious. Yes, in a rage, Kat was capable of committing this act of barbarism which no civilized soldier could condone. It would have horrified the Normans as well as the Spanish. Certainly, it explained Don Miguel's polite acquiescence; he regarded his life and the lives of his officers at the mercy of a madwoman and he was anxious not to stir her to wrath. The silence of her own officers was likewise clear: the captains, her own companions especially, were too loyal to speak against the commander who had led them through the Terrojos gate and inspired them during the tedious days of siege. Kat was their hero. Which of them, from Uismarde to the least footsoldier, would carry tales of her disgrace?

Mara tried to offer her personal apology on her cousin's behalf. "Don Miguel, I must tell you how sorry I am-"

"You have no need, Prince Margueryt. I understand. Marchion Frederik was my friend. I mourn his death as well."

Mara believed that Miguel was sincere, in spite of the fact that one of his own archers had been responsible for Frederik's death. That was the way of war; they all understood it. If circumstances had been different and Don Miguel had died at Norman hands, Frederik would have sorrowed just the same.

Hundreds had died in the conquest of Terrojos, but the loss of Frederik was most widely felt. Kat had lost more than a lover: the Marches had lost their governor. The Dennefort guard lamented. Khrystophania bore her brother's death stoically; taught from childhood that such a tragedy might one day call her to take Frederik's place, she solemnly prepared to assume the duties of Marchion. Kat mourned, silently, angrily. Even the Spanish expressed sorrow at the death of a respected neighbor and foe. Mara alone was not allowed to grieve. She'd been seen to disapprove Kat's plans to marry Frederik. Knowledge of this seemed to be widespread now—perhaps not surprising in light of her behavior on the morning before the battle—and it was generally assumed that she hadn't liked the young Marchion. Often, Mara caught a slight hesitation or awkwardness whenever someone spoke of Frederik, as if his name wasn't to be mentioned in her hearing. Khrystophania was particularly reserved. Mara wanted to protest that she *had* liked Frederik. She hadn't wished for Kat to marry him, but she'd always found him to be a pleasant young man of excellent capabilities. She had never wanted him dead. But now that Frederik *was* dead, such protestations would sound more like contrition than honest admiration. Any show of sorrow would seem insincere. Kat would despise her for it.

In August, news reached Spainfort that Arnauld's armies on the coast had successfully engaged the reinforcements from Spain, but another transport ship had landed further south, beyond their reach. More troops now marched inland. Mara's shoulder had healed completely, and Kat officially relinquished her command and returned to Dennefort. The common soldiers whispered that grief for her beloved had unsettled the Irish Prince's mind, but

Mara and her Shieldmaids were privileged to the truth. The truth had been suspected for some time before Kat's departure.

"She didn't look well at this morning's review," Bel observed in late July. "Pale. Weary. I don't think she sleeps."

"There's no mystery to that. It's barely been six weeks."

"I don't believe it is sorrow that makes our commander ill," Sataumie said obliquely. "Though Frederik is certainly is the cause of it."

"Oh, Taumie, you don't think–?"

"Haven't you thought of it yourselves? She shows all the symptoms."

"The symptoms are easily mistaken," Alyx answered. "A dozen ailments might produce the same pallor. Christ knows this heat is enough to make us all turn away from our food."

"And none of us is accustomed to this thin mountain air," interjected Bel.

"True. You are no more a midwife than I am. How can you know?"

"I can't know with certainty," Sataumie admitted. "But I have eyes and ears and I have observed enough to wonder if it's true."

"Can it be true?" Bel wondered as well. "Oh, poor Kat."

Mara put a stop to these speculations before the scandalous rumor was whispered all around the camp, but she couldn't stop her own worst imaginings. She had heard her cousin being quietly sick in the adjoining chamber early every morning. If she asked, Kat always insisted that she was fine; she bathed and dressed and attended to her duties without complaint. Indeed, her illness might be attributed to other causes: the high altitude, the muggy, summer heat, the windowless little room, formerly occupied by Miguel's attendant, which Kat insisted on keeping even after Mara no longer required a nurse—any of these might make her pale and sickly. Her sorrow still fresh, it wasn't strange that Kat spent so much time in the chapel, nor—though the walls were thick and Mara heard only the faintest sobs—that she wept at night. All might be explained, but Mara thought again and again of that night when Kat had returned exultant from her lover's arms. She counted the days since. Like Sataumie, she couldn't be certain, but she saw enough to be worried.

On the morning after Arnauld's news reached Spainfort, Mara

went into Kat's room to find her cousin sitting on the floor in her nightdress, chamber pot set before her—by this time, a familiar sight.

"Kat, are you carrying a child?"

Kat pushed her unraveling braids away from her face and looked up at this blunt question. "I think so."

Her fears had been confirmed, and yet Mara's moral sensibilities were not so outraged as they might be. It was useless to scold now. Kat sat before her, still shaky from her recent bout of morning sickness. With her rumpled nightdress, disheveled hair, and eyes wide with worry, she looked quite young and vulnerable. It was as if her beloved Kat had returned, the little sister who had admired her, followed her, wanted so to be like her before Frederik had come between them. Now, in this time of trouble, Kat turned to her again.

"What are we going to do?"

Mara couldn't refuse this appeal for help. "Don't be frightened." She tried to reassure the girl. "Let me attend to everything." Leaving Kat to dress, Mara turned to practical matters.

The morning review of troops was postponed while Mara's chief officers and confidants quickly assembled in the private closet in her chambers.

"There is a personal problem before me which I require your aid to address," the Prince began. "It concerns my cousin Kat, but it mustn't pass these rooms."

"You can't hope to keep this secret for long, Mara. I don't intend to."

Kat had emerged from her own bedchamber in full dress uniform, her braids freshly woven. She stood at the closet door and looked at each member of the little group Mara had gathered—Bel and Alyx at the window overlooking the terrace, Sataumie on a chair facing Mara at the map table, and Khrystophania apart from the others on the bench beside the door. "What is this?"

"I've called a counsel," Mara explained. "Our friends must hear of it first. They can be trusted."

"Trusted with what?" asked Bel. "You haven't told us your secret." But she glanced at her fellow Shieldmaids as she spoke.

"Kat?"

"It will become obvious soon enough." The last traces of the vulnerable girl had disappeared. In her pressed, white linens, bronze-trimmed armor, and imperial sash bearing the golden lions, Kat looked every inch a stern warrior-prince. Impossible to imagine this forbidding young woman asking for aid! She stood alone, feet planted firmly, shoulders squared, chin up and hands loosely clasped at the small of her back, and delivered her announcement with the air of a commander addressing her subordinates. "I'm pregnant. I'm not ashamed of it, though I would rather the father had lived to see his child."

Sataumie threw an *I told you* look back to Bel.

"Oh, Kat." Khrystophania leaned forward as if she meant to embrace her, then hesitated. Kat's military posture was not inviting. The younger woman blushed and looked very embarrassed.

"Shame or no, certain changes must be made to accommodate this," Mara pressed on before further sympathetic outbursts delayed her. "As my cousin observes, it won't be possible to conceal her condition for long, but I will not have her become an object of gossip among the common soldiers in her command. The matter must be conducted with discretion—I rely on all of you."

"Yes, of course," said Alyx.

"There will be modifications in the chain of command. Though I meant to resume my place at the head of the armies before the Spanish reinforcements reached us, I did want you, Kat, to continue your duties as commander of Spainfort. It will remain our base in Terrojos throughout this campaign. Now, I must appoint a new commander. Obviously, Kat cannot remain here much longer."

"Why not?" Kat turned to her.

Mara was astonished at the question. Killing a pregnant woman was an atrocity according to the codes of civilized warfare. None but barbarians and monsters would dare deliberately lay sword against a woman with child; like cutting down a foe who had surrendered or executing a ransomed prisoner, it simply was not done. In consequence, civilized soldiers were horrified at the thought of a pregnant woman entering battle. Among Northlanders, the horror was so deeply fixed in their traditions that it had become visceral. Even the sturdiest Shieldmaids were barred from active service in the months before childbirth. Kat couldn't stay. So much was obvious to Mara. Why did Kat refuse to see it?

This was another example of Kat's new perversity. For all their lives, Mara had imagined Kat to be the person most like herself. Their moral standards, their spiritual beliefs, their understanding of what was and was not proper had always seemed to be the same. But in these past months, she'd seen that Kat would cut down surrendered foes, would pledge herself to a man with a seduction, and now this–! Had Kat always been like this? Mara felt as if her sister were truly a stranger. Did she know this woman at all?

"It's been less than two months," Kat continued. "The child hasn't yet quickened. I won't ride to battle, but I am capable of continuing my duties here."

"That's beside the point. Pregnant women have no place in war."

"If I am pregnant, I was so when I charged the Shieldwall gate. I have been so all the weeks I governed this fortress in your place. None contested my abilities then."

"None contest them now, Kat," Sataumie offered in placating tones.

"You've proved yourself wonderfully capable," Mara added. "But it isn't proper for you to be here while the Spanish march against us. We did agree that I would care for you. You asked for my help."

"This is not at all what I expected," Kat answered dryly.

"It's the best I can do. Believe me, Kat, I do not send you away as punishment. It is meant for your own safety. What if there is a siege? It is unthinkable that I allow you to face such danger. "

"But I don't want to go."

"Then you should've guarded yourself against this."

"I never meant to bear a child so soon."

"Didn't you?" After Kat had shown such calculation in taking Frederik as her lover, Mara could easily imagine her deliberately foregoing the contraceptive techniques known to Shieldmaids. Consummation might have sealed their illicit betrothal; pregnancy would ensure their marriage. None would wish to see Kat's child in the uncertain status of a bastard when it might be avoided. The imperial family endured enough complication with Ambris's family and Kharles's acknowledged children. Dafythe would not only approve the match, but hasten it so that there could be no question of the child's legitimacy. Everything would have happened exactly as Kat had hoped. But Kat hadn't foreseen Frederik's death. "You would not be troubled now if Frederik had lived. This would be your triumph. If he were here, I would have seen you wed long before this day."

She was aware that the others were extremely uncomfortable witnessing this scene, particularly hearing her speak on this sensitive topic, but she went on.

"I would not have seen him harmed—nevertheless, he is gone. All of us must alter our plans for the worse without him. Your plans for the baby must change. I don't imagine you wish to abort?"

Kat's vehement "No!" was echoed by Khrystophania.

"Then you must accept the consequences of your choice. If you mean to have this baby, you must think of its welfare before all else. You are not well. Oh, you deny it and carry on your duties without regard for yourself, but we can all see how you've taxed your health. You cannot continue to do so. It won't be easier in the months to come. If you don't have a care, you may lose the baby. Don't scoff—Heartier women have miscarried." Her words were more harsh than she had intended. Mara didn't wish to bully, but she had to make Kat understand that she was right. "You don't belong in this place."

"I took this place," Kat retorted.

"I know. And I know how. `Tis why I would not have you face the Spanish again even if you were fit to fight. I can't know what you'll do."

In spite of this oblique phrasing, Mara's meaning was clear. Kat went white and drew back as if she'd been slapped. There was a quick intake of breath from Khrystophania, and the Shieldmaids shifted from foot to foot and glanced at each other.

"Who's spoken to you?" Kat asked, barely above a whisper.

"None of your officers betrayed you," Mara assured her.

"It was that damned Spanish puppy," Bel growled. "Always

underfoot. If I lay hands on him–"

"Captain, you will not touch him," Mara snapped. "No prisoner, not even a Spaniard, will come to harm in my custody."

She'd never meant to let Kat or her companions know that she knew what had occurred, but Kat's willfulness was infuriating, goading her into saying things better left unspoken. This conversation had gone wrong from the first. When she'd left Kat in her room not an hour ago, she had genuinely desired to help her cousin. Her first thought was to protect Kat from any form of disgrace. Indeed, she had called this meeting of her sister-Shieldmaids—including Khrystophania because it seemed right that she be here—to enlist their aid. They had proved themselves trustworthy; they would provide invaluable assistance in silencing wild rumors, assuming Kat's duties and seeing her safely away before the Spanish troops approached. Every difficulty she could think of had been attended to. That Kat should resist her efforts was incomprehensible. What more did she want?

Mara regretted her hurtful words, but it was too late to take them back. She wouldn't continue to dash herself against that implacable barrier between them. Nor would she encourage the suspicions and hostile intentions of her Shieldmaids. If she had to give orders as their liege to make them obey her, then so be it!

"No more of this. We must address the disposition of the fortress before the morning's review runs too late. Everyone bears unexpected duties as it is and my cousin's absence will leave a greater gap. Khrysta is heavily burdened without the added responsibilities, and at any rate she leaves us soon." Though she was prepared to take up her brother's duties, Khrystophania could not lead the armies of the Marches until Kharles appointed her as governor. Pending her confirmation as Marchion, she would return to Dennefort. "Alyx will continue to ride as my left-arm ward as well as act as my liaison with the March lieutenants. Bel, you'll captain the archers as always. These are the tasks you are best suited for, though I may ask other offices of you both later. Khrespian will captain all my knights. I cannot spare Uismarde or Tortos from their regular duties. Taumie, you have assisted my cousin through these weeks and you know her routine as well as she does. Do you think yourself fit to govern Spainfort in her stead?"

"I will try if you require it of me, Prince Mara," Sataumie answered formally. Like the others, she was surprised by these swift decisions. "Though I doubt I'll do so well as Kat."

"You'll do admirably. I want you to begin to relieve Kat of her lesser duties this week so that you will be prepared to take up the appointment and she may depart as soon as possible."

"Yes, My Prince."

"If you insist," Kat murmured. While Mara issued her orders, she had moved from her place at the door to sit beside Khrystophania. She had ceased to fight. "Where will you have me go?"

"I can't send you home," Mara said. "It looks too much like disgrace."

"Kat can come with me," Khrystophania offered. She'd been silent throughout the discussion, but now she addressed Mara. "If Pendaunzel will not acknowledge Frederik's child, I shall. It is all of my family that survives. It ought to be in the Marchion's line. None will deny it." Abashed at her own boldness, she ducked her head and shyly invited Kat, "Will you? The baby will be born at Dennefort and christened in the Princes' chapel where Frederik and I were named."

"It would be best," Mara told her cousin. "It isn't far to travel and you'll be safe there."

Kat looked up at her, lips drawn back tightly and teeth bared in an unpleasant smile. "That's settled then."

treten

The Sonnedragon rose, displayed, *vert* figured in *gules* on field *d'or*. Nothing like the *passant* herald of Gallys, nor after the style of the writhing Cathay beasts—the dragon revealed itself in its fearsome glory as Mara had first beheld it, snakelike head thrown back against the rays of the sun, great jaws open, wings spread wide. With painstaking care, she mixed the colors—gold, green, red—and cut the tufts of stiff horsehair for her brushes. She painted over the battered hartshead and drew her outlines on the fresh, pale yellow surface. Even if a professional limner could've been summoned from Dennefort, Mara would have done this herself. Her sign must be made by her own hand.

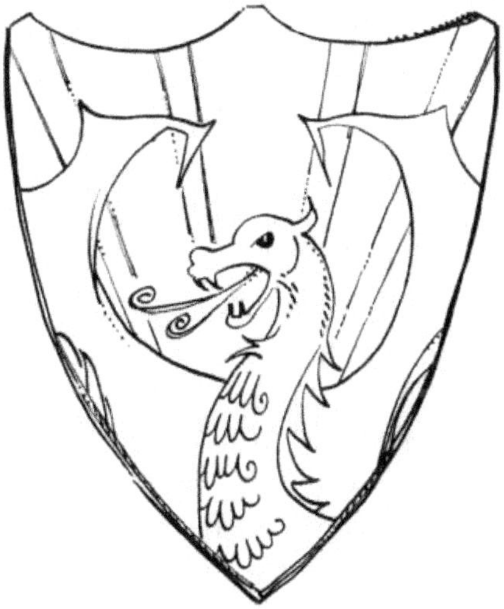

These alterations to her arms drew considerable attention. As she worked in the late mornings, when the sunlight fell on her terrace, the officers who came out to receive her orders observed her progress with increasing curiosity.

"What's it meant to be?" Bel asked, viewing the freshly painted wings and head. "A phoenix?"

"In green?" said Alyx. "It's a dragon, simpleton."

"The Sonnedragon," Mara corrected her. "It is my talisman."

"You had your vision?" Bel exclaimed. "Mara! You never said a thing!"

"I meant to reveal this new shield in our forthcoming battle. Alyx, what news from Uismarde's scouts? How far off are the Spanish now?"

"At last report, approximately one hundred and fifty miles to the southeast."

"Within the week, then. When I ride at the front of the armies to meet them, I shall bear this device before me." This had been her resolve from the first, but as she spoke, she doubted. Although the image of the dragon remained vivid in her mind, the figure created by her brushstrokes was an unimpressive copy. The shape was right, but it didn't inspire awe. The Sonnedragon had promised to strike fear in the hearts of her foes. What faint-hearted Spaniard would be fearstruck at the sight of *this* feeble beast? Indeed, Don Miguel had been here with her half the morning—although he'd retreated to the far balustrade at the arrival of her companions—and while he expressed an interest in her talisman, the dragon was obviously no object of terror to him.

"You'll both have to alter your own arms in its likeness. God pray your skill with a limner's brush is better than mine. I've no talent for this, I'm afraid." She sat back to examine her work. "My hartshead was much easier. That, I simply copied from one of the Northlander coats of arms about the Palace. Here, I must work from memory."

"But you never spoke a word of it!" Bel persisted in her amazement. "Mara, when did this revelation occur? Was it during your illness?"

"No, before that," Mara answered. "The dragon appeared to me on the battlefield as I lay wounded."

Alyx was likewise surprised. "All the days you and I sat out here and spoke of nothing! If I'd been blessed to receive a sign from my talisman beast, I would've introduced the topic to our conversations at some point."

"There isn't much to tell. As I lay wounded after the battle, the dragon flew out of the sun and landed on the hill—as you see it here. Then it came down to me."

Like the half-finished portrait before her, any attempt at a more detailed description would be a faint imitation of a most remarkable experience. She had never mentioned it to her friends for the same reason she'd never told Kat: there were so many peculiar points to her story that she knew they wouldn't believe her. Alyx, Bel—What did these clear-headed women know of visions? Even Sataumie, who had joined them to hear the end of her brief account, had seen nothing so strange as the revealed Sonnedragon. Could she tell them of the ancient wisdom in those amber eyes? Could she tell them she had received the creature's blood in a sort of communion? They wouldn't understand. Could she tell them that the dragon had kept vigil at her bedside during her days of illness? They would call it fever-dream. She couldn't think of saying that she believed the dragon had caused the explosion which brought the curtain wall down. They would think her mad. Indeed, she wasn't entirely certain that they would be wrong to think such things. She often wondered about it herself.

A few drops of red darkened the remaining yellow to golden-orange. With this, she painted a series of rays emanating from the dragon to the border of the shield to create an *en soliel* effect. "It wasn't at all as I imagined. Tell me, Sataumie—did your wolf speak to you?"

"No."

"The dragon spoke," Mara explained. "At least, I think it was the dragon. I heard the voice in my head. It sounded dragonish—deep, ages old, melodious, and so wise." The green paint was drying. Carefully, with her finest brush, she picked out the eye and serpent-tongue in thin crimson lines.

"Well, what did it say?" Bel pressed.

"Strange words: the dragon is the eldest of all beasts. A talisman of kings." There was a wicked curve to the upper rim of the eye; it gave the beast a menacing expression. "It said all would know me by the name of Sonnedragon. It spoke of the virtues of its flesh. It offered me gifts."

"Gifts?"

"Is that usual?" Bel looked to Sataumie, as if her one vision were the pattern for all.

"Beasts who proclaim great fortunes and victories often appear to heroes," said Sataumie. "Think of the unicorn who bowed before Elfgifu. Or the white hart which Pwyll chased through many days and promised that he would become king of Gallys. Even Jack's cat-in-boots. Bard Delphyn could tell a dozen such tales."

"No, not foretellings. The dragon promised me gifts," Mara answered. "It offered its scales as a shield."

"What can it mean?" Alyx wondered aloud. "Are you to wear

a dragon's hide as armor? 'Tisn't sensible."

"I wasn't sensible at the time. I simply tell you what I heard." As she formed rows of tiny red *v's* across the green breast to represent these same scales, Mara continued, "No weapon can breach a dragon's hide. Its blood heals all wounds. It spoke of the surpassing sharpness of a dragon's tooth."

"Dragonsfang?" asked Bel, and Mara looked up quickly.

"Denys's sword." She hadn't thought of this before. "The dragon's tooth is sharper than the lion's," she repeated the words she'd heard in her vision. She had pondered over them in many quiet moments. Did the gifts refer to material objects to be bestowed upon her, or did these tokens signify qualities that she bore with the Sonnedragon? "Do you think that's what it means? Am I meant to take up Dragonsfang?"

"If it is so," said Sataumie, "then the other gifts may be real as well. The blood, an elixir. The scales, a suit of armor. Perhaps you'll find them here, in Spainfort's treasury."

Miguel, who'd been listening to the conversation, drew nearer at this point as if he meant to speak. A fierce look from Bel stopped him.

Miguel and his officers remained here as hostages to bargain with if the fortress were besieged. Because of his place as former commander of Spainfort and his noble rank, Miguel was permitted more liberty than most, but Mara liked to keep him under her eyes. This wasn't because she would have liked to meet with similar courtesy if she'd been taken prisoner, nor because she'd grown rather fond of the young man—though both were true. No, she kept watch over him because she had promised his safety. Kat had departed Spainfort two weeks ago, but the rancor of her Shieldmaids toward him for his suspected tale-bearing had not abated.

They had all changed since the beginning of this campaign. The girls' games of sword and bow had ended; they were true warriors now. They had killed and they'd seen comrades fall around them.

Sataumie, always the most thoughtful and clear-headed one among them, was also the most unassuming. She had become Kat's aide-de-camp when all other suitable officers had been injured or otherwise occupied and in Kat's absence, she was given command—a promotion she hadn't expected. She doubted her capabilities, but that same careful thought which made her a trusted advisor to her quick-tempered friends also made her an excellent manager. Mara did not regret the appointment; Sataumie had grown to fill it. Alyx too, beneath that urban cynicism, had been uncertain of herself. Street-spawned wharf brat—What right had she to ride in the company of princes? At the Shieldwall, she had proved herself fit to be there. She bore proud scars in defense of her liege. There was a subtle difference in her bearing, a new surety, but Mara had noticed it. Again, she didn't regret that she had chosen this woman not once, but twice, to serve as her left-arm ward.

These hard weeks had brought out the best in them. Bel, on the other hand, had disclosed a part of her personality better left hidden. The petite captain had always been assertive; now, that pugnacity had a keener edge. Her eagerness to have revenge on the Spanish archers was, like Kat's madness at Frederik's death, something Mara could understand and sympathize with, but the depth of brutality revealed in both was disconcerting. This hatred of all things Spanish surpassed her own casual contempt. More chilling, it hadn't been put away with the last battle. Mara truly feared for Miguel's safety.

And herself? The Sonnedragon had changed her too, though she couldn't say precisely how. Had her vision made her more sure of her purpose? She had never doubted. Had it given her courage? She had been born with that. Did it confirm Magician Peter's forescrying? She'd believed in it from the first. These things had not altered; nevertheless, she *felt* different.

If anything, the Sonnedragon had focused her mind to her mission. The taking of Terrojos had been her goal in sweeping terms. She was a woman of grand and broad-ranged plans, settling the particulars only when faced with them. Now, she saw clearly all that must be done to defeat the Spanish. She knew each step in the path from here to the Ciudadela de Tolo Invencible. Even if it were not the Gobernador's seat, this citadel raised by the legendary Spanish hero was sufficient challenge, and more-than-sufficient prize. Its capture was the final step in her victory. The first was this shield bearing the dragon.

As she added the last touches, curved scarlet claws on the

upraised forelimbs, she thought that her efforts were not so bad after all. It was a pale reflection of the true Sonnedragon, but rather fearsome. It would serve.

Three days later, the Spanish advance troops rode into the foothills and Mara charged down to meet them, freshly painted shield before her and five thousand soldiers at her back. The first battle was won with astonishing swiftness. In the next fortnight, the armies of the Northlands and Marches drove back wave upon wave of Spanish reinforcements as they pressed southward and cut deeply into Terrojos. They spread through the hills, knocking out strongholds as if they were wasps' nests and suffering barely a sting.

Though she was always at the fore of her troops, Mara did not suffer another injury. Luck was always with her. Wherever she marched, bizarre mishaps plagued her foes: a captain's blade flew free from the hilt as he brandished his sword, beheading one of his own soldiers and impaling another. A charging knight tumbled from his mount and accidentally stabbed himself. The fortress of Riovista suffered an incapacitating attack of food poisoning just as Mara's armies lay siege. Spanish archers secure in the hills above the Norman encampments were forced to abandon their strong tactical position when unexpected heavy rains caused the very earth to slide out from beneath them. The supplementary forces called to relieve the garrison at Dolorosa were mysteriously delayed. Such instances of ill fortune were too numerous to overlook.

Mara was never certain what had happened at Con Permiso. She had targeted this fortified town—chartered "with the generous permission of the King"—as a place where her troops might quarter and replenish their supplies before they advanced on to the greater prize of Alcazar Norte. Intelligence reports indicated that the expected reinforcements were still several days away when they charged through the valley and met the knights and pikes who defended the town. Alyx's horse caught a pikestaff in the foreleg and she was knocked from her saddle; Mara swung down to her defense. They took the double-faced position, back to back, shields upraised and blades flying.

In the midst of the battle, she heard a screech like a giant bird.

Alyx, still at her back, said, “Christ’s blood, what was that?” but Mara didn’t stop to answer nor look about. At that moment, she was in a contest with a Spanish knight and to give way to distraction was to leave herself open to death.

Some minutes later, after she had brought her opponent down and driven Dentelyon through his ribs, she became aware that the Con Permiso guard was in retreat. She and Alyx were no longer encircled. She heard shouts from the Spanish captains, but there was too much confusion on the muddy field to make sense of their commands. Once the last Spaniard had fled, Mara advanced to a small rise above the town where she could watch her Norman soldiers in eager pursuit of the retreating lines of Spanish pikes.

Alyx embraced her, delighted that they were both still alive. “But what do you think happened? They’re running like rabbits.”

“I don’t know.”

They flagged down a young knight and sent him ahead to discover what news.

“I think we’ve won,” Mara told her friend, “but I’d like to hear them say it.”

She located her horse and found another for Alyx after they put the broken-legged animal out of its pain. This horse had been Alyx’s own since she’d received her commission at Storm Port; she grieved as Mara cut its throat.

As they rode to the town gates, they met the young knight again. “The Spanish have put down their arms,” he explained. “They await you, My Prince. They plead for your mercy.”

A battered Spanish captain met them at the town gate to offer terms for surrender. He claimed he spoke in place of the Teniente, now dead.

“Was he killed on the field?” Mara inquired.

“No, Fearsome Prince.” And the captain crossed himself.

She never did learn what exactly had happened to Con Permiso’s Teniente. The Spanish prisoners whispered of it, but some of their stories were so strange and fabulous she could only attribute these wild rumors to the ignorance and superstition of the rabble or the poisonous deceit of the more sophisticated. The most plausible tale Mara heard was that the Teniente had been mauled by some sort of beast. There were lions in these mountains, she knew; one had perhaps been flushed from its cover by the fury of the battle and in its panic attacked the first luckless person it met. But this didn't explain why the Spanish prisoners held her responsible for the man's death. Whatever evil had befallen the Teniente, they blamed her for it. They feared and despised her as the captives at Spainfort never had.

The image of the Sonnedragon *did* strike fear. Mara's device was ever-present now: her Shieldmaids displayed its likeness. Young Arthur bore it on her standard. Flags bearing the green dragon flew over every captured town and fortress. The Spanish knew her by it and they cursed the sight of it. They called her a bloodlusty conqueror who cut down her foes without mercy. Tales of her cruelty in battle preceded her on her march to the heart of Terrojos. She heard the furtive murmurings of the captured; their name for her, *Destazadora*, had an ugly sound to it.

Well, she was ferocious on the battlefield. Alyx called her fighting style "a blind rage," but Mara knew that it wasn't rage that drove her. Rather, she felt as if her moving body were a separate thing from her essential self, as if her consciousness had risen to some more abstract level where she observed her own actions with dispassionate interest. She saw what she had to do to defeat her opponents and she did it swiftly. Neither fear nor anger nor doubt influenced her; nothing caused her to hesitate. She might have been mowing grain in a field.

The sun was bright as she cut down the onslaught of foes. All her attention was focused on the flashing metal before her. She fought, action and reaction. Swing, duck, charge. She didn't pause until the last Spaniard fell before her, or Alyx gripped her shield-arm elbow and said, "Mara, for the love of God, stop!"

But she wasn't merciless. She gave a quick and clean death whenever she could and she withheld her sword when her foes cried for quarter. She acted without malice; now that she had met the Spanish, she didn't hate them—not as many of her company did. She was as adamant as ever against the mistreatment of prisoners and the civilian population. No brutalities were committed in her name. If she was harsh on the battlefield, she was equally harsh in punishing her own soldiers when they transgressed against her laws. And they adored her for it. For them, the Sonnedragon was an object of veneration. Her troops roared in admiration at the sight of her shield.

She thought that her good fortune must be the Sonnedragon's doing. What else could she think, when victory after victory was so easily obtained? She was a good general and her troops well-seasoned by the end of the summer, but this streak of peculiar luck could only be attributed to divine intervention. Mara gave ardent prayers of thankfulness after each successful battle.

Her prayers were heard; Mara was certain of it. Surely, God had turned His favor from the Spaniards. They were Christian too, and they must pray for victory as she did, but nothing seemed to go well for them. Mishap followed mysterious misfortune. The portent was clear: God had bestowed His highest blessings on her enterprise.

In these weeks of battle, she learned a great deal about the nature of the God she served. This wasn't the Heavenly Father of her childhood, but a more ancient aspect of the Deity. This was the jealous, lightning-bolt hurling Jehovah, the vengeful Wuldorfaeder of her Anglo-Saxon ancestors, the Crusaders' Lord. This was the God of War in Righteous Cause. His enemies were hers. Blood was His worship.

Daily, she was anointed. This was the sacrifice demanded—the price of her service to Higher Powers. Blood splashed into her face, trickling hot down her cheeks beneath her faceguard. Her war-paint, a green device upon her brow like the dragon's wings, was obscured by it. Her braids were stiff with it. The leather lining of her mailshirt was soaked and even the linen beneath was stained. Her boots were caked thick with red. Mara didn't notice while she fought, but in the evenings she was always astonished at how quickly the water turned red when she bathed. It disturbed her to think of how many she must have killed to drench herself so, and it disturbed her more that she couldn't recall them. Her memory of the battle was a confusion of flailing arms and glinting mail and steel.

At the end of October, they stormed the Ciudadela de Tolo Invencible and the Gobernador Francisco formally surrendered Terrojos. Mara intended to rename it Kharlesmarch in honor of the Emperor who had given her this glorious opportunity. She called it by this name in her first dispatches. Yet it remained the Redlands on the lips of the common soldiers—the Redlyon's old name for the conquered territory, a simple translation from the

Spanish. And so it became.

Spain demanded Naufarre as recompense for the captured march, but Kharles replied that they had first broken the treaty and all rights to the land were forfeit. Spain would have Naufarre only if they could take it from him. It was possible that they might do so; the war there was not going well.

In the newly-named Redlands, there were spoils and riches for all. The wealth of the city treasuries was distributed among the soldiers as pay. Spanish citizens and peons paid tribute and were allowed an unmolested retreat to Iardinez. Captive officers and the Gobernador himself were ransomed. Don Miguel's family paid handsomely for his release and he too departed under safe escort—and with great relief, Mara imagined.

Before Miguel left Spainfort, he presented her with a gift.

"I thank you for your kindness to myself and my officers," the young nobleman said during the inventory of the chapel treasures—this had been delayed until after the chaplain was ransomed. "You have sheltered us with your gracious protection when your own officers might have cut our throats. You sent your own kinswoman away when you learned how she had conducted herself in the capture of this fortress. I call you most civilized, Dread Prince."

Mara smiled. Miguel didn't know the full story of Kat's dismissal, but it was natural for him to assume that she'd done it for his sake, after their confidential conversation, and be grateful. "I might say the same of you, Don Teniente."

"The chaplain showed me this hidden treasure when I first took command of *Los Ojos*." Miguel went to the crucifix behind the chapel altar. Reaching above the stripped tabernacle, he removed the metal rods which pinned the bleeding hands of the Christ to the cross, and to the wall. The crucifix swung to one side. Miguel extracted a small, polished wooden box from a niche behind the feet. "Such a prize ought not be divided with the common spoils. It belongs to you alone." He offered it to her with a slight, ceremonial flourish. "Prince Margueryt, I give you the gem missing from the famous Prince Denys's swordhilt."

"The Black Ruby?" Brief examination revealed that it was neither a true ruby nor black, but an inferior gem the dull color of dried blood with a dark flaw at its heart, refracted through its multiple facts. "This can't be it."

"My Prince, I assure you it is. It has been kept in the care of the chaplains for many years."

Mara unfolded the parchment square tucked into the bottom of the box beneath the silk wrappings. "Can you read this? It's in Spanish."

"Certainly." Don Miguel came to her aid. "It is a verification written in the hand of a Padre of this chapel many years ago. The first line reads: *Herein lies the red stone taken from the sword of Prince Denys.*"

Mara studied the incomprehensible lines of faded script. She had picked up a useful phrase or two of Spanish in her contact with Miguel and other prisoners, but not enough to make sense of this. Strung through the *el*'s and *de la*'s were words she recognized: *Denys* was there, unmistakable. The name wasn't used by the Spaniards; it could only refer to the one Norman Prince of that name who was well-known in this part of the world. *Infant* was Prince. *Roja* was red. *Espada* was sword. She knew that much. *Joya* might be jewel or gemstone. Miguel's translation seemed to be accurate. Could this truly be the famed, long-missing hiltstone?

"And what's the rest of this? There is more written here."

"The good Padre tells the tale of how the gem came to be in the possession of *Los Ojos*. I thought of it when I heard of your vision, Prince Mara. The stone from the sword named Dragonsfang is the Dragon's Eye. Therefore, it is yours."

"If it belongs to anyone rightfully, it is Marchion Khrystophania," answered Mara. "It ought to be restored to her."

She meant to return the stone to Khrystophania, but somehow it didn't seem worth the trouble. Legends had built the Black Ruby into a magnificent stone, and this lackluster gem would be a disappointment if she were to present it to Denys's one living descendant. Besides, she began to think that Miguel had been right to give it to her. Was not the dragon's eye one of her promised gifts? If any true object was represented by that name, this must be it.

In the end, Mara kept the gemstone. The pressing matters of warfare occupied her for many weeks and after that, she was engaged in the important business of governing the Redlands in her Emperor's name until Kharles could give his attention to the land she had conquered.

In mid-November, Lieutenant Uismarde was appointed Provisional Governor of the Redlands. A residual force was left in her command while the remainder of the Northlander troops withdrew and disbanded to their homes and city garrisons.

Mara returned home by Christmas.

Pendaunzel
1955

quarten

"Peter, I think I am accursed."

Peter Scholar, the court magician, looked up at Mara in the doorway of his private chambers, startled by her presence as much as by this strange announcement. "You, My Prince? You've never been more victorious."

"But that's exactly why. I think the Spanish have put a curse upon me in revenge."

Since her return to Pendaunzel two months ago, she had been plagued by dreams. Night after night, the Sonnedragon wove its way through her sleep, manipulating the circumstances of her triumph: its serpentine length slithered soundlessly between the kegs of cannon powder at Spainfort and exploded them with a gentle blast of fiery breath. The beat of its vast wings drove the rainclouds into the hills where the Spanish archers hid. A taloned claw swept down, disemboweling the Con Permiso commander. When she awoke, her heart pounded, her nightshirt was soaked with chilling perspiration and she was a-tremble, but not with fear.

What she felt was exaltation. The Sonnedragon rampaged through her blood. It thrilled to the fight. It desired more. It urged her to repeat her past glories and promised even greater victories. Mara had imagined that once she attained her goal in Terrojos, this craving for activity would be sated. And yet she was restless. Throughout the winter, she felt the beast pace within her; she couldn't endure to sit still at Pendaunzel.

She sought the Duke's physician, Dr. Dimitrios, first. He found no sign of illness. Her wound had healed beautifully. Her health was excellent. He suggested more exercise. After her campaigns last summer, she was strained by the idleness of courtly life. On his advice, Mara sparred with any available partner. She rode with the Pendaunzel courtiers on the Christmas hunt; the gallop through the snowy hills in pursuit of deer had quieted her. After the holidays, she rode out on her own, at first with a falcon or dogs but more often unaccompanied. She brought down rabbits and turkeys; her skill as a bowswoman seemed much better than it had ever been before. On mild nights, when there was little snow and the wind wasn't strong enough to cut through her woolen hose, she roasted her day's kill over a campfire and bedded in the wildwood above the city. She slept better in her impromptu camps than in her own bed and she returned to Pendaunzel rested, certain there would be no further trouble. Until she dreamed again.

Ordinary medicine had no power to aid her. What she needed was the advice of an experienced magician. Although she didn't often speak to Peter, he was in her father's service and obliged to serve her as well. She didn't doubt he would be willing to do as she asked.

She unknotted the leather tether about her neck and held out the red stone. "Do you know what this is?"

"No," Peter answered as he took the stone dangling before his eyes. "A charm?"

"It was once called the Black Ruby. It belonged to Prince Denys. The Spanish took it as a prize at his death and it's been in their hands these one hundred and twenty years—or so I was informed by the Spaniard who gave it me." Miguel had been meek and well-mannered, but he had also been a prisoner in fear of his life. She would never know what he truly thought of her. Was his gift a parting shot of revenge? "This was in the box with it." She had brought the parchment square with her, and gave this to Peter too. "Can you read Spanish?"

"Not well, but there are many people in the Palace who do." Peter tucked the parchment into the breast pocket of his loose-fitting robe.

"My Spaniard claimed that the stone was rightfully mine, that it betokened my talisman beast. It may be true—who can say? I only know I haven't worn it with comfort since I came home. I think I have been ensorcelled."

"Your pardon, My Prince, but I don't think that's possible. I've never heard of such a spell save in a fairytale. Such magic is a thing of superstition, I assure you."

Mara wasn't convinced. Peter hadn't been witness to the bizarre streak of good fortune she had enjoyed since the gemstone had been given to her. He couldn't know how the Sonnedragon raged within her even now. "You once told me that you had the power to divine the secrets of an object in your clasp. Peter, will you do it now for me? Can you receive any impressions from this?"

"I shall try."

Peter rose to poke up the dying embers of his sitting-room fire, then sat down on the hearthrug with his legs folded beneath him, leaving his one comfortable chair to his guest. Mara sat and watched the magician bow his head as if he were at prayer and press the stone between his palms.

"Two brothers," he said softly after a moment. "One red-haired, armed for battle, red with gore. The lion on a field red. Red as blood. The other is fair. Handsome. Honey-colored hair. His gear is also blood-stained. Red. He bears the *fleur-de-lys*."

"Eduarde and Denys," said Mara. "It must be."

"A treasure-room," said Peter. "They've kicked in the door. A holy Brother. The red-haired brother falls upon the sealed caskets. He breaks the locks with his swordhilt. Treasures spill on the floor. Colors in the light. Gemstones. Gold cups. Silver crucifixes and ivory beads. Rosaries. Holy artifacts. Saints' blood and bone. He plays with them. The fair one wades through his brother's toys. He looks– He sees something else. A box? A long box. Polished. Bright wood. A golden lock, a seal. A castle keep.

"*Goode Brother, what's in here?*"

Mara started at the abrupt change in Peter's voice. These last words were not spoken in the magician's normal accent of an educated Anglo-Saxon, hard on consonants, clipped on vowels, but in the more flowing accents of an old-fashioned imperial courtier. The *r*'s were trilled and there was a soft slur at the ends of the words, turning *brother* to *brothah*, *here* to *heah*. It might've been called effete if not for the steel-edged hint of authority underlying the simple question. Though the voice was pleasant, it demanded an answer.

"*'Tis no treasure, My Lord.*" Now, Peter sounded tremulous, halting, as if he were foreign-born and had difficulty with the Norman tongue. Mara had heard more than enough Spanish-speaking people in this past year to recognize the accent. Was this meant to be the voice of the monk? "*'Tis not worthy of your notice, when there is so much greater wealth that is yours to take.*" Peter gestured as if gems and holy relics were scattered on the floor before him.

"*Then why do you keep it here among your treasures? It bears the crest of the house of Castile. Surely it must be worth something.*" This was the courtly Norman's voice again. Denys? The tone was amused, yet doubting. He didn't believe the monk but he was willing to wheedle the truth from him.

"*We preserve,*" the monk-voice struggled with this word. "*It is our grave office. Dread Prince, I pray you do not look upon it.*"

"Does he open the box?" asked Mara. If she were in this situation, her curiosity would only be increased by such hesitant warnings. "What's in it?"

"*A sword!*" the voice of Denys cried. "*Eddie, we have an accursed sword!*" Peter moved his arms as if he unwrapped the sword from its wadding cloths and held it up to examine the blade.

"*What curse lies upon it?*" This was a new voice, similar to Denys's but a half-tone deeper. Gruff while Denys laughed. The young Redlyon?

"*It gives great triumph to he who bears it, Lord Prince,*" the Spanish voice explained. "*It makes great temptations. Our kings bore this sword in days long past, 'til the sainted Ignatius brought it to our care. It is no thing of God's design. Only a warrior of the purest heart may be so bold to wield it and not be swayed by its corruption.*"

This vision enacted by Peter confirmed what Mara had already guessed. Miguel had not lied; this unimpressive little gem was truly the famed Black Ruby stolen from Prince Denys's swordhilt. All she had heard seemed to fit the known history of Dragonsfang: the sword had been part of the spoils of a monastery, won by Denys in his first campaigns at Madehef.

"A sword," said Peter, "Silver spells engraved at the blade's edge. Spells on its hilt. Bind it to the steel. A worthy vessel. *The sword, O Prince, is so sharp as the dragon's fang.*

"Put the accursed thing away! Let it never see daylight nor touch another human soul. Unclean thing!

"It is no thing of evil. It is only the instrument.

"The sword on the sand, its blade red. A sealed box, a holy place. *We preserve.*

"I want it."

Then Peter laughed. *"Didn't you hear, Eddie? Only the pure of heart may wield this sword. Little brother, that certainly isn't you."*

Mara tried to follow this babble. The voices of Eduarde and Denys were easily distinguishable from Peter's own trance-whisper, but there were other voices she didn't recognize. Someone had called the sword accursed, just as she thought the stone must be. Was this meant to be the voice of the sainted King Ignatius?

She wished she knew more of Ignatius's reign. All she could recall from her schooling was that he had been an extremely pious king who had ruled Spain more than a century before Denys's first African campaign. Long before that, hadn't Spain been ruled by generations of powerful kings and queens? There were legends of their might, centuries past now. Mara wished, again, that she'd paid more attention to her Spanish history. Until now, she had scorned it. What patriotic Norman cared to hear of the glorious achievements of their most hated enemy? She recalled that the kingdoms of Andaluz, Castile, Leon, and Aragon had united after the Moors had been driven from their lands. She knew that Spain had captured Naufarre in those long-ago days, and Portugal too, and then they had sent their ships to conquer the New World. Even today, Spanish colonies occupied more of the Atlantean continent than either the Norman or Scandinavian domains. But the names of the conquerors, the details of their victories, were not remembered. Had there been tales of a fabulous sword which belonged to these victorious Spaniards? Mara thought she'd once heard something like this, but her memory of it was vague and the fragments she did recall were so fantastic that the tale seemed more likely to refer to mythic Excalibur than to the early history of Dragonsfang.

Peter spoke suddenly in a hissing whisper: *"You are his*

squire, Margad. You can take it. One sword is like another to a warrior such as our brother. Put another in its place and bring Dragonsfang to me. He won't notice the substitution."

Mara drew a sharp intake of breath. This was the Redlyon's voice.

"Spaniards!" Peter yelped. "The camp invaded. *Where is it? Margad, my sword!* There are too many! Oh, he is lost!"

Mara sat silently, watching Peter yet not seeing him. She was stunned. Could this be true? Could such treachery lay at the heart of the most famous tale in modern Norman history? Mara had too much faith in the powers of magic to mistrust Peter's visions, but the scene he had just described was too appalling to accept without question.

Could it be true? Eduarde had envied his brother's success. No, that was no surprise. He had attributed Denys's inexorable progress to his bespelled sword. Again, this wasn't so strange a thing. But could he have stolen it? And, more disturbing still, had both Denys and Margad died because of this theft? This was more than Mara could bear to consider. Her heroic grandfather a thief and betrayer! The murder of the Princes had been the great tragedy of the pre-Eduardian era. Indeed, it had been the making of the Eduardian era, for the Redlyon had waged every war against the Spanish with his brothers' names as his battle-cry. How could Eduarde have brought it about?

Jealous, the young Redlyon might have been, but Mara believed he had truly loved and admired Denys. Even if he envied his elder brother's glory enough to think of stealing it, he could never have wished to see the Bright Prince dead. The results of his treachery—if there had truly been treachery—must have horrified him. His guilt must have been unassuageable.

"The broken sword," said Peter, as he emerged from his trance.

The broken sword. The device of the Dennefort family.

Eduarde had not kept Dragonsfang. He had left the sword to the first Khrystophania. She might have been Empress; he had made her Marchion. Had he sacrificed the prize he'd betrayed his brother to gain as an act of atonement? Had Eduarde, in taking what he desired, discovered he couldn't live with it?

Perhaps, thought Mara, Peter did not speak of the symbolic

shattered blade of Dennefort, but of a sword with its hilt damaged, with a stone torn from its setting. Dragonsfang. The broken sword. The Black Ruby had been stolen.

Another thought more sinister occurred to her: perhaps Eduarde hadn't surrendered his prize out of repentance. Had he left Dragonsfang to the Dennefort family because he thought it wasn't worth keeping? His wars against Spain—Were they fought to seek revenge for Denys's murder, or did Eduarde attempt to recapture something he thought the Spanish had taken from him? Did he believe what Mara now suspected, that the famous sword was not the true source of Denys's uncanny success?

Mara had negotiated to have Dragonsfang herself during her brief stop at Dennefort on her way home, but Khrystophania, still mourning her brother, wasn't willing to surrender it. Mara might have taken it by force, but even if she considered herself its rightful owner, she felt it indecent to insult her allies by snatching the sword from the possession of the grief-stricken Marchion. It was then, when Dragonsfang had not fallen into her hands, that she'd begun to doubt that she was meant to have it. Her literal interpretation of the Sonnedragon's promise must be wrong.

Peter blinked, dazed. Perspiration beaded his ginger mustache and pale brow. He was obviously shaken by the intensity of his scrying. The stone dropped from his fingers.

Mara hunted about the room until she found a nearly full decanter of pinkish wine on a sideboard and poured out a tumbler. "Peter, drink." As she knelt to offer the wine, she scooped up the fallen stone. "Are you well?"

The magician lifted his head from his hands to sip. He breathed in and out slowly, sipped again, then nodded. "I've never *seen* so vividly before," he told her with an apologetic smile.

"But you've given me my answer. The stone is the talisman, not the sword." She squeezed it in her fist. "My little gem gave Denys his victory. Its bearer cannot lose."

Miguel couldn't have known of the stone's power; he would never have given it to her if he had, but kept it for himself. The siege at Spainfort, the conquest of Terrojos, might have gone very differently if Miguel had possessed the gemstone. But he had given it away, to a Norman Prince. Perhaps he thought it cursed.

Perhaps he thought it worthless. Obviously, it hadn't aided the Spanish while sealed in its box in the chapel. It must be possessed by one master. Mara could only think that this was truly a piece of the Sonnedragon's promised legacy; it was meant to belong to her.

"You said you thought it was accursed," said Peter.

"I did," Mara agreed. "I know better now. Perhaps the gem is a blight to one whose heart is tainted. Eduarde–" She hesitated to allude to this betrayal. Her grandfather had always been a hero to her. "The Redlyon sought to take it by dishonest means, and so it leapt from its setting—or else Margad knocked it out by an accident of fate—and no good came of his treachery. But Denys..."

Mara thought of the laughing voice she had heard Peter imitate. Truly, it belonged to a noble Prince, for it was so like the handsome, fair image of Denys she'd seen all her life. No, nothing evil had ever touched that brave heart.

"If the Spanish legend is true, the thing is dangerous. A great wizard must have impressed it with remarkable magics—though I have no idea how. There are no marks of spellcraft upon it." Peter's fingers brushed the hearthrug and he discovered that Mara had taken the gem. "It may be nothing but a flawed gemstone and the legends no more than fancy tales. May I keep the script you found with it for further study, Prince Mara?"

"Yes, of course," Mara answered absently; her mind was already racing on. Whatever uncanny power the stone retained, it was not cursed. The possessor brought his own influence to it, for good or ill. She had taken it honestly. She bore no taint. She wouldn't be corrupted. With this talisman, she might ride to any battle of her choosing and she would never be defeated. Her restless desire for warfare might be sated. The Sonnedragon had promised as much and she'd seen enough to believe that such promises could be fulfilled.

She tossed the gemstone up into the air and caught it again.

The next morning, when the court assembled at the Othelie chapel for Ash Wednesday Mass, Mara sought out Bel. The captain was the only one of her companions who had accompanied her back to Pendaunzel.

"I think of leading another campaign against the Spanish this summer," she said softly as they took seats in the forward pew. Although the benches behind them filled rapidly with bleary-eyed courtiers who had been up late at the Grand Tuesday revelries, none would join the Prince and her captain without explicit invitation. Their conversation wouldn't be interrupted.

"Mara!" Bel was delighted at the announcement. "So soon?"

"So soon as I can." After a night during which she had turned more restlessly than usual, she knew she must choose her course of action swiftly.

"What of My Lord Duke? Will he allow it?"

"I fear not."

"I hoped that after we had marched once, he would have no reason to refuse a second time–" Bel stopped abruptly as the murmuring courtiers behind her fell silent and rose to their feet. The Duke had entered the chapel. Dafythe moved slowly down the center aisle past them, a herald supporting each elbow, and took his usual seat in the boxed pew to the immediate right of the altar, beneath the stained-glass window depicting the Sainted Othelie converting the pagan tribes. The chaplain had only been waiting for the Duke's arrival to begin the Mass. Once Dafythe and his heralds had settled themselves, the priest blessed the congregation—*In Nomine Patris, et Filii, et Spiritus Sancti*—and began the penitent's prayer:

"Spare me, Almighty Lord Our God,
For I have sinned in thought and word and deed.
Mea culpa, mea culpa, mea maxima culpa."

Mara and Bel knelt for the invocation, elbows upon the rail and heads bowed. Bel glanced up at the Duke.

"Where?" she hissed.

Where indeed? Mara had spent the night at this question and had not yet formed a satisfactory answer.

"Iardinez is the logical target," the Prince whispered, her face hidden against her upraised arms. "Much of our army remains in the Redlands, not one hundred miles from the new border. But now that the Redlands have been restored to Norman rule, we can expect no threat from *that* quarter. The Spaniards to our south go in terror of me these days, since we filled their sanctuaries with

Terrojos refugees. Tales carried."

Bel chuckled.

"*Kyrie eleison*," the priest intoned.

"*Christe eleison*," the congregation responded.

"*Kyrie eleison*."

"If not Iardinez, where?" asked Bel. "The nearest Spanish territories elsewise are the marches north of Tenochitland. Not that I mind where we go. Wherever you choose, Mara, I'll ride with you. Only give me the opportunity to have at those bastards again—*Christe eleison*!"

More than once, Mara had observed that Bel was too eager to lay her hands on the Spanish. She hated them with a passion. She looked forward to another war only because it enabled her to spill more of their blood. But were Mara's reasons any more noble?

> "Cast me not from Thy presence, O Lord, but embrace me to Thy Bosom.
> Deliver me from blood-guiltiness, and I shall sing of Thy Glory.
> When Thou open'st my lips, Lord God, praise of thy works shalt flow.
> Thou desirest no greater sacrifice, else would I give it Thee."

Her God demanded blood spilt in his name. That, more than her restless craving for excitement, more than promise of victory, drove her on. But she didn't act from hatred. This was no base lust for revenge. Her desire served a higher purpose. The blood was her sacrifice. It was the praise she offered to the Almighty. His foes were her foes. With her sword, she cut her obeisance.

> "O Merciful Lord, wash from me my wickedness and cleanse from me my sins.
> Against Thee have I sinned and evil have I committed in Thy sight.
> For I was conceived in wickedness, and in sin hath my mother borne me.
> But Thou shalt grant divine truth unto my heart."

The blood spattered hot on her face. It stained her princely tunic. It ran down her face like teardrops. And nightly, she washed the blood away.

"My soul shall be purged of all corruption and be made whiter than snow."

The prayer concluded, the priest moved among the congregation to place the ashes upon each brow. As he passed from one penitent to the next, he repeated the same phrase: "*Memento, pulvis es et in pulverem reverteris.*"

Remember: Dust thou art and to dust shalt thou return.

The priest smeared the ashes upon her brow.

"*Memento.*"

Bodies lay dead and dying on the battlefield. Blood seeped from the wound in her shoulder. The sun blazed into her eyes.

Pray for us sinners, now, at the hour of our death.

"Amen," she whispered. Her hand went from her brow to her breast to form the sign of the cross, but she stopped in mid-genuflexion to clasp the red stone.

She offered a prayer of her own: *O Lord Almighty, as I am Thy most humble servant and the instrument of Thy will, guide me to Thy use. You give me gifts of great power—show me how I am to wield them. You grant me victory in all battles—show me the land I shall conquer. Show me the way I am meant to go.*

Next came the presentation of the holy gifts. The priest's attendants filled the silver communion chalice with red wine; the host was brought from the tabernacle and placed on the silver salver. The priest moved toward Dafythe first. Rank and age gave the Duke the privilege of remaining where he was, while the rest of the congregation filed in turn to the altar to receive the body and blood of Christ.

Mara and Bel rose first. Ambris, shepherding the heralds, joined them. They knelt on the single step before the altar, in the dapples of green, yellow and rose-colored light from the tiny panes of Othelie window. Colors danced over them.

Vast green-scaled wings spread into translucency.

The priest offered Mara the host.

"*Accipite. Hic est corpus meum.*"

The host was placed upon her tongue. The chalice was offered.

"*Accipite. Hic est sanguines mei.*"

A single tear of blood dropping from the Sonnedragon's curving claw.

This is my blood.

Mara drank, dissolving the wafer with the wine before she swallowed it.

There was the final prayer, and then Mass concluded. The congregation rose.

"Bel, I pray you that no word of my plans reach my father's ears `til I am ready," Mara whispered as they shuffled toward the doors. I ought to decide where I'm going before I speak to him–"

She stepped out of the chapel, and a blast of heat nearly knocked her back.

The sun was dazzling. Mara blinked and lifted a hand to shield her eyes. The scene before her was not the little churchyard she'd known all her life, with its twin rows of shrubbery flanking the path to the ducal mausoleum, and the bare trees not yet in flower obscuring the walls of the Manor.

This was a desert. The sky was brilliant blue without a cloud, the sun searing white. Heat scorched her cheeks and dry air cracked her lips and reached even into her lungs. Tough-looking tufts of tall, faded grass studded the dirty yellow hills before her.

Atop a massive platform of wind-sculpted rock in the distance, dark in silhouette against the blazing sky, sat a fortress. This was no Spainfort, nor even the size of Alcazar Norte or the citadel of Tolo Invencible. It was tiny, but inaccessible upon its perch. The broad, glistening line of a river curved about its base and another, smaller stream flowed into the greater.

In her head, she heard the voice of the dragon: *It is thine, O Prince.*

"Mara?"

She blinked. There was a hand on her shoulder. Bel stood at her side.

"Mara, what is it?"

They stood in the churchyard of the Othelie chapel on a dreary and grey February morning. "What happened?"

"I would ask you the same," Bel answered. "You've been staring at the sun as if you'd never seen it before. I thought you were in a fit."

"No, I'm fine." She took the hand from her shoulder, squeezing once before she released it. "Everything's going to be fine. We're going to go."

"Iardinez?"

"No, somewhere else." That desert land she'd seen couldn't be any part of swampy Iardinez. But where could it be? She'd been shown her goal; now, she must find the path.

The large, square map featuring the eastern half of Atlantea was spread flat on the table in the Hall of Record, its curling corners weighted with an inkpot, a seal of office, and two candlesticks. The Northlands was tinted pale blue. The Norman marches, to the south and west, were lavender. In the upper right corner, not far above the circle of gold paint which symbolized Pendaunzel, was Scandinavian Uinland in green. The Spanish territories bordering the southern edges were yellow. The coastal regions were represented in great detail, with the smallest villages, rivers, and roads clearly labeled, but as the map progressed westward, fewer details were provided. Only the principal rivers and towns of the western marches were given their names. Beyond the Michelne River, so it was said, lay vast, green forests, a grassy desert populated by nomadic pagan tribes, and a range of mountains far greater than the Spirit Mountains which provided the Northlands' western boundary. Unclaimed and unexplored, these fantastic features did not appear.

"Here." Mara placed her left hand upon a yellow-tinted cluster of territories in the south-western corner of the map.

"The Apostolistas," said Ambris. "What do you wish to know of them?"

"They are a mystery to me," Mara answered. "This map gives their names—Santiuan, Santemarco, Santeluq, Santematteo, Santiago, Santomasso, Santebartolo—but nothing more. I know they are desert lands, but where are the cities, the fortresses? Who governs them? I know nothing of their history. I don't even have an answer as to why there are only seven of them, and not the twelve which ought properly to be there. Not that I'm not glad of it, else the Spanish would try to make up the other five from our marches."

Mara didn't normally visit the Hall of Record. Her presence

here alone had excited Ambris's suspicions. He must guess why she took an interest in these Spanish lands and, caught in the act, she could only explain herself as if she'd meant to seek his counsel from the first.

She had several reasons for avoiding Ambris. First, would he believe her? He'd been skeptical the last time they'd gone to hear Magician Peter's visions. He would call her mad if she said she'd received one of her own. Mara was glad she'd left the Spanish parchment with Peter; Ambris, no doubt, could read it in an instant and solve her mystery for her, but even faced with that evidence, he would question her belief that she could achieve any victory she desired through the powers of an unimpressive red gemstone. Second, Ambris was her most trusted advisor, but he was also Dafythe's Chancellor. His duty to the Duke must come first, and Mara would rather not place him in a position where he must choose between them. Third, he would tell Father of her plans, and she wasn't ready for *that.*

"What can you tell me about them?" she asked again.

"They are not greatly peopled," her brother answered. "There is a military presence, but the inland territories aren't settled, not by very many Spanish citizens at any rate. Wild, aboriginal folk live there. The principal fortress in each is governed by a *conde*, which is something like a marchion, a military governor who may be of noble birth. The marches along the coast of the Tenochitland Sea are more populous and more valued because of their ports. Tenochitland itself is protected from the north by the Great River—*Rio Grande*, they call it—as the Northlands' marches are protected by the width of the Michelne. That land between the two rivers has always been of worry the Spanish, and so they established these marches to guard their principle colonies. Our westward marches are there for the same reason."

"Yes, I see. Santiago borders the Jamesmarch." The two marches were separated by the blue line of a smaller, unnamed river which ran southward into the Tenochitland Sea.

"Iago is the Spanish version of James," Ambris explained.

"Have we a more detailed map of the region?"

"The Apostolistas have never been surveyed by Norman mapmakers, but perhaps there are copies of Spanish maps about. The clerks will look. Mara, what are you planning?"

She smiled at him. "My next campaign."

Ambris nodded, as if this was no more than he'd expected to hear. "Have you spoken to Father?"

"No, not yet." Mara paused. "Will you tell him?" she asked in the tone of a young girl caught in some naughtiness.

"He suspects that you intend to march again, though he could never guess the particulars. I am surprised myself at your choice."

"Will you tell?" she repeated.

Ambris considered, and answered honestly, "No, Mara. You ought to. It will go best for you if you present him with a coherent plan. When do you propose to go?"

"This summer if I can. As soon as possible."

"Have you thought of how you will reach the Apostolistas? That journey isn't like the march to the Shieldwall. There's no paved road to lead you past every town and city capable of supporting thousands of soldiers."

"There is the Guylliamesburghe Road."

"Which stops at Guylliamesburghe, hundreds of miles short of your goal. Past that, you'll find nothing but small towns, farms, and hamlets. The western fortresses are not half the size of Dennefort. Some are simple camps circled by walls of wood. The roads are footpaths and woodland trails. If you travel alone, it is a journey of three or four months. How can you place an army there by the summer?"

"I shall send them through the ports of the Eduardesmarch and the Redlands," Mara answered after some thought. "I can commission ships to transport them to here–" She tapped the blue line some hundred miles north of where the Michelne flowed into the Tenochitland Sea. "As you say, there are small towns and fortresses along the great river. No more than one or two companies will burden each. From there, `tis a short journey across the Jamesmarch. Those who travel from the north with me will ride along the Guylliamesburghe Road `til we meet the River Myame. Barges will convey us down. That cannot take more than two months."

"Where will you get the barges?"

"If none are available, I shall have them made," Mara answered promptly.

"And how will you feed so great a number?" Ambris

continued the catechism.

"Supplies can be shipped along with the troops, and after the armies are in place, convoys can carry them from the river ports."

"You will do all this by the summer?"

"I must go as soon as I can. I promise you, Ambris, one good strike, and you and I will see no trouble from Spain for the rest of our lives."

Ambris smiled at her enthusiasm. "If you conquer all the world before you are Duke, Mara, what will you do afterwards?"

"I shall have other duties to attend to then. A Duke can't go riding off to make war in the borderlands every year. What better way to begin my reign than with those borders safe?"

"You are very certain of victory."

Mara nodded.

Ambris was right. On all points, his advice had been sound. Mara blushed now when she thought of all the practical matters she hadn't considered, but had leapt impulsively from the promise of her vision to the first likely target. Sure of her eventual success, she had thought only of the place. True, given the Sonnedragon's elusive but awesome powers, Santiago might suffer an earthquake and slide into the sea before she ever approached it, but she couldn't rely upon so miraculous a conquest.

Victory required planning: strategy, supply, weaponry, deployment of troops. It also required an extensive knowledge of the territory in question. Mara was ashamed at her ignorance of the lands which bordered her own dukedom. She knew their names, but little else. When she had not looked upon them as potential targets for invasion, she hadn't cared. What were marches hundreds of miles away? But Ambris had been so well-informed. As Prince and future Duke, she ought to possess this same information. There was so much she needed to know about Santiago and its neighbors before she could lead an army there. Rely on magic to carry her victory? She knew better than that!

She simply would not be able to prepare an army for war this summer. The time wasn't right. Most of her important officers were in the Redlands, but they were there because the Emperor continued to wrestle with Juan Maria's rebellion in Naufarre and had no time to appoint his own governor or garrison imperial troops. She couldn't remove her own troops until Kharles provided replacements. In addition, her personal staff was in disarray. Of her Shieldmaid companions, Bel alone was in Pendaunzel. Sataumie remained in command of Spainfort and Alyx aided Lieutenant Uismarde with the provisional government at Cuidadela de Tolo Invencible. Kat was still at Dennefort; her child wouldn't be born for another month. Mara didn't even have a squire: after their return to Pendaunzel, her nephew Arthur had entered the city's chapter house of the Order of the Holy Knights of Saint John—the Hospitalers—to prepare for his knighting. She hadn't yet chosen another. Once he turned sixteen, Bertrande would leave his place as Dafythe's herald to become squire to his brother Eadrik. Ambris's next children, Marcius and Mathilde, were at school at the Abbey of St. Samandra and were not old enough to be presented at court. She didn't know any of the unclaimed Pendaunzel children well enough to bestow this particular honor upon one of them.

Mara considered Ren. She had consulted the girl's mother at Storm Port and received permission for Ren to continue in her service. Alekeeper Adyna was delighted at the request, preferring to have her daughter in the protection of the Prince at Pendaunzel rather than in the Marches, even though Ren had been no nearer the battle than Dennefort. Mara didn't know why the girl was necessary to her future, but Peter had *seen* her and the Prince trusted this vision. Ren was a respectable gentyl-maid and she might as well stay on, but Mara was bound by her promise not to receive the girl as her squire. Though she gave the girl lessons in the battle-arts from time to time, Ren would not bear her shield or sword.

So, her quest must be postponed for a time. A disappointment, but one she could endure. She would reach Santiago eventually—it was inevitable—and even though she would not march this summer, her months of waiting wouldn't be wasted. This delay gave her time to plan. She would learn all she could of the Apostolistas, and discover exactly where the fortress of her vision lay waiting for her. She had time to contract barges for her river journey, commission ships, gather supplies. She also had time to think of effective arguments to convince her father to let her go.

Ambris had been right about Father too. She ought to speak to him.

She'd seen very little of her father since she'd returned from the Redlands. Though Dafythe appeared at public ceremonies, such as Wednesday's Mass, and held audience in the small reception hall in his apartments, he had withdrawn from the court. When he wasn't summoned by his duties, he shut himself in his private chambers.

When Mara ventured to the Duke's apartments, she found Martleanne occupied with petitions Dafythe had received from various court factions while the little herald Andemyon played chess with his lord. The Prince sat down without speaking. She already felt herself to be an intruder upon Dafythe's peace; it would be discourteous to interrupt and she was anxious to avoid displeasing her father before she made her request.

Mara watched the game, not understanding the elaborate maneuvers her father and the boy conducted with the decorative little warriors of ivory and ebony. She never saw the point of chess; it seemed a feeble imitation of warfare. She thought it odd that Dafythe enjoyed such a game.

Suddenly, the boy laughed out loud, seized a pointed-capped black token, and slid it across half the board to flank the cluster of white castle-keeps and horse-heads surrounding a larger, crowned piece on Dafythe's side of the board.

"Check," said Dafythe, smiling. "And if I move out of the bishop's path, your queen's knight awaits. Clever lad!"

"You let him win," Martleanne said mildly.

"Indeed I have not. The boy learns even more quickly than you did." He rumpled Andemyon's curls. "Gramercies for a delightful game. You may go now. Martleanne, attend to those tomorrow. Go to your supper. I have one last petition to receive."

The Duke gathered up the chess pieces. "You haven't been to visit me here often lately, Daughter. What have you been up to?"

He knew. Ambris hadn't told—she trusted her brother's promise—but Dafythe knew her well enough to understand that she wouldn't sit still at Pendaunzel for long. Surely he had observed her whispered conference with Bel at Mass and guessed what they spoke of.

She told the truth. "Father, I'm going to lead another

campaign."

Mara expected immediate disapproval, but Dafythe only said, "Kharles has called you to aid him in Naufarre, has he? I'm not surprised. I understand that our Emperor doesn't share your battle-prowess, nor your good fortune."

"No, Father, Kharles hasn't called upon me."

"You form your own plans, then. Where do you intend to go?" He sorted his pawns, black and white, and ranged them down opposite sides of the board.

"Santiago."

"The westward march?" The Duke laughed. "Now what has Santiago done to warrant invasion?"

"The Spanish are still our enemies," Mara answered. "Even now, they make war with our Emperor in Naufarre. The loss of the Redlands wasn't enough to quiet them. Father, if I have to take every bit of Spanish land in Atlantea to extinguish the threat of them, I will do it. I can take all of Atlantea if I wish– "

The Duke put the last chess-piece into its proper place. "Mara, no. I will not allow you to campaign for no better reason than to have a fight."

cinqueten

Mara sat at the window of her reception chamber, the gemstone dangling before her eyes. A pretty bauble: Though it appeared unimpressive in normal circumstances, it shone bright red when held up to the sunlight. The flaw, she saw now, was a single *v*-shaped streak of dark matter at its center. Held at a certain angle, it looked like a pair of outstretched wings.

She didn't call this gem the Black Ruby any longer. This was Dragonseye, the talisman of her herald beast. Who knew it had once belonged to Denys? Miguel, who had given it to her, but he was in Spain. Her companions, but Bel alone was in Pendaunzel. Even so, all three of her friends had expressed disbelief when she'd first told them of Miguel's gift. Bel and Alyx, cynical Storm-Porters, had scoffed as if the young nobleman were a suspect merchant plying worthless trinkets at the bazaar. They wouldn't carry tales. Since she'd returned from her campaigns, she had confided only in Peter.

She had asked Bard Delphyn about the legendary sword of great Spanish kings. That was safe: Delphyn had been with her at Dennefort and had seen her negotiate for possession of Denys's sword. The minstrel wouldn't think it odd if she continued to express an interest in its history.

"If there were such a sword, My Prince, it was lost long ago," Delphyn had answered her questions. "Spanish tales tell of a magical sword which the great warrior-kings of Castile bore into battle in days of old. It had many names: the Sword of the Valiant, Sword of the Blood—that's a reference to the royal Castillian line, not to bloodletting, by the way. There is a ballad which tells how the hero El Cid received his sword from the wizard Ystrafael. For generations, Spanish princes claimed that they carried this same sword, but whether there was one sword or many, I cannot say. No, it was never known as Dragonsfang or anything like it. Denys named his sword. The Spanish wouldn't use such a name, you know. To them, the dragon is a sign of the diabolical. Could Dragonsfang be this sword of legend? Prince Denys *did* recover it from the treasury of a Spanish monastery, but I doubt the Spanish would cast aside so valuable an object. Magical or otherwise, a sword of kings must be an enormous historical treasure. No, Prince Mara, I can't believe the two swords to be the same."

But Mara needed to hear no more to convince her. She was certain now that Dragonsfang *was* the Spanish sword of legend. Denys had found it.

Last night, she had dreamt of Denys on the hot, white desert sand. Winds blasted his honey-colored hair across his face. He stood in the green-tinted shadow of the dragon's outstretched wings.

Be thou unafraid, Bright Prince.

If he were frightened, he betrayed no sign of it, but drew his sword as if he meant to fend off this glittering monster with the ancient steel.

Thy victory here hast been granted so that thou receivest thy rightful prize. The sword, O Prince, is so sharp as the dragon's fang. No steel may hold against its might. Kingdoms are thine while this gift is in thy hand.

Dragonsfang. Denys had named it for his talisman beast. The Sonnedragon had appeared to him as well.

It is no thing of evil. It is only the instrument.

There was a knock at the door and Ren, who'd been sitting quietly in attendance, rose to admit Magician Peter.

"May I have a moment's audience with you, Prince Mara?"

"Yes, of course." She turned from the window, slipping the gemstone's tether quickly about her neck, and waved to dismiss the little maidservant. Ren exited, shutting the door behind her. "What is it?"

"I have the translation of the script you left with me, My Prince. It tells the tale of how the stone came to be in Spanish possession."

"Don Miguel, the Spaniard who gave it me, said as much."

"But he didn't read it for you? Prince Mara, I inferred when we first spoke of this that you believed the stone had fallen into

Spanish hands immediately after the murder of Denys."

"Didn't it?"

Peter shook his head. "The Black Ruby wasn't kept at Spainfort nearly so long as that, My Prince. It wasn't taken from Denys at his death, but brought to the chapel in 1895—seventy years later."

Miguel had not translated that part. "Damn that Spanish puppy."

"In 1895, Spainfort was Norman," Peter continued. "The Treaty of Naufarre had been signed two years before, but the exchange of lands wasn't yet fully accomplished."

"Yes, I know. We kept a garrison there."

"This records the arrival of the stone. It was written by a Par Maryz, who was chaplain of the fortress in its last days as a Norman stronghold. He was a native of the Eduardesmarch, and spoke Spanish as well as our own tongue. The fort was to be surrendered according to the terms of the Treaty, when the stone was given into his keeping. Maryz wrote this account of the event for his Spanish successor."

"Well, what does it say?" Mara's patience could bear no more. "Who brought the stone to Spainfort?"

"The stone was brought to Par Maryz by two couriers in the livery of the Prince of France."

Mara sat upright in surprise. "France?"

"According to Par Maryz, the Prince's agents presented him with a box bearing a wax seal upon the lock, which they then broke away to reveal the stone within. They told him it was the missing stone from the sword of Denys, but didn't explain how it came to be in their possession. The Prince's agents then conjured him to swear in Christ's name that the item be kept in a secret place and left to the care of the chaplains thereafter. Maryz adds that he doesn't understand this mysterious tribute, but he prays that the chaplain who comes after him will likewise place his honor in Christ above loyalty to any worldly emperor. He doesn't describe its hiding place, but he must've shown his successor where he placed the stone. The secret was kept `til the gemstone came to you, My Prince. I don't believe the Spanish ever knew the importance of what they held."

Mara's mind was a riot of confusion. Uncle Kharles had once

possessed the Black Ruby. But *how*? Until this time, she'd assumed that the stone had fallen from its setting during Denys's final battle and been stolen by the Spanish assassins. Had it lain on the battlefield at the Shieldwall for those seventy years? Had Kharles discovered it there? So far as she knew, the late Emperor had never visited Dennefort. Even if he'd done so, what reason could he have to return the gem to Spanish hands?

"Uncle Kharles had it," she said thoughtfully. "And he deliberately abandoned it. He hid it. Where could he have gotten it? From *his* father?"

Had Eduarde's theft been successful after all?

The Redlyon had had Dentelyon made as a replica of Dragonsfang; Mara had the opportunity to examine both closely in this past year: one was made after the style of the other. Eduarde couldn't duplicate the lost arts of the Moorish swordscrafters who had forged Dragonsfang, but the length of the sword, the breadth, the configuration of the hilt and pommel, the minute, spidery intricacies of the spells inscribed on the flat of the blade were all the same. But where the famed red stone had been set on Denys's sword, Eduarde's featured a snarling lion's head. The opposite side of the grip was unadorned.

If Eduarde had possessed the Black Ruby, would he not place it there? It wasn't unreasonable that the stone would come to him after Denys's death. If he had claimed it lost, then why not announce it found?

Perhaps, Mara conceded, if the gem had come to light in Norman hands, courtesy would demand that Eduarde offer it to the first Marchion Khrystophania just as he'd given her the sword. If the Redlyon knew what he held, he couldn't have contemplated *that*.

She gripped the edge of the window seat and sat forward suddenly. "Peter, did you sense my grandfather Redlyon's influence upon the stone when you handled it?"

"The Redlyon's touch is deep upon the stone, My Prince," the magician answered, "But I received no clear impression beyond– ah–" Peter paused, not wishing to allude to the disgraceful event that must tarnish the name of one of the most honored Norman heroes.

"And the late Emperor Kharles?"

"No, Prince Mara. You must understand that my talents are not so reliable as the magics of a full wizard. A wizard's spellcraft will produce the same effects again and again each time it is performed so long as it is properly cast. A magician of mental powers cannot cast spells. I depend solely upon my own ability to perceive. I've tried to explain—all I *see* is true, but my perceptions do not always provide me with the full truth. So it is here. I can try again, if you wish."

"No, Peter. Not now. I have another task for you. I need to verify what we've discovered."

"What I've seen of the Black Ruby's history is accurate," the magician replied.

"I do not question your ability," Mara assured him. "I pray you, don't take offense. But what can we know of that Spanish monk's honesty? His story of Dragonsfang's history may be no more reliable than the Spaniard who gave the stone to me. What truth is there in the words of a prisoner who will say whatever he can to please to his conquerors? And what of Par Maryz? Can we trust his tale?"

"What reason would he have to lie?"

"I don't know! There is much here that I don't understand..." Her fingers went to the gemstone on its tether.

She had first turned to the storyteller, but Delphyn wasn't in her confidence; she must reveal a great deal to learn a little. Besides, the bard only knew stories of centuries past, while Mara needed certain facts. Peter knew the old tales as well as Delphyn, but he also had studied wizard-lore.

Mara imposed upon the magician, but Peter was a scholar at heart. He might welcome the prospect of research on a worthwhile subject. "Peter, do you know the name Ystrafael?" she asked.

The young man didn't understand the purpose of this question, but he answered: "The magician? I've heard of him. He's a sort of Spanish Merlin, My Prince."

"There is a tale that he bestowed an enchanted sword upon the hero El Cid."

Peter smiled. "My Prince, one might as easily say that Richard Lionheart received Excalibur from the Lady of the Lake. That sort of thing cannot be taken as true history. Ystrafael appears in hundreds of tales."

"Was there such a true wizard?"

"If there was such a living person, he lived in the Dark Days before the ranks of wizardry were established."

"Could he have enchanted this stone?"

Peter didn't believe so. "I've read some texts on the subject of magical gems and crystals since we last spoke. There were quite a few stones of power in the Dark Days—or so 'tis said. The notions of some early wizards are entirely erroneous on matters of basic science. A perfect gemstone was believed to possess the ability to focus and amplify a wizard's powers. Such gems were popular. Wizards wore them on rings and pendants or fixed them at the ends of rods. The crystal globes and crystal bowls that the carnival seers sometimes use are the remnants of that craft, but the opinion of professional magicians today is that there's nothing in it. If a modern wizard wears a gemstone, it is as a curiosity."

His eyes dropped briefly to her breast, where the red stone spotted her white tunic like a dried bloodstain.

"That stone of yours wouldn't do, Prince Mara. According to the books I've read, the focal stone ought to be a precious gem—a diamond or true ruby, or at least a quartz of perfect cast. Yours is flawed. Even if it were perfect, and if it truly worked, such a stone could only amplify an existing power. A wizard might employ it, but not you nor I. That little stone simply cannot perform the marvels which have been attributed to it. I promise you, My Prince, that it can't do what you claim it can—not by the natural laws of magic as I understand them." Then he added, almost as an apology, "Have you shown that gemstone to My Lady Laurel?"

"I haven't shown it to anyone."

"Magicians of great power have astonishing perception of things beyond the normal senses. If there is any spell upon that stone which I'm unable to detect, she may be able to perceive it."

"Perhaps..." Mara caressed the stone again. "Peter, will you look into the stone's history for me? I am especially interested in those years between the death of Prince Denys and the day it was brought to Spainfort. I want to know where it was for all that time."

"Yes, My Prince."

"And speak to no one of this, will you?"

"Of course."

She held her destiny in her hands. All battles were hers. All dreams fulfilled. She saw herself becoming a warrior-maid of legendary proportions—the hero that so many already believed she was. But how was she meant to wield the power of this little gem? Did she control it at all? Could she use the magic to influence her father?

If the gemstone held any influence over Dafythe, it wasn't immediately apparent. Nothing that took place in her first interview with her father had been unexpected: Dafythe hadn't been angry with her. He had not scolded. He simply refused to consider her request.

"Will you at least tell me why?" she insisted.

"The Apostolistas are no threat to us," Dafythe had answered. "Santiago is far from our borders. The Michelne, the marshes of Uoldor, and the mountains guard us from them. Why do you not plead for Iardinez?"

"Would you let me lead an army there?"

"No, but it's a far more sensible target. I would say you showed a better sense of strategy if you wished to secure the Spanish territory upon the border of your last conquest than you do yearning after Santiago. There is no reason for it!"

"And you will not consider it."

"No, Mara. Your thirst for excitement is not reason enough to make war on our neighbors. I let you go once. I allowed my realm to sink into barbarity—I will not condone another bloodletting so long as it is in my power to prevent it. Oh, we have heard the same tales here of your campaigns, Daughter, as they tell in the marches—the execution of prisoners, the ravaging of farms and villages, the butchery–"

"Lies!" Mara protested, seriously grieved by these accusations. She'd heard the same tales herself. In fact, she had encouraged them among the Spanish: a village that believed it was about to face merciless pillage and indiscriminant slaughter was more likely to surrender than a village that fought an honorable foe. She took advantage of the Spanish terror—and her ferocity on the battlefield gave credence to the wildest tales. But it pained her to hear Dafythe repeat those same rumors and believe them.

"I have never committed an act of barbarity! My soldiers to the least squire and baggage-boy know that I do not tolerate the wanton slaughter of civilians. No prisoner can complain of mistreatment while in my custody."

Dafythe had remained doubtful. "Then these tales I have heard—these atrocities have not occurred?"

"Of course there was bloodshed," Mara answered. "A great deal of blood. I meant to take Terrojos. What other choice did I have but to fight when the blasted Spaniards refused to surrender? If they came at me with their swords drawn, I had to cut them down. They would've killed *me* if I hadn't killed them first. I did what was necessary to survive."

"But is it so easy to live with your actions afterwards?" Dafythe countered. "I couldn't kill, even in my own defense, and sleep well thereafter."

"I do not always sleep well," she admitted. "I see the dead in my dreams. I see their blood on me." But she didn't see their faces; she could never remember the faces of the foes she had cut down. "It isn't easy to kill living men and women—but I'm not ashamed of my victories. I conduct myself as a knight within the chivalric codes of honor and all my wars have been fought in my Emperor's name and won by God's grace. It is no crime to win under such circumstances. Are you angry, Father, at my success?"

Dafythe waved the question away. "No, of course not. I have no desire to see you sacrificed. If you must go to war, I would rather you return victorious than return dead—just as I would rather you carry yourself as a virtuous knight instead of a butcher. But I would rather you not go at all. There must be a reason for a war."

"Spain–" Mara began, but the Duke continued to speak as if he continued his own thoughts aloud and didn't hear her.

"In Terrojos, there may have been reasons for what we did." But he shook his head as he said it. "I do not say there were. I remain steadfast that we might've made my brother Juan peaceable and kept Spain at bay if I hadn't allowed you and Kharles to have your war for glory. You would've had your way eventually, but I might've stood against the tides of the time for a little while longer—long enough to see out my days in peace. Five years, ten, this war might've been delayed. I cannot help but think of those who are dead because I surrendered too soon. Their souls weigh upon me. My subjects, buried so far from home. The Spaniards. That poor young man. What might he have done in ten years' time? Lived, at the least. Seen his child born."

This reference to Frederik surprised Mara. She had never imagined that her father regarded the Marchion as more than a fellow nobleman and Norman governor. Did he mourn so deeply for a young man he'd never met and could not acknowledge as kinsman?

"If Kharles summons you to Naufarre," Dafythe continued, "I have no choice but to grant his request for aid. I shall give you my blessings and wish you godspeed. I will also pray that you are not forced to kill my brother Juan, as I pray you will not be killed yourself. As for this reckless scheme for Santiago—Mara, do not think of it."

Dafythe would not recapitulate. Mara was certain of it. He wouldn't even hear her out. Unless she took extraordinary measures, her plans for Santiago would come to nothing.

What would happen if she deliberately invoked this magic to sway him? Would he miraculously change his mind? Or would something more sinister occur? Mara thought of the things the Sonnedragon had done to her enemies, and she shuddered. No, she didn't dare.

"I can't go through this all again," she confided to Lord Rafenshighte. "The endless rounds of *yes* and *no*. I only had my way last summer because Kharles commanded me to go and Father couldn't oppose him. Father concedes he'll let me march again if the Emperor calls for me."

"Will you appeal to My Lord Emperor?" he asked.

Mara shook her head. "I don't wish to invite the Emperor to involve himself too much in the Northlands' affairs." Also, if she marched under Kharles's direction, she would once again claim her victories for the glory of the Empire, not for the Northlands.

That was the irony of her last conquest: the Redlands were not hers. Northlander troops occupied the territory now, but she'd taken it in her Emperor's name. When Kharles named his own governor and sent imperial troops, Lieutenant Uismarde and the Northlander garrisons would retreat like dismissed servants who'd been hired by a chatelaine but were of no use to the master of the house. She meant no disrespect to her Emperor, but she wanted something she could claim for her own.

"'Tis unfair to use such influences to force Father to yield against his own will. I won't do it unless I can find no other way."

Rafenshighte might be an odd choice of confidant, but Mara had seen more of him than her father these past months. He'd ridden with her on the Christmas hunt and he offered to accompany her on her more recent rambles, though Mara had spared him that duty. His inevitable presence invited personal conversations. Mara knew he had little understanding of military matters, but he was knowledgeable of how to get things done at court. His amorality she normally found distasteful, but she acknowledged that he was capable of creating sensible-sounding reasons for doing what he desired. If anyone could provide a scheme by which she might win Dafythe over by ordinary means, it was he.

"Is it right to manipulate him?" she asked.

"Certainly! We all use our wits to get what we want from each other. My Lord Duke is a master of winning his subjects to his will. Why should you not learn from his example? Such skills of persuasion will be of inestimable value to you when you are Duke."

"It smells of guile and trickery."

"Perhaps. But so long as you have your way, My Prince, what does it matter? If your goal is worthy, then the means by which you obtain it are unimportant." His tone suggested that whatever she planned must be unquestionably worthy. "Of course, there are degrees of usage. If you mean to persuade My Lord Duke, you must choose your words carefully."

"I never know what to say to my father," Mara confessed. "Our words glance off each other and never strike true."

"If the question comes before the Council...?"

"It won't," she answered glumly. "It will never go so far."

"Perhaps I might introduce the subject myself?" Geoffrey offered.

"No. Father would know that I prompted you to it."

The young nobleman grinned. “My Lord Dafythe is always suspicious of my motives.”

She knew what he hoped to gain by courting her, but she didn’t resent it. In fact, she gave it serious thought. If she must marry, why not marry Geoffrey? There was no other suitable young nobleman of her acquaintance. And there was no better way to secure his loyalties and his talents than by keeping him at her side as her consort.

Geoffrey raised his arms in a gesture of helpless apology. “I’m afraid I’m not much help to you, My Prince. It must be frustrating to be without the aid of your military advisors at so crucial a time—save your rapacious little captain.”

Mara chuckled. “Bel has no influence with anyone at court except myself. If Lt. Uismarde were here to speak on my behalf, Father might listen to her. Or Kat. He always called *her* reasonable. Now, if Kat were here...”

“Have you heard from your cousin, Prince Mara?”

“Not since Christmas. She wrote Father.”

“You miss her very much,” Geoffrey said quietly, as if he understood.

Kat had greeted her courteously when she’d stopped at Dennefort in November. They might’ve been strangers, not women who’d once been close as sisters. In her fifth month of pregnancy, Kat had been preoccupied with the coming child. Encouraged by Khrystophania, she embraced her memories of Frederik. Mara didn’t matter anymore; Kat didn’t even trouble to be angry with her.

“She would be there now if she had married,” Mara said.

Although she missed her cousin terribly, Mara knew it was useless to wish for Kat’s return. Even if Kat were here now, their friendship wouldn’t be restored.

This loneliness had caught her unprepared. It wasn’t simply that Kat had gone; Mara had been taught to expect that from childhood and, even though she’d ceased to believe it would ever happen, she thought she could bear it. This was more than Kat’s absence. No, this was a dozen times worse. She’d always believed that she and Kat might be separated by thousands of miles but they would somehow always be connected in spite of the distance. They would think of each other. They would write. The intimacies that had bonded them together as sisters would remain throughout their lives even if they never met again. Frederik's death had severed those bonds. He would always be between them.

She'd wished for Frederik to be gone so that Kat would be restored to her, and she'd lost Kat just the same.

In May, Kharles appointed an imperial governor to the Redlands and Uismarde and her officers led the Northlander troops on the long journey home. Kat accompanied them, bringing her newborn daughter.

syseten

The war in Naufarre hadn't gone well for Kharles. The royal family had slipped from his grasp when he'd taken Pamplona: the Dowager Marianne retreated to the sanctuary of a convent on Majorca long before the Emperor lay siege to the city. Likewise, Serafina and her Spanish retinue fled to Toledo. Prince Juan Maria escaped capture during the confusion following the city's fall and had been maddeningly elusive since. It was said that he was somewhere in the Pyrenees with his armies, where he took one small victory after another through surprise attacks and infuriating strategic retreats.

Juan's soldiers knew the mountains well; they held hundreds of tiny strongholds in the clefts and passes and could slip from one to another via footpaths unknown to the Emperor's forces. The large imperial army simply couldn't keep up with them. In addition, the peasant folk were fiercely loyal to their rebellious prince. Juan might find aid in any one of a number of farms or villages.

Although Kharles captured Pamplona early in his campaign, his possession of it was never more than tenuous. The city's inhabitants were as sympathetic to Juan's cause as the country folk, and they made their resistance to the occupation known in dozens of spiteful little ways. Food supplies were contaminated. Trip wires and caltrops were placed in narrow and dimly lit streets. Banners and graffiti appeared in public places: some messages were cheerfully pro-Naufarre—*Viva King Juan Maria!*—while others were obscene ditties regarding the peculiar sexual tastes of the Emperor. Caricatures of the French and English soldiers were also popular. These were torn down or washed away daily, but fresh ones were put up again in the night. Attempts to investigate this subversion met with hindrance and evasion; no Pamplonian questioned ever gave a straight answer. Kharles ordered several troublemakers executed, which produced the first surge of riots in the city and created even greater heights of hostility. And though he would rather his troops confront the elusive armies of Naufarre than try to quiet the outraged civilian population, the frustrated Emperor wasn't yet prepared to put a city full of nominally Norman people to the sword.

Kharles spent nearly a year at the forefront of his troops, but the pacification of Naufarre was far more difficult than he had anticipated. The struggle might go on for years. Shortly after Mara's return to Pendaunzel, the Emperor finally relinquished command of the Norman armies to his generals and returned to Paris. Matters of state demanded his attention.

One matter of great concern was that the present Marchion of the Eduardesmarch and Princeland—a crucial person in the borderlands—was an unmarried young woman and the continuation of her line depended entirely upon her brother's posthumous bastard. This precarious situation couldn't be allowed to continue; Khrystophania's first duty as Marchion was to secure a legitimate heir. As an inducement, Kharles provided her with written permission to marry whatever man she liked so long as he was a Norman citizen of respectable station. He also promised to be godfather to her firstborn himself if she bore the child within two years.

Khrystophania chose a Northlands nobleman she had met during Mara's campaigns and become friendly with while he served as liaison officer between Dennefort and Uismarde's government in Cuidadela de Tolo Invencible—the Eadeshire knight Khrespian. They married on May Day. Kat might have remained at Dennefort. In the months since Frederik's death, she'd been an enormous comfort to Khrystophania as well as a great help as the young Marchion grew accustomed to the duties her brother was meant to bear. Kat's little daughter might yet be the next marchion if Khrystophania and her husband produced no children. They were welcome to stay, but evidently Kat felt herself superfluous in the newlyweds' household.

She arrived at Pendaunzel at the beginning of summer with Uismarde, Sataumie and Alyx. Once there, the question of her future immediately arose.

The birth of Tyrelspethe lowered Kat's value as a bargaining bride, but she still might be married if she chose. She was a

Norman Prince and an attractive young woman. A royal bastard might be an embarrassment, but it wasn't a complete disaster. Many royal bastards had been born before this. Especially here at Pendaunzel, where Ambris held so prominent a position, Kat's indiscretion was barely a scandal at all.

But Kat herself showed no inclination to marry. She had loved once, lost her love, and given birth to his child; she was now indifferent to the matchmaking which had consumed so much of her girlhood. Dafythe seemed entirely sympathetic. Mara knew that in a private interview soon after Kat's arrival, he had assured her that he would've been happy to consent to her marriage to Frederik. Of course, it cost him nothing to say it now and it gave Kat some comfort, but Mara believed her father had meant it.

There was some discussion of Kat taking up the government of Eireland upon her father's death, but that day was remote. Count Egan was not yet seventy. For the present, Kat had come home and had no idea of going anywhere else.

Mara spoke little to her cousin in the first weeks after her return. This separation was not of her choosing; she had so many things she wanted to tell Kat, but there was never a moment for private conversation. Kat seemed to be deliberately avoiding her.

The Irish Prince had not taken her old rooms near Mara's, but instead chose a new apartment on the opposite side of the Manor, in the west wing near the nursery. Although a nurse had accompanied her from Dennefort, she spent most of her time with her baby and Laurel's little ones.

Mara only ventured there tentatively. From time to time, she passed through the west-wing corridors and stopped at the nursery doorway when she glimpsed Kat within. Usually, her cousin sat beside Tyrelspethe's cradle. Sometimes Kat spoke playfully to the baby or sang her lullabies, but most of the time she simply watched the child sleep. She looked pale, these days, and more thin than Mara remembered her. The set of her mouth was more solemn. Her own, dear Kat, but different.

Some women put aside their swords forever once they bore children. Others only deferred until the baby was weaned or had reached an age to be fostered at an abbey school. Others left the baby with a wet nurse and resumed their duties right away. Mara wondered which Kat might be.

Could she tell her cousin everything she wanted to?

With Alyx and Sataumie, she'd been as forthright with her intention to lead another campaign as she'd been with Bel. There had been a conference in her chambers the day after their arrival in Pendaunzel; the Shieldmaids knew everything about her plans for Santiago. With Uismarde, who was Dafythe's officer, Mara had merely hinted that she thought of her next battle. But what could she say to Kat? Would her cousin even be interested in her schemes? Would Kat want to come with her?

Once, and not so long ago, Mara wouldn't have needed to ask. Kat would've followed her on any cause to the ends of the earth.

Once, Kat would've been the one person she could entrust with the secrets of her destiny. She might have heard of Mara's visions of the Sonnedragon and the little fortress on the wind-blasted desert. She might've known all the history of Dragonseye and its connection to Denys and Eduarde. Once, Kat wouldn't have disbelieved this extraordinary gift which Mara had received—or, at least, she wouldn't have scoffed. But what would Kat say to her now?

Mara loitered one morning outside the nursery. Andemyon, who always seemed to be in Laurel's company when he wasn't attending the Duke, played on the floor with little Tomyas, now a robust if ash-pale toddler. Laurel's second child, born that winter and christened Laurel Ambrosia but called Lauret, squalled and babbled in her mother's arms. The Lady herself and Kat were in the midst of a commonplace conversation about their respective infant daughters. Since Kat had returned with Tyrelspethe, she had formed a new intimacy with Ambris's wife.

"I used to do that when Tomyas was first born," Laurel was saying. "I'd fret at his every whimper and panic if he howled. I'd wonder what harm I'd done to the poor little thing this time to make him squall so. But my nurse had more experience with little children and she assured me that I wasn't half as dangerous as I imagined. A baby will scream to wake the dead over nothing at all."

"I'm not very good with babies," Kat admitted. "I know so little."

"No less than I did– Tommy, stop it!" Tomyas had been banging a wooden soldier rhythmically, persistently, against the hearthstones. "Wizards seldom keep their children with them even when they're small. My Uncle Redmantyl is an exception. I never thought I'd spend my days in the nursery. Fortunately, I had Ambris's children to gain some practice before I had children of my own– Tommy, stop! Do you want to wake Tyra? Demy, will you take him out, please?"

Andemyon lifted the little boy up by the arms, spun him, and swung him over his shoulders. Tomyas laughed and crowed in delight as he was carried off to the adjoining nurse's chamber.

Laurel sighed. "In truth, two children are enough for me," she continued. "A boy and a girl—that seems sufficient and Ambris needs no more. They say I had an easy time of it. If so, I have the greatest pity for women more frail." Mara knew what she referred to: Laurel's cousin Igren was a delicate young woman who had had several difficult births and miscarriages; it was now doubtful that she could carry a living child. "I intend to have no more."

"You know how to do that?" asked Kat.

"My Uncle taught me in my 'prenticing."

"A man?"

Kat looked up to meet Mara's eyes—she hadn't seemed aware of her cousin's presence a moment before—and silently conveyed her astonishment at this information. Mara understood her perfectly. Contraception was a part of every Shieldmaid's education; no active soldier wanted to be encumbered by an unwanted pregnancy and, for some, chastity wasn't easily maintained. But such things were considered intensely private, known only to women. Shocking that a man, even a wizard, was familiar with these techniques!

Laurel laughed and, following Kat's gaze, glanced over her shoulder. "Oh, he was embarrassed, but if my master had been a woman, *she* would've done the same and he couldn't leave me ignorant," she told them both. "He said that he had no regrets for his own children, but he hoped I'd be more careful. He thought pregnancy might be too much a distraction for a young wizard-woman."

Kat glanced at Mara again; for the first time in nearly a year, they shared their old, unspoken understanding. "In truth," Kat said to Laurel, "I wonder that you chose not to become a wizard. Was it because you wanted children?"

"No, it wasn't that," Laurel answered with caution. Little Lauret had quieted since her brother had been taken out, and her mother placed her in the cradle beside the sleeping Tyrelspethe. "Shall I tell you? My duty as a magician required me to kill a child, a maid not yet sixteen. I refused."

"My Lord Redmantyl cast you out for that?"

"No," said Laurel. "I cast myself out. You see, I should've killed her when I had the chance."

Laurel had never told them so much about her past; the princes wondered if she spoke the truth now. What reason would the ranks of wizardry have for asking one young maiden to kill another? And how could Laurel speak of her regret so easily? Practiced soldiers, Mara and Kat both shuddered at the thought of cutting down a child.

"What was she, this girl?" Mara asked. "What became of her?"

"I don't know," Laurel answered after a moment. "That story isn't finished yet. At any rate, I'm well out of it." She smoothed the blanket over the sleeping children, and left the nursery.

Mara remained in the doorway. She was about to leave as well when Kat turned suddenly and smiled at her. "You didn't come to hear us prattle about babies, Cousin."

After so many months of cool formality and distance that surpassed the miles between them, Mara needed no more encouragement. "I came to see you."

"We haven't spoken much together," Kat admitted. "My fault, I know." She gave Mara another smile. "So, what have you been planning?"

The question startled Mara. "Who's told you? Father?"

"No, not Uncle Dafythe. No one, quite. I guessed for myself that something was afoot. I see how my uncle and Ambris are troubled over you. And I couldn't help observe your conferences with the Shieldmaids, though I've never been invited to join you." She spoke this last without resentment; it was a playful chide.

"I didn't think you were interested in war councils anymore," Mara answered.

"Where is it you think of going?"

"To the westward marches. Santiago."

Her cousin was surprised. "So far? What about Iardinez? I thought– That is, I expected you'd return to the south on your next campaign."

"In all your months so close to the border, did you once hear one breath of danger from Iardinez?" Mara asked in reply.

"No," said Kat.

"Then Santiago is our next best choice. You've missed nothing in my meetings with the Shieldmaids, Kat. They all make the same points regarding Iardinez—but they'll follow me to the west all the same." Here, Mara hesitated. Did she dare ask? She and Kat were on much better terms today than they'd been in months, but this would be the final test to prove that their friendship had been restored. "Will you come with me?"

"Do you ask?"

"I thought you might've changed." Mara explained, speaking quickly in relief. "Women do, you know, once they are mothers. I thought you might've lost your taste for battle." *I thought*, she added silently, *you would want nothing more to do with me.*

Kat shook her head. "No, I haven't. I'd rather go with you, Mara, even to the godforsaken western marches."

Mara was lightheaded with happiness. This interview had gone far better than she'd dared hoped. Whatever her reasons, Kat had shown herself willing to reconcile, had even agreed to join her! For the first time in many months, Mara began to hope that everything would be just as it had been. They would be friends again. If she didn't retain some little part of her caution—the breach between them was so newly healed—she would've embraced her cousin fiercely.

Instead, she said, "I meet with my Shieldmaids tomorrow. You are welcome to come." Then she paused. "Please? I'd like you to be there."

Kat smiled and consented.

They met in the ladylike parlor that had once belonged to Mara's mother. Warrior-women with copper-clasped braids and daggers strapped to their leather jerkins or thrust into the tops of their tall boots lounged on velvet-cushioned chairs meant for more gentle females at less serious business. Ren served them wine and honey-cakes, then retreated to the windows, where she usually sat during the Prince's conferences.

"The removal of our troops from the Redlands complicates

matters," Mara told her Shieldmaids. She knelt on the carpet, a map of the Northlands spread open before her. "Our armies are now disbanded, or else returned to the towns where they were garrisoned. I have no hope of recalling them swiftly for the journey westward, but I've given the problem some thought since we last met. It is to our advantage if the army isn't so large as it was during our last campaign. A smaller force will be more easily supplied and more readily moved by ship and barge. However, it also requires a more specialized soldier—only the most fit and able will be chosen to go. You three will act as my agents: Alyx returns to her command of Storm Port's garrison this summer. Taumie, you remain here as Uismarde's aid for the present, but I will contrive to have you commissioned elsewhere when the opportunity arises. Bel will be my liaison with the garrison captain at Pendaunzel. When the time is right, we can reassemble the army of the Northlands in a matter of weeks!

"Ships will gather at Storm Port—here," Mara tapped the map. Bel left her chair to stand behind the kneeling Prince and look over her shoulder. Sataumie, on the coucherie, sat forward. "Also at Ystre Harbor, Johnesport, Lammouthe, Heofon, New York, and the Frankeshire ports to the south. Our greatest numbers will already be stationed at these towns, and the rest will be no more than a few days away."

"Save the Gilleshires," said Alyx.

"I do not forget them," Mara answered. "Those regiments will travel by river—the Myame flows into the great Michelne and it is navigable by barge. I shall take that route myself."

Kat leaned forward to view the map. "Where do we reunite?"

"On the westward banks of the Michelne. 'Tis not on this map." Mara waved in the general direction of a larger, rolled sheet of parchment on the sideboard behind her; Alyx rose to get it. "I can show you on the full Atlantea map, if you like, Cos. We land at the river-ports of the Jamesmarch and assemble our troops there."

"Have you written the governor there?" asked Kat.

"No, not yet."

"Our plans haven't gotten beyond this room," Alyx added, smiling as she helped herself to a second glass of wine as long as she was near the decanter. Bel glanced up to scowl at her for speaking so lightly of this solemn matter.

"Nothing we say here may leave this room 'til Father gives his consent," Mara continued as she rolled out the large map purloined from the Hall of Record. "We land here," she tapped the thick, blue line of the Michelne River with her fingertips. "The troops will assemble and resupply themselves at the port towns. We'll march across the Jamesmarch to the Santiago border. Once we are there, our first target will be the fortress which sits above this little river. It is built upon a tower of rock and is nearly impregnable, but we shall take it."

"This fortress," asked Kat, "What's it called?" She looked to the others: Sataumie shook her head; Alyx shrugged. Bel, still at Mara's shoulder, watched the Prince trace the thin line of blue which marked the border between the Jamesmarch and Santiago and didn't look up. "Where is it?" Kat joined her cousin on the floor. "This map makes no mention of a fortress, upon a rock or otherwise," she announced after a close examination of the pale yellow cluster of Spanish marches. "Mara, where did you learn of this?"

Mara looked up at her from the other side of the parchment. "I've seen it—a fortress above the desert. It was promised me."

"Promised?" Kat glanced from one Shieldmaid to another; they had all heard this before. "By whom? Not your talisman dragon?"

Mara smiled. "I knew you'd be skeptical."

"I'm not skeptical," Kat protested. "I only wish to understand. Do you mean that you're going to invade Santiago because you saw it in a vision?"

"Yes, of course. Oh, I know it sounds odd to you—you haven't seen your talisman beast yet. You haven't heard it speak to you of wondrous gifts. Victories which will be yours for the taking." Mara gripped the gemstone dangling at her throat as she spoke. "Kat, if you'd seen that desert land as I have and known that it was meant to be yours, you would do the same as I've done."

"Perhaps," said Kat. She sat back against the legs of her chair, frowning as Mara continued to explain the deployment of her troops.

When the group disbanded, Kat took Bel's arm in the corridor outside Mara's apartment. "You've been with her these months while we've all been in the south," the Irish Prince whispered.

"How long has she been like this?"

"February," Bel answered. "She had her vision of Santiago at the beginning of Lent. I was at her side when it happened." There was a distinct note of pride in her voice.

"Did you see anything?" asked Alyx.

"No, of course not. I've never seen the Sonnedragon either, but I don't doubt its truth. *She* sees it." Bel looked from one to the other defiantly, challenging them to deny this evidence.

None of them could. Question a talisman beast? They might as well question the existence of the Blessed Virgin Mother.

"Is it sensible to you, this plan of hers?" asked Kat.

Here, Bel faltered.

"No, Prince Kat," Sataumie admitted. "We thought it strange when Mara first told us."

"But you said nothing to her?"

"Christ's Mercy," cried Alyx. "Are we to contradict our Prince?"

"We did ask if Iardinez might not be a more reasonable target," Sataumie added. "She would have none of it."

"Your pardon, Kat, but if our Prince and General wishes to lead us halfway across the continent to conquer a desert land on the advice of a visionary dragon, then we will march with her," said Alyx. "Won't you?"

"If Uncle Dafythe consents to this venture, I will go," Kat answered. "Mara will need sound advisors for this peculiar campaign."

Alyx nodded. "If it eases your mind, Prince Kat, I was at Mara's side every day of our campaign through the Redlands and I've seen her as frightening—in battle, her eyes were fixed upon nothing, yet she struck true at whatever foe stood in her way. She's never miss-stepped when the spirit of her dragon guides her. I don't pretend to understand it, but trust her in it."

"We've all been frightening at one time," Kat agreed. "It's easier to act when you don't think, and you find yourself doing things you couldn't have imagined before."

"All of us, save Sataumie," the Storm-Port captain answered, grinning. "She's never known a moment's madness. Her wolf would never send us on a thousand-mile quest."

"Santiago, Iardinez, Naufarre," Bel said impatiently. "It matters not the least to me. So long as it's a Spanish land and we *go*."

Ren emerged from Mara's apartment, her arms filled with rolled parchment maps to be returned to the Hall of Records. The gathering in the hallway dispersed.

"Alyx, what's that stone that Mara wears?" Kat asked as they walked on. "Have you noticed it? Red." Her hand went to her breast, mimicking Mara's gesture.

Alyx glanced to Sataumie. "Is it the one Don Miguel gave her?"

"Miguel? The Spainfort commander?"

"Yes, Prince Kat. 'Twas after you left. He made her a present of a gemstone, told her it belonged to Prince Denys or some such nonsense."

"I'm pleased to learn that you and Kat are friends again. You haven't truly been happy without her," the Duke said to Mara the next time they met. "She's joined the little circle gathered about you, has she?"

"Who's told you that? Kat?" While Mara was personally delighted at her reconciliation with her cousin, she couldn't help recalling how Kat had questioned her plans at yesterday's conference. She felt a stab of suspicion. Was Kat carrying tales to her father?

"Ambris told me," Dafythe answered. "He has noticed your sessions with your Shieldmaids and wonders at them as much as I. Tell me, Daughter, what is it you discuss? You aren't still fixed upon that ill-conceived plan of yours, are you?"

So they'd come to the true reason for this interview! Father already knew the answer to his question; Mara was certain of that.

She said nothing.

Dafythe frowned. "And now you've dragged your companions into your schemes. Mara, I do not like this."

"I do no harm to speak of it," she protested.

"It is dangerous! You do yourself no good service if you place yourself among such friends, who consent to your every wish."

"What do you mean?" Mara asked. "Do you suggest that my Shieldmaids are not trustworthy? Alyx has been tested at my back a hundred times. And Bel—"

"I'm fond of your Bel," Dafythe stopped her. "You know I am. I'm certain the rest of your companions are equally loyal. I mean, Mara, that they are not the best advisors you could choose. They champion your cause, regardless of its merits. Right or wrong, they will follow you to the corners of the earth and be ready to die at your side. But will one of them disagree with you? I don't doubt their sincerity. They do not mislead you deliberately, as I know Geoffrey does. It confounds me, Mara, that you favor him."

The Prince seized this opportunity to change the subject. "Geoffrey is your advisor, Father."

"He sits on my Council. I do not hear his advice on all matters. He hangs upon you, whispering his lies. I don't like it."

"You dislike him for the same reason you disapprove the rest of my friends," Mara retorted. "They agree with me. Bel, Geoffrey—they say I'm right and you are wrong, and so you call them unreliable!"

"They tell you that you are right whether you are or not," Dafythe answered tersely. "How can you know? Mara, if you are to govern well, you must learn that those who cheer you on in all pursuits and offer only the advice you wish to hear will fail you when you have need of them most. Whether they act from blind loyalty or courtly deceit, they betray your best interests. Yet you surround yourself with such people! I cannot allow this to continue. Dream of Santiago if you like, Mara, but henceforth you are forbidden to make plans. You have called your last war-council. One word from you is a promise to your followers, and you are in no position to promise them anything. Not one soldier shall be alerted. Nothing will be commissioned in your name. No rumors of a second campaign will be spoken outside the Palace. The tales within will die away if there is nothing for the court gossips to feed upon. I don't wish to be harsh, but if you will hear no other voice of dissent, you will hear mine. Daughter, I command you: not another word of Santiago."

There was no help for it. Her father was also her liege lord. She had sworn obedience to him and could not refuse his command.

"Yes, Father," she answered. "As you wish it."

"It could be worse," Rafenshighte consoled her that same afternoon once she'd spent her outrage in repeating this latest quarrel with her father. "My Lord Duke hasn't forbidden you your Shieldmaids, only limited the topics you may discuss with them. He might've sent your friends from court. He might have forbidden you to speak to me."

"It is unfair!" Mara continued her tirade. "Father warns me against the advice of those who support me—he thinks you sycophants—but he gathers his own favorites about him. His legal lass, his pretty pet herald–"

"Andemyon?"

"Yes, *you* would notice that one," but Mara smiled as she said this. "The boy is always in Father's chambers. He's made himself indispensable. He sings." She often heard that soprano voice trilling in the corridor when she passed by Dafythe's apartments. "He plays chess. He's become a second secretary. He knows where everything is—he's sorted all of Father's papers and tied them up with cloth tapes of different colors *and* made up indices. Father calls him a marvel. He sits in attendance night after night at Father's request when the other heralds are meant to share the duty. Father hasn't doted upon any child since Martleanne first came to his service."

"No, he rarely makes such a fuss," Geoffrey agreed. "I know that it displeases some to see it."

"Why?" Mara wondered. "What harm could Andemyon possibly do?"

"It isn't the boy himself," Geoffrey spoke as if he were reluctant to explain the truth of the matter. "I have the highest regard for My Lady Laurel and a healthy fear of her wizard-uncle, but they rise too fast to please some here at court. That overly fair family has come from nothing and risen to the Duke's household in two generations. They stand amidst the oldest noble families of the Northlands and My Lord Dafythe picks them out for special honors. Where did they come from? What was Lord Redmantyl's father? A farmer? A wheelwright?"

"He was a village miller, I believe."

"And the grandchild is the Duke's pet. He has the Duke's ear."

"I doubt the boy gives my father advice good nor bad that need concern anyone at court. What will you wager, Geoffrey, that my father's favorites never speak a word of disagreement when he seeks their opinions?"

"I wouldn't take such a wager, My Prince," her confidant replied. "My Lord's personal secretary and his herald would no more disagree with him than I would disagree with you." Observing that she was calmer now, he continued in more serious tones, "Take heart, My Prince. This ban can't go on forever. The Fates may conspire to see that you have your way yet."

Mara looked a little guilty. "What do you mean?"

"My Gracious Lord Dafythe is very old," Geoffrey answered obliquely. "Even if the Almighty in His Infinite Mercy allows him to reign twenty years more, his resolve isn't so strong as it once was. He relented once before, bending to the wishes of our Emperor. He may again."

"Oh."

"Your cause isn't dead yet, Prince Mara. If I were you, I wouldn't be ready to abandon my plans—but surely you don't need my humble advice on this point."

"No, I'd like to hear it," said Mara. "No one else offers such interesting options."

Rafenshighte smiled, gratified. "I suggest that you cease your conferences with your Shieldmaids, just as My Lord Duke commands. Open defiance will only distress him. He may forbid you the counsel of your friends but, if I may speak frankly, even so prominent a nobleman as the Duke of the Northlands and son of the glorious Redlyon cannot keep a freeborn woman from her own thoughts, even if she be his daughter and a knight sworn to his service. Can he prevent you from reading what books you like, My Prince? From looking upon maps of your own land and its neighbors? He cannot stop you from taking notes for your own personal memoranda." The courtier paused to be certain Mara understood. "And, should My Lord Dafythe relent one day, these same private writings may be of interest to others."

This level of subterfuge was unfamiliar to Mara, yet she found it appealing. Nothing Geoffrey proposed directly contradicted her father's orders. She wouldn't discuss Santiago with her Shieldmaids. No word of her plans would escape the Palace. Father would have no reason to complain… if he even knew. She wouldn't be the one to tell him.

"I will not disobey my father," she said, "but I'm going to

Santiago. If he places me under such arbitrary restraints, then I am justified in using whatever means I find at my disposal to evade them."

For the second time, Mara considered using the power of the Dragonseye. Under its influence, Dafythe would relent tomorrow and hear her proposals for the invasion of Santiago; the consequences of invoking this strange magic, however, were too unpredictable. She wanted her own way, but not if she must injure her father to get it.

"It would be best if I had the proper words to persuade him," she continued. "But I never am able to say the right words. We don't understand each other, Father and I. He doesn't think of war, even when the cause is most reasonable and urgent. He calls my plans impractical. Certain victory means nothing to him. If I rode into Toledo and captured the Emperor of Spain, Father would only shake his head and say *Mara,* as if I were a child up to some naughtiness."

Geoffrey grinned. "I must confess, My Prince, I don't always understand you myself. Oh, I'm in full sympathy with your desire to drive the Spanish from our borders even though I have no wish to march with you. But I am also unceasingly amazed at your soldierly intensity. It astonishes me that a woman born to the luxury of soft beds and silks should choose to ride in from the woods so many mornings with mud on her cloak and last autumn's leaves in her hair. Most of the world sleeps on dirt and straw, you know. They dream of the feather-stuffed mattress you scorn."

Mara laughed. "Geoffrey, you've never given a thought to most of the world's discomforts!"

"I don't pretend to. I present myself as I am."

"Ambitious, glib, self-interested," she counted these qualities on her fingers.

"Exactly, My Prince." Rafenshighte's indomitable grin flashed again. "I refuse to apologize for it. Is there evil in honest ambition?"

"If I thought so," Mara answered, "I'd banish you from my company exactly as my father wishes."

"Yet you do not."

"No, Geoffrey. You've been of service to me." She knew

where this turn of conversation was leading, and she didn't discourage him.

"I hope I may be of greater service in the future." He paused, meeting her eyes with something like uncertainty. "Margueryt– May I address you so? Mara, you know my ambitions, but you also know that you alone possess the power to fulfill the summit of my hopes."

"A Duke's consort?" she asked. "Is that as high as you wish to climb?"

Geoffrey's eyebrows went up in surprise. "How much higher can I go? True, you may become Emperor by the Grace of God one day if My Imperial Lord Kharles is unfortunate in the health of his children—but that's too much for either you or I to fix our hopes upon. My dear Prince, reassure yourself I have no intention of overtaking you. Supplant the Sonnedragon of the Northlands? I'd be a fool as well as a knave! No, I'm content to be a satellite and reflect the luminescence of a greater light."

"That sounds very humble," said Mara. "How do you intend to serve as my reflector?"

Geoffrey was still smiling. "I shall counsel you and hope that the words of a husband have at least as much influence as the words of a mere courtier. Have you found complaint with the advice I've offered you so far?"

"No, of course not."

"And then, when you're away from Pendaunzel on your campaigns against the Spanish, someone must take up the burdens of governing in your absence. My Lord Ambris will not be able to bear all your responsibilities. Do you trust me less?"

"Than my brother? Yes, certainly."

This was probably what Geoffrey had sought since the beginning of their friendship, but Mara didn't mind. At least, he was honest about his reasons for proposing this marital alliance and didn't insult her by trying to make love to her. Geoffrey wasn't the sort of man for it, and she wasn't the sort of women who would enjoy it. He *was* of use to her; today, especially, he had been enormously helpful. Would she have found so simple a way of slipping past her father's restrictions if she'd consulted anyone else? As long as she could rely on his support, and as long as Ambris was here to keep a check upon him, there was no reason why Geoffrey wouldn't be a suitable consort.

Geoffrey was watching her hopefully. "Well, Mara, what do you think?"

"I'm not afraid of your ambition," Mara answered. "I think I can control you."

If Rafenshighte was startled by this strange reply, he was too courteous and circumspect to reveal it. "I am always yours to command, My Prince," he said smoothly, "whatever honor you choose to grant or refuse me."

"I'll think on it, Geoffrey."

senneten

Dafythe was credited as architect of the *pax normania*, but Dafythe himself knew that it was his brother's doing. He'd only been a boy when he'd been introduced to Kharles's plans. The red still swam before his eyes after he'd witnessed his first execution at Tyburn, when his elder brother had taken him by the shoulders and said softly: "I couldn't tell you before this—you wouldn't have understood what it was like until you'd seen for yourself."

"But *why*?" The words had burst from him. "Why do such terrible things happen?"

Kharles had answered, "It's Father's doing, Davy. It wasn't always this way."

That night, they'd sat up talking of the Empire's glory days. The plans they'd made! Together, they'd imagined a world where imperial purges and pogroms were as illegal as murder by common cutthroats. Where physical punishments were only given for the worst physical crimes. Prisoners would not be tortured, Jews and heretics not persecuted, witches not burned. If a sentence of death was given, the execution must be swift and clean and *never* carried out in a public square before crowds of howling commoners. It was barbaric for Norman citizens to stand and witness such suffering.

On that night, as he rested his weary head on his brother's knee, Dafythe realized that one day he and Kharles would wield the same power that Eduarde held. They could put a stop to every symptom of his madness. They could make the Norman kingdoms into whatever they chose.

His brother had always guided him. Kharles had given him the books to read: Plato's *Republic* was a favorite. They'd discussed what in this imagined society was suited for a Christian state and argued over the true role of a philosopher king. They read Roman historians, Suetonius, Tacitus, Plutarch's *Lives*. Dafythe was particularly fascinated by the strict moral codes of the Republicans. It seemed to him that Rome's earliest citizens held a stronger sense of virtue than modern Normans. For Normans, honor was a matter of manners, not of moral scruples; beneath their veneer of good manners, they were truly no more civilized than the barbarian Gauls and painted Brits their ancestors had been two thousand years ago. He had a theory: Rome had reached its heights when its citizens valued their personal honor so highly that they were prepared to die rather than forsake it. When they feared death more than dishonor and sacrificed their virtue to survive under the rule of a series of madmen, their empire grew decadent and eventually fell to ruin. The Normans faced a similar crisis under the Redlyon. Could they avoid the same fate?

They discussed democracy. Each city and shire reflected true Athenian democracy in its local elections, but both princes agreed that this wouldn't be practicable on a larger scale. An empire-wide election would be impossible to coordinate and, besides, what would the provincial folk know of the merits of imperial ministers? They agreed that all Norman citizens were freeborn and deserving of respect regardless of their places, but it was dangerous to give lesser folk powers to challenge the great. A leveling attitude toward one's inferiors was a privilege of the aristocracy. A good governor ought to hold republican sentiments. No loyal subject should.

Should they educate the common folk? Dafythe had argued that if the strength of the Empire lay in allowing the most intelligent to rise to positions befitting their talents whatever their birth, then surely the promotion of literacy, basic mathematics, and the science of logic would best further that goal. Kharles had disagreed. He believed that the clever would come to their own even if they were discouraged on all sides. God had decreed the fate of all; if a common-born child were meant to rise to prominence, he would do so eventually in spite of the obstacles placed before him. Also, he thought that the common folk never valued anything easily obtained. They would despise education if it were offered them freely. A treasured thing becomes meaningless if everyone receives it for the asking. Universal education only gave dangerous knowledge to fools and rouges. An illiterate dissenter was always dismissed as ridiculous; the dissenter who presented himself as an educated man and quoted great words out of context might sound plausible and gain the ignorant and credulous to his cause. What Empire could withstand such subversion? Dafythe had reluctantly conceded to this last point.

They argued over what they meant to do with their perfect civilized state. Civilization should mean an end to cruelty. In a truly civilized world, war would be unheard of. The execution and mutilation of criminals would be unthinkable, but then so would murder, battery and rape. Pain could not be eliminated entirely—even so young, Dafythe wasn't naive enough to believe *that*—but once they governed this great empire, they could put a stop to its institutionalized forms. They would not condone rituals that were brutal simply because they were tradition. When he became Duke, young Dafythe had once vowed, he would outlaw those customs that were based upon misery: Manhood tests which involved rites of mutilation or excessive bloodletting; bear-baits, cock fights, dog fights, and other such beastly entertainments. These things encouraged the worst in humanity. As governor of his own dukedom, Dafythe meant to encourage the best.

Kharles had listened to his fancies and laughed. "Davy, *you* are the most civilized person I know!"

Their plans had continued to develop as they grew from boys into young men, even up to the days of their mother's last illness just before he assumed his duties in the Northlands.

Dafythe knew he wasn't a practical planner. He was a dreamer. He'd been fortunate to have practical attendants. Ideas he'd never thought more than pleasant fantasies were made real when he became Duke of the Northlands. He had only to express a desire and his Council worked to make it fact. A new palace where the crumbling ruins of the old castle stood? Architects and builders were summoned. Restore the old laws? Copies of the original writs were retrieved from the archives and presented for his consideration. Dafythe had been blessed with a series of talented advisors who understood his philosophy of good government and were swift to shape policies to reflect it. There were limits, of course, to what he could accomplish while his father lived, but he fulfilled what he could of his dreams. Kharles didn't have those same opportunities.

When they'd met in Kharles' private apartments at the Paris palace in the summer of 1888 after their sister's christening and their step-mother's funeral, Dafythe hadn't foreseen how close they were to the beginnings of the *pax normania*. In those last, dark years of the Redlyon's reign, it had never seemed less obtainable.

"His madness grows worse," Kharles confided as he poured out wine for them both. "He knows no limits these days. He sees traitors everywhere. You are spared the full horror of his purges in the Northlands, Davy."

"I remember them," Dafythe had answered quietly, reaching up to accept the offered cup.

Kharles shook his head. "No one is safe now. You noticed who was absent from poor Aline's funeral?"

"Arned–" A chill had run through him. "Oh, Kharles, Aline's own brother? Surely not!"

"He was arrested last week. Father goes to oversee his trial. The Old Duke dare not speak against it, or he'd join his son in London Tower and follow him to the block. He may at any rate. Father's taken a dislike to the Kent family lately."

"Is there no hope?"

"Arned's been too incautious with his opinions since his sister became Empress. He's opposed Father's tax to fund his next campaign, and to Father that's the same as treason. He's accused Arned of collusion with Spain. And, Davy, if one of our own kinsman can go to the Tower so easily, even you and I are not safe. Father's always been mad, but his present insanity will bring the Empire down around us in ruins while he looks for spies and traitors in every noble house. There'll be no one left. Even his most loyal adherents must see that he can't be relied upon to govern rationally. He's talking of Naufarre again—as if that little patch of land were worth the thousands of soldiers he slaughters upon it!"

Dafythe swallowed his wine at one gulp. Even here, in private conversation with the person he trusted most in the world, the next words were not easy to say. "How are we going to stop him?"

"I don't know yet," Kharles answered after a moment. They both understood the dangerous step they were taking. "We dare not speak to Father's ministers. Even those who are in sympathy are not bold enough to stand with us against him. And it's useless to try to speak to *him*. Even when he was more reasonable, Father wouldn't heed my advice. Father never listens. When has he ever heard any opinion but his own? If there were a way to capture his attention..." He sipped his wine thoughtfully. "Play upon his superstitions."

Dafythe sat forward, intrigued. "What do you mean?"

Instead of answering, Kharles announced, "I'm following Father to London."

"I'll come with you."

"No." His brother had stopped him before he could even rise from the chair. "I take a great risk, Davy. If all goes well, I'll need your help in a hundred ways, but you are safest if you stay far from Father. One of us must survive to see our hopes fulfilled."

Dafythe didn't like this mystery, but he acknowledged that his brother's reasons for protecting him were valid. Reluctantly, he conceded. "Our dreams," he'd said wistfully.

"*Your* dreams, Brother." Kharles had smiled. "You are more likely to see our grand plans realized. When we were boys, I saw that things were monstrously wrong and I was angry. *You* wanted to change them, and you made me believe we could. You've done so much already. I envy the way you govern your Northlands, Davy. Assigning the surplus armies to serve as auxiliary to the city garrisons. Taking the burden of supporting them off the Treasury and putting them to regular work! I've wished for years that I could do the same for France, but Father always overrides my endeavors to make changes. He prefers to keep things just as they are. Return to the Northlands." Though he'd only been in France ten days! "You've done your part. This is mine alone. If I succeed, you'll hear from me soon enough. If I fail, then you are innocent of all complicity. Perhaps Father's wrath will not touch you, so far away."

Dafythe never did discover exactly what Kharles had done to wrestle control from the mad Emperor. Their father *was* superstitious: the Redlyon's faith in his own warrior-ability had always been a strange amalgamation of true magic, religion, and an infantile attachment to charms and tokens. The fetish he'd made of Dentelyon was the most striking example. Even though the famous sword had been rune-woven by a Redmantyl, Eduarde seemed to believe it held powers far beyond those any wizard's spell could provide. In fact, Dafythe suspected that Kharles's successful coup had been brought about somehow via the sword, for Kharles had taken it from Eduarde and sent it to his care not very long after the peace accords.

He was flattered that Kharles believed that the *pax normania* was his doing, but Dafythe knew that his dreams had primarily come to fruition through good fortune and happy accident. The accomplishment had truly been his brother's work.

"You are restless, My Lord."

Dafythe lifted his head from the pillow to find the golden-haired child sitting at the foot of his bed like an attending cherub. "I'm sorry, Demy. Did I wake you?"

"I wasn't asleep," the boy answered, yawning.

The Duke grinned at the obvious lie.

"Shall I sing for you, My Lord?"

"No, it's too late in the night for a lullaby. Talk to me."

Dafythe enjoyed hearing the boy sing and dreaded the day when that astonishing voice must inevitably be lost, but he also saw more interesting qualities in Andemyon which people who observed the child's beauty and had never gotten past his shyness hadn't discovered. Andemyon possessed a remarkable young mind. He was bright and fanciful, his head filled with myths and strange stories; he was, after all, the child of a thespian and a wizard. Dafythe found him delightful to listen to. How different his elaborate imaginings were from the grunted *Yes, M'Lord*'s, *No, M'Lord*'s, and *Dunno*'s of the other heralds.

It pleased Dafythe to imagine that Ambris might've been like this during his boyhood years away from Pendaunzel. This delicate, fair little creature was nothing physically like his own dark son, who must have been all arms and legs at fifteen. But Andemyon was possessed of that same sharp intelligence, that same quiet thoughtfulness. Dafythe would have liked to be able to say as much about his own grandchildren. Ambris's sons at court, who ought to have inherited some of their father's intelligence, were dull little lumps. Young Eduarde alone showed a spark of wit.

Andemyon was a timid child, not easy to draw out in conversation, but Dafythe had made the effort and he was pleased at the results. On nights when the Duke was unable to sleep, it was comforting to speak with the little herald at the foot of his bed. He looked forward to Andemyon's nights on duty and often requested that the boy attend him even when it was another herald's turn.

"What have you been about lately, Child? I hear you assist Magician Peter. You think to apprentice yourself to him, do you?"

Andemyon acknowledged the gentle jest with a smile. "No, My Lord. We study the lore of gemstones."

"Gemstones?" Dafythe laughed. "What odd things scholars take interest in! I never would've imagined that mousy magician to care for diamonds and rubies."

"'Tis for Prince Margueryt, My Lord."

"That ugly stone she wears about her neck?" Now, Dafythe was truly curious. Kat had told him that his daughter was making a fetish of the gem. Mara had changed since her campaigns in Terrojos; she was more restless, impatient than ever before. She fixed upon pointless goals for no reason he could fathom. Did this gemstone have something to do with it? At the least, it was another symptom of her irrational behavior and too much like his father's old superstitions for Dafythe's comfort.

The boy nodded. "Peter researches its history. He says it may have once belonged to your father the Redlyon or Prince Denys. Somebody told Prince Mara so, and she wants to find out if it's true. She thinks it may be magical, or so Peter says. That what he has me to help with, since I used to read magical books in Lord Redmantyl's library."

"Magical gemstones…" Dafythe murmured in disbelief. He would have to speak to Peter or Mara directly to learn more about this. To Andemyon, he said, "Well, it's good of you to aid Peter in his researches, my boy, but you mustn't let him keep you out quite so late. Old Toppet tells me that you came into the heralds' chambers last night long after the other boys were abed. You're not afraid to walk through the palace gardens alone at night?"

"Oh no, My Lord, not when the moon is up and I can see my way. And I don't always go alone. My Lord Rafenshighte sometimes walks with me."

This unexpected information brought Dafythe's head up with a jolt that painfully wrenched his neck. "Geoffrey? What business does *he* have at the magician's house?"

"I don't know, My Lord. He's there some nights when I'm helping Peter, and he offers to come with me back to the Manor."

Dafythe didn't like the sound of this at all. He made note that, tomorrow, he must also have a word with Geoffrey.

At last, Mara had found the name:

"Full wroth! Full wroth!
The might of all the Northlands
Could not cross the river's froth.
Maud's knights stopped upon Jamesbank

Iagoburso stood proud to tempt her,
but `twas not hers to take."

Iagoburso. The impenetrable Spanish stronghold upon a rock. Norman lands lay to its east, across the river boundary—a most vulnerable position. It must have a most powerful guardian.

Though she couldn't convey her triumph to Bel in explicit terms, the little captain seated on the coucherie at her feet was smiling as she heard the words spoken and didn't look up as Ren admitted Kat to the Prince's sitting room.

"What's that you're reading?" her cousin asked.

"Poetry." Mara held up the book to show Kat the pages she'd been reading aloud from. "A ballad of Duke Maud's last campaign."

Kat glanced from Mara to the cheerful-looking Bel. "I thought you'd both be heartbroken by my uncle the Duke's ultimatum, but you seem to be bearing up well."

Bel's grin only widened. Mara answered, "We take our solace where we can."

The Irish Prince nodded, her eyes fixed on Mara. "Leave us, Captain, I pray you," she requested and once Bel had gone, she spoke her mind. "You haven't given it up yet, have you, Mara?"

"I'm forbidden to speak—even to *you*, Cos—but there's no reason in the world I shouldn't edify my companions with a rousing ballad celebrating the adventures of one of our venerated ancestors."

"An ancestor who once rode to battle on the same frontier where you wish to campaign," replied Kat, who had paid more attention to her geography lessons than Mara had.

Mara scowled. "I don't forget Santiago. I promise you, Kat, we shall see Iagoburso one day."

"Iago– What?"

"It is in this song," Mara told her. "The Spanish fortress Maud couldn't take. The fortress upon the rock! It's the same one that I saw!"

"Oh, Mara," Kat said softly.

"Do you doubt it?"

"No, Cousin. But it's a subject we cannot discuss. Uncle Dafythe hoped that you'd abandon this scheme if you were kept from conferring with your companions. I ought not encourage you."

Mara was baffled by this reticence. Once, there'd been a time when Kat would've damned Father's restrictions and received her confidences eagerly. The Shieldmaids, even Bel, might be forbidden her secrets, but never Kat.

"And you ought not encourage *her*–" Kat waved toward the door Bel had gone out of. "She feeds off your promises of further battles against the Spanish and inspires you to make more elaborate plans. If Alyx, Taumie, and I had been here to advise you, this would never have gone so far."

"But you weren't here. There was only Bel, and I'm satisfied with her advice."

Kat sat down at Mara's feet, where Bel had been. "Have you taken her into your confidence in defiance of your father's wishes?"

Mara shook her head. "Not a word! But she's no fool, my captain. She sees without being told the significance of the fortress Maud couldn't capture. I don't make her promises, Kat—I'm not permitted to—but she understands without my speaking."

Her cousin stared at her. "I never thought I'd see you twist your way out of an oath, Mara," she said after a moment of incredulous silence. "You once knew the importance of fealty."

"I know fealty!" Mara shot back, shocked herself that her

cousin could accuse her of such deceit. "I feel it both as liege and vassal. I'm bound by my obligations to Bel and the others and the armies who have marched with me and to *you*, Cousin, as much as I am to Father and to the Emperor. I've kept my word to the letter. I haven't disobeyed Father, and I haven't betrayed the faith of my friends." Suddenly, a dark pang of suspicion struck within her. "Can you say the same?"

Kat frowned. "I don't know what you mean."

"Don't you? You speak very well for my father's interests. You seem more in sympathy with him than with me."

"I worry for you, as he does."

Mara pursued her point. "If I tell you I haven't ceased to make plans for Santiago, will you carry tales to him?"

"I can't if you don't tell me!" Kat replied with some heat. "Whatever is it you do in spite of Uncle Dafythe's wishes, `tis best kept to yourself. For your own sake, let me hear no more of Santiago and the Jamesmarch and fortresses set upon rocks."

This reply confirmed Mara's worst suspicions. "Cousin," she asked, sick that this question should ever arise between them, "Have you been spying on me?"

"Uncle Dafythe's worried for you," her cousin repeated, rising from the coucherie. "He sees much that alarms him. Your passion for this campaign. Your visions. Your secrecy. I will not fly to him if you tell me you continue to make plans, but I would much rather not know what you're up to if he should ask. I would rather not lie, even for your sake."

"I read," Mara flung at her. "I study maps. I keep my little book of notes. No one has read it yet, but there will come a time when I can make my thoughts known and all will be revealed. Tell Father *that*."

It was a challenge flung down between them. A test of Kat's allegiance. If Father did find out that she hadn't abandoned her plans, Mara would know his source.

She didn't wait long; her father summoned her to his private apartments that same afternoon. "Mara," said the Duke, "it has come to my ears that you continue to think of your campaign to Santiago."

"Has it?" Kat must have gone straight to Dafythe with the

news. Only two other persons were privileged with any part of her secrets: Bel, who wanted another chance at the Spanish so badly that she would never dare breathe a word against Mara even if she *could* doubt her purpose or think of committing an act of disloyalty; and Geoffrey, who wasn't trustworthy, but who had everything in the world to gain if he were loyal to her and nothing to gain by betrayal.

Her father was puzzled by her calm response. "You don't deny it?"

"I'm certain your source was reliable." It was her own fault. In her eagerness to have the old days back again—as if Kat were still that same girl!—she'd rushed foolishly into confidences better kept to herself. Indeed, Kat had warned her that she ought to.

Dafythe continued to regard her with concern. "I confess, Daughter, I'm lost as to what more I can say to you to return you to your proper senses. You hear no words you do not wish to. You've become mad in your pursuit of this meaningless goal. My commands are disregarded. You continue speak to Captain Belinde and your cousin as if your army were ready to march."

"I haven't!" Mara protested. "I haven't spoken to anyone about going on a new campaign since you said I must stop all plans. I've *thought* of it, `tis true. I can't help that, Father. But my thoughts are my own. In my chambers, I read whatever I can find in the libraries about the lands to our west. Is that madness? Bel is sometimes with me when I read."

"That's a petty distinction, Mara. Your captain comprehends your motives as well as I do, and it stinks of duplicity for you to pretend she doesn't. Such tricks are beneath you. You used to have a finer sense of honesty."

Those last words stung. Mara felt her father's disappointment.

"And what's this I hear about you and Magician Peter searching for the history of that gem you wear? Does that have a part in your thoughts for the marches?"

Mara's hand went to the stone tethered at her breast. Dafythe's eyes followed the gesture; he'd seen it before. "It's nothing, Father," she answered. "I wish to find out where it came from. That's all." This was a blatant lie, but her father already thought her mad. If she told the truth about the Dragonseye, it would only confirm his worst fears.

"You don't think it magical?" Dafythe asked.

"I don't know that it is. It's what I was told, and I've asked Peter for his help in finding out if all I've been told is true."

Dafythe seemed somewhat doubtful of this answer, but he accepted it. "You might not like Peter's answer when he finds it, but I suppose these researches of yours are a harmless pursuit. They distract you from other interests. As to those other interests, Daughter, they must cease. Hear me in this if you hear nothing else: so long as I am Duke and have my voice to speak with authority in this land, you will not go on campaign to the western marches. I forbid it. Do not plan. Do not look at maps or histories of those far lands. Speak no word of it to anyone. I don't like to be reduced to giving such tyrannical orders, but you've made it necessary. Look westward no more."

"What did you expect him to do?" Ambris asked when Mara sought him out immediately after leaving the Duke's rooms. "Father is Father. He stands firm on what he believes to be a matter of principle. You've done nothing to make him change his mind. In fact, if I may speak frankly, all you've done is make him stand more firmly against you. You've acted contrary to all his wishes. You've ignored his direct commands. You've taken counsel with his courtiers, including myself, behind his back. Even if he'd been persuadable at the first, Mara, he couldn't bend before such defiance. He'd never be able to stand again. A duke can't be seen as weak, particularly where his children are concerned. And since he's made his will in this known, I'm afraid I can't aid you any further. I must be his councilor before I am yours."

"I didn't mean for you to choose between us," Mara answered, chastened. She knew that Ambris was right in all he said—her persistence had only made her father more determined to suppress her—but she also felt the awkwardness of the position she'd placed her brother in. Ambris had shown great loyalty to her by answering her questions and offering his advice. He'd done as much as he could for her without betraying his oath of fealty to Dafythe. "I'm grateful for your help. I know you have your own principles. You don't like the Northlands going to war any more than Father does. Yet you've supported me in this."

"I believe that Father is right," said Ambris. "War is humanity's greatest atrocity, encompassing all lesser evils, and a sign that in spite of our civilized manners we are no better than barbarians. But war it will be one day, whether I like it or no. As you are Prince of Gossunge and the Duke's presumptive heir, I am bound to aid and counsel you. My opinions on the subject are of no consequence."

He spoke without bitterness, simply stating facts, but Mara wondered at his seemingly calm acceptance of so unfair a fate. Usurped as he was, how could he not feel some resentment toward her? She would be Duke, but he was Dafythe's firstborn. Even now, he wielded more power in the Northlands as magistrate, chief administrator, and the Duke's closest advisor than she did as Prince. Ambris was well-liked and respected by all who knew him. If he put himself forward as the rightful heir after their Father's death, she was certain he would have no lack of adherents. And yet he not only deferred from such ambitions to supplant her, he supported her. He seemed as willing to champion her causes as he'd always championed Dafythe's. Could she behave so well if she were in his position?

"How horrid it must be for you," she said with sincere sympathy, "to be at a younger sister's bidding. You might be Duke yourself. You're far more fit to govern than I am."

"I have my place," Ambris told her. "I do not begrudge you yours." From his expression, Mara saw that he was astonished that she could imagine such a thing. "Mara, if I schemed against my sister and betrayed my father's trust, I should be a monster. I far prefer myself as I am."

"I'd give it to you if you'd only let me have my armies."

"Mara, never say that! Even in jest, never say it before another person." Then Ambris added in lighter tones, "If I were Duke, you'd have a harder time winning me to your will than Father. When you are Duke, you can do as you choose and I will stand by you. Until then, you must wait. Father will not relent."

"I pray he relents of his own accord," Mara said softly. She spoke more to herself than to Ambris, but he couldn't help hearing her words. He looked puzzled by them.

"How else might he relent, Mara? What would compel him?"

"I have it in my power," she answered reluctantly. "But I fear to use it, especially against someone so dear to me. I would have my way at last, but only at some terrible price."

This reply only increased Ambris's bewilderment. "Mara, what are you talking about?"

"*This*." She grasped the tether about her neck and held out the murky red stone.

"I've seen it," Ambris answered. "You've been wearing it for months. Kat tells me it was given you by the commander of Spainfort, who claimed it once belonged to Prince Denys."

"It did," said Mara. "Peter and I have confirmed that. He held it in his hands and saw in a vision how Denys and our grandfather discovered it. It was once in the hilt of Denys's sword and it was the power behind all his great victories." She hadn't dared to tell her father the full truth, but she felt she could confide in Ambris. "I think that the Redlyon may have known of its power. He tried to steal it from his brother. Peter saw that in his visions too."

"The Redlyon..."

"But it was Uncle Kharles who sent it to be hidden in the chapel at Spainfort. I can't say why, except that perhaps he didn't want in it his own hands and didn't want it in anyone else's. We don't know how it came to him. Peter is looking into that on my behalf. It is the same stone, Ambris. I've made certain of that. As it was Denys's, it is now mine. I haven't lost a battle since it came to me."

Ambris heard all this with astonishment. "A gemstone that grants you victory regardless of the circumstance?" He tried not to smile. "Mara, that is the silliest thing I've ever heard you say. I know that soldiers are given to superstition and keep talismans for good luck, but to hear a reasonable and well-educated noblewoman speak seriously of such ridiculous notions–! I can scarcely believe my ears."

"I knew you'd think me mad if I told you. You're too much like Father."

"I don't think you mad, Mara," her brother assured her in more gentle tones. "But you've let your imagination fly wildly over what can only be a string of coincidences. That gemstone you wear might once have belonged to Denys. If you and Peter have found proof that this is true, then I accept it as fact. I will even agree it's possible that Denys and our grandfather believed as you do, that that stone possessed some sort of magical power—though I find it difficult to credit such superstitious foolishness to a man of Uncle Kharles's intelligence. But I refuse to believe that it actually holds any such fantastic powers. Remember, Mara, that Denys lost in the end. No doubt, a certain amount of success lies in having bravery and confidence, but even if you go into battle believing yourself invincible, you'll be killed sooner or later."

"What about my victories in the Redlands?" asked Mara.

Ambris couldn't help smiling. "Everyone attributes them to your abilities, Sister. You seem to be the only person in the Northlands who questions your competence as a general."

"I don't. I am fit to lead. My commanders are the finest in the Northlands and our soldiers the bravest and best in the world. But our success in battle hasn't been entirely due to good soldiery. Sometimes, our victories fell to us through extremely odd luck. You've heard the tale of how the Spanish troops were forced out of their strongholds in the mountains by heavy rains."

"It was autumn," Ambris answered. "The rainy season in the south. Such landslides due to the rains are not remarkable."

"And the Con Permiso commander?" Mara knew that her brother had heard this tale too.

"He was attacked by a wild creature. Black bears and lions live in those mountains. I grant you these are fortunate coincidences for you, Mara, but they aren't magical. Why do you think they are?"

Ambris's rational explanations were no different from the ones she'd often told herself, and yet she felt in her heart that these events weren't rationally explicable. "Peter isn't the only one to have visions. I have also had dreams." She could tell Ambris. "I've dreamt of my dragon."

"Your talisman beast?"

Mara nodded. "The one who appeared to me as I lay wounded at the Shieldwall. He promised me gifts that day—this stone is one among them. The Dragonseye. It is his power I summon through it. In my dreams, I see him commit these acts to aid me. *He* destroyed the curtain wall at Spainfort. He killed the Con Permiso commander." If Ambris hadn't thought her mad before, surely he must now.

Whatever he thought of her, Ambris replied patiently, "Dreams are not always prophetic. I've dreamed of the palace garden all in bloom and Mother–" He meant Mara's mother, "still alive and walking with me along the paths. I've dreamed of wandering through the woods near Eadbury in search of Laurel. What do these portend? Nothing! A dream can be simply a dream. It isn't the same as a magician's visions. But I see you are unconvinced. Very well. May I propose a test?"

"A test?"

"There's one way to prove whether or not you're right about that stone's powers, Mara: employ it now. If you're so certain of the power you wield, let's see how it influences Father to change his mind."

Mara balked at this suggestion. "I couldn't!"

"What is it that frightens you more?" Ambris asked her. "That you may do some harm to Father, or that your magical gem will do nothing at all?"

After his interview with Mara, Dafythe sent for Lord Rafenshighte to have a private conversation. "Geoffrey, I've heard reports of your conduct which do not please me," the Duke began in his most authoritative tones. He was gratified to observe that Rafenshighte had the decency to look surprised and abashed. "It must stop—*now*—before you've brought irretrievable disgrace upon yourself. This is a dangerous game you meddle in."

"Dangerous, perhaps, My Lord," Rafenshighte agreed, his spirit rallying. "But disgraceful, how?" Dafythe began to bluster, amazed at the young nobleman's reply, when Rafenshighte went on, "The Prince your daughter is a grown woman. Your pardon if I offend, My Gracious Lord, but it is for *her* to decide if she finds me a fit companion. I assure you that my conduct with regard to her has always been irreproachable. My intentions are of the most respectful and honorable nature."

It was obvious that they weren't speaking of the same thing. "You and Mara–"

"Surely, My Lord, you've heard ugly gossip which twists the truth of the matter."

"Indeed," Dafythe answered, as if this was what he'd meant to discuss from the first. "There are so many odd rumors going about the court these days. I should like to hear the truth from your own lips, Geoffrey."

Rafenshighte nodded. "The truth is simple, My Lord: I've asked Prince Marguerytfor the undeserved honor of her hand in marriage. She hasn't yet given me an answer, but she promises to consider it."

The Duke had known for some time that Rafenshighte was courting his daughter for political reasons, but he'd never imagined that the strange relationship had advanced so far. Rafenshighte must be lying. He meant to be provoking. Even if he had dared to ask her, surely Mara couldn't mean to accept a proposal from such a glib and ambitious puppy? "I can stop it."

"You can delay it, Lord Duke," Rafenshighte answered. "Both Prince Margueryt and I realize that you must grant your approval as our liege before we are permitted to wed. I'm sorry you think me unsuitable as a husband for the Prince, but I'm not surprised to hear it's so. I didn't expect you to approve when you learned of it. Still, the proper forms must be preserved where fathers are concerned. It's only fair that you know how matters stand between us."

Dafythe didn't know how to answer this respectfully phrased but insolent response. Rafenshighte gave every appearance of humble courtesy, but his eyes were merry. He was enjoying Dafythe's discomfiture.

"I find it a remarkable match," the Duke answered. "I can't imagine why either of you thinks of it." But he did know very well why Geoffrey sought this marriage: as husband to the next Duke, Geoffrey would have more influence over her than anyone except Ambris. He would flatter her more than Ambris ever did. Dafythe didn't believe for a moment that he was at all fond of Mara. He meant to use her power. Why Mara intended it—if she did—Dafythe could only consider it as further evidence of her increasing irrationality. "You are so different, Prince Mara and yourself."

Rafenshighte grinned. "That's precisely why we're suited to each other, My Lord. I don't mind having a wife who rides off to campaign at the ends of the earth, and *she* will not be disappointed if I'm not the conventional sort of husband. `Tis no worse a match than the arranged marriages made between strangers these past thousand years or more. Prince Margueryt might've been married at your discretion to one of a dozen noble youths for political expediency—men she might like less well than me and men less fond of her. I expect we'll get on far better than most."

Dafythe's temper rose at this smirking response. "My daughter may put up with a great deal from you, Geoffrey," he answered tersely, "but she will not tolerate your chasing after boys."

"My Lord?" Rafenshighte looked confused for a moment, not expecting this accusation, then he laughed. "I see. You've heard other rumors too! Is there a particular boy you refer to?"

"You know whom I refer to! Andemyon tells me you've been hanging around the magician's home at nights, waiting to escort him through the gardens. You can't deny it's true. The boy has no reason to lie. He doesn't even see the danger in it. Geoffrey, I've endured quite enough of your predatory behavior. No more! Have you no decency? Andemyon is still a child!"

Rafenshighte was unabashed. "Never fear, My Gracious Lord. As it happens, I agree with you. Andemyon is too young to engage in the sort of pursuits you accuse me of. If it soothes your moral outrage, I assure you that I haven't harmed that splendid innocence of his by one word or deed."

"Then why do you seek him out?" Dafythe demanded.

"May I be honest?"

"I doubt it, Geoffrey."

Rafenshighte grinned. "Surely, My Lord, you see as well as I that our little Andemyon is going to be an extraordinary young man." Rafenshighte's tone was now conspiratorial, as if this understanding of Andemyon's qualities was something the two of them alone shared. "I wouldn't see him subverted from that fate. At present, he is a deliciously tight bud which can be ruined if it's forced to open too soon. I seek his friendship. I encourage the slow unfolding. I hope to be nearby to observe when that bud blossoms in a few years' time. Three or four years. Even five. Patience is one of my virtues."

"Then you do mean to have him eventually," Dafythe accused.

"I can't deny that I'd like it." Having promised truthfulness, Rafenshighte was apparently committed to its delivery. "But I doubt it will ever come to be. You know as well as I, My Lord, what happens to people who meddle with Lord Redmantyl's children. I have my weaknesses, as all men do, but I'm too fond of my own life to dare risk being struck by lightning even for the sake of such a beautiful boy."

"You will keep away from him while he is under my protection," Dafythe insisted. He might've been reassured by Geoffrey's last words, but the young nobleman's refusal to be ashamed of himself was too outrageous to endure. "In seventy years, I've never seen any beauty cause such a stir among my courtiers as much as that one innocent boy has done, especially among your sort."

"My sort," echoed Geoffrey. "What do you know of 'my sort'?"

"I know your wickedness."

"My Lord, when I was no older than your innocent little pet, I knew that I was condemned to Hell for what I was and no amount of prayer could alter that fact. What was there to do but ensure that I paid the full price of admission? I must say, you've usually been quite understanding in spite of my unrepentant wickedness."

"I've always tried to be tolerant of my courtiers' foibles in private life as long as they harm no one, but you–! You pass all boundaries! I may be able only to delay your plans with Margueryt, but she is a grown woman and must answer for herself in the end. Andemyon is another matter. As long as he is my herald, he is under my protection. I've sworn it. I warn you, Geoffrey—keep away from that boy!"

"Ah, of course." Rafenshighte's eyes brightened. "If you place the matter in *that* light, My Lord, I must obey. There are stories about the court to such effect, but I didn't believe them. I humbly pray your pardon for my intrusion."

Dafythe wasn't reassured by this sudden acquiescence, but it wasn't until after Geoffrey had bowed and retreated from the room that he realized what the young man meant by it.

Mara sat alone in her bedchamber, clasping the Dragonseye between the palms of her hands as if in prayer. She'd dismissed Ren for the evening and shut her doors against all visitors. For this, she needed to be alone.

Since her conversation with Ambris that afternoon, she'd begun to doubt all she believed to be true, and that was almost as frightening as being right. Her brother was always so reasonable. Did she dare to test the gemstone's powers as Ambris suggested? She'd never done so deliberately before, and the thought of evoking the Sonnedragon against her father was terrifying… but tempting. He would yield to her by no other means.

What if nothing happened? If her father didn't change his mind, that would mean that Ambris was right. This gem was only a flawed and ugly stone. Whatever its history, it held no powers. Her victories were due entirely to her own skill and some strange twists of luck. The Sonnedragon existed only in her imagination.

There was only one way to know.

She tightened her hands about the gemstone and shut her eyes. It was done.

For one moment, she was horrified at the irrevocable step she'd taken, then she felt a sense of great relief. For better or worse, events had been sent into motion. The gem would do its work. Father *must* come around.

heyghten

One evening just after midsummer, the Duke's thespian troupe performed a new play titled *The Dragon Displayed*—a dramatization of Mara's conquest of Terrojos. The aged Duke, his family, and courtiers walked in a solemn group down the Processional from the Palace gates to the Duke's Theatre to attend. This in itself was a remarkable event, for Dafythe hadn't gone out to his theatre in many years. While he continued to patronize the troupe, as he'd done since the theatre was first built more than sixty years ago, he rarely saw them unless they were invited to the Palace for private performances. But tonight was a special occasion. The Duke's presence had been particularly requested, and Dafythe graciously accepted the invitation. Like everyone else in Pendaunzel and the Palace, he was curious to see the play.

The Duke's box had been refurbished in anticipation of his acceptance. New blue velvet curtains were held back by golden ropes. The crest of the Northlands over the box—a hartshead, not Dafythe's lions nor Mara's dragon—was freshly gilded, as was all the ivy-vine trim. The chairs in the front row, with their high-backs like little thrones, were likewise freshly varnished and the cushions new. A row of less impressive chairs stood behind these royal seats and a bench ran along the back wall, though it was nearly impossible to see the play from this position. The Duke's box hung above the far right side of the proscenium; from its left end, it was possible to look down into the wing beyond the stage and see thespers changing their costumes and waiting for their cues while backstage hands rushed about to perform mysterious theatrical business with innumerable ropes.

While most of the courtiers who accompanied Dafythe into the city had taken their own boxes for the play, Ambris, Laurel, Mara, Kat, Geoffrey, and those heralds whose good behavior warranted a special treat were permitted to sit with the Duke. The theatre was already crowded when Dafythe and his family arrived. Attendants sternly policed the forward benches immediately around the stage; these were the cheap seats, and the theatre management was determined to have no rowdiness among the commoners tonight. Some excited murmurs and cries of "God bless his Grace!" could be heard as the Duke took the middle seat at the front of the box. The murmurs continued until Mara appeared, then the entire audience rose and cheered.

Mara stepped up to the rail to wave and bow her head in modest recognition of Pendanzel's enthusiasm for her. Walking down the Processional with Geoffrey at her elbow and three or four young boys in tabards arrayed on either side, it had been easy for her to imagine that this was how she would make public appearances when she was Duke and Geoffrey her consort—except, of course, her own heralds would be girls. When these cheering people were her own subjects, she would receive their accolades in this same way. How far away that day might be, she couldn't guess. Dafythe was very old, but his health remained good. Mara had kept a close eye on her father since she'd employed the Dragonseye against him; several weeks had passed and she saw no sign of his relenting or of his growing ill so that he was no longer able to stand in her away. While this might mean that the gemstone held no real power, she was nevertheless relieved that Dafythe had come to no harm through her.

As the applause subsided, she took her accustomed seat at her father's right. Ambris and Laurel sat to the Duke's left, and Kat was on Mara's other side. While a coolness had grown between the two Princes since Kat had carried tales to Dafythe, both were too eager to see this performance about their own adventures to feel uncomfortable seated so close to each other. The heralds, Rafenshighte, and the other members of the Council took their seats behind. Andemyon stood at the rail beside Laurel so that he could see the stage.

Little lads and maids in short tunics scrambled up on ropes to put out the lamps dangling above the rows of benches. The crowded theatre lay in darkness and the rushlights placed along the foot of the stage glowed all the brighter for it. The play was about to begin. A hush of expectation fell over the audience, but

Mara could still hear some excited whispers in the dark.

The story of *The Dragon Displayed* was set entirely in the marches, represented on stage by canvases painted with rocky red mountains. A castle cleft between two peaks was meant to be *Ojos des Mantegnas* though, as Kat whispered to Mara, it looked nothing like it. Tall wooden walls, painted in dappled gray to look like stone, stood in the foreground to represent the fortress of Dennefort. These were drawn backstage by burly hands once the armies of the Northlands marched.

The woman who played Prince Kat was pretty and petite, and she seemed weighted down by her relatively light, tin stage armor. Mara had seen enough performances by the troupe to know that this woman usually played romantic roles. Frederik was also played by one of the usual lovers and looked no more like a true soldier than the stage-Kat did. The two enacted a tragic love story against the backdrop of the war. The thesper who took the role of Prince Mara was the woman who normally acted as the troupe's jester. Mara's first thought that this was meant to be a joke and she wondered why her father's troupe meant to insult her, but as the play progressed, she realized that they had made a good choice. The jester's athletic skill as a tumbler gave her the energy to carry off the part. Her tin armor didn't weigh her down; she wore it as naturally as Mara wore her own battle gear. And no other woman in the troupe would have been so convincing as she leapt about the stage in battle and cut down the innumerable Spanish soldiers that came at her from all sides. She also performed surprisingly well in the dramatic role—as valiant and princely as Mara herself could wish, without a hint of burlesque.

The Dragon Displayed was a rousing pageant about the Northland's new heroes, but it wasn't the truth. Some parts of the true story no one but Mara and her closest friends knew. Other parts had been discretely altered to avoid giving offense to the Duke's family. Frederik's ancestry was never mentioned, even though Prince Denys featured heavily in the story. While the Bright Prince never actually appeared onstage, his presence was felt as vividly as any character who did; his name was spoken so often, and his sword, displayed prominently on Dennefort's wall, had its part to play in several scenes. The stage-Mara approved her cousin's love-affair with the Marchion. In a scene that was nothing like their quarrel by the campfire the night before the first battle, the fictitious Mara and Kat planned a wedding as part of their victory celebrations. Gone, too, was Kat's rage of grief at Spainfort. Frederik's death occurred offstage.

To Mara, the most interesting part was the recreation of her vision of the Sonnedragon. An image of a fiery red dragon appeared, flapping its wings above the wounded warrior-prince as she lay alone on the stage. This incredible effect was achieved with mirrors, cheesecloth, and firelight shining through an orange glass. Mara had glimpsed these items backstage before the show had started. The words this dragon spoke were not quite the words Mara herself had heard, but then she'd never repeated them accurately to even her closest confidants.

The play ended with the surrender of the Terrojos governor. The stage-Mara gave a speech of thanks to the Highest Lord for sending her the Sonnedragon to guide her. Good fortune was foretold for her future reign.

"Was it very strange to see yourself portrayed on stage?" Dafythe asked his daughter and niece after the last scene had concluded. "I hope it didn't distress you too much, Kat, seeing the death of poor Frederik again."

"No, Uncle. I was afraid it might, but it was so different from what really happened to us, it was like watching something else happening to other people. They weren't us at all. I ought to have felt more, shouldn't I? As if I were seeing Frederik fall again. But that wasn't him." The thesper who had played Frederik was at that moment standing on the stage with the other members of the troupe, taking his bows.

"It's the way they tell the story in Pendaunzel, Prince Katheryne," said Geoffrey from his seat immediately behind Kat's. "The tale as it will be told for generations after we've gone. Who can say that it isn't more suitable than the truth?"

"I'm not sure that I didn't like this story more than my own, even if it wasn't true," Kat answered. "What about you, Mara? Do you prefer your own story to this one?"

"I prefer what's true," Mara answered, but she was thinking how odd it was. This play *was* her story. She'd seen everything that had happened to her in the marches played out again here tonight on stage, but none of it was the same. Most of the facts remained, but the truth behind them had altered in strange and subtle ways. Did the difference lie in who was telling the tale? A different story might be told by each of us who were there, Mara realized. Kat's story will not be the same as mine, nor will Taumie's nor Bel's, nor Alyx's even though she was at my side for most of the war. None of us have all the pieces of the tale. I have more than most, but not everything. The common soldiers in my army will speak of their part in the battles we led. Khrystophania will have another tale entirely to pass on to her children. And the people of the Northlands who weren't there to see will remember it this way. We will be remembered as great and valiant heroes, and not as mere women. Do they think of us as heroes now?

She gazed down at the crowd, who were rising from their seats and shuffling toward the open doors at the back of the theatre. Many paused to gaze up at the Duke's box with wide-eyed expressions. Yes, they were heroes to the folk of Pendaunzel. At three and thirty, she had already slipped from the living Prince into legend.

"Ought we go down to congratulate the thespers on their performance?" asked Ambris.

"I believe they are expecting it," said Dafythe. "You and Kat must certainly go and praise the thespers who played you, Mara. That is simple courtesy."

Mara consented and the group in the Duke's box prepared to leave. Andemyon had remained perched on the arm of Laurel's chair throughout the performance. The two were still talking about the dragon and how the trick had been done. Some of the less-favored boys had fallen asleep on the bench at the back of the box, and courtiers gently shook them to wake them.

A private stair led down from the corridor behind the boxes to the wing on the right side of the stage. The stage-manager was waiting below to welcome the Duke and his party, and offered to escort them to the dressing-rooms. The thespers were half out of their costumes—wigs cast off and tin armor discarded, but still in shirts and hose. They had all expected or at least hoped that the Princes would favor them with a visit, but the appearance of the Duke took them by surprise. The meeting took on the air of a formal presentation in spite of their informal attire. The thespers gracefully bowed low and expressed themselves to be honored by Dafythe's compliments. Kat said a few kind words to the couple who had played Frederik and herself, but made no critical remarks about the truth behind the tale. Mara was more fulsome about her counterpart's performance. Everyone spoke highly of the dragon.

"We were most impressed—it was almost like a magical spell," said Laurel. The stage-manager assured her that there was no magic involved. "Can't we go and see how it works?"

The stage manager bowed low. "It would be the greatest pleasure to grant your request, My Lady, but we humble thespians have our secrets that we must guard."

"That's all right," Laurel responded. "Andemyon was once a thesper, and I traveled with a company too when I was young. We won't give away secrets."

"Andemyon–?"

Laurel indicated the herald at her side. "His mother was a famous thesper, head of my uncle Lord Redmantyl's troupe."

"Mother's troupe had a dragon made of cloth that they worked with long sticks," Andemyon offered. "It fought with St. George."

One of the thespers laughed at this. "You hope to trade one secret for another, lad?"

The boy blushed, and Dafythe came to his defense. "Surely you can make this one exception? The Lady Laurel has given you her word, and I give you my own that she and Andemyon are to be trusted."

After this, the stage-manager would have permitted the entire group to view the apparatus behind the dragon's appearance if Dafythe had wished it. A backstage hand was summoned and asked to escort the lady and herald across the stage to the other wing.

As they walked away, Mara heard one thesper whisper to another, "So that's the one, is it? The pretty, fair-headed lad?"

"Yes, that's him," came the reply. "They say he's the Duke's Cat."

Mara had heard this same phrase around the court lately—and even among the excited murmurs in the theatre tonight—but she'd assumed that they were referring to her cousin Kat. Now, she realized that they meant Andemyon, although she didn't understand why.

Dafythe hadn't overheard this exchange, but she could see that Ambris had. Drawing closer to her brother, Mara gripped his arm and asked, "What do they mean?"

"Not here," Ambris replied in an undertone. "I'll tell you all I know about it when we are home."

"There've been terrible rumors around the court," Ambris told Mara and Kat later that night after they'd returned to the Palace. Dafythe had gone to his bedchamber; the rest of the courtiers had likewise retired. The halls of the Manor were dark and silent and the only lighted candles were in Mara's room, where the three now sat in private conference. Ambris was obviously embarrassed to speak of the matter, but after the incident at the theatre, he felt it necessary that his sister and cousin know all. "It's rumored that Father has taken that boy into his bed. As you heard tonight, Mara, they call him 'The Duke's Cat.' It is an abbreviation for 'catamite.'"

"Christ's Mercy!" Kat cried out, shocked.

"That's absurd!" Mara was first struck by the ridiculousness of the accusation. "Father's one hundred! Even when he was younger, there was never any gossip that he fancied little boys."

"Andemyon is sixteen now—of an age to give consent—but only just," said Ambris. "If anything has happened between them, it may have begun before this spring."

"Nothing could happen!" Mara insisted. "They must be mad, those who say such things. It's madness to believe it."

"I'm not mad, but I am afraid Father may be," her brother responded. "I would be happy to reject these tales as filthy lies. I too thought at first that it was impossible. As you say, Mara, Father is far too old for such activities, and his reputation has been impeccable these last fifty years. But there was more than this to consider. I've been told of strange behavior by Father that would be unthinkable for him if he were in full control of himself."

"Told? By whom?" Mara demanded.

"It was Othel who drew the stories to my attention last week. Talk has been going on for much longer than that, but no one dared repeat these ugly rumors before one of us. He thought I must hear about them before the matter was spoken of openly.

I've conducted discreet inquiries among Father's personal staff, and discovered one or two points that are disturbing. First, they all say that Father is overly familiar with the boy. He openly prefers Andemyon to all his other heralds. Andemyon sings for him. He accompanies Father on private walks, reads to him, plays chess with him."

"Yes, we've all seen *that*," Kat said impatiently. "But I've never seen anything in it to alarm me. Have you?"

Mara shook her head.

"Nor have I," Ambris agreed. "But there's more. You also know that the heralds watch over Father through the night in case his health should suddenly fail. One boy is assigned to take the duty each night, yet Father requests that Andemyon stay with him three and four nights in a row. The next point is more suggestive: on one night recently, when Andemyon was in attendance, Father woke and complained of chest pains and shortness of breath. The boy was sent to fetch the physician—dressed in his shirt and a loosely-laced tunic. The heralds are meant to wear their livery during this night duty."

Mara and Kat glanced at each other, but had nothing to say to this.

"I've conducted certain private interviews with various persons around the court and heard more alarming stories," Ambris continued. "Some claim that Father has been seen kissing the boy in the gardens. Others say they've heard that Andemyon has received extravagant gifts, such as jewels, or that he's been promised a prestigious position at court once he leaves the heralds. But these stories are unsubstantiated. I've found no proof that of any of this has actually happened and believe it to be no more than wild gossip. People repeat the tales they've heard, but no witnesses have come forward, save for Father's physician."

"What does he say?" Mara asked.

"For his part, it seems the tale is true. On the night that Father suffered his pains, the boy came to summon him and wasn't dressed in full livery."

"It could be perfectly innocent," Kat spoke up. "You can't expect a boy to sit up in that stiff tabard night after night."

"That's so," Ambris agreed. "But one boy shouldn't have the duty night after night. The court has noticed Father's preference for Andemyon, and this one fact has surely been the root of all the gossip that's followed. Whether or not any other part is true, this surely is. The rest remains to be examined."

"It *can't* be true, not the rest of it," Mara insisted, though not with the same conviction she'd shown at the beginning of this discussion.

"I don't like to believe it either," Ambris answered, "but we can't ignore it at this point. If the tale has carried to Pendaunzel, then it's become too widespread to be disregard. We must confront it."

"What are we to do?"

"I intend to continue my investigation until I discover the truth. If there's nothing more to this ugly story but lies, then Father's reputation must be cleared and his slanderers brought to account for their crime against him as well as against a young boy. If there *is* something to it, then I can only assume that Father is in his dotage. He's no longer entirely in his right senses and become madly infatuated with a pretty youth—though we may hope, due to the infirmity of his age, that the worst has not occurred."

"And if the worst has occurred..?" Mara allowed the sentence to trail off. She didn't know how to finish it. What if the worst rumors *were* true? What would they do then? What would they be able to do? Ambris surely knew the law pertaining to governors unfit to govern. If their father was no longer in full possession of his faculties and had abused a boy under his protection, they could certainly remove Andemyon from danger and hush up any scandal. What else did they have the authority to do? Could they prevent Dafythe from committing greater abuses? Could they remove him from power?

The thought of it frightened her. In spite of her differences with her father, she never wanted to usurp him. No, the worst couldn't be true. It was impossible to imagine Dafythe doing such a thing. Even in his dotage, he never could harm anyone. If there was any truth at all behind these stories, there must be another explanation.

Another explanation occurred to her so suddenly that it was almost as if someone had spoken the words near her ear. "There's another possibility to be considered," she said. "This may be

Andemyon's doing, not Father's. Perhaps he isn't so innocent as he seems."

"Oh, Mara!" Kat protested. "You must be joking! You can't truly be saying that that young boy–"

"No, nothing so bad as *that*. Andemyon is very young, but he's not a child—perhaps a bit backward for a boy of sixteen, but no fool. Everyone says he's remarkably intelligent. You've often said so yourself, Ambris." Mara turned to her brother. "He thinks more deeply than boys his age are wont to, and he keeps his thoughts to himself. What if he's ambitious? He must've seen how his family has risen under Father's favor. You can't deny that they haven't, since Laurel has become your wife. Who's to say that the boy hasn't taken some advantage of Father's affection for him? He needn't have done anything really *wrong*–" she added quickly, for Ambris looked as astonished as Kat at hearing such thoughts from her. "I refuse to believe anything of the sort has happened between them. All Andemyon would have to do is look like an angel and be attentive to Father. He can't help doing that much! If poor Father's mind *is* turning, then he'd grant whatever favors Andemyon asked of him."

Her brother and Kat were silent for so long following this speech that Mara began to wonder if either would speak at all.

Then Kat said, "It could be so, Ambris. I don't like to think anything has happened either, but I'd much rather it be as Mara says than Uncle Dafythe preying upon an innocent boy. At least, we can protect him from Andemyon."

"Andemyon must be removed from Father's service immediately," Ambris agreed. "I'll see to that."

"It won't stop this awful gossip," Kat said dispiritedly. "It might even start more talk. Some people will see it as proof—if there was nothing behind the stories, we wouldn't have to take Andemyon away."

"I know," Ambris answered. "That can't be helped. But it will at least prevent both from suffering further harm. If Father has forgotten himself in his dotage, it will take the boy out of his reach. And if Andemyon is playing up to Father, then Father will be safe from such blandishments."

"Then you think I may be right?" asked Mara.

Her brother shook his head. "I don't yet know where the truth lies. There are only two people who can tell us. We can't approach Father until we are more certain. The one to be questioned is Andemyon."

Ambris spoke to Old Toppet, who was in charge of the heralds, early the next morning to ensure that Andemyon would no longer be given night duty with the Duke. He intended to bring the boy into his own office as soon as he could do so without drawing undue attention. So much was easily accomplished. Finding Andemyon alone so that he could be questioned proved a more difficult task, for Andemyon was never alone. He continued his daily duties of attending Dafythe with the other heralds, and when he wasn't thus occupied, he spent his time with Laurel. It was impossible to summon him away without having to explain why he was wanted; Ambris was more anxious to keep this state of affairs from his wife than he was to keep it from his father, for Laurel was very fond of Andemyon and almost as protective of him as her own small children.

They found no opportunity for several days, until the night of the Duke's 74th anniversary of his coronation. All the court and half the city turned out for this grand celebration on the Palace grounds. The lawns and gardens around the State Hall were ablaze with lights and the Hall itself crowded when Dafythe made his appearance with his seven heralds.

Andemyon stepped forward from this group to shout out the well-practiced announcement, "Gentle nobles, good citizens, all hail thee Dafythe Gabriel Holyrood Ambris Lyonsbloode Plantagenet, Prince of the Norman Empire, Grand Duke, Sovereign Lord Governor and Protector of the Northlands, Preserver of the Peace, Defender of the Faith, by Grace of God!"

Mara watched this angelic child in his velvet and ribbons, bright curls tumbling about his shoulders. Was he no more than an innocent boy? Was he an ambitious young schemer, or was he a victim of the aged Duke's misplaced affections?

Andemyon returned to his place at Dafythe's immediate right. As the small procession came slowly down the ancient stone steps, Dafythe reached up to place a hand on Andemyon's shoulder to keep his balance. His fingers brushed the boy's curls. Mara shuddered. It was an innocuous gesture, but with such thoughts in her head, it was unbearable to see. From the murmurs in the crowd around her, she knew that others had seen it too and were wondering as well. She began to feel sick.

"Can't we get Andemyon away tonight?" Kat whispered to her and to Ambris, for the three of them stood together near the foot of the stairs. "Surely Uncle Dafythe won't keep his heralds in attendance all evening? It isn't a formal ceremony—it's a party! He must let the boys go and have their fun once he takes his seat. At his age, he won't be wandering around greeting his guests for long."

"We'll have to be quick if we want to draw Andemyon out without being observed," said Ambris. "Mara, you're the strategist. What do you recommend?"

"If we can, one of us ought to take him out into the courtyard," Mara suggested after a moment's thought. "The other two must watch and follow. We'll be noticed if we all go out together. The best time for it will be when everyone's gone out to the great lawn to see the rockets set off. There are sure to be people wandering about the gardens even then, but we've no better chance of speaking to him privately without being interrupted or overheard."

"What are you whispering about?" Laurel asked as she approached them. "You look as if you're planning a conspiracy."

"We've been discussing Father's intended activities," Ambris lied—a remarkable event!

"I was wondering if he planned staying up late for all the festivities," Kat added quickly. "Uncle Dafythe gets tired so early in the evenings, I don't expect he'll remain with us long enough to see the Cathay fire-rockets. `Tis pity—he's always had a liking for such tricks from foreign and faraway lands. But he's sure to hear them, even from his bedchamber!" The conversation continued along these lines while Laurel was with them.

"Doesn't she know?" asked Mara after Laurel had gone to speak to Dafythe herself.

"She guesses that something troubles me, but I haven't told her of the gossip, nor confided our plans," Ambris replied. "I am most reluctant to. It isn't usual that I keep things from her, but I dread to imagine what she might do if she believes the worst."

"Do you mean what she might do to Father, or to the people

who've carried tales against Andemyon?" asked Mara.

"Both."

"Then we must take care she doesn't learn of it 'til Andemyon is safely away from Father." She glanced at the Duke, who had taken his seat on the dais beneath the Northlands' hartshead. Laurel was with him among a group of courtiers offering their good wishes and hopes that Dafythe's reign would continue for many years more. The heralds stood arrayed at either side of the Duke's throne. Some of the boys were trying not to look bored; others had their eyes on the refreshment tables laden with countless delicacies. "Watch for the first chance that presents itself," Mara said to her brother and cousin, and they went their separate ways.

Each made the motions of enjoying the celebration, took refreshment, chatted with the courtiers, but all three kept an eye upon the Duke. When the musicians struck up cheerful music, Geoffrey humbly requested to lead the first dance with Mara.

"You seem distracted, My Prince," he teased her after they'd taken hands and led the long column of dancing pairs through the opening steps. The dance was a simple promenade, with no complicated maneuvers; Mara had learnt it in childhood, but she faltered tonight, for she paid little attention to her movements and cast frequent glances at the Duke's dais. "What can be more important, I wonder, than a dance?" Geoffrey turned his head to see where she was looking. "Are you concerned that My Lord Dafythe mightn't approve of my partnering you, even for half an hour?"

"No," Mara answered absently. "I'm not troubled by that."

"I'm most gratified to hear it! I gives me greater hopes." Geoffrey lowered his voice. "Your father has heard that you've considered honoring me above all other men, and he means to put a stop to it. Did you know? He called me to his chambers not long ago to speak severely about our presumed betrothal and said he would never consent to it. That is of course his right, so we must abide until your choice of consort is your own to make. While I trust My Lord will continue to reign for some time to come, I don't imagine we will have to wait as long as *that*."

But Mara gave less attention to these attempts at flirtation than she did to her dance-steps.

More than an hour passed before Dafythe retired. Before the Duke departed for his chambers, he bid the festivities go on and his guests enjoy themselves. He gave his heralds liberty until their bed-time.

Andemyon, now free of his duties, wandered shyly around the edges of the crowd, then went to a table bearing crystal decanters and enormous silver bowls of wine-punch. At the end of this table stood tall doors open to the courtyard. Ambris followed the boy as if he meant to refresh his own cup from the same bowl where Andemyon was filling a cup for himself. He took Andemyon by the elbow. “Come with me, Demy.”

They went out into the garden. Mara and Kat, who had been covertly watching from positions on either side of the open doors, waited until the pair had gone past them, then fell into formation like a phalanx of guards at the rear. It was done so quickly that Mara was confident their exit went unobserved. Andemyon, however, heard their footsteps on the flagstones behind him; he turned and looked from one Prince to the other, then up at Ambris, but didn’t ask what was going on, nor did he try to break free. When they reached the fountain at the center of the courtyard, he sat on the stone rim where Ambris indicated.

“Andemyon,” Ambris began gently, “we must ask you certain questions about what has passed between you and my father the Duke. You are often alone with him during the nights.”

“I attend him at night, My Lord,” the boy responded promptly, as if this were the information Ambris sought. “That is, I did until this past week. Toppet says I mustn’t anymore, for I’m to begin new duties soon.”

“Yes, but tell us: what occurred when you were called to this duty?”

“I would sit up with My Lord Duke. If he couldn’t sleep, I would amuse him as he requested me. If he were taken ill, I was to fetch the physician.”

“As you did one night shortly before Midsummer?”

“Yes.” Andemyon nodded. “He—My Lord the Duke—awoke in the night and said that he had a terrible pain just here.” He placed his own hand on the left side of his chest. “So I ran to Dr. Dimitrios’s room and brought him back. He said that it was something My Lord Dafythe had eaten before going to bed, and not his heart, that distressed him, and gave some physic to soothe his pains."

"When you went to fetch the physician, you were not in your full livery," said Ambris. "We have confirmed from Dr. Dimitrios that this is so."

Andemyon first looked frightened, then relieved. "Yes, that's so," he admitted.

"You are aware, Andemyon, that it is the custom for the herald who attends my father in the night to remain fully dressed."

"Yes, I know," the boy answered meekly.

"Then why did you remove your tabard?" asked Ambris.

"My Lord Duke said I might."

"Did you ask if you could, or did he invite you to?" Kat asked. She and Mara had allowed Ambris to take the lead in questioning Andemyon, but they were growing impatient with his roundabout, lawyerly way of asking questions.

Andemyon turned to her. "My Lord saw one night that I wasn't able to sleep comfortably in it, Prince Kat. He said it was foolish for me to keep it on, and I needn't wear it again whenever I spent the night with him so long as no one else saw. I should've put it on when I went for Dr. Dimitrios," he added in apologetic tones, "but I was frightened for Lord Dafythe and didn't think of what was proper."

"Do you truly know what's proper?" Mara wondered. "What else has Father bade you do, Demy? Is there nothing more you have to tell us?"

"I don't know what you wish me to say, Prince Mara."

"We want to know what Father's done with you—or what you've done with him."

The boy gaped up at her, but gave no answer.

"Andemyon, we must have the truth," Ambris spoke more sternly now. "Before God and upon your honor. This is a very serious matter. My father's reputation may depend upon it, and yours as well. You are very young and mayn't comprehend the danger you are placed in. I vow to you that we will not be angry with you so long as you tell no lies. You spend many nights in the Duke's chambers, at his request. You say you've been bid to sleep without your full livery. Tell us more. Where do you sleep on these nights? On the coucherie at the foot of Father's bed? On the bed? Have you ever lain in bed beside him?"

"What is this? Why are you asking him such things?" The unexpected voice from the darkness of the shrubbery startled them all. Laurel stepped forward. She had obviously overheard the last part of their interview. "I guessed that something was going on. Is *this* what you three have been whispering over and making plans for—the filthy questions you meant to put to Demy?"

"I didn't want you to know," Ambris explained. "Rumors are wild about the Palace and Pendaunzel, and perhaps beyond. We have to discover the truth behind them."

"You can't believe such rubbish, Ambris! You–" Laurel looked from Kat to Mara. "Do you truly think that there's been something scandalous between them? Mara, by your own words, you seem to be implying that Andemyon's done wrong."

"We don't wish to believe it," said Ambris, "but Father's behavior toward Andemyon has been most peculiar lately. The gossip can't be ignored. Demy is the only one who can answer for the truth or falsity of it."

"The truth is that you're too frightened to confront your father, who can answer for himself more readily than Demy can. `Tis far easier to interrogate a little boy than a Duke, isn't it? You don't have to be careful of what you say. You can bully him into giving whatever answers you choose. I don't believe a word of it, but if there *was* any wrongdoing, I'd suspect the grown man first, not the child."

"You speak of my father," Ambris reminded her.

"And you speak of my brother!" Laurel spat back.

This answer jolted Andemyon from his confusion at the quarrel going on over his head. He hadn't guessed. The others were likewise surprised. There'd been much speculation around the court about the Lady's true parentage, but Laurel herself had never before declared that *she* knew whose daughter she was.

"You know well, my love, that Lord Redmantyl will not forgive you for our marriage," she told Ambris as she lay a protective hand on Andemyon's shoulder. "He thinks it the ruin of me. And you know what he did when he thought that Orlan had been deceived and disgraced by the Mayor of Storm Port. Demy is his darling pet, more dear to him than even Orlan or I. What do you imagine he'd do to those who threaten the reputation of his best-beloved child? Pendaunzel and all those courtiers who tell lies wouldn't stand long before his wrath."

Sparks of some previously untapped power rose in Laurel with her anger. She "blazed with it"; the Princes had heard this phrase used to describe the glamour of powerful magicians, but they'd never before seen it manifest. Laurel shone more brightly than the light from the torches at the State Hall's doors. She'd given up her apprenticeship to marry Ambris, but she kept the full force of her magic all the same. If she employed it, she might truly be a wizard to match her father.

The intensity of this speech stunned Ambris, but he responded evenly, as if he'd seen his wife in a blaze of fury before and was undaunted by it. "If Andemyon is your brother, then he is also mine in law. I must care for his best interests as I would for my own brother, or for one of my sons if they were in this same position. It's my duty to protect his reputation as well as Father's."

Laurel nodded. "So he is, and it's well you remember it."

"I will speak with my father, Laurel, but I cannot confront him with questions about such terrible deeds unless I'm certain what crime has been committed. We know nothing of what's passed between them—has Father actually taken Andemyon into his bed, or is he merely infatuated? Has Andemyon encouraged Father's affection for him?"

"You can't accuse Andemyon without proof either," said Laurel.

"I don't. I seek the proof—if there are such proofs to be found—now. We brought Andemyon out here so that we could question him in confidence. If I see any cause to believe some improper act has in fact taken place, I will also ask Dimitrios to examine him," Ambris answered. "No one has made accusations."

"I heard questions that sounded very like accusations." His wife looked pointedly at Mara and Kat.

"We meant no harm to him, Laurel," said Kat.

"Then you needn't have gone about this in such a bullying way! Very well—If you must have the truth of it, I'll ask him." Laurel sat down beside Andemyon and forced herself to be calm as she spoke to him. "Demy, we must clear your name, and the Duke's too. You needn't be afraid, for I will defend you. Tell me: when you attended My Lord Dafythe at night, what did you do?"

"I would tell him stories," Andemyon answered.

"What sort of stories?" asked Mara.

"Mama's–" he looked to Laurel for assistance.

"His mother was a storyteller as well as headthesper," Laurel explained. "She used to tell wonderful tales of the old myths—Oedipus in medieval trappings, the fall of Troy, Arthur's knights."

Andemyon nodded.

"And you repeated these tales to Uncle Dafythe?" Kat asked.

The boy nodded again.

"What else?" asked Laurel.

"I would sing to him. When he couldn't sleep, he asked me to sing his favorite hymns, or else a lullaby. He taught me a Galsh one that his nurse used to sing to him in the nursery when he was a little boy."

While this wasn't the sort of detail they were dreading to hear, there was something vulnerable and intimate about it that made Mara feel uncomfortable. They were prying into her father's secrets and learning things that they had no right to know. "What else?" she asked.

"We talk, Prince Mara," said Andemyon.

"What did you and Lord Dafythe talk about?" Laurel prompted him.

"Different things. I would tell him about Wizardes Cliff, and Mother's troupe. He wanted to know what sort of place I would be suited for at court when I was of an age to leave off my service as a herald." Growing more confident under Laurel's protection, and anxious to give whatever information would help him out of this frightening situation, Andemyon was finding his voice.

"Has Father promised you advancement at court?" asked Ambris. "Have you asked him to grant you some prestigious place?"

"My Lord Duke says that I ought to go to the university to be educated," Andemyon volunteered. "He said that was how I would serve him best. He promised to write to Father about it."

This was touching and interesting, but it still wasn't what they wanted to know. Although she was careful to speak gently to the boy, Laurel had to be more specific. "Andemyon, has My Lord the Duke ever put his hands upon you in a familiar way or kissed you—not as he might touch or kiss one of his grandchildren, but in a way that felt wrong to you? Has he offered you gifts? Has he spoken to you of love?"

To each question, Andemyon answered, "No, Laurel," with an ever-increasing look of puzzlement.

At last, Laurel sighed. "Demy, do you understand what's been said about you?" She explained patiently, "Do you know of how a man and woman will lie together in love? They embrace so that they join together. Do you know about such things? Has the Duke done such a thing with you?"

Andemyon's eyes were wide. "But, Laurel–"

"Has he?"

"No."

Laurel looked up at her husband triumphantly.

"But, Laurel," Andemyon continued his protest. "I'm a boy." He twisted to look up and around at the others, wondering that they hadn't considered this most pertinent fact. "I'm a boy."

"Yes, my darling," Laurel embraced him fiercely. "A most wonderful boy. Go along now. You don't want to miss the fire-rockets. Speak to no one of this, not even My Lord Dafythe. Do you understand?"

"Yes, Laurel." Andemyon rose and darted back into the State Hall. There was a loud, sizzling hiss from some distant point on the lawn. A bright point of light shot high into the dark sky to explode in a burst of red and yellow sparks like an enormous flower overhead. The first rockets were being set off, but their colorful light was nothing to the flash of anger in Laurel's eyes as she turned back to the Princes and Ambris.

"Innocent? Beyond all doubt, he is! Have your father's physician confirm it if you like. He'll find nothing amiss. Demy's done nothing. He knows nothing about it. The poor child didn't even understand the questions!" She left them and followed after Andemyon.

nyneten

The delicate task of speaking to Dafythe was left to Ambris. Mara never learned precisely what was said during that private conference, but she saw the effects of it upon her father. That anniversary celebration was to be the Duke's last public appearance. Dafythe withdrew, first from all official duties, then to his chambers, then deeper and deeper into himself. Only a few select people—his children, his physician—were admitted to see him. No boys attended the Duke in the night now; Dr. Dimitrios's assistants, grown men and women, took that duty. Though the physician said that there was little physically wrong with Dafythe beyond the ailments common to a man of his age, Mara was shocked at how much her father was changed in only a few days' time. Dafythe had truly become old. Not merely his face, but his hesitant voice, his impersonal tone of conversation, his uncertain demeanor, were unlike the father she'd always known. It was as if the news of the gossip had struck at his mind and his heart and caused greater damage than the physical pains he'd suffered on that night when Andemyon had gone to fetch the doctor.

She and Ambris had agreed that an open denial would only give credence to the rumors by acknowledging their existence and might make matters worse. They would behave publicly as if they'd never heard a word whispered against Dafythe. Ambris, believing firmly now that Dafythe had done nothing disgraceful, privately made efforts within the court to dispel the rumors, but the stories had spread too far to be effectively suppressed. Some people would always wonder if there'd been something to it after all.

Andemyon along with four other heralds were quietly given posts elsewhere within the Palace. He worked now assisting the scribes in the Hall of Record. Andemyon had also been moved to chambers near Laurel's and Ambris's; in fact, his two little rooms, intended for an attending maid or lady-in-waiting, were connected to Laurel's. She had charge of him during the evening hours while Ambris oversaw his days. Both protected the boy though they remained at odds. Laurel hadn't completely forgiven Ambris for doubting the boy's innocence. She hadn't forgiven Mara or Kat either, but they could avoid meeting each other. Husband and wife, however, must see each other every day.

"Laurel has written to Lord Redmantyl, to gain his permission to send Andemyon to Maryesfont in the autumn," Ambris informed his sister and cousin at the beginning of August. "Since Father spoke of it when he was in his own mind, it must've been what he wanted for Andemyon's future. I believe it is the best course. We can't keep the boy here at court much longer. He's become too dangerous."

"Dangerous?" echoed Mara. "What do you mean? He and Father haven't been allowed to see each other in weeks." Since she overheard no recent whispers about "the Duke's Cat," she'd believed that the gossip was dying away, having nothing to sustain it.

"It isn't Father I refer to, but myself," Ambris answered with a note of embarrassment. "You mayn't have heard, but since I've taken charge of Andemyon, he's become notably attached to me. When he isn't occupied with his new duties, he follows me about and wants to be of service in any way he can."

Mara was astonished and yet she couldn't suppress a slight smile at this strange turn of events. "I would've thought he'd resent you for the way we questioned him, as Laurel does."

"No. I've become his champion. People told wicked lies about him, and I've made them stop—that's how he regards it. Laurel doesn't like to see it, though it's difficult to say if Andemyon or I anger her more. It's a child's admiration for one who's defended him, no more, but he doesn't realize how others perceive it after the propriety of his relationship with Father has been put to question. Laurel is quite right. He's too innocent to understand the impression he leaves."

Mara was trying not to smile, when Kat laughed aloud. "Poor Ganymede! I don't suppose he ever meant to draw the eagle's attention."

Ambris wasn't amused. "It isn't a joke," he said. "What's said in jest today may be ruinous gossip tomorrow. We can't afford a second scandal, not after what's happened to Father. Andemyon will be safer at Maryesfont. His mother's family lives there. They will house and look after him while he completes his education. I must also tell you that Laurel intends to leave for Eadbury with the children as soon as Andemyon is sent off."

"She's not leaving over *this*?" asked Mara.

"In part. She says she's sick of the court and its vicious gossip, but there is another reason too. She sits up late at night in her bedchamber, watching the sky from her windows. She's sensed something… out there, and it frightens her. I can see that much for myself, but when I ask what disturbs her so, she refuses to explain. Magicians will keep their secrets, and I've always known that she has her own to guard. Whatever the reason, she's anxious to be away from Pendaunzel, and I will not detain her if that is her wish."

As Dafythe abrogated his responsibilities as Duke, it became clear that those duties must be shifted to another. The Council considered appointing a Regent. They met frequently during those summer weeks to debate the merits of the only two possible candidates: Dafythe's Lord High Chancellor and firstborn but illegitimate son, or his daughter and heir. Ambris and Mara were summoned to hear the results of these conferences.

"We've voted more than once," Lord Tuxsetau informed them, "and we find ourselves divided evenly each time. For the sake of future accord, I will not reveal who has voted for whom."

"I'm not ashamed to declare where my loyalties lie," said Lord Rafenshighte.

Tuxsetau glanced at him disapprovingly, but didn't otherwise acknowledge this interruption. "I'm certain that no one here wishes to be disloyal, nor intends offense to either you, My Prince, nor to you, My Lord Ambris." Brother and sister nodded graciously to indicate that they took no offense. "Both of you in your respective positions have certain rights, and there are precedents of tradition to favor each in the case of a Norman governor becoming unfit to govern. It is with the deepest sorrow that we must acknowledge that it is so with My Lord Dafythe. His physician's reports give us little hope of his eventual recovery.

We've discussed the advantages of appointing our Chancellor, who has many years of experience of governance in his father the Duke's service, versus the appointment of our Prince, who will of course become Duke in her own right when My Lord Dafythe goes to his final rest, as we all must one day."

Though Tuxsetau made every effort to express himself diplomatically, Mara understood the source of the Council's division very well. She was certainly less experienced in administrative matters than her brother. Many of the councilors would be relieved to have Ambris take up the duties of their Duke. At the same time, the Council was wary of giving Dafythe's son a position of power that might tempt him to usurp his younger sister's rightful place. No member of the Council would dare say so openly to Ambris or herself. The first implied that she might be incompetent to rule her own future dukedom. The second was an even greater insult to her brother's impeccable integrity. Ambris was surely as aware of this as she was. Tuxsetau and the other members of the Council were hoping that the two of them would consent to a compromise that allowed the government of the Northlands to continue without disruption and without either of the Duke's children feeling as if they'd been slighted.

Were they expecting her to accept the title of Regent and Ambris to agree to aid her? This solution wouldn't deprive her of her rights as Dafythe's heir, but at the same time it would make use of her brother's greater political experience. But it would also mean that, as Regent, she must remain in Pendaunzel indefinitely.

If this was their hope, then she intended to surprise them. "I believe I have an answer to the problem that will suit us all," she announced to the councilors seated around the great table, then turned to her brother. "Ambris, you once told me that, if you were Father's heir and Duke after him, you would agree with him and not allow me to go to war against the Spanish on our western borders as I wish. Would you do so now if it were in your power?"

"It isn't in my power, Mara," Ambris answered. He seemed as taken aback by her question as anyone else at the council table. "Nor will it ever be."

"It might if you were Regent. I would prefer that place for you, if I were certain you wouldn't stand in the way of what I desire most. I say it plainly: I will not oppose your governing in Father's stead if you do not oppose me taking an army to the western marches."

"You can do whatever you like once you are Duke," Ambris answered with the same circumspection.

"I'd rather not wait like a crow upon Father's death. Besides, once I *am* Duke, I won't be able to do as I like. I'll have my dukedom to see to first. I won't be able to attend to my duties here if I'm hundreds of miles away. If I am free to march now, as soon as troops can be made ready, I will leave Pendaunzel confident that the Northlands are in the most competent of hands. You'll look after things for Father, and for me if I'm gone for very long. I trust you beyond all others." *That* declaration of her faith should quash any fears among the Council that Ambris would attempt to usurp her. Treachery was not in him. "Will you agree, Brother?"

"What does the Council say to it?" Ambris asked back. "If they consent to your plans, I won't stand in your way and I will assume the responsibilities of Regent while you are gone."

"We must hear more about this Spanish venture," said Lady Peaque.

"If it's what you want, My Prince," Rafenshighte spoke carefully, "then I will vote to approve it."

Others too agreed, some more reluctantly than others. Mara explained her intention of going to Santiago to lay siege to the fortress on its rocky heights above the desert, but this was little more than a formality. If the Council was astonished to hear that she'd seen this fortress in a vision, they didn't express it aloud. There was some discussion on the subject, but since Mara had made it clear that she wasn't interested in assuming the regency herself and would give it to her brother on this one condition, then they would grant her one condition. In the end, enough votes were cast to support Mara's proposed campaign to the western marches. The whole matter was settled with remarkably swiftness. She'd won.

She left Hartshall, walking swiftly toward the Manor to find her cousin and Bel and tell them her good news. Rafenshighte raced to catch up with her.

"I must say you surprised me today, Prince Mara," he said once he'd gained her side and matched her pace. "I thought you would be pleased to become Regent, otherwise I wouldn't have voted as I did. Well, I daresay you know best about obtaining your own ends, but it delays some other important matters. We'll have to wait to make any personal announcements. I'd hoped I might be allowed to continue to serve you as your consort intended, if not consort in fact, while you were away on your campaigns. Whatever else he allows in order to become Regent, My Lord Ambris as certainly won't stand for that! I simply don't understand why you refused this power when you've sought it so ardently."

"I did seek power—to do as I wished," Mara answered. "I'm not eager to be Duke yet, though I see that it must come to me one day soon. I've no desire to take up the burdens of governing before I have to. Ambris is welcome to those. He thrives upon such business."

"And so you surrendered the regency to him in exchange for leading an army into the desert." There was an asperity to this blunt statement that made Mara stop walking and regard him with surprise.

"You voted in my favor, Geoffrey. You said you approved."

"It's what you said you desired, and it is *my* desire to aid you however I can." Rafenshighte resumed his usual deferential tones. "However, I must confess that I don't understand *why* you desire this. I've heard you speak many times of your plans to march westward. You've spoken to me of little else for months. But I'd never heard the plans themselves until today."

"I wasn't allowed to speak of them," said Mara. "You know that my father forbade it."

"I grant you that I'm not military-minded. Perhaps your strategy eludes me. It isn't my place to question, when you've had such great success in your previous campaigns. Your pardon, My Prince, but it's a very long way to march for so little gain, and you gave up a great deal simply for the opportunity to do it. You might've got so much more. It seems a sad waste, after all the effort I've made on your behalf."

"What efforts have you made for me?" Mara asked lightly. She remembered how Geoffrey had declared his loyalties to her at the Council meeting today and imagined that he'd been making similar declarations in her favor during these past months while their alliance had developed. What more could he have done? Then a strange and terrible, sickly feeling overcame her. He seemed to be alluding to some specific service he'd performed for her benefit. Seizing her companion by the upper arm, she pulled him abruptly off the path and into the shade beneath a copse of young trees so that their conversation might not be observed by anyone else passing by. "Geoffrey," she hissed, "what did you do?"

Rafenshighte smiled confidentially. "Surely you don't imagine that this situation has come about entirely by chance?"

"Situation?" she repeated the word without immediately understanding. "You mean, concerning my father? This awful gossip—you didn't start it, did you?"

"No," he answered with a quick shake of his head. "There've been jokes and odd stories going around the court since the lovely Andemyon first came into My Lord Dafythe's service. I never believed there was anything it. Low-minded people will gossip, and the tales they whisper need not be true. There's been much worse gossip about *me*, so I know well how the smallest and most harmless act can be distorted by one's enemies. But I've since seen more for myself."

Mara felt another chill creep through her. After questioning Andemyon, she'd been satisfied that both he and her father were innocent of any wrongdoing. Was she mistaken after all? "What did you see?" she asked, dreading the answer.

"I wasn't the only one to notice how My Lord the Duke kept Andemyon close to him. You told me yourself, Mara, how he favored that one boy above the other heralds. If you'd seen how fierce he was when last I had audience with him, it would've astounded you as it did me. Lord Dafythe spoke of Andemyon being under his protection, but there was more behind his words than the usual noble obligation to look after the weak and defenseless. He was jealous. He thought I was infringing upon what he considered his own prerogative. I couldn't bear the hypocrisy—to accuse *me* of having designs on his pretty herald when *he* has the boy in his bed half the nights of the week!"

"Geoffrey!"

"Oh, I don't doubt My Lord Duke is too old to get up to any sort of buggery," Rafenshighte assured her, "but the passion was there. I saw it, beyond a doubt. It was the same day he forbade our betrothal, but he wasn't as hot against *that*. Of course, I said nothing to Lord Dafythe but agreed not to speak to his precious Andemyon again. When I later heard Dr. Dimitrios's curious tale, I wasn't so indiscreet to tell my own tale in turn, but I hinted to the good physician and to others that I knew more besides."

Mara could scarcely believe what she was hearing. "You mean, you helped to spread this ugly gossip that's ruined my father?"

"I saw an opportunity to do you a service. I thought it was what you wanted, My Prince. You've often spoke to me of your wish to have your father cease to stand in your way. I couldn't imagine you meant assassination. This has effectively unseated him from power without doing harm to his life or his rank. He is still Duke, but he no longer opposes you. You have what you wanted, and I've had my own small part in assisting the inevitable along."

"I never wanted *this*. I wanted my father to reconsider, not–" What had she wanted? Not Dafythe's death. Not his abdication. His capitulation, no more. Even when she'd held the Dragonseye in her hands and wished with all her might for Dafythe to yield, she hadn't foreseen such a terrible ending as this.

She was furious at Geoffrey, but she couldn't blame him alone. Whatever despicable acts he'd committed, she'd been the one to instigate them. He was acting in her interests as well as to further his own ambitions. That didn't mean, however, that she was able to forgive him.

"You've gone too far and presumed too much," she told him. "As you say, my choice of consort is my own. Whatever was between us before cannot continue. Leave me, Lord Rafenshighte. I do not want you in my sight again."

Rafenshighte's mouth popped open. He was on the point of expressing one perfectly honest sentiment before he regained control of himself. "As you wish it, My Prince." He bowed low, a sharp movement that gave an angry edge to his courtesy and made it plain he considered himself ill-used by one he had faithfully served, but Mara was in no mood to think of Geoffrey's feelings, nor her own. Her deepest sorrow now was for her father.

Though he never spoke a word about it to her, Mara knew how deeply it must have hurt Dafythe to realize that his court, his subjects, even his family, could think him capable of such heinous actions. Whenever she went to Dafythe's chambers, he looked ashamed. He kept his head down and avoided meeting her eyes, almost as if he were guilty.

Mara felt ashamed too of the part she'd played in bringing this about. She wished she could tell Dafythe how she had wronged him, but she was unable to confess. Her father wouldn't be able to understand what she'd done, would most likely believe her mad for thinking herself responsible for his downfall. And if she told Dafythe or Ambris about Geoffrey's actions on her behalf, he would bear the brunt of the punishment that *she* deserved. Angry as she was at Rafenshighte, honesty prevented her from trying to shift culpability to him. She had already dealt with Geoffrey herself. She kept her silence on this point, as well as on the progress of her plans to march before the autumn was far advanced. She and Dafythe talked of trivial things.

It was just after one of these visits, as she was returning to her own rooms, that she found Peter waiting for her. In his hands he held an object that looked to be made up of old leather.

"This has been sent me from London, Prince Mara," he announced as he came eagerly toward her, holding the object up. "I know you've been preoccupied with more pressing matters, but I thought you'd wish to see it right away." They went into her boudoir, where Peter explained himself further. "You recall that there wasn't much to be discovered in my own library about magical gems, only some old folk tales and information about wizards' experiments with crystals. To seek the particulars on the history of that gemstone you wear, I corresponded with My Lord the Emperor's court magician, Ainaulfe. We were students together at Wittenberg. In reply to my inquiries, Ainaulfe has sent me this." He presented her with the packet.

Mara turned it over in her hands. The leather was indeed very old, stiff, yellowed, and cracked. It had long been bound tightly shut by cords of aged string, which she observed had just recently been cut. "You've read it already?" she asked Peter. "Does it contain the answers I sought?"

"It does. It seems the history we've been searching for, Prince Mara, was already gathered by a previous magician or scholar at the imperial court. This work was done in the 1820's or `30's."

"For Denys or Eduarde," said Mara.

"I guess that it was done on behalf of Denys, My Prince. The emphasis of this research is upon the origins of the sword, not the gemstone, though of course the history of the two was identical for many centuries. I haven't read all that's within, but I was up 'til the early hours of last night with it. The famed sword carried by Spanish kings of old into battle was said to have been forged by the finest Moorish swordsmiths according to the secret traditions of their craft. Spells were wrought upon its blade by a wizard, who isn't named here, but who was said to have given the sword in gift to his king. Not to El Cid, as the old tale has it, but to a later king of Castille in 1200 or thereabouts. The sword is mentioned now and again in Spanish history, but the person who gathered these tales makes note that it's sometimes difficult to know if they all in fact refer to the same sword. The descriptions vary. You may read them for yourself, Prince Mara. One account is of a coronation in which the new king bore a ruby-hilted sword. Another tells of a king who led his armies into battle wielding a sword with an opal or black gem in its hilt. In another, the stone is said to be a flawed carbuncle. The last record of a sword with a similar description is from the days of the Sainted King Ignatius. The Sword of the Blood is listed as part of Ignatius's inheritance, as an heirloom passed down from king to king for generations. There's no indication here that he ever used this sword in battle, nor that he was the one who put it away at the abbey where Denys discovered it. It isn't mentioned among the treasures that Ignatius passed on to his heir, and simply disappears from Spanish history after his reign. But the author of this research notes that Ignatius did travel in progress through the Madehef Marches early in his reign and may have visited that abbey, though no record of it remains."

"Then the Spanish Sword of the Blood may be Denys's Dragonsfang."

"The person who conducted this research seems to believes it possible, Prince Mara, though he couldn't confirm it beyond all doubt. He would naturally be reluctant to disappoint his prince." Peter seemed to share this reluctance with regard to his own prince. "In answer to my questions about the fate of Dragonsfang's missing hiltstone after Prince Denys's death,

Ainaulfe says that he's found no written history of the Black Ruby's whereabouts, but he refers me, or my patron, to portraits of Eduarde Redlyon."

A portrait of the Redlyon, painted early in his reign, hung in the gallery of the Manor next to a similarly larger-than-life-size portrait of his consort, Duke Diana. Mara and Peter left the packet in Ren's care and left her chambers to go down the stair to the gallery to examine it closely. Though Mara had walked beneath this painting nearly every day of her life, she'd never given it more than a glance.

Peter was the first to find it. "There it is, Prince Mara! Look!"

Mara stood close beneath the painting's frame and stood on tip-toe to peer upwards at the spot Peter was pointing toward. Among the massive chains of office that hung heavily covering the late Emperor's breast was a single dark-red pedant—a blob of paint like dried blood. Could it be...? She held up her own gemstone by its tether; the two appeared to be identical. "So he did have it!"

At last, she had proof enough to confirm that all she believed about the Dragonseye was true. She might even convince Ambris, but she wouldn't bring her evidence to him. Her brother had enough to trouble him at present as he assumed the responsibilities of Regent. He had probably long forgotten his challenge to her to test the power of this little stone.

She could trace the path of the thing easily now. Denys the Bright Prince, hacking his way to victory with this stone on the hilt of his Spanish sword. He had discovered it on his first campaign and had enjoyed enormous success thereafter until the gemstone was stolen from him by Eduarde. Then he had been tragically cut down. Eduarde Redlyon, undefeated throughout his glorious reign, wearing this same gemstone hung about his neck. Uncle Kharles had somehow seized it from his father, and the valiant Redlyon had thereafter sunk rapidly into madness and degenerative idiocy. Kharles had used the stone's peculiar power for only a short time, long enough to wrest control of the Empire from the Redlyon and set up the framework of this modern, peaceable world, then abandoned it before becoming Emperor himself. Kharles had, in effect, returned the gem to the place where Denys had found it. It had been discovered in a Spanish chapel, and had been sent back to another. Thereafter, Kharles had enjoyed a respectable but uneventful reign.

What had made her uncle renounce so wonderful a power? Had he believed it too great for him to wield? Had he thought it dangerous? Had he sensed some corrupting influence from it? Perhaps he'd learned something about the nature of the stone, which Mara was herself only now beginning to perceive. It would grant whatever its master desired, but with an unexpected and often unbearable price attached. Eduarde had wanted Denys's success, but he'd only obtained it at the price of his beloved brother's death. Terrojos had been conquered, but it wasn't hers to govern. Her father no longer opposed her plans to march against the Spanish fort at Santiago, but poor Dafythe was in no position to oppose anything now.

What of Uncle Kharles? He'd remade the Empire to suit himself—but what price had he paid for that reconstruction? What had made him put the stone away as the Sainted Ignatius must have done centuries before?

There was only one person here at court who might tell Mara something about the true nature of the Dragonseye, though they were presently not on good terms. While Peter had been of enormous help to her in her researches, she couldn't consult him on this point. Peter, like her brother Ambris, understood magic only as a set of natural laws that obeyed certain principles: Just as heavy objects always dropped to the earth at a certain and constant rate, ice and wood floated while metal and rock sank, and the angle at which the catapult was launched predicted where the stone would land, so it was with magic. But they weren't magicians. They didn't truly understand the principles by which these laws operated any better than she did. They didn't know how to manipulate them, to cast spells. That ability was beyond most mortals. Laurel had forsaken her education, but she couldn't have forgotten what she'd once learned.

Peter had suggested that she ask Laurel when they'd first begun to seek information about the stone, but Mara had delayed doing so for fear of the answer. At the time, she'd been afraid that that the Dragonseye would turn out to be an ordinary gem with a minor historical importance, and its powers all a delusion. Now, she was more afraid to discover that the power the stone held *was* a very real and dark magic and its influence would corrupt her even as it fulfilled her every wish. She didn't want to learn that it was useless, nor that it was an instrument of evil. She needed it to be the sign of her talisman beast. No other truth would suffice.

The day for Laurel's intended departure drew nearer; Mara saw that she must ask her sister-in-law now, or never have another chance. She went to Laurel's chambers. The gentyl-maid who answered the door informed Mara that her Ladyship wasn't well but, after consulting the Lady, admitted Mara to see her.

Mara entered a darkened room. The draperies were drawn over the windows and no candles were lit. Laurel reclined on the coucherie at the center of the room in her dressing gown; Mara could only see the plaits of silvery-white hair until her eyes adjusted to the dim light. "I hope you're not very ill," she said. "I don't wish to disturb you, Laurel, if you are."

"You don't disturb me, Mara. Why have you come?" asked Laurel without rising. "Not to apologize?"

"No—although I am sorry, more than I can say." As Mara stepped closer, she could better discern the figure on the coucherie. She also saw that a circle—in chalk?—had been drawn on the floor around it. "That isn't what I've come about." She stepped inside the circle and stood over the coucherie. As Laurel looked up at her, Mara could see that her sister-in-law was very pale, more than usually so even for her strange fairness. There was no glimmer about her today; Mara had recently seen Laurel blazing with fury, but that light had since been put out. Was Laurel suppressing it herself? Ambris had said that she'd been frightened by something she'd sensed in the night sky.

"You may have heard about the gemstone I found in the Redlands," she plunged on, regretting now that she hadn't come sooner.

"Yes, Ambris told me of it."

"He thinks my ideas about it are nonsense and superstition, but I know they are not. Magician Peter and I have searched its history and confirmed that it once belonged to Prince Denys, and that my grandfather bore it also during his reign. I believe there is some extraordinary magic in it, though we haven't the ability to discern what it is. I hoped you might, Laurel, as only a true wizard can. You have perceptions that we lack." Mara had drawn the gem up by its tether and removed it from around her neck. "Can you–?

She held the stone out toward Laurel, who sat up and began to regard her with increasing interest and curiosity as she listened to this explanation. A white arm extended from the dark fabric of the dressing-gown sleeve. But just as Laurel's fingertips were about to touch the polished surface, she recoiled.

"For God's Sake, Mara! Throw that thing into the river! Drop it in the deepest well you can find and pray it never sees the light of day again!"

"Why? What's wrong with it?" Mara's hand closed protectively around the stone as if she expected Laurel to try and destroy it on the spot. "Do you say it is evil?"

"No." Laurel shook her head. "'Tis only a gemstone, neither good nor evil. But it draws–" She stopped suddenly, on the point of saying more.

Mara knew that the young woman before her had abruptly left her apprenticeship with Lord Redmantyl and abandoned her magic over some mysterious disaster; she would never tell anyone about it, not even Ambris. Would Laurel reveal the secret to her now? Mara felt as if an important magical mystery were about to be revealed to her.

But instead of confiding wizardly secrets, Laurel retreated back into her old, well-guarded state of vigilance. "Mara, I pray you put it away from you. Mortals shouldn't play with such trinkets. You don't realize what you've stumbled upon, but ignorance won't save you from the consequences of employing it. A thing like that will draw the attention of... forces you can't possibly comprehend, nor defend yourself against. If I couldn't stand before them, what hope have you?"

On a misty early October morning, the Pendaunzel garrison and local volunteers marched out of the city to join the rest of Mara's army on their long westward journey. The city-folk and half the court turned out to see them off. From his closet windows, Dafythe had watched his daughter and niece, Captain Bel, and their squires ride from the stables across the lawn toward the

Palace's gates, but he wouldn't attend the parade. Today of all days, he had no wish to expose himself to public view.

He had opposed this war from the first, but he'd become powerless to prevent it. Since Ambris had been appointed Regent, he consulted Dafythe every day and made a polite pretense of deferring to his father's wisdom, but both were aware that Dafythe's opinions mattered very little now. Mara's campaign had been approved by the Council before the Duke had even heard of the bargain she'd made to obtain her goal.

Ambris had told him about it afterwards in tones of apology. "She was determined to do it sooner or later, Father. I like it no more than you do, but if it must be, better that it comes now than when she is Duke."

Mara herself and Kat had come to see him last night, to kiss his cheek and tell him that they were "going away." Neither had said where they were going, though they surely must know that *he* knew. They meant to spare his feelings. Mara wouldn't wish to gloat over her triumph; in fact, Dafythe thought he saw something apologetic in her demeanor too.

Though his children had benefited most from his disgrace, Dafythe couldn't blame them for it. They'd each done what they'd perceived to be necessary, and his retirement was his own choice. He might've disputed the rumors. Instead, he'd sunk before them, wounded at the blow. He'd first been stunned, not so much by the vicious nature of the gossip, for he knew what people were capable of, but that those who knew him best had believed it possible. Then, he'd been too mortified to go out among his people and ignore their whispers. Now, he felt sorrow at his own folly in falling prey to evil-minded gossips who could perceive no other reason for his fondness for a young boy—or, had deliberately made it seem so.

Dafythe wasn't naïve; he understood that certain court factions observed the recent prominence of Lord Redmantyl's family. The wizard himself had been elevated by Dafythe from the traditional title of Redmantyl to Lord of Greenwaters Island. His niece had married Dafythe's own son. His adopted son was a recognized court favorite. In three generations, they'd risen from obscurity to form an alliance with the Norman imperial house. They were therefore a threat to the established court influences.

That these upstarts were a magical family must be especially alarming.

This vile slander had achieved its purpose. Since Andemyon had been taken from him, he hadn't even be able to say farewell when the boy left Pendaunzel. A serious rift now separated Laurel and her husband. She too was leaving Pendaunzel. These interlopers were effectively removed from the court.

This disaster had given him a peculiar gift, rare among rulers: he'd survived beyond the end of his reign and had the advantage of looking back upon it from its promising beginnings to its final days. He could, in effect, read his own epitaph. While he'd done much to be proud of as Duke of the Northlands, he wouldn't be remembered for his great work—his *pax normania,* his prosperous reign, the splendid palace and city he had built here—but for this ending. History would recall him as a doddering old man who'd made a fool of himself over a pretty boy.

Santiago
1956

tuentye

Iagoburso sat high atop its massive platform of craggy and wind-sculpted rock above the curve of a wide green-grey river, which was called Rio Amarillo by the Spanish; a lesser river, called d'Iago Pescador, flowed into the greater just below the rocks. All was exactly as Mara had seen it in her vision last spring. When she'd first set her eyes upon the fortress at the end of the long march westward, it had seemed like a dream. Now, after nearly three months encamped on the river's opposite shore, she had not only grown accustomed to the sight, but was weary of it.

It had taken eight months for her army to assemble at Guylliamesburghe and make the journey downriver to Jamesfort, a frontier town on the western banks of the vast Michelne and on the eastern border of the Jamesmarch. From there, they had crossed the Jamesmarch on foot and on horseback, and settled here in their present camp in the midst of a sweltering June. And here they had remained through a blazing July and August. It was early September now. Cooler nights were beginning to promise some relief from the heat, though they couldn't expect the temperate autumn of their homeland in this desert. Many hoped that they would not still be sitting here when winter came.

When Mara's army had first made camp beside the Amarillo, Bard Delphyn had frequently sung that ballad featuring Duke Maud's siege upon this same fortress, with the arch implication that Mara's venture would be more successful than her famed ancestor. But Delphyn hadn't sung of Maud's failure in weeks.

Iagoburso was not hers to take. That might describe Mara as well as Maud.

Her vision of Iagoburso and the Sonnedragon's foretelling that it would be hers sustained Mara's hope and gave her the will to persevere. She had no inspiring visions now; the clarity of purpose that had led through the conquest of the Redlands was no longer there to guide her during this campaign. The restless rage in her blood had quieted. Had her Dragon abandoned her?

She saw that her troops were growing restless and even her most loyal followers were beginning to wonder what they were doing here. This sparse land wasn't hospitable to Northlanders. Most of them had grown up amid green hills, forests, and farms, and they yearned for their verdant homeland as they camped day after day by the banks of the glittering yellow river under the merciless summer sun.

At least, they hadn't been sitting idle all this time. Several expeditions had ventured across the river to scout the Spanish territory on the other side. Raiding parties had also crossed, finding little to raid. Santiago, they reported to their Prince, looked to be nothing more than empty grasslands, inhabited by spike-horned antelopes, huge, shaggy bison that ran in thunderous herds, and smaller beasts such as wild fowl, hares, and burrowing rodents colored the same shades of dusty brown and yellow as the tall prairie grasses in which they hid. The Northlanders hunted these animals to supplement their regular food supplies with fresh meat. Most of their supplies were sent to them in barges down the Michelne River and brought across the Jamesmarch in carts.

The scouting expeditions had discovered a number of farms on the Spanish side of the Amarillo, chiefly along the banks of the smaller river, but these had been abandoned and the crops harvested some time before the Normans reached them. Nothing remained but fields of stubble and the occasional stray cow. The farmers had presumably retreated into the fortress for safety and taken their harvest with them. Also along the d'Iago Pescador about ten miles west of the fortress was a tiny anchorite monastery within a cave in a less imposing rock face. This had been left empty for years, with only a stone crucifix above the entrance, some religious carvings on the walls and the remains of an altar and cells for no more than half a dozen monks to indicate what it had been.

The scouts reported sighting a few native tribesmen on horseback in the wilderness, but hadn't confronted them. The

Norman quarrel was with the Spaniards, not the aboriginals; Mara had given orders that her soldiers were not to do battle with the natives unless they were first attacked.

She might have sent more troops across the river to establish permanent encampments, but Mara realized that she couldn't overrun and lay claim to Santiago until the fortress was taken. As long as the Spaniards held it, her occupation of Santiago would not be secured. The fortress stood like a single sentinel guarding Spanish interests, a sentinel that couldn't be budged by all her efforts.

There had been one or two small skirmishes when they'd first arrived. Spanish soldiers had emerged from their fortress to meet the Northlander troops. Mara's captains had not only driven these forays back, but found the passages up the cliff face by which they had come down onto the prairie-land. These paths were too well defended for Mara's troops to breach them, but they had set their own guards at the foot of the cliffs to prevent further assaults. Since then, they'd seen no Spaniards. Rocks were occasionally flung at them from catapults fixed on the fortress battlements to keep them on their own side of the river, but even these defensive measures had recently ceased. It was assumed that the Spanish garrison had run out of rocks.

Mara had sent Alyx with messages to Luiz, the Conde of Santiago at Iagoburso, to request that he surrender the fortress peaceably. Mara's first requests were polite, promising that all inhabitants of the fortress, soldiers as well as non-combatants, would be allowed safe passage out of Santiago if they offered no resistance. When these first requests were refused, subsequent messages were sent in more threatening terms. Mara stopped sending her emissary altogether once it became clear that she had no means to carry out her threats. No army could scale those sheer walls of rock—and her army had tried. The winding paths carved into the cliff face were too narrow to allow more than one person to pass at once; the Spaniards could easily waylay her soldiers by shooting arrows, dropping rocks, or pouring hot oil down on them from strategic positions above. The Northlanders had no catapults of their own that could reach the fortress walls. There was no means by which she could oust the Spaniards and claim the fortress for her own.

"If we can't get up into their fortress, at least we've assured that they can't come down," Alyx consoled Mara during one of their strategic meetings. Alyx had been placed in command of the troops guarding the foot of the rock, but every evening she crossed the river to return to the Northlander encampment to report on their present state of affairs and have dinner in the Prince's pavilion, which was merely a roof of canvas on tall poles, providing shade and leaving all sides open in hopes of catching any breeze. Because of the heat, the Prince and her companions wore their lightest white linen garments and dined on cold roast game and beer that had been stored in jugs in the river to keep it cool. The meal had now ended and they sat gazing out at their goal as the sun set behind it in a blaze of red-streaked clouds. This too had become part of their daily routine.

"It's only a matter of waiting them out," Mara agreed confidently. "Iagoburso must eventually be starved into surrendering. Once their store of food is depleted, they'll have to agree to our terms. Their last harvest can't sustain them very much longer."

"Their supplies must be scarce," Alyx answered, "but I believe that Conde Luiz will hold out `til the last stale crust of bread is eaten and his people are skin and bone."

"Is he so stubborn?" asked Mara.

"It's more than stubbornness. You haven't met him, Prince Mara, but you've heard my reports of how he received me to hear your demands."

"You said that the Conde wasn't a nobleman."

Alyx nodded. "Merchant-born, I'd say, or even a peasant. He has the hard look of a man who's fought his way up through the ranks. If we learned one thing in the Redlands, it's that Spanish peasants keep the most unaccountable, old-fashioned prejudices. Conde Luiz was always courteous when we met, but I could see he didn't know quite what to make of me. He has women under his command, but none of my rank. That I was the representative of a woman of far greater rank—a female Prince—astounded him."

"`Tis odd," said Kat. "Spanish queens of old rode to battle against the Moors long before Norman noblewomen did."

"Queens 'of old'," Mara repeated, emphasizing this last, key phrase. "Ambris told me those same tales too, of Ysabella, Juana, and Katerina. But it's been hundreds of years since a queen ruled Spain or led their armies to war. We must seem to Don Luiz like figures out of a history book or legends of long ago rather than like people who live today.'

"Conde Luiz had heard of you, of course, My Prince," Alyx told Mara, "but I don't think he truly credited the tales of you leading a victorious army in the Redlands. I'm not certain he credits it even now."

"Is that why he stands against us?" asked Bel. "He thinks he can defeat our armies in the end?"

"No, I don't imagine he hopes to win, but he can't allow himself to lose. I believe it would shame him to surrender to a woman."

Mara and her companions laughed incredulously at this strange attitude, though they'd encountered it among the Spanish they'd done battle with before. "It's fortunate then that so many of the commanders in the Redlands were nobles of the highest birth," said Mara. "They know how to surrender with dignity and grace, like sensible men."

"Could he be waiting for relief troops?" Kat wondered. "He might've sent messengers to seek aid when he saw our army coming, and he expects them to arrive any day."

"It's possible, of course," Alyx answered. "They had enough forewarning of our coming to bring even the farm-folk into their fortress. Conde Luiz must've had time to send out a rider or two, or to launch a boat downstream. Someone might even have stolen out through one of their hidden passages before we found and blocked them all. But no one's come to their aid yet. The scouts Sataumie has taken to the south report no Spanish armies approaching. They've sighted nothing at all."

"Well, where could they go for aid in this godforsaken waste?" said Bel as she finished her beer. "The nearest fortified towns with Spanish garrisons lie along the coast of the Tenochitland Sea, hundreds of miles away. A messenger on horseback would take a week or more to reach them, if they survived so long a ride through these desert lands. It'd take weeks more for the Spanish to assemble troops and march here. I say there's little hope of an army coming our way."

"Little hope?" Kat repeated this phrase with a small smile. "You hope for a Spanish army then, Captain?"

"Don't you, Prince Kat? I pray nightly for Spanish relief troops to appear," answered Bel. "They'd give us a good battle, instead of all this waiting upon those cowards hiding up on their rock."

"That's so. At least, a battle would give us some reason for being here," Kat said.

Mara didn't like her cousin's tone. "All of us would like to see some sort of activity, even if it means fierce battle," she said. "I don't blame my captains for their impatience. I feel the same myself. Rather than wait for that stubborn commander to be starved out of his fortress, I'd prefer to knock down the walls of Iagoburso somehow and make our way in, but it's impossible. Our catapults can't strike high enough. If Conde Luiz doubts the might of our forces now, he'd laugh to see us flinging rocks against the cliffs and never coming near him! I don't like this sitting any better than you do, but what else can we do? If Conde Luiz refuses to surrender now, then we must abide 'til he has no other choice. The day must come. You'll have your chance at the Spaniards before we leave this place, Bel. I promise you that."

"Oh, I believe that, My Prince," Bel responded with simple and unwavering faith. "I only hope it will be sooner rather than later."

This wasn't the first time that Kat had alluded to the pointlessness of their campaign, but Mara grew more concerned at each disparaging remark. While all the Northlanders were impatient at their weeks of inactivity, it had become obvious that her cousin's forthright opinions were the greatest threat to their eventual success. Her soldiers might grumble privately, but as long she had their loyalty, they would obey orders and follow wherever she led them. It was the same with her commanders; if Bel, Alyx, or Sataumie wondered why she had brought them here, they kept their questions to themselves. Kat alone felt free to speak her mind and, as Mara's kinswoman and a Norman Prince herself, her words had weight. If she continued to do so, discontent might spread among the others and destroy their morale. Once the troops lost faith, this venture could only end in disaster. Kat must therefore be stopped.

Mara could guess why her cousin was speaking against her. There had been a tacit reconciliation between them once Kat had agreed to join her on this campaign, and no discussion of their private differences while they made their plans and embarked on the long journey westward, but those differences remained. Mara would like nothing better than to mend the breach and have Kat as her trusted friend again—and not merely because she wished to have her cousin's mouth shut—but that meant that they both must speak of things they'd avoided discussing for a very long time.

After they'd bid goodnight to Alyx and Bel and seen the former on her way back across the river, the pair walked together around the perimeter of the camp as an informal review of the troops to confirm that all was well, but also as a chance for a private conversation. There were few opportunities for them to speak without others overhearing their words. It was a windless night with a sliver of moon high in the sky overhead as they went along the well-trodden path on the river's eastern bank. The lights of campfires dotted the darkness, and voices raised in shouts, laughter, and song could be heard. These boisterous sounds diminished to murmurs when the soldiers caught sight of the two white-clad figures moving past their rows of tents. The occasional guard standing watch saluted them. On the opposite side of the river, pinpoints of flickering yellow light from torches and candles could be seen high atop Iagoburso.

"Are you still angry with me, Cos?" Mara asked.

Kat stopped walking and turned to her. "No, Mara."

"You disagree with me at our council meetings. You think we've come here to no purpose."

"I wonder what purpose brings us here. That isn't exactly the same," Kat answered. "I trust you have good reasons of your own for making us all sit around that stump of a rock these long weeks, but I'm afraid you'll look a fool whether we take it or not. I'm not the only one to wonder if it's worth the trouble we're giving it. The others mayn't say so to you, but you know how they feel about it."

"So I do, but I can't stop anyone thinking what they like. Your speaking aloud what others only think is worse. Say what you like to me in private, Kat, but I can't have you scorn my hopes of seizing Iagoburso when there are others around to hear. It creates ill feeling."

Very humbly, Kat apologized for her disrespect and promised that it wouldn't happen again. Mara accepted this graciously.

"You don't want to be here—so much is plain," she said after they'd walked a little farther along the path. "Do you wish to go home?"

"I think often of home," Kat admitted. "In this– what did Bel call it? This 'godforsaken' place, I can't help remembering what it's like to live where it's cool and green. I dream sometimes that it's raining, and I wake up disappointed to see that there's no rain and the land is as parched as ever. I miss my baby, but I know that Ambris is looking after her, as he looks after everything else. But I won't go home. I'll stay as long as you do, Mara, 'til whatever you brought us here to do is finished, or 'til you give up this idea of capturing Iagoburso."

"I can't give it up. It was promised to me."

Kat chuckled. "Then we may be here `til the end of time."

They continued to walk until the path turned away from the river and led around the northern end of the camp. Scrub oak and twisted, dwarf pine trees grew here on the rising ground. The path would eventually take them southward again, toward their own tents. "You never used to doubt me, Kat," Mara said once she was sure they wouldn't be overheard. "I once could rely on you beyond all others."

"It's not that I think it impossible," her cousin conceded. "I wouldn't have come so far with you if I didn't think you might have some chance of taking that blasted fortress. We've had remarkable successes before. You haven't forgotten the curtain wall at Spainfort. Who knows how long we might've sat and waited there if that hadn't fallen on its own?"

"No, I haven't forgotten what happened that day," said Mara, "any more than you have." She felt as if they were approaching the heart of the matter and plunged on toward it boldly. "It's where this all began, when Frederik was killed. Everything went wrong between us then. You never forgave me for disapproving of how you behaved with him—but I never wanted him dead! You can't blame me for that."

"I never blamed you for *that*," Kat told her. "That was a

Spanish archer, and I served him and as many of his fellows out for it as I could. I'd do the same for you, if it came to it. It's not poor Frederik's dying—it's what happened afterwards I find hard to forgive."

"I don't know what you mean."

"Don't you? You took the command of Spainfort away from me to punish me over Frederik, and because I was having his baby. I turned to you in a time of need, and instead of comfort I faced a tribunal and banishment. You turned my victory there against me, suggested I was unfit to fight and might go chopping up Spaniards indiscriminately—as if you and Bel and others wouldn't do just the same!"

Mara was astonished at this accusation. Was this the grudge Kat had been nursing against her for so many months? "I did no such thing!" she protested. "I meant to help you."

"I would rather you'd sat and wept with me awhile instead up jumping straight up and calling for your captains."

"What good would that have done? Women who sit and weep are soon run down." Mara made a gesture of impatience. "Your problem required swift action. It wasn't meant for a punishment, Kat. I thought only of your safety and the baby's. A woman with child has no business in battle." Kat, who was walking swiftly a little ahead of her, made a scoffing noise. "Is this the reason why you betrayed me?"

Kat stopped again. "Betrayed you—how?" she demanded.

"You told Father, didn't you?" Mara made her own accusation in turn. "I took you into my confidence about my plans for this campaign even after he forbade it, and you told him. You can confess to it now. It doesn't matter, but I want to know."

Her cousin shook her head. "Uncle Dafythe didn't need to be told by me, Cos. He knew you well enough to guess what you were up to by himself. If you must know the truth, he asked me about you once. 'She doesn't intend to give up these wild plans of hers, does she?' That's just what he said. How was I to answer? Was I to lie for you and tell him No, or betray you and say it was true? As it happened, I was called to say neither. He saw it all without my saying a word. Poor Uncle Dafythe was never a fool when he was in his right senses. `Twas lucky for you he lost them in the end so you can have your own way. You always do. I suppose this campaign will turn out well for you too, though God alone—and perhaps that dragon of yours—can imagine how."

With that, Kat turned and followed the path into the trees. She hadn't gone far, however, before Mara heard her cry out.

"Kat!" They might be in the midst of a quarrel, but that didn't matter now. Mara dashed after her cousin, ducking to avoid the clutching branches of the trees on either side of the path as it led down from the top of the ridge into a slight dip. She had to slow her pace when she stepped into a slick, wet patch like a mud-puddle and felt her boots slip beneath her. As she put out one hand to save herself from falling, she saw that Kat stood just ahead of her, eyes wide and glinting in the faint light and lips moving soundlessly. She stared at something in the underbrush to Mara's right. Hand at her sword's hilt, Mara turned to see what it was.

Half-hidden by the underbrush, a corpse sat propped against the trunk of a tree. The hot, metallic, familiar smell of blood suddenly rose to her nostrils, and it occurred to her that the puddle she was standing in was probably not mud. She stepped back quickly onto dry ground.

"Is it one of our men?" Kat asked in a hoarse whisper.

"I think it is." Mara delicately pushed aside the underbrush with the tip of her sword. "He's got on a sergeant's uniform, what's left of one." She was accustomed to the sight of mutilated bodies on battlefields, but this was more disturbing somehow. The man's head was thrown back, and beneath was a dark mess; he had been torn open from throat to abdomen. It wasn't a sword wound, Mara's professional eye perceived immediately, nor a wound from any weapon she was familiar with. It looked more as if a great claw had swept down through the body to eviscerate it. "He wasn't murdered by the Spaniards, at least."

"No," Kat agreed. "What could've done this? A bear?"

"It must be, or some other beast like it." They hadn't seen any bears since they'd arrived in this desert land, but that didn't mean one couldn't be lurking and waiting to prey upon them. "It couldn't have happened very long ago. The blood is still fresh."

"It's a wonder we didn't hear him cry out. Someone must have."

The light of many campfires were visible through the trees. In the darkness, they seemed very far away, but it was in reality only a short distance; a few minutes' walk would have brought the luckless sergeant from the nearest fires to this point. If he had screamed, surely one of his fellows would have heard him and come to his aid? But the soldiers were all sitting peacefully, undisturbed. Whatever had happened therefore must have occurred so swiftly that the man had had no time to call for help once he was attacked. Nor had he had time to attempt to defend himself. His sword was still in its scabbard at his side.

"We'll have to puzzle it out by the morning's light," Mara decided. "Will you go down and fetch up some of the footsoldiers there to carry him into camp?"

In the morning, they held a brief investigation. The sergeant had last been seen alive by his company at dusk, less than an hour before his body had been discovered. He had left the gathering around the campfire, presumably to relieve himself in the privacy offered by the trees. No one among the troops at the northern end of the camp reported hearing a scream or sounds of a struggle. It was assumed that the unfortunate man had been surprised by some sort of wild beast while in a vulnerable position and unable to defend himself. A bear was the best guess by general consensus, in agreement with Mara's initial opinion, but some also spoke of lions and the smaller, wolf-like creatures they had occasionally seen in the area. The peculiar but similar death of the commander of Con Permiso was also remembered by those who had been with Mara on that campaign.

The sergeant's body was buried that afternoon with appropriate rites performed by the Princes' own chaplain. Mara ordered more guards to patrol on night duty around the camp's perimeter, all within sight of each other, to prevent the beast from preying on her soldiers. The matter was then considered settled, until a second body, one of the posted guards, was found at the river's edge four days later. This one hadn't been mauled. In fact, there was no obvious injury to be found.

Thereafter, bodies of Northlander soldiers were discovered at the edges of the camp frequently, every two or three days, and none of them disemboweled as the first had been. They were all given respectful burial in the ever-growing graveyard. Mara issued orders for everyone to keep themselves armed and remain alert whenever they were separated from their fellows even for a few minutes, but these measures seemed inadequate. With each new death, unrest among the troops increased and Mara and her commanders were afraid there would soon be a panic. The soldiers were already beginning to make up stories to explain these strange deaths.

"They say it's a vampyr, My Prince," Ren reported to Mara one evening as she performed her nightly task of aiding the Princes in preparing for bed.

"Don't talk such nonsense, girl," Mara scoffed at the idea.

Ren ducked her head, "'Tis what they say, Prince Margueryt."

"You can't blame the poor child for simply repeating what she hears," Kat pointed out from her seat on her cot as she stripped off her own hose. "It's important we know what the company is thinking. You say so often yourself, Mara."

Mara acknowledged this. "But it's an absurd notion, Kat. There's no such thing as vampyrs. Shapeshifters, ghouls, and such-like only exist in tales nursery-maids tell to frighten little children." She handed the garments she shed one by one to Ren. "It's a sign of how frightened they are that they make up so ridiculous an explanation for these deaths. Besides, not one of the dead soldiers was bitten. We must look for a more reasonable cause: a poisonous snake or spider, or even scorpions in the brush."

"Bel would be happy to believe that the Spaniards are behind it," Kat said, smiling.

"So would I, but we've seen no sign that points to them. Conde Luiz and his people are still besieged within their fortress and can't possibly get out with our knowledge. They couldn't cross the river without being observed. No one in the companies stationed with Alyx on the Spanish side of the river has yet fallen victim, and it would be more reasonable for the Spanish to strike at them first if they were responsible."

"It's odd that we weren't troubled by scorpions or spiders when we first came here, but that they've struck so often recently. We never saw that beast that killed poor Sergeant Gilamus either," Kat mused once Ren had put away Mara's clothes and gone to her own bed in a smaller, adjoining tent. They hadn't continued the conversation that had been interrupted when they'd discovered the sergeant's body, but both were a little more at ease with each other now when they were alone. Mara hadn't spoken again of sending Kat back to Pendaunzel. "You don't think it could be something… else, do you?"

"Of course not! What else could it be?"

"Odd things have happened during our campaigns before, Mara, some much odder than this."

"And there's always been a reasonable explanation for them." Mara insisted. "Wild tales and old superstitions won't solve this problem, Cos. That sort of talk only feeds the troops' worst fears." While these losses were far fewer than those they would normally expect in a battle, their inexplicable nature made them more distressing than the easily understood deaths in combat, as well as more damaging to the troops' morale. Mara was aware that her soldiers were beginning to feel as if they were sitting prey for whatever was stealthily working to diminish their numbers. They yearned for action, but this attack by an unseen foe who struck at them one by one in the darkness was not the sort of combat they desired to face. "It's snakes or scorpions we must battle, not vampyrs."

"How shall we defend ourselves against snakes and scorpions? Have the soldiers wear good, solid leather boots whenever they go out of their tents? And see that they give them a good shaking out before they put them on to be certain nothing's hiding within?" Though she'd taken off her boots a few minutes earlier, Kat picked one up by the heel and turned it upside-down, shaking it to demonstrate. Mara smiled in spite of herself.

"That would be a suitable measure," she agreed. "I'll issue a general order to all the troops to that effect first thing tomorrow."

Did Kat guess that she was lying? Mara lay awake in the darkness long after they'd both gone to bed. While she was certain that vampyrs didn't exist, she wasn't as sure that some small, poisonous desert creature was the true cause of these odd deaths.

Kat was right; this wasn't the first odd occurrence to happen during their campaigns. There were always reasonable explanations, but she'd never entirely believed in them, preferring to attribute these occurrences to the magical power that aided her. Until now, however, such inexplicable events and strange disasters had always happened to her advantage. Where was the advantage in these deaths among her own troops? For the first time since the battle of the Shieldwall, she felt as if Fate was not favoring her. Was there some ultimate purpose here she didn't yet perceive? Or was the Dragonseye turning its power against her? Was this why St. Ignatius and Uncle Kharles had given it up rather than wield it?

She hadn't forgotten what Laurel had said about the gemstone, though she tried. She had thrust the warning aside as soon as she'd heard it, for Laurel's words terrified her. She didn't want to consider that her talisman might be a thing of evil when she needed its powers most. But a dreadful fear that Laurel was right had remained at the back of her mind all these months. She couldn't help thinking of it now, as women and men under her command mysteriously died.

The next morning, the day of All Hallows, Mara went out to review the troops under a sun that had already baked away the night's cooler air even though it was barely above the horizon. As she issued her orders about boots and avoiding poisonous vermin, she could see that the soldiers looked relieved. They might still have their fears about some monster, natural or supernatural, preying upon them, but this common-sense approach to the problem was reassuring. It gave them a measure of defense against the unseen.

As the troops dispersed to go about their daily routines and duties and Mara walked away in the direction of the pavilion to join her commanders for breakfast, a small, dark girl in a common guard's uniform appeared and follower her shyly.

"Prince Margueryt?"

Mara turned and saw the girl for the first time. "Yes, what it is?"

The girl bowed her head humbly. "A word with you please, Prince Margueryt."

"A word, no more," Mara granted this request graciously. "I have my duties to attend, as you must also."

"None so important as this, My Prince."

Kat, who accompanied Mara on the review of the troops, had gone on a few steps more after Mara had stopped walking. She paused now and looked back over her shoulder at her cousin with a puzzled expression; Mara waved for Kat to go on, and turned her attention to the girl who stood so timidly before her. Mara didn't know what to make of her. This little maiden was smaller than Ren and looked even younger. She couldn't possibly be a full guardswoman, in spite of the uniform. Was she someone's squire? The child was all thin arms and legs and looked barely old enough even for that service. After all these weeks among so small a company, Mara knew all her officers, their squires and attendants. She didn't recall seeing this girl before. "What is it?" she repeated her question.

"It's the fortress across the river, My Prince," the girl answered without lifting her eyes from the ground. "I know you want to break its walls down so you can capture it."

This was no secret; everyone in the camp was well aware of their Prince's objective. It was why they remained here. Mara acknowledged it was so.

"I can do it."

"Do what?"

"Give the fortress to you, and without breaking the walls down. I can remove the Spaniards from it."

Mara couldn't help laughing aloud in astonishment. Whoever she was, the child must be mad. "It would take a greater army than ours, or most powerful magic to do that, my lass. You're no magician."

"No, but I can do it, if you wish me to, My Prince."

"Of course I'd like it if you could do it," Mara answered, still smiling in disbelief. "I would be grateful to anyone who could perform such a service on my behalf. Who are you, lass? If you are to have my gratitude for this remarkable feat, I'd like to know your name."

"Alys, My Layn Prince." The girl bobbed in a curtsey. "Alys of Lyngreen."

"Lyngreen? Where is that?" The name sounded vaguely familiar, but Mara couldn't quite place it.

"`Twas a village in Oerykeshire, My Prince. It's gone now. It burnt to the ground."

"Then you are in an Oerykeshire company? Who is your commander?"

"Captain Silban was, My Prince, `til he died two days ago. I was in service to Sergeant Gilamus, but he's dead too."

This struck Mara as strange; traditionally, body-servants were the same sex as the officers they served, and sergeants weren't allowed to keep servants at all. If Alys were a little more mature, Mara might suspect the dead sergeant of smuggling the girl out here to live with him as a doxy. Could she have been his daughter? Not very many camp-followers or soldiers' families had accompanied the army out into this unwelcoming land, but Mara was unofficially aware that there were a few. It would explain why she'd never seen the girl before, but it didn't explain the child's uniform. "You're very young to be a guardswoman," she said. "Are you rightly one, Alys? Or does that uniform you wear belong to someone else?"

"`Twas given me by one of the guardswomen, Prince Marguerýt, so that I might stay with the company," Alys explained. "They lost so many."

This sounded plausible. Since it would be extremely difficult for the girl to be sent home now, with or without an escort, the company had obviously adopted her as a sort of mascot. Understandable, but it wasn't the way Mara liked to see her troops manage themselves. Boys and girls who worked as servants to officers frequently joined the regular troops when they were of an age, but Alys could hardly be old enough yet. She must certainly lack training in the soldierly arts—no thin little maid like this should face the possibility of battle without at least learning how to wield a sword! In addition, Alys's outlandish claim that she could bring about the fall of Iagoburso suggested that the poor girl's mind must be unhinged. She needed to be looked after, not pressed into service and asked to take up duties she wasn't yet able to assume. Mara thought that she'd speak to the late Captain Silban's lieutenant about the girl as soon as the opportunity presented itself.

She dismissed Alys and headed for the pavilion. On her way, she turned back once and saw that Alys was no longer in sight.

"Lyngreen?" Captain Alyx said that evening when Mara told her friends about this strange encounter. "I remember it—it wasn't very far south of Storm Port. There was a great fire that consumed the whole village in one night, and everyone who lived in it."

“Except for this one child,” Kat pointed out.

“Except this child. She must’ve been very young,” said Alyx. “Lyngreen was destroyed ten years ago. If she’s not yet sixteen now, she couldn’t have been more than five at the time. A toddling little thing. It’s a wonder she survived when no one else was so fortunate.”

“I wonder how she made her way at so early an age,” Kat replied. “If her family was killed, who looked after her? How did she feed and clothe herself? Such a tragedy so young must surely have disturbed her mind. Then having her sergeant torn apart so brutally! I couldn’t fault her for going mad. You said you thought she might be mad, Mara, after talking with her.”

“So I did,” Mara answered. “I still do. But I haven’t told you the strangest part of the tale yet. I asked Lieutenant Kesandra about her—*she’s* never heard of the girl. She says she’s never seen such a little maid among the company, nor heard any gossip that Sergeant Gilamus was keeping a maidservant. It’s against regulations, after all.”

“The company’s been hiding the girl and keeping her secret from their officers,” Bel offered the obvious explanation.

“If that’s so,” said Kat, “then what’s more peculiar still is their letting the poor, mad child come and speak to you, Mara, and give herself away.”

Mara agreed. “She must’ve slipped past them, believing she could do me a service.”

“By knocking the Spaniards out of Iagoburso and off their tower of rock,” Alyx laughed. “If it comes about, Mara, you’ll know who to credit.”

“Aunt Mara!”

Mara was immediately on her feet, alert and alarmed. She looked all around for the boy who had shouted her name. Three of her nephews had accompanied her on this campaign: Arthur, her former squire; Eduarde, Lord Laufegcrike, Ambris’s second son, who had been knighted last Christmas; and Bertrande, who was Eduarde’s squire. The voice sounded like Eduarde’s, though Mara knew that he ought to be on a scouting patrol in the south of Santiago.

She spotted him as he emerged from the shadowy twilight, scrambling up the path from the landing point on the river and headed toward the pavilion. Now in the torchlight, she could see that his normally tanned face was chalky-white, and his eyes were large and glinting with tears.

Kat was also on her feet and spoke first. “Eddy, what is it? What’s happened?”

“It’s Bertie,” the young knight answered. “He’s dead.”

All the women made shocked and dismayed sounds at this terrible news; Bel cursed the “bastard Spaniards!”

“No, Captain, it wasn’t the Spanish,” Eduarde told her, then reported to Mara. “No one can say what happened to him. I don’t know. Aunt Mara, Captain Sataumie bids you come right away.”

tuenty-et-un

Even before she and Kat crossed the river and began the long moonlit ride southward to the encampment Sataumie had established as the base for her long-range scout patrols, Mara knew what they would find. Bertrande lay on his cot in the tent he shared with his elder brother, looking like a child asleep, but pale and still; there was no obvious wound on his body.

"Was he found in this same manner this morning?" she asked.

"Bertie was fine this morning, Aunt Mara," Eduarde answered. Standing over his brother's body, he was shaken anew. "He helped me put on my armor, as he always does, and we rode out together. We were together all day."

"When did you see him last?"

"We returned about three hours ago. I went to make my report to Captain Sataumie." Eduarde bowed his head respectfully at the captain, who had accompanied them into the tent. "I gave Bertie my horse and shield."

"Bertrande returned Lord Laufegcrike's horse to the corral along with his own," Sataumie added. "He must've come here to his tent immediately afterwards. Lord Laufegcrike found him lying on the floor and summoned help. We moved him to the cot when we tried to revive him. We made every effort, Prince Margueryt. I'm very sorry."

"Father will blame me," Eduarde said mournfully. "I promised I'd look after Bertie." Kat stepped closer and, though the young man had grown taller than she, brought his head down to her shoulder and bestowed a sympathetic pat. Tears were shimmering in her own eyes.

It's not your fault, Eddy," Mara reassured him. "You could've done nothing to prevent this. I will write your father tomorrow and explain to him how it happened." Ambris was more likely to hold her responsible for his son's death. The fact that Bertrande hadn't fallen in battle would be but a small comfort. "You know that Bertie isn't the first one of our number to die in this way. We've lost nearly a dozen among the troops on the eastward side of the river."

"Have you found any bite or mark on Bertie's hands or ankles that some crawling little creature might've made?" asked Kat.

"No," said Sataumie. "We found nothing."

Mara hadn't expected a different answer. "Have my nephew conveyed with all state and dignity back to our camp in the Jamesmarch," she gave the order. "He was a prince of the Northlands." It would be impossible to convey the boy's body home to Pendaunzel; because of the hot weather, Bertrande must be buried with no undue haste among the other fallen soldiers in the graveyard they had created on the outskirts of their camp. "I will write my brother and father tonight. A messenger must be sent at daybreak to Pendaunzel to bear the news of poor Bertrande's death to them."

"The first to fall victim on this side of the river—and it's one of our own kinsmen!" Kat said angrily as she and Mara rode back through the dark and empty miles. Mara had invited Eduarde to return to the main camp with them, but the young knight insisted on remaining beside his brother's body until it could be carried back in the morning. The moon had risen high in the sky by this late hour and the rocky tower beneath the fortress of Iagoburso rose to the north ahead of them, still several miles distant. Mara kept her eyes fixed upon it as a guide, for it was the only feature of note in the landscape. A long ride lay ahead of them, but they went slowly. Neither prince expected to sleep once they reached their own beds.

Mara had rarely ventured on to the western side of the river before this—not from lack of curiosity about the territory she hoped to conquer, but in order to avoid giving the Spanish opportunities to see her. She hadn't used her Shieldmaid companions as proxies in royal garb during this campaign, as she had in the Redlands, for their duties were too widespread and various. Only Kat served in that capacity by wearing princely white robes and the Norman lions bannered across her breast. Mara intended to make it difficult for the Spanish to identify her, and difficult for their assassins to target her. On this occasion, however, she felt she was safe. She and Kat would cross the river well before daybreak.

"If the Spaniards aren't behind this, it's blasted convenient for them," Kat continued speaking. "To strike at our own family strikes at the very heart of us."

"It will rebound against them. If the Spanish *are* behind Bertie's death somehow, they'll pay for it threefold." But Mara couldn't feel any great outrage toward the Spanish, for she didn't believe that the Spanish had anything to do with her nephew's death, nor the deaths of the other soldiers. This devilish work was not in their power.

"Poor Ambris will be heartbroken," said Kat. "What will you write to him?"

"I can say no more than the truth: Bertie died suddenly from some cause we don't yet understand. I'll say that he didn't suffer, if that will make it easier for Ambris to bear the loss of a son so young. He's never lost a child before, and will not have faced such grief. I'm sorry that we won't be able to take the news to Pendaunzel ourselves. Father will be devastated too. He was very fond of Bertie, not only as his grandson, but as one of his heralds. He always takes particular interest in those boys and keeps a place in his heart for them even when they aren't our kinsmen."

Kat made a slight, muffled sound at this statement, as if she had been ready to make a remark and then thought better of it. Mara knew that her cousin was thinking of Andemyon and waved a dismissive hand. "There was never anything in *that*, Cos, save folly."

"Ah, but whose folly?" Kat replied.

"Father's. Ours. Geoffrey's and Dr. Dimitrios's, and the rest of those evil-minded gossips who made much of so little. No one emerges very well from that shameful incident, and the Northlands will no doubt feel the effects of it for years to come. At least it got us here, where I most longed to be." Mara set her eyes again on the towering rock in the distance. "Though it wasn't how I would've wished to win my own way. It seems that someone else must always pay for my victories." She was thinking primarily of her nephew and the others who had fallen so mysteriously these past weeks, but when she heard Kat sigh, she knew that Bertrande wasn't whom her cousin was remembering. "You do blame me for his death, don't you?" she asked.

At the question, Kat started in her saddle. "Who? You mean Frederik? I told you once I didn't, Mara, and I meant what I said. It wasn't your doing. Any of us might've fallen at Spainfort. I can't fault you for his death because you didn't want me to marry him, and his dying spared you that. It's not as if you wanted him dead." She pulled her mount to a stop; Mara did the same. "Remember the night we found Sergeant Gilamus? Oh, of course you remember *that*—but do you remember what we were talking of before we found him, the conversation that was stopped?"

"Yes, I remember. We were speaking of Frederik that night too."

"There was more that might've been said then, or I might've said to you since if I'd found the right chance for it," Kat told her. "I've wanted to speak, Mara. This mightn't be the best time, but it must be said between us."

"About Frederik," Mara prompted Kat to go on.

"No, not Frederik, though he has his part in it. I've come to understand a good many things I didn't that night we quarreled before we went to battle at the Shieldwall," Kat said quietly. "It wasn't Frederik you disliked. I think you *did* like him when we first met him, `til you saw how I was growing to love him. It wasn't `til I declared myself his beloved and said I meant to stay and wed him that you disapproved. You opposed our love-affair, not because he wasn't a fit match for a Prince of Eirelande, but because you were jealous."

"Kat!" Mara cried out incredulously. "What are you saying? That's absurd! Jealous of your Frederik? How could you think I wanted him myself?"

"No," Kat answered in the same quiet tone, "that's not what I meant."

"What then?"

Instead of explaining explicitly, Kat asked, "Have you ever considered how much less complicated our lives would've been if you or I had been born a boy? Uncle Dafythe would've brought me over from Eireland as a child intended for you instead of for Ambris. Instead of spending my youth waiting for a suitable match, you and I would've been wed as soon as we were of an age to sign the contracts. It would've suited everyone wonderfully. We'd be perfectly matched, Cousin."

Mara couldn't believe what she was hearing, and tried not to understand it. "You're joking, Kat. This is nothing but nonsense."

"Is it nonsense?" Kat went on, "Since I was a little girl, I've dreamt of a Prince who was strong and brave, with a lion's heart of courage, an angel's purity of resolution and righteousness, a true knight's honor. One who was my equal at least in skill and will and intellect. I couldn't respect anyone lesser, but I could admire one greater. I didn't believe any such man truly existed. He must belong to a fairytale. No living man could match my ideal. Frederik–" She paused. "I loved Frederik. If he'd lived to be my husband, we might've lived happily together at Dennefort for all our lives, bringing up our daughter and perhaps other children too, but I knew from the first that he wasn't my Prince. After he died, I thought nearly as often of that imagined Prince as I did of him, until I saw the truth of it. I realized that I sought all those virtues in a man because I'd learnt from my cradle to love them in a woman. Mara, *you* are my Prince. The one who exactly fits my ideal is you."

She waited for Mara's reaction to this announcement, but Mara was too shocked to say anything.

"I thought it ought to be said, and I don't regret it," Kat declared with her old defiance. "I don't expect it will alter the nature of our friendship. Whatever talk there might be of sapphites among the Shieldmaids, I know you've never countenanced it. You like to pretend such things don't exist. You care for me as much as you're able to—I daresay more than you care for anyone—but love isn't your business and never will be."

Mara could hear no more. Spurring her horse, she rode away across the dark land. Kat did not try to catch her.

She rode as fast as she could until she had left Kat far behind, then slowed to an easier pace as she headed for Alyx's camp. The hour was late, but the captain had waited for her return; after she had left her horse to be watered and tended, Mara told Alyx briefly about Bertrande's death and asked her to send a small honor guard at daybreak to bear his body back for burial.

"And where is Prince Kat?" Alyx asked her. "Will she be

returning from Sataumie's outpost tonight?"

"She was riding after me," Mara answered. "She should arrive here within the hour. Tell her I've crossed the river." She had no desire to see her cousin right now, not after that terrible confession of feelings better left unspoken.

"Shall I wake the boatman to row you over?"

"Not yet. I'd like to stretch my legs first." The rock upon which the fortress of Iagoburso was set towered above them, enormous in the darkness, blocking the stars and even the setting moon. She'd seen it in a vision last winter, and had viewed it for months from the other side of the river, but had never been so near it before. Already, she was taking the first steps to draw closer. "You needn't accompany me, Alyx. I won't be gone long."

She strode quickly through the sleeping camp and within minutes was close enough to place one hand on the surface of the rock face. It was warm to the touch, still holding the sun's heat from yesterday. From a distance, the face of the rock appeared solid, but now that she stood before it, Mara could see that there were innumerable deep crags and vertical crevices. Some of these, Mara recalled from Alyx's reports, concealed the entrances to secret tunnels that led up into the fortress. They had blocked all the tunnels they'd found and guards were placed to keep watch over them. Mara glimpsed some of these guards as she walked around the base of the rock; they regarded her with surprise, jolting themselves to attention and saluting or bowing as she passed. The foot of the open pathway that wound up around the rock was also under guard.

Though she hadn't originally intended to go all the way around the enormous rock base, Mara was still troubled by her conversation with Kat. In her efforts to dispel it from her mind, she walked rapidly with one hand outstretched so that her fingertips brushed the rough surface. Before she knew it, she had gone out of sight of Alyx's camp and circled to the moonlit side of the rock. Although she'd passed the last guards mere minutes ago, Mara felt as if she were entirely alone in this still and silent landscape. Then she heard a movement close behind her.

Several soldiers were emerging from one of the deep crevices. They weren't her men—she saw that at a glance. There were Northlanders as black-haired and bronze-skinned, but the uniforms worn by these men bore the device of a large bird of prey with its wings spread, perched on a tall rock like the one that currently towered above them. So, in spite of their searches, Alyx hadn't found all the secret tunnels and entrances to the fortress; at least one remained that the Spanish could still use to come and go as they chose.

For a moment, they seemed as astonished to see her as she'd been to see them. Then one of the soldiers stepped toward her, his hand on the hilt of his sword. "You wear the golden lions," he spoke in heavily accented Norman. "If you are not the Infanta of the Drakon, then you are one of her ladies—a most important person."

Mara didn't respond to this. It was more prudent to keep the Spanish uncertain of whom precisely they had discovered. She wouldn't give them her name.

"At last, we have gained a great prize," the same Spaniard spoke again, and gestured to bring his companions forward. "It would give us great pleasure, Lady, if you would come with us. The Conde will be delighted to meet you."

If she'd believed that she was in physical danger, Mara would've tried to fight them, to flee or call for help, but she was still in her dinner robes with neither mail nor armor for protection, and no weapon but a light sabre. She didn't think they would harm her. She *was* too great a prize. If they'd wanted to kill her, they could have easily struck her down before she had seen them. As they had stricken so many of her people—including her own nephew? The answer to that remained to be seen. Surrendering quietly would also gain her the one thing she'd sought for weeks: entrance to Iagoburso.

She let them take her into the cleft in the rock.

The crevice went deep into the heart of the rock, a passage so narrow at first that they must turn sideways to squeeze through, then widening into a cave where more soldiers were waiting with torches. A conversation in Spanish followed. Mara had learned a little of the language during her Redlands campaigns, but this flow of words was too rapid for her to make sense of. Even the words she recognized didn't help her to understand more than she already anticipated. One of the soldiers took her arm, firmly but not roughly, and escorted her toward a stair cut upwards into the walls of a long shaft.

Up and up they went. The stairs were uneven in both height and width, and so steep at points that they were often forced to use their hands to climb. A single torch carried by one Spanish soldier going ahead of the others lighted their way; another torch was carried by the last person in the procession. Mara was kept carefully in the middle of the group.

At last, they reached the top of the stair and arrived at a thick, wooden door. This door was unbarred and opened for them when the first soldier pounded on it. There was another rapid exchange in Spanish between this soldier and the doorkeeper, and the latter darted away down a level corridor. Mara was taken down this same corridor, then up more stairs inside a stone tower to a round chamber. They must now be at the very top of Iagoburso. The room appeared to be a council chamber or dining hall, for there were many chairs around a rectangular table at its center. A large book that looked like some sort of journal lay open at one end of the table, a bottle of ink and a quill beside it. There were several cluttered shelves against the outer walls. The setting moon shone brightly through the windows on one side, and Mara could glimpse the silvery course of the river from another beyond the fortress battlements. Atop a shelf just below this window sat the long tube of a scrying-glass.

The soldiers who had brought her here remained with her until a man in an officer's uniform finally came up the stairs and entered the room. He was large and heavy-set—not fat, but a certain slackness in his cheeks and jowls suggested that he had once been, and might be so again if he had regular, hearty meals. He must be suffering from short rations during this siege as much as any of the men he commanded. His hair was dark and pulled back tightly, but several loose strands straggled free, and he was unshaven. Mara felt certain that he had been awakened for this meeting at such a late hour of the night. Given the obeisance and apologetic tone of the words the soldiers offered him, plus the use of the word *Conde* in all the conversations she had so far overheard, Mara had no difficulty in identifying him.

"You are the commander of this fortress, Conde Luiz," she said in common Norman; she knew from Alyx's reports that he was fluent in her own language.

"At your service," he replied with a bow. "You are the Infanta Marguerуt. They call you the Infanta of the Drakon. I welcome you to Iagoburso. It is a great honor for us to welcome a lady of the highest birth as our unexpected guest. Pray be seated, Infanta. Make yourself comfortable."

Once again, Mara refused to acknowledge her own identity. "You don't know that I am the Prince," she answered as she sat down in one of the chairs around the table.

"I think I am right in calling you so. You see, I know the Infanta and her ladies. I've watched them many times from here. I have an eye-glass—*como se dice?*—a spying glass." He indicated the long tube on the shelf behind him. "I cannot come out of my fortress, but I see what goes on around it. The tall, fierce capitan with long hair the color of wheat who keeps watch upon *me* I know well. I have met with her in this same room. Capitan Alyx, she is called. Peasant-born, like myself, yet she is the friend and companion of an Emperor's granddaughter! The one with the black hair, who rides in on her horse from the south, I also see often though I have not the honor of her acquaintance. It is not so easy to see so far across the Amarillo, but I sometimes see the little one with her hair in curls. I should like very much to see her more closely, for she looks as if she might be pretty and I see few pretty women here. But she is no more an Infanta than the other two. No, there are two Norman Infantas I have seen. They dress in white robes. They look much alike, but I am told that the taller of the two—but not so tall as Capitan Alyx—with shoulders so broad as a man, is the daughter of the Northlands Duq, the Infanta of the Drakon. You must be she."

It was difficult to continue to deny who she was after hearing these descriptions of herself and her closest companions. Mara simply chose not to say anything.

"May I have your sword please, Infanta?" Conde Luiz requested.

Mara drew her saber from its scabbard and formally handed it to him, hilt first. Conde Luiz took it, holding it horizontally in both his hands as he examined it.

"This is not the Lions-tooth," he observed. "The famous sword of the Redlyon."

"Of course not," said Mara. "That's much too heavy to be carried around every day. The Redlyon's sword is to be saved for special occasions."

"I am surprised that any woman, even the Redlyon's own granddaughter, has the strength to wield such a manly sword, but I have heard many times that you do. You are as feared and famous as he in parts of the Empire. They say none can defeat the Infanta del Drakon."

"You may see the truth of that for yourself, Conde, if you will come out and meet our armies in battle."

"Come out?" Conde Luiz looked astonished that she should suggest such a thing. "Come to meet an army far greater than ours and be slaughtered on the open lands where there is no shelter? I haven't arisen so far from my most humble beginning as a common footsoldier by making so foolish an error."

"Have you come no closer to spy upon us?" Mara asked him. "Your people still seem free to come and go as they please."

"Not so free as that! There is nowhere to go in this desert. Sometimes, I send out those who speak your Norman tongue to learn what news they can from those who live below us. This night was such a time. I saw that there was some disorder among your people this evening, and wondered what had occurred."

"Haven't you heard? A young prince of the Northlands has died," Mara told him. "He was Bertrande of Eadeshire, a son of Lord Ambris. You know who he is?"

"Lord Ambris? Of course," Conde Luiz answered. "I know much of your family, Infanta. Your brother is known the world over as a man of great learning and judgment. He is half of Spanish blood himself—a Spanish peasant's blood." This might've been meant an insult, but it didn't sound like one to Mara; as Luiz freely acknowledged, *he* was from the Spanish peasantry and he seemed to hold Ambris in higher esteem because of this common bond. "I sorrow to hear of the death of his son."

"You had nothing to do with it?" Mara demanded.

"I was not aware of the young prince's presence in Santiago."

"He may have been bitten by some poisonous desert animal," Mara persisted. "A snake or a scorpion. Many of our people have died in this same way, but no bites have been discovered on any of them. It's very strange. I wondered if there might be some other poison at work—a poison not from by the bite of an animal." Mara watched Conde Luiz closely to see how he responded to this implicit accusation, but the Conde received it with equanimity. "You haven't suffered the same among your own people?"

"Such creatures are common in this land," Conde Luiz answered. "I have lost men to them, but we are above such dangers here in the fortress. It is one additional protection we have by staying here."

"You were given the opportunity to leave Iagoburso peaceably," Mara reminded him. "Captain Alyx has brought you the Prince's terms for surrender."

"Yes, I have spoken with her many times. All the same, we choose to stay where we are safest."

"But are you safe? Your supplies here must be very short. You can't provide for your people for much longer without relief. What is it you're waiting for, Conde?" Mara asked him bluntly. "Are more troops expected from the south?"

Conde Luiz shook his head. "No. I have known for a long time that we can expect no aid. I was sent here to oversee this blighted desert because no other commander would have it. It is an exile. I would be pleased to be in any other part of the Empire, but is my sworn duty before the Lord God and in the Emperor's name to defend Santiago from invasion. I have long doubted that even the maddest of Normans would desire to invade such a worthless place—but you and your army are here and I have my duty. I have done my best to protect this land without hope of aid, and we here are prepared to die to the last man before we surrender to you. No, it is not more armies from the south I have waited and prayed so long for. I've waited for the opportunity I knew must come to save us. You have at last given it to me. Tonight, you've given us what we most needed—a hostage to bargain with. If you are not the great Infanta after all, then I have no use for you." For the first time, he sounded menacing.

"You'll get nothing by keeping me prisoner," said Mara. "The Northlanders are instructed not to pay ransom for any captured officers, even their Prince. If I am she, then you must surely know that my capture will only anger them and drive them to fight all the more furiously on my behalf."

"They will fight, yes, but they haven't taken my fortress for all their efforts," Conde Luiz replied composedly. "They can merely batter themselves against the mesa for so long, as they have done. They will not reach us. Eventually, they must wear themselves out and will agree to hear my demands. I have been patient so long. I can wait a little longer." Two of the soldiers who had brought Mara into the room had remained during this interview; Conde Luiz now turned to them and gave an elaborate order in Spanish before he told Mara, "Will you please to go with these guards, Infanta Marguerryt? They will take you to a room, where you will wait as well. The accommodations are the most comfortable I have to offer. I regret I have no gentlewomen such as you are used to, but I will send a woman to attend to your needs while you are my guest." He turned to look out of the window behind him: the sky to the east was growing pink with the approach of dawn. "Your people must by this time see that you are missing. When the sun has arisen, I will send a messenger down to Capitan Alyx to inform her that you are here with us and have not been harmed, but I will also tell her what she must do to see you returned to your own people."

tuenty-et-tu

The room was not very comfortable, but it wasn't a dungeon. Conde Luiz had placed her in what appeared to be empty quarters for a low-ranked officer in a lower level of the main tower. There was one narrow bed and a narrow window high on one wall. After sleeping in a tent for so many weeks, Mara found it adequate. A guard was placed outside the door. When she climbed up to stand on the bed and look out of the window, she found no means of escaping by that route; even if she managed to squeeze herself through the tall, thin slit, a sheer drop hundreds of feet down the outer wall of the fortress and the rock it was built upon awaited her. She wasn't certain that she wanted to escape yet. She wasn't afraid for her life or person. Conde Luiz had only threatened her with harm if she wasn't the Prince. While she hadn't yet acknowledged that she was indeed Marguerыt, she saw that there might come a time when it would be more advantageous to admit it. For the present, she could only wait and see how her friends and her armies responded to the news of her capture. Alyx was sure to arrive before long. Would her captain inadvertently reveal her identity?

Mara had spent a sleepless night, much of it on horseback, and while she sat on the bed and waited, she soon dozed. She woke abruptly, startled by the sound of the door opening, but it was only the guard, admitting a woman in peasant garb, bringing her breakfast. Since it was now long after her usual breakfast hour, Mara accepted this food: a clay pitcher of yeasty water, or perhaps extremely watered-down beer, and a crumbling piece of dry, unsalted blue-grey bread made from ground maize. Mara assumed this was the same diet that the Spanish inhabitants of Iagoburso were living on but, when she asked, she found that the woman didn't understand a word of Norman and looked bewildered at the question. Mara thought the woman was also a little frightened of her even though she was captive, and dismissed her with a "gracias" as soon as she had finished her sparse meal.

The sun had climbed high, out of the range of her narrow window, when at last Mara heard the sound of boots in the corridor outside. The guards who had come for her spoke little Norman, but enough that Mara understood she was to be brought to Conde Luiz.

The Conde was in his tower room where Mara had left him, but a visitor had joined him. Alyx stood in the middle of the room, flanked by the two Spanish guards who had escorted her up through the fortress.

When Mara was brought in, Alyx bowed her head respectfully, but didn't salute nor address her commander with the usual obeisance given to the Prince. Mara took note of this, and only said, "It's good to see you, Alyx."

"And you. We were frantic with worry when we realized you hadn't gone back to the camp," Alyx told her. "I was almost relieved when I received Conde Luiz's message. I was afraid something much worse had happened to you."

"You see that your Infanta is unharmed," said Conde Luiz. "She will tell you herself that she has been treated well." Mara confirmed that this was so. "If you will agree to my terms, Capitan, then there is no reason why she cannot be returned to you."

"What are your terms, Conde?" Alyx requested. "I am commissioned to hear them, and I may accept or refuse them as seems fit to me."

"They are simple, Capitan, and may easily be complied with. I wish no ransom. It is not wealth I seek, merely the continued safety of my people, as you surely wish for the safety of your Infanta. To ensure this safety, you will withdraw all Northland troops from Santiago immediately. This must be done today. When I see that all your men and women, including those riders to the south, have returned to the other side of the river, I will know that this much has been fulfilled. You will then remove your encampment from the eastern bank of the Rio Amarillo and cease all threats to Iagoburso and claims to Santiago. This must be done in seven days. I must have your word of honor on this—both yours, Capitan Alys, and the Infanta's. When I see that you are breaking your camp and have begun to move, Infanta Marguerýt will be set free to join you. Do you agree to this?" He looked from one woman to the other. "Do I have your word?"

Alyx gave Mara a quick glance that warned her something was afoot. The Prince was therefore not surprised when Alyx replied in respectful terms, "I'm sorry to say, Conde Luiz, that we cannot accede to your demands. What you ask is impossible."

The Conde *was* surprised by this blunt refusal. "I think you speak in haste, and will repent of it," he responded with a note of asperity. "You are foolish and prideful—it is often the way of women who do not wish to lose a quarrel, but there is more than an argument here to be lost. You may expect to hope that because I am a man of honor, I will not kill a defenseless woman, but desperation will often lead one to act against the codes of chivalry. If you are truly soldiers, you know this is so. I pray you believe that we in Iagoburso are desperate. If you do not withdraw your armies, then it is with the greatest regret that I must execute your Infanta."

"I believe you, Conde Luiz, and I will be grieved if you should execute this woman—as will many in our company," said Alyx. "Nevertheless, I cannot agree to your terms. My Prince will not allow it, even to save one who is nearly a sister to her. She is that firm in her resolve to take Iagoburso."

Conde Luiz looked utterly bewildered, as if his understanding of Norman weren't sufficient to take in this strange speech. "Your pardon—you say your Prince...?

Alyx nodded. "Believe *me*, Conde Luiz, when I tell you that you are mistaken. You have not captured the prize you imagined. This woman is not Prince Marguerýt. Our Prince stands upon your battlements even now, prepared to avenge her cousin."

Conde Luiz was skeptical of this announcement; Alyx moved toward the window overlooking the courtyard before the fortress's main gates.

"Will you come and see?" she invited him.

She opened the casement, and as if in response to this signal, a voice cried out in badly accented Spanish:

"Yo soy Infanta del Drakon!"

The Conde rose from his seat and went to the window. Mara joined him.

A woman stood atop the wall above the barred but conspicuously unattended main gate. Over her mailcoat, she wore a princely white tunic and a banner with golden lions across her breast. The gold circlet of a battle crown upon her helm shone brightly in the late morning sun. In one hand she held the Redlyon's famous sword; the other arm was guarded by a shield bearing a dragon—the very shield Mara herself had painted.

Luiz turned to regard his prisoner in renewed confusion.

"I'm not Prince Margueryt," Mara told him. "I'm her kinswoman, Katheryne of Eireland."

The four guards who had escorted Mara and Alyx were likewise confused, for they had also believed that they were holding the Northlands Prince hostage. The sight of the Sonnedragon upon the shield was enough to strike a chord of fear among them, but the woman who stood on the wall appeared to be alone. Then two other women and one young man armed for battle clambered up to stand beside her. No Spanish soldiers were in the courtyard below—a fact that seemed as unexpected to the rescue party as to Conde Luiz. The Conde, however, recovered swiftly from his momentary surprise and gave terse commands to send the guards in the room down to confront the invaders.

As the proclaimed "Infanta del Drakon" and her companions climbed down from the wall to meet the Spanish guards in the courtyard, they passed out of view of the window. Mara, Alyx, and Conde Luiz could hear voices shouting in Norman and Spanish and the sounds of clashing metal. There was a scream or two. Then there was silence. A strange silence. Not only had the sounds of fighting completely ceased, but they heard no voices or other sounds of people in motion.

"What's happened?" Mara wondered. Had Kat and the others been ambushed? The absence of soldiers in the courtyard suggested that some sort of trap had been laid for any Northlanders who had followed Alyx up to the fortress. But if that were so, then the trap hadn't been of Conde Luiz's devising, for he seemed as uncertain as she about the outcome of the battle.

"Shall I go and see?" Alyx offered. "Conde Luiz will keep you good company while I am gone." She bowed and went out.

They listened to her boot heels on the stairway beyond the closed door, until this sound receded and they were left again with a silence that became more disturbing as it continued.

At last, Conde Luiz met his prisoner's eyes. "Your pardon, Infanta Kateryne," he said. "I must see for myself. If your kinswoman has triumphed, it is my duty to receive her. If my men have won this fight, then I may have more prisoners to welcome."

He didn't invite Mara to accompany him. In another moment, the Conde too was gone and she was alone in the tower room. Who would he find at the bottom of the stair, Mara wondered. Her rescuers, or dead Normans and triumphant Spaniards?

Conde Luiz had locked the door behind him. Mara immediately confirmed this by trying the latch and peeking through the large keyhole to be sure that the key hadn't been left in the lock. No, the Conde had taken it with him. In spite of this, Mara believed she might be able to escape. She had to try. It was impossible for her to sit here, patiently waiting, while a battle was going on somewhere in the fortress below. She had to join the fight. Her friends might have need of her. The saber she'd surrendered to Conde Luiz was still lying on the table at the center of the room, and surely there was something—a slender-bladed knife, perhaps—that she could use to open the lock.

She was searching the shelves for some such tool when she heard someone calling out from the corridor at the foot of the stair.

"Where is she?" It was Bel's voice. "My Prince! Prince Mara! Can you hear me?"

"I'm here!" Mara shouted, rushing to the door and thumping her hands on the wooden surface. "Up here, Bel! The door at the very top. I can't get out."

"Wait! I have just the thing." After a moment, Mara heard her friend running up the stair, then the rattling of a ring of keys and the click of the lock. The door opened.

Bel stood on the small landing beyond the door and looked Mara over anxiously from head to foot. "You're all right, My Prince?" she asked. "They haven't harmed you?"

"Not in the least," Mara assured her, and took up her sabre from the table. "Let's go. Where are the others? Have you seen Alyx?"

Bel shook her head. "Not since she left with the Spanish messenger and came up the path ahead of us. The rest of our party separated to search for you once we'd taken care of the guards at the gate—a poor showing, I thought," she spoke as she went down the stairs ahead of Mara. "Only four men to match the four of us. They've left their fortress sadly undefended. I've scarcely seen another Spaniard since Prince Kat sent me up this way, only one oily-looking bastard who tried to stand in my way."

In the corridor near the foot of the stairs lay Conde Luiz. His eyes were wide open, but unseeing. A stain of fresh blood spread across the front of his tunic from a wound in his chest.

"Wouldn't he tell you where I was?" Mara asked, recalling the first words she'd heard Bel speak.

"I didn't wait for his answer. He stood there, blocking my way and grinning at me like a lecherous fool. Once you called out my name, I had no further reason to seek his cooperation."

"You didn't need to kill him, Bel. He wouldn't have murdered a woman, save out of desperation. He said so himself and I believed him."

"He was a Spaniard," Bel replied. "He might've stabbed you in the back at any moment, and smiled all the while." She stepped easily over the body to lead the way down the corridor. "I'd stab a thousand Spaniards for you, My Prince, if I were given the chance."

Although she'd only known the Conde a very short time and he had threatened her life, she couldn't help feeling pity for him now that he had paid with his own life. He had indeed been a desperate man, acting for what he'd believed was the best defense of his people, his fortress, and the land he'd been given to govern. She could respect that desire to protect what was his, even as she wished he'd been more reasonable about surrendering the fortress and the land on her terms. It shouldn't have come to this bloody ending.

"What's happened?" Mara asked as she followed her companion. "Why is it so quiet? Have we taken the fortress?"

"It's ours," the captain assured her, "though I can't say *how* it came to be. We were expecting that we'd have to face a terrible fight to free you. There were only a pair of guards stationed outside the gate—we dispatched them easily enough, but we thought there'd be a dozen more inside. Prince Kat climbed up onto the wall, posing as you and hoping the sight of the

Sonnedragon upon your shield would strike fear into their Spanish hearts, but no one was there to be frightened! Once we were over the wall, we met with a few more soldiers, as I've told you, but they gave us little trouble. I'm disappointed. I was looking forward to cutting some of their throats."

"Where are they?" Mara knew that at least two hundred soldiers were stationed at Iagoburso—she'd seen at least twenty herself since she'd been captured this morning—plus an untold number of peasant farmers who had taken shelter inside the fortress.

"I don't know, My Prince. They must've hidden themselves before we arrived, but we haven't yet discovered where."

"Then it's best we be ready for a fight when we do find them."

Swords drawn in case the Spanish soldiers should suddenly emerge from hiding to attack them, Mara and Bel cautiously made their way down through the great tower. At the foot of the tower, they looked into the armory and found it unattended, then went out into the courtyard where the rescue party had met and defeated the Spanish guards. Here, blood had also been spilt. Three of the four Spanish guards Conde Luiz had sent were dead; the other was wounded and held at swordspoint by Eduarde. The young knight looked relieved and overjoyed to see his aunt. Captain Alyx, he informed her, had gone for reinforcements. And where was Kat? In answer to this question, Eduarde pointed across the courtyard to a large portal, its wooden doors open. "After she sent Captain Belynde into the tower, she went to search for you there."

Mara ordered her nephew to keep watch over his prisoner and ensure his safety until her return, then went after Kat. Bel accompanied her.

Once they had gone through the portal, Mara and Bel walked down a broad, cobblestone path and into a less well-kept yard than the one just within the front gate. The lower parts of the fortress appeared to be used as a stable and farmyard, for loose straw was scattered across the stones, and there were empty pens stinking of animal droppings along the walls. A bony, short-haired dog came out to bark at them, then retreated timidly as the pair continued toward it. There were no people in sight.

"Where could all they be?" Mara wondered again. "They

couldn't have fled, not without being seen by Alyx's guards below."

"They had horses," said Bel, indicating the stable. "They might've gone in the night, though how they could take the beasts up and down that narrow path along the cliff-edge is beyond my understanding." She peeked into the stable and reported that there were indeed several starved-looking horses and donkeys within. "They didn't ride out."

"They must still be here somewhere. If Kat's found–" Mara began, when a high-pitched wail stopped her. For a horrified moment, she thought that Kat was screaming, then quickly realized that it was the cry of a child. With one hand on the hilt of her sabre, she ventured toward the sound, hoping to trace it to its source.

It was then they found the first bodies, a group of soldiers lying in a passageway leading away from the stable yard. Could this be Kat's work? Even though she was armed with Dentelyon, it seemed a mighty task for one woman alone against so many. But Mara and Bel saw no blood, nor any sign that the men had been engaged in battle at the moment of their deaths. Most looked as if they'd simply fallen in mid-step. They were all facing the same direction, as if they'd been headed together toward some destination farther along the passage.

Ahead of them along this same passage, rose a cluster of round buildings that looked to be storage chambers. The child was still wailing.

As Mara and Bel went on, they discovered more dead Spanish soldiers, their skin still warm to the touch. Though the sun was now high overhead, baking the exposed stone and clay of the fortress walls, even those bodies in the shade retained some natural warmth of life.

"What could've done this? Is it a plague?" Mara wondered. Whatever had stricken them down, it must have occurred immediately before the Northlanders had arrived. She would've liked to question Luiz about the condition of his people, but he was dead now too.

The storage chambers at the end of the passage had been used as housing for the Santiago farmers who sought shelter from the Normans during the siege. They too were all dead. As they ventured within, passing through a series of semi-circular rooms against the outer walls, they found a dozen families huddled among their belongings, lying on makeshift beds or gathered around meager, half-finished breakfasts. They had obviously died some time before the soldiers outside, but not more than a few hours ago. The prevailing smell within the close rooms was a mixture of cooked food, unwashed bodies, mildew and middens, but not the stench of the dead. Clouds of black flies swarmed everywhere, more flies than Mara had ever seen at once; she could hear them buzzing even before she and Bel had gone inside, and their noise once they were disturbed nearly drowned out the sound of the crying child. Mara was accustomed to the sight of corpses in far worse condition, but this inexplicable disaster made her feel sick.

They found the single survivor, a little girl of about three or four, in one of the inner chambers, among a group of farm-folk who must have been her family. In the single shaft of light that shone down from a hole in the ceiling, she seemed nothing more than thin, pale arms and legs, a tangle of black curls, and a pair of enormous black eyes. Her howls grew even louder when she saw the two women with swords.

Mara had no great affection for small children, but she knew better than to give the care of a Spaniard, even one so young, to Bel. She handed her sabre to the captain before she stepped closer and said, "Hush, little one. We mean no harm to you."

The child couldn't possibly understand her, but her tone was gentle and reassuring; the little girl ceased to scream, but it took more soothing-sounding words before she let herself be taken up.

"She doesn't look as if she's suffering from more than fear and a lack of good food," Mara said once she held the child in her arms. "If only she were a few years older! She surely saw what happened here. Well, where there is one alive, there might be others who are able to tell us more."

"Hush," Bel spoke suddenly in a hissing whisper. "Someone's outside, and they may not like to answer our questions."

Mara also heard the sound of heavy boots treading slowly through the interconnecting chambers of the storage building, moving carefully past the same groups of bodies they had discovered. A long shadow was cast from one of the slits of a window high overhead on an outer wall, and it grew longer and larger as it approached.

Bel brandished the sabre and positioned herself beside the open doorway, ready to defend Mara from whatever danger threatened. “Who’s there?” she demanded. “Identify yourself!”

The shadow shape stopped. “Bel?” came the surprised response. “Is that you? How came you here? Is Mara with you?”

“I’m here, Kat!” Mara called out.

Her cousin appeared in the doorway. Mara could scarcely recall that awkward scene that had sent her flying from Kat; that was mere hours ago, though it seemed ages. So much had happened since then, and all she could feel in this moment was delight. If it weren’t for the little girl she was still holding, she would’ve embraced her cousin.

Kat looked ready to embrace her as well. “It’s good to see you alive,” she said, lowering the heavy Dentelyon as Bel likewise lowered the sabre. “There aren’t many here who are.”

“Are all the Spaniards dead, like these poor folk?” Mara asked. “Is there no one left alive?”

“None that I’ve seen, `til now.” Kat glanced at the child in Mara’s arms. “I’ve been all around this part of the fortress. The soldiers’ quarters are here, and they’re all just the same—in the refectory, in their beds, or lying out and about, as if they were all struck dead at once by the Hand of God.”

“It wasn’t God who struck them down,” said Mara. “We must look about, and find the others living, if they are any. Will you set our people to the task, Cousin? Bel, I leave you to lead the search. I must go down to our camp below and show myself, so that everyone can see I’m alive and unhurt. I’ll bring the child with me. I’ll have Eduarde take his prisoner down, and you must send down any other Spaniards you find alive. I want them to stay alive. We must see them fed and cared for. If any speak Norman, I wish to question them. Someone must tell us how this came about.”

With the little girl clinging to her, Mara made her way out of the storage chambers and lower part of the fortress. As she passed through the courtyard, more Norman soldiers were coming up through the front gate and the tunnels that had long been guarded at both ends. She spoke briefly to Eduarde and Alyx, giving each her orders, then she left Iagoburso. It was hers at last, but she wanted nothing more than to be far away from it.

tuenty-et-tre

By the late afternoon, Mara had returned to the eastern side of the river and her camp in the Jamesmarch. She would occupy Iagoburso eventually, once the scores of bodies had been cleared away and decently buried. Whole squads were assigned to this task. Other Northland troops were spreading through Santiago unhindered, taking official possession of the captured territory. Once she had issued her orders, however, Mara had left the management of these tasks to Kat and her captains. Bertrande's body had been brought to the camp at dawn and she felt that the burial of her young nephew, and the letter she had planned to write to his father, took precedence over all other concerns.

The troops in the Jamesmarch were relieved at their Prince's safe return and delighted at the news that Iagoburso had at last been taken, but their joy at these events was oddly subdued. Already, they whispered that the Prince and her cousin Kat were somehow responsible for the deaths of all the Spaniards; Mara's capture and rescue had only been a ploy to gain access to the fortress so that they could enact their bloody plan. While Mara was pleased to let her soldiers think that she'd been that clever rather than careless, the indiscriminate slaughter of non-combatants also attributed to her wasn't as gratifying.

The lone surviving Iagoburso guard could provide no explanation for the deaths of the other Spanish inhabitants of the fortress; he insisted that they were not afflicted with disease. His fellow soldiers and the officers had all been alive and well the last time he'd seen them that morning, less than an hour before he'd escorted Captain Alyx up from the front gate to the Conde's room in the tower. He hadn't seen the farm families since the night before, when their rations had been doled out. They complained of the small amounts of food they received, but there was no sign that they were ill in great numbers.

The only other living witness to the disaster spoke no word of Norman, nor even enough of her own language to describe what she had seen. The little girl could only repeat her universally understood cry for "Mama!"—a cry that would never be answered.

"What will happen to her?" Kat asked when she met her cousin in their tent that evening. She was still dressed in Mara's battle gear and bore the Sonnedragon arms, for she'd been too busy overseeing the occupation of Santiago all day to return and change her clothing before this.

"I'll see that she's cared for," Mara promised. "Delphyn is looking after her now. She's been fed and bathed, and she seems to be thriving. Since she has no living family here, and we've no means of finding out if she has other relations elsewhere, I'll see that she's provided for as my ward once we are home. An Abbey will be the best place for her. The Sisters at Samandra Abbey are accustomed to take orphans in."

"And our other prisoner?"

"Keep him away from our troops, save the guards who must watch over him. If he shows no signs of falling prey to the illness that struck his fellows down, then we will set him at liberty in three days' time. I have no use for prisoners. See that he is equipped with a horse and sufficient supplies to carry him safely to the Spanish lands to the south. He may bear my message to the Conde there that Santiago is now mine. I doubt they'll contest my claim. If they meant to fight, they would've done so long before this instead of leaving Conde Luiz to fend for himself." She regarded her cousin in her clothes. "Was that ruse your idea, Kat?"

"That I should bear your arms?" Kat indicated the shield painted with the image of the Sonnedragon, which she had set down by the entrance to their tent. "Yes, that much was. When I came back here to arm myself, I saw how I might cast the Spaniards into confusion about who their prisoner was. But I can't claim the rest of the plan as my own. It was Alyx who said we ought to follow her up to the gate once the guards accompanied her—she knew she couldn't have stopped Bel from doing so if she had her held at swordspoint. I felt the same myself. We couldn't sit by and leave you at that Conde's mercy. Who knew what he might do? Oh, Mara, you don't know how I blamed myself when we found you were missing. We searched all around the base of the rock, where Alyx said you'd gone. I was afraid to imagine the worst. I knew how it was all my fault. If I hadn't said what I did and set you riding off alone–"

Mara didn't want to talk about *that*. She would prefer to pretend that it had never happened; that was the only way she could continue to treat her cousin as she always had. "We must see to occupying Santiago—and rechristen it with some more suitable, Norman name as well. I've been thinking of calling it Bertrandesmarch, in memory of poor Bertie. When the fortress is made ready, we'll take up residence. I'll station a garrison to remain there with us."

"If they dare live in that place after what's happened!" Kat exclaimed. "I don't know if I'm brave enough to lay my head to rest in one of those Spaniards' beds after what I saw there today. Those poor dead peasants will haunt my dreams for nights to come."

"Civilians are often killed in battle," said Mara, as much to herself as to Kat. "It is a fact of war. I wish it weren't so, but it is. We've seen old men and women, even children, dead in Spanish towns before this. These are no different, though I would almost rather we'd cut them down quickly instead of letting them die in so slow and terrible a way. We besieged their fortress, and left them prey to starvation and disease."

"They looked as if they were going hungry, but I don't believe they starved to death," Kat replied. "They were very short of food, `tis true. They'd eaten all their livestock except for the horses. We found all sorts of bones piled in the rubbish—cows and pigs, goats, chickens, and even what looked like rats, though none that were human, please God! But they had grain enough to last them another week or two on small rations. If they had starved, they wouldn't have all died at once as they did. I doubt even plague would take so many in an instant." She lowered her voice, though no one but Ren could overhear their conversation. "You know what it looked like, Mara. They were struck down just as our own people have been, but by the score rather than one at a time. No spider or scorpion, nor even a thousand of them, could've done such terrible work."

Before she met with her captains at dinner to hear their reports of the day, Mara walked the path by the river's edge. Kat, nervous at letting her cousin go on another walk by herself, had offered to accompany her, but Mara insisted on going alone.

It was now dusk, and torches blazing atop the fortress across the river showed her that Northland soldiers were still at work within. Would she dare to reside at Iagoburso when the time came? Kat had claimed to doubt her own bravery to do so—words spoken partially in jest, but Mara felt a slight shiver run up her spine at the idea of quartering troops in same barracks where so many had died, or sleeping in the same bedchamber that had so recently belonged to the late Conde Luiz. At this moment, she hated the sight of the place. She wouldn't mind seeing the whole edifice crumbling into dust so that she could rebuild it anew from untainted stone.

The mysterious deaths of the Spanish was in itself disturbing, but Mara felt a deeper dread at what these deaths portended. She had wanted them to leave Iagoburso so that she might occupy it, and they were now gone. Once again, she'd gained her victory, though at a grotesque and appalling price.

"It is thine, O Prince."

The words of the Sonnedragon had repeated often in her head for many months, but it wasn't the Sonnedragon that spoke to her now. This was a woman's voice—a voice she had heard before. Who could know the words of the Sonnedragon's promise, words she alone had heard? And did she detect a hint of mockery behind them?

As Mara whirled to locate the person who had spoken, a small figure stepped from the long evening shadows to reveal itself: Alys, the mad little serving-maid dressed in the uniform of a guardswoman.

"It is done, Prince Marguerуt," the girl said. "The fortress is yours."

Once recovered from her initial startlement, Mara had to smile. "Do you claim responsibility for it, Maiden?"

"I've done what I said I would," Alys stated simply. "There are no longer any Spaniards in Iagoburso. It is as you wished."

The girl's strange jest, which was not very amusing in the first place, seemed less so with every word she spoke. "The Spaniards are all dead," said Mara. "You believe this is *your* doing?"

Alys smiled as she replied, "You have far more deaths to your name than I, Dread Prince. Why should these matter more than any others? You have what you desired. `Tis better not to ask how it came about. You called upon me, and I came to do your bidding. That must be enough."

This sounded like madness, but an uneasy feeling crept through Mara as she regarded the tiny young maiden standing before her. It might be no more than coincidence that Alys should repeat the Sonnedragon's words, and yet there was something very odd about the girl. Alys tonight was different. There was nothing timid nor deferential in her demeanor. She was bold and unafraid, as if she approached an equal and not a Prince. When her eyes met Mara's, something more disturbing than madness could be seen in them.

"I never summoned you," Mara answered. "I don't even know who you are. I never saw you before yesterday."

"You've enlisted the aid of my masters, many times. You called out to them to see you win this last venture, and they sent me. You know that you aren't the first great Prince to bear the talisman. Others greater than you have employed it to their own ends, or refused to."

Mara's hand went to the stone on its tether around her neck. "You refer to the Dragonseye?"

Alys nodded her head, dipping her chin once while her eyes remained on Mara's. "It's been called by many names. It is but a small relic left from an earlier era of magical warfare before the modern rules of magic were laid down upon this world. They do not apply to this."

Mara didn't understand this further preposterous claim. A wizard might. Nevertheless, it disturbed her to hear that Alys not only knew about the gem, but knew something of its history and seemed to know what it meant to her. It was as if the peculiar little creature had peeked into her thoughts and seen her secrets. She was afraid that she was faced with a lunatic… and more terrified that she was not. "What is it you want of me?"

"Only that you continue as you have done, O Prince. It's all that can be expected of anyone, and all that my masters require of you. They tell me you will not disappoint."

This answer was even less comprehensible than the last. "Who *are* you?" Mara demanded. Whatever she might be, Alys was certainly no ordinary young maid.

"Alys of Lyngreen, at your service." The girl curtseyed, just as she'd done the day before. But in this, as in all her words and actions, there was now a trace of mockery. "You know who I am. I've been with you, Prince Marguerуt, from the beginning. When you first fell in battle at the Shieldwall, I gave you the power to rise again. You drank my blood. You received my gifts. Since that day, you've borne my name and my image upon your shield, and I've led you from victory to victory. So long as I serve you, you must triumph." That smile flashed again. "I am the Dragon."

"That can't be true!" Mara protested.

"But it is true, My Prince. You know in your heart that it is." Alys laughed and, as she took a step backward into the deepening shadows, it seemed to Mara that she vanished. But her laughter could still be heard.

It wasn't possible, Mara told herself after Alys had gone. It couldn't be. Neither Alys nor her "masters" had played a part in the remarkable events that had occurred during this campaign. Alys's masters did not exist; they were demons conjured up by the imagination of a mad young girl. Alys was surely mad. She possessed a talent for making acute guesses about other people's secrets, and the conviction of insanity made her astounding claims seem believable while she was speaking. That was all.

In fact, all of it from first to last was entirely the delusion of a madwoman. Not Alys, Herself. A bear had attacked Sergeant Gilamus, just some beast had killed the Con Permiso commander. Poisonous snakes or scorpions had bitten the hapless soldiers among her troops, including her nephew Bertrande. Plague of some unknown kind, aggravated by the conditions of close quarters and privations during the siege, had ravaged Iagoburso. To attribute these strange events to the influence of supernatural agencies was plainly madness.

What more had she imagined? That the Dragonseye was something more than a stone of minor historical interest and that it held ancient magical powers. That she'd won her victories because she wielded these powers, and not because she was a capable general and favored with good fortune. That her vision of the Sonnedragon had been as real as flesh and blood, and not the delirium of a wounded soldier lying dazzled by the hot sun on the battlefield.

There was no Sonnedragon. The only bloodthirst that coursed through her veins was her own.

Mara repeated these thoughts to herself, but in her heart she didn't believe a word of it. Alys had spoken the truth. In using the Dragonseye, she had unwittingly called upon powerful and malign forces she didn't understand, and now she was bound to them. How was she to free herself from this Devil's bargain?

In the moments after Alys had vanished, Mara had uttered a prayer for God's protection, but she knew that more was required before she could truly feel she'd been redeemed. Continue as she had been doing? No. If Alys and her masters desired these campaigns of hers against the Spanish to continue, then they certainly must cease. Her friends and followers wouldn't understand why she had so abruptly changed her mind, but this was a sacrifice that must be made if she were to save herself. She would leave Santiago in the command of a capable and trusted captain, and travel homewards as soon as she was able. She must then do penance, confess herself and pray for forgiveness.

There was also another, more practical action she could take right away. Seizing the stone dangling from its tether, she pulled it free and flung it into the river. It would eventually be carried down to the sea and out of human hands forever.

"Prince Mara!"

She'd seen the lanterns on the boat crossing the river several minutes earlier, and knew that Alyx, Bel, and Sautamie had returned from the fortress. They would be waiting for her. Turning away from the dark water, she hastened back up the path the way she had come, heading toward the lights of the pavilion. Her friends were standing beneath the foremost part of the canopy with worried faces, until they saw Mara coming up the bank from the river's edge.

"You shouldn't go about alone, My Prince," Alyx scolded her. "Prince Kat and your guard here shouldn't have let you. When she told us that she'd left you to walk by the river by yourself, it recalled me to last night."

"No harm came to me," Mara assured her friends. "There are no more Spaniards to threaten us even in solitude. I am as safe tonight as any mortal Christian soul may be. I've been thinking about my plans for Santiago. Know first that I intend to leave this place as soon as possible...."

A memorial service was held for Bertrande the next morning in the burial ground in Jamesmarch, and another later that week for the Spaniards buried in a common grave in the shadow of the fortress which had already been renamed Marasfort by the Norman soldiers. Although Mara hadn't authorized this or any other changes of place names, the Northlanders were quick to replace Spanish words with one from their own common tongue: Rio Amarillo was now the Yellow River, and d'Iago Pescador had become Fisherman's Creek.

By the end of the week, the fortress was fit to be occupied. The assigned garrison moved into the barracks, but Mara didn't take up residence in the quarters that had once belonged to Conde Luiz. She offered these instead to her cousin, whom she appointed as commander of the new territory. Mara hoped that this gesture would make up for Kat's removal from the command of Spainfort and heal that old breach between them. It was also a way to keep Kat far from her until she could overcome her discomfort at being in close company with her cousin.

In spite of her intention to depart immediately, Mara had duties to her army and officers; she couldn't simply abandon them at a few day's notice. There was much to do in the preparation for the decampment of the army in the Jamesmarch, as well the deployment of the forces that would remain behind under her cousin's command.

While Kat oversaw the occupation of the Bertrandesmarch with Alyx's and Sataumie's assistance, Mara continued to sleep in her tent on the other side of the river. Messages were sent to Pendaunzel bearing news of her success and announcing her imminent return. When the single surviving Spanish guard didn't fall ill, he was set free to bear his message south. Though Delphyn had been given the care of the younger survivor of Iagoburso, it was Kat, missing her own daughter, who spent the most time looking after the little girl. In spite of frequent coaxing in the few words of Spanish Kat possessed, she could never learn the child's true name and instead called her Perdita. When Kat took up her quarters in the fortress, Delphyn and the little girl went with her. No illness nor mishap befell those who dwelt within the fortress.

No more Northlander soldiers in either the Bertrandesmarch or Jamesmarch were found mysteriously dead. Mara hadn't seen the strange creature that called itself Alys of Lyngreen since she'd cast the Dragonseye away. She hoped that that abomination was forever banished. As the days passed, her encounter with Alys seemed less and less real. Had that scene by the river's edge truly happened?

November ended and the bleak desolation of the prairie winter was upon them—a winter without snow nor rain, but grey skies replaced the merciless summer sun. Northlands troops were well established throughout the Bertrandesmarch by this time and were ready to defend the conquered territory if the Spanish should attempt to challenge them. Things were well in hand, and Mara hoped to be away before the year's end.

Mara was writing another letter to Ambris to this effect when a messenger who had arrived at the camp was brought to her in her tent. He wore the Duke's livery, a blue and gold costume very like the garb of Dafythe's heralds, but this was no boy; he was a grown man, dusty and weary after long days of riding. Mara offered him some warmed, spiced brandywine to drink before he conveyed his message to her.

"Gramercies, My Gracious Layn," the messenger replied as he accepted the drink brought to him by Ren.

As he spoke the words, "My Gracious Layn," Mara realized what news had brought him so far. "When did my father die?" she asked.

"Nearly six weeks past." The messenger dropped to one knee and bowed his head. "I beg your pardon, My Layn Duke, for bearing such sad tidings so clumsily. My Lord Ambris had writ a letter I was to give you along with this packet." He produced these items from a flat leather pouch he wore strapped around his waist beneath his livery coat. "He would write more gracefully than I can speak."

"I would rather hear such news spoken than read it." Mara held out her hands to receive the packet, which contained her father's ring and seal of office. They were hers now. "Tell me:

how did it happen?"

"He died peacefully abed," the messenger assured her. "When Lord Ambris went to the late Duke's apartments, as was always his custom in the evenings, he found My Lord Dafythe—God rest him—at the chair in his private closet with one of his histories in his lap. He thought him asleep at first, and only sent for the physician when he couldn't rouse him. They brought Lord Dafythe to his bed, where he lay for some days in a state between wake and sleep. He suffered no pain, Duke Marguerytt, and at times would speak. He made such farewells as he was able to to those who were near to him in the Palace. He asked for you, and for the Irish Prince. At the end, he fell to sleep and didn't wake again. Your brother Lord Ambris stayed by his side until the last."

Mara didn't know whether or not to be comforted by this information. It sounded like a peaceable way for an aged man to end his life, but she'd seen many younger men and women die lately. Was it God's choice to take Dafythe now, or was this more malignant work from that creature who called herself Alys? Dafythe's death had occurred after the last of the strange deaths here, after Alys had been banished. "Did he receive last rights?" she asked.

"Yes, My Layn. The ceremony was performed before his last breath departed his body. Lord Ambris bids you not to fret. Lord Dafythe had made his peace with a Greater Lord in these past months, and a soul such as his must surely see Heaven."

"Certainly," Mara agreed, and crossed herself. Her father's soul, at least, was safe. But it was odd to think that, when she returned home to Pendaunzel, Dafythe would no longer be there.

She wouldn't weep for him—not now, when others might see. Her grief as a daughter was a private matter. She would spend her tears later.

She'd been brought up to become Duke of the Northlands one day. That day had arrived. Mara suddenly felt the weight of her new responsibilities pressing down upon her. There was so much that must be done. Her coronation must be planned. Members of her cabinet must be appointed. She wouldn't arrive home in time for her father's funeral, but she must commission memorial masses for his soul in churches throughout the dukedom. She must gift those who had been loyal to Dafythe. There were a multitude of ceremonies, small and great, to mark the transition of power and policy; Ambris would surely take care of many of these in her absence, but others required her presence. The entire Empire, if not the whole of the civilized world, would go into mourning. Everyone would look to her to lead them. Ambris and Kat would aid her, of course, but the duty was chiefly hers.

What must she attend to first?

The messenger had taken out Ambris's letter, and was reading from it. "My Lord your brother also sends to inform you that he maintains his position as Regent in your absence at the request of the Council. Lord Dafythe lies in state in the Hartshall. Lord Ambris will delay the funeral `til you and Prince Katheryne are able to attend, but he desires your return to Pendaunzel as soon as you may travel."

"Yes, of course. We'll come at once." Kat would have to accompany her home; Alyx would be given command of the new march in her stead. Mara must be the one to tell Kat about Dafythe's death, for Dafythe had been like a father to the Irish Prince as well.

"My cousin Kat is across the river at the fortress," she informed the guards who had escorted the messenger to her. "Go and tell her I wish her to come to me here immediately. I also bid you find my nephews Eduarde and Arthur and have them brought to me. Do not tell them what you've heard spoken of here. I shall tell them of Lord Dafythe's passing myself. Then send for my captains. After I've spoken to them privately, you may announce my father's death to the troops and declare most solemn mourning for the Duke of the Northlands." She turned to Ren, who had heard the news as well. Tears flowed down the little maid's cheeks. "Rennie, pack a light traveling bag for me and one for yourself. We must travel ahead of the troops, and the rest of our belongings must follow with them. We'll ride with my cousin and nephews at daybreak tomorrow to reach Jamesfort as soon as we can."

The girl curtseyed. "Yes, Prince Mar– I mean, yes, My Layn Duke."

Pendaunzel
1957

tuenty-et-quar

Mara returned to Pendaunzel late one evening at the beginning of April, more than four months after she'd begun her long homeward journey. Her entourage had been small to facilitate rapid travel; when she'd left the Jamesmarch, only Kat and her nephews and their squires, Bel, Ren, Bard Delphyn, and the Spanish child had accompanied her. These last two wouldn't travel all the way to Pendaunzel with the rest of the party, for Delphyn had been charged with a special errand to convey the child safely to the Sisters of St. Samandra, where Mara's own younger nephews and niece were being educated. She and Kat had agreed on this.

In spite of Mara's plans, travel was slow. In addition to the more arduous work of navigating boats upstream on the Michelne and Myame rivers, the journey was fraught with small delays at every town and village where they stopped. All the Northlands had heard of Dafythe's death before the news had reached Mara. While the Northlanders sincerely mourned the passing of the only Duke all but the very oldest had ever known, those who had the opportunity were eager to see his successor. Mara couldn't refuse them: being viewed by the public was one of the primary duties of royalty, and this journey home from the westward marches was unofficially her first progress as Duke. She was obliged to stop, if only for an hour or two, to show herself to her subjects before taking a meal or finding a bed for the night. But there were many such stops along the way.

By the time they reached Pendaunzel, she and the other members of her family were past their initial grief, and Mara had had plenty of time to make plans. These, she discussed with Kat.

Though she'd received a hint of Mara's plans in her refusal to occupy Iagoburso, Kat was openly baffled by her cousin's declaration that she would never again campaign against the Spanish territories at their borders. "Not ever, Mara?"

"Not unless they become a clear threat to us," Mara had answered. "If the Spaniards dare attempt to invade the Northland marches, of course I will defend what is rightfully Norman land. No good Duke would do otherwise. Even Father would've granted that such defense is necessary. But I will not seek war for its own sake without provocation."

"What will you do instead?"

"Strive to see that the Northlands are governed by a Duke as worthy as the last. I will give all my life to that cause."

Kat had smiled at this. "You hope to become more like Uncle Dafythe?"

"I doubt I can ever be so good as he, but if God will it, I shall try."

Mara hadn't confided, however, her reasons for this decision. She never told her cousin what had occurred on the day when Iagoburso had fallen, what Alys had said to her. If Kat or any of Mara's other companions had noticed that she no longer wore the Dragonseye, they didn't remark upon it, nor connect its absence with her abrupt change of heart.

Along the final stages of her journey, Mara had been met by messengers from her brother, keeping her apprised of events in Pendaunzel. She knew that her news regarding the capture of Santiago and the death of Bertrande had been received by Ambris. She knew that her father's body had been embalmed and lay in state upon draperies of imperial purple and gold, as befit an Emperor's son. Liveried palace guards kept vigil, while monks from Belminstre knelt and intoned constant prayer for the departed soul. The obligations of royalty to be seen did not end with death; per long-standing custom, Dafythe had initially been available for viewing in an open coffin, but a carved wooden cover bearing an effigy of the late Duke had since been placed atop the coffin lid. Thousands of people from all over the Northlands and beyond had come to view him and, according to Ambris, were still coming every day. Distinguished personages from all parts of the world were converging to pay their respects to a man they had greatly admired. Many were lodged within Pendaunzel, but those of the highest ranks were made welcome as visitors within the Palace. Dafythe's final resting place, a grand tomb of marble and granite was being prepared in Othelie Chapel; he would be interred there beside his predecessors during the performance of the final funeral rites, which would be held once the new Duke was present.

In reply, Mara sent these same messengers riding back to Pendaunzel more swiftly than she was able to travel herself, informing her brother that that day was not far ahead.

The streets of Pendaunzel were still festooned with banners of white crepe, symbolizing the city's state of mourning, but it seemed as if the inhabitants were also past their first grief. Mara and her companions sensed a curious air of excitement within the city as they made their way toward the Palace. It was more than the arrival at last of their new Duke, though those who spotted Mara riding down the Processional with her entourage shouted their delight and good wishes to her.

"It's the Emperor, My Gracious Layn!" the sergeant at the Palace gate told Mara after he had let them in. "He's here! I was here on duty this same hour last night, when there was news from the docks that a ship with purple flags had come in, then a herald came right here to this very gate and announced it was the Emperor Kharles himself."

"He must've come for Father's funeral," said Mara, touched by this gesture from her kinsman.

"That's right, My Duke. He was expecting to meet you, but Lord Ambris went down to the ship to welcome him in your stead, and they came back together with all the imperial guards and attendants marching in front of them as well as behind so that I could scarce catch a glimpse of him even though he passed nearly as close to me as you are now yourself. The Emperor's been up at the Palace since."

Mara sent Ren to see to her rooms and Bel to announce her arrival to the Palace guard and take them in hand as their new commander. Then she and Kat gave their horses to the squires and went to seek Ambris. Eduarde and Arthur were already crossing the lawn ahead of them for, even from the gates, they could see lights blazing in the State Hall.

A somber sort of celebration was going on in the ancient hall. There was no music, but everyone was dressed in their finest garments and wine and dainties were abundantly available. As Mara and Kat entered through one of the open doors to the lawn, they gazed upon a crowd of faces, some familiar, others belonging to strangers. Laurel was present, but this came as no surprise to Mara, for Ambris had written that she'd brought his younger children from Eadeshire to attend the funeral. Andemyon was here too, and that *was* a surprise. The boy was inconspicuously dressed in the sooty grey of a wizard's son, but he'd grown tall in the year and a half since he'd been sent from the court and his bright golden curls drew her attention even with so many fair-haired Europeans among the crowd. He was in the company of a gaunt and awkward-looking dark-haired youth in the black robes of a magician; Mara had no idea who this could be.

But what struck her foremost was the number of guardsmen, attendants, and nobles wearing imperial livery—golden lions on cloth of rich, reddish purple. The hall seemed awash in the royal color, which overwhelmed the finery of the other guests. This must be the moment Magician Peter had foreseen.

The crowd fell silent at Mara's entrance. Everyone bowed low, except for one man who remained upright, regarding her with frank curiosity. This attitude of superiority alone would have told her that she faced Kharles V, Emperor of the Normans, even if he weren't wearing a gold crown. Kharles also had the Plantagenet face; like Frederik, he bore a strong resemblance to her own father. Dressed in long velvet robes, he reminded Mara of the portrait of young Duke Dafythe at his coronation, which hung in the gallery of the Manor—but Kharles's face wore an expression of amused cynicism that she'd never seen on Dafythe's face nor Frederik's.

Under her imperial cousin's appraising gaze, Mara felt a little shabby. She and Kat had only just left their horses and were still in their riding leathers with muddy boots and hair pulled sloppily back into braids. They might easily be taken for messengers from the new Duke instead of the Duke and Irish Prince themselves.

Ambris had been embracing his sons, but left them now to

cross the hall and greet Mara. "I hadn't expected you to arrive tonight, My Duke," he apologized, and dropped to one knee at her feet. "We've kept watch for your return for many weeks, but I received no notice that you were so near Pendaunzel."

This formality of address from her brother was jarring, but Mara understood that it was a public declaration of his loyalty to her. Ambris meant to make it clear to everyone present that, although he'd taken charge during her absence, he'd been acting all the while in her service and didn't intend to remain in charge now that she was here.

Mara held out her hands to take his and raise him before she responded. "There was no time to send notice. We rode as fast as we could these last few days, since we were so near to home and eager to be here. `Tis wonderful to see you again, Ambris, even under these circumstances." She hugged him without formality. This was *her* public declaration; she meant everyone to witness how much she loved and trusted her brother. She didn't intend to govern the Northlands without him.

"You mustn't mind that you weren't ready for us, Ambris," Kat added. "We're hardly ready for such a party as this ourselves."

Others around the room were rising now. Kharles came forward, smiling. "My dear cousin Margueryt!" he said. "I've looked forward for so long to this meeting."

Mara bowed to him as her liege and sovereign lord. "No more eagerly than I have, sire."

"Ambris has given me news of your success at the frontier. So we have a new march to protect the Northlands! I expect you'll expand the borders of this Dukedom to double its size before the end of your reign if you carry on this same course."

"You honor me," Mara responded modestly, though a dry tone in Kharles's voice confused her. She wasn't entirely certain that this was meant to be praise. "But I have no intention of continuing any further campaigns against the Spanish on our borders. The governing of the Northlands as they are is my principal concern."

"I'm astonished to hear it, Cousin. From all I've heard of you, you enjoy nothing better than fighting the Spanish wherever you find them. You might well spend half your life on the frontier and safely give little thought to the mundane tasks of government. Your brother seems to have done very well in this respect during your absence," Kharles observed.

Ambris likewise did not appear pleased at this remark even though it sounded like a compliment.

"'Tis strange we haven't met before this, Cousin Marguerуt. Your brother Ambris, of course, I've known since I was a child, and I had the great pleasure of welcoming our cousin, Katheryne of Eireland, to our court in London when this trouble over Naufarre began." Kharles nodded to acknowledge Kat, who also sank neatly down on one knee and rose again.

There were many other dignitaries and grand nobles beyond the Emperor in the State Hall, though they hadn't come forward: German and Italian princes, or their representatives, the Tsar of Russe's emissary, the Doge's, the Duke of Burgundy, even courtiers from Spain. Ambris had undoubtedly extended the proper courtesies to each of them on their arrival, but Mara would have to make them welcome personally once she was fit to do so. It might be seen as a slight if she greeted them while she was still mud-spattered and disheveled from her travels.

"Your pardon," she said formally to Kharles, as well as those who were near enough to hear her. "As our cousin of Eireland has observed, we weren't expecting to return home in the midst of such festivities. I pray you await while we make ourselves more suitable to receive such company as are gathered here."

"And I'd like to see Tyrelspethe—my daughter, sire," Kat told Kharles. "I've thought of little else during the months we were away. She must've grown greatly since I saw her last. I don't doubt she's walking and speaks full sentences now."

"Indeed she does, though she isn't always easy to understand," said Ambris. "You'll hardly know the child when you see her."

"Nor she me, I'm afraid."

"Yes, certainly go, Cousin Katheryne," Kharles responded with a generous laugh. "I understand how it is. I'm devoted to my own children, my little Prince and all his base-born brothers and sisters."

Some appeared shocked, and Mara herself was startled to hear the Emperor speak so frankly of his illegitimate children but, after all, Kat had mentioned her own daughter first. "I shall return shortly," she promised, and with another bow to Kharles, accompanied Kat out.

Ren had had time to order hot water brought to Mara's chambers and laid out clean linen for her, so that Mara could wash immediately and make herself presentable. Months of living in camps had taught her how to dress swiftly; within a very few minutes, she had changed into a clean shirt and hose, and put on a plain velvet tunic of dark blue. With Ren's assistance, she unbraided and combed out her hair so that it fell long and unbound in the fashion of the nobility, but she put on no ornaments nor devices of her rank. Since Dafythe's death, she was no longer Prince of Gossunge, but she wouldn't be consecrated as Duke of the Northlands herself until she was anointed and received the ducal coronet at her coronation. That ceremony would not take place until after her father's funeral.

These refurbishments completed, Mara went down the corridor to the nursery, and found that her cousin was still reacquainting herself with her small daughter and Ambris's younger children. She hadn't changed her clothes yet.

"Make my excuses, please, Mara, and go on without me," Kat requested. "It's you they want to see. No one'll regard my absence at all."

As Mara made her way back through the Manor alone, she passed the rooms that had been given to the Emperor for his visit. These were the finest apartments in the Palace, except for those usually occupied by the Duke's family. More servants and attendants in imperial livery were here. For one horrifying moment, Mara glimpsed the figure of a small and dark-haired young woman walking down the corridor some distance ahead of her. Alys? But, no. The resemblance was merely superficial. That creature couldn't be here in Pendaunzel.

Once she returned to the State Hall, Mara performed the proper ceremonies of welcome, then thanked all her guests for honoring her father's memory with their presence. Surely a golden age had passed with the death of Dafythe. The world was diminished without him. As for what the future foretold for *her*, she could only do her duty and serve the Lord's will.

She next sought out the members of the Council—*her*

councilors now—Peaque and Tuxsetau, Lt. Uismarde, and Rafenshighte, to speak to them about her plans for new appointments. Places must be found for her trusted companions, not only Kat and Bel, but her other friends still in the Bertrandesmarch. They must be rewarded for their loyalty, but she would discuss this with Ambris before she made any decisions. There would be additions among her advisors, but those currently in the Council could be assured that she wouldn't dismiss them.

"Even me, My Duke?" Rafenshighte asked. "You know that I've been as loyal to you as any of your Shieldmaid companions, and it has always been my hope to serve you as I served my late lord."

Knowing how Geoffrey had served her father, Mara didn't find this a reassuring prospect. Nevertheless, she answered carefully, "If you are willing to serve me better than you served my father, Lord Rafenshighte, then I will be pleased to keep you as my diplomatic officer. I can't deny you have great skills in making yourself agreeable, and you'll be of use when we must have dealings with the Spanish." This much was true, but Geoffrey mustn't be allowed to hope that he would ever be more to her than one among her many advisors. She had no plans to choose a consort but, if she ever did, it would not be him.

Thereafter, she went about the room, speaking informally to those she met. She embraced Laurel and her eldest nephew Eadrik, who hadn't gone on the westward campaign with his brothers, and had a brief but civil conversation with Martleanne, who was now serving as Ambris's secretary. She found Magician Peter and promised him a longer talk when time allowed about the fate of the Dragonseye. Andemyon shyly presented his young magician friend, Mikha, who had only just been confirmed a full wizard and was looking for a position to begin his career.

At intervals, she spoke to both Ambris and Kharles, and again perceived a peculiar tension between the two men. She was well aware that her brother disapproved of the young Emperor's personal conduct, even when Kharles had been a boy. Ambris couldn't forgive the cruel and dismissive treatment of the princess who had later become Ambris's first wife. But that had been more than twenty years ago, and this resentment seemed fresh. Was it simply that she was seeing her brother with Kharles for the first time, or had they quarreled anew since the Emperor's arrival yesterday?

When she asked Ambris, he told her, "Be wary of him, Mara. In spite of his smiles and semblance of good cheer, I believe he doesn't mean well by you."

"What do you mean?"

"Last night when we first met, he questioned your fitness to be Duke. He's heard some muddled tale about your vision of the Sonnedragon and asked if you truly believed in it. He seemed to me to be suggesting that you might be mad."

"And that you might be more fit to govern?" Mara saw now why her brother had made such a public declaration of his loyalty. "Well, he can see for himself that I'm not mad. You'll be pleased to hear that I've given that all up as nonsense, dear Ambris. My dragon was a dream, no more."

As the evening's festivities drew toward their end and people began to retire, Mara thought longingly of her own bed. She'd spent a long and weary day riding hard for many hours without stopping long enough to have a proper meal, only to come home and find the duties attending this occasion awaiting her. She was exhausted.

She made her apologies to the persons still in the hall and bid them continue to enjoy themselves as long as they pleased. Kharles was among those remaining; as Mara was about to leave, he caught hold of her sleeve and said softly, "A moment's conversation, I pray you, Cousin Margueryt, before you go to rest. There's a matter of grave importance to the safety of the Empire that you and I must discuss between ourselves. It cannot wait `til tomorrow."

"Ambris..." Mara turned to look for her brother. Surely he must also be apprised of this serious matter? And, after Ambris's warning to be wary of the Emperor, she would be glad to have him at her side during this conference.

"No, this doesn't concern him," Kharles said quickly. "What I have to say is for you alone to hear. It is the chief reason I came to the Northlands at the news of Uncle Dafythe's death. Will you come with me, Cousin?"

Together, they walked across the torch-lit gardens to the

Manor, and went up to the rooms where the Emperor and his attendants were lodged. Kharles waved aside those lordlings, grooms, and servants who bowed low as he and Mara entered, and escorted her to a private closet adjacent to his bedchamber.

"What is it?" Mara asked once they were alone. "Is there some danger?"

"Yes, I suppose you could say there is a danger," Kharles replied as he took a seat with his back to the door. "It is a delicate and most difficult problem, and I consult you so that we can find a resolution to it that safeguards us both."

"Do you ask my aid in your campaign in Naufarre?" Mara guessed that this must be the 'problem' Kharles was alluding to. "You haven't subdued Prince Juan?"

"Alas, not yet," said Kharles. "Uncle Juan continues to evade capture, but I have no need of your assistance there. Naufarre will soon be brought under my hand and order restored. It isn't Uncle Juan who troubles me. He is no threat to this Empire. There is another relation, closer to me in blood, dear cousin Marguery t, whom I fear more."

Mara couldn't imagine who Kharles was referring to. "Uncle Egan, Kat's father?" she guessed a second time. "Is there rebellion in Eireland?"

"No," Kharles answered. "Our upstart Irish uncle has been behaving himself of late."

They had many other relatives beyond the Empire's borders but, as far as Mara knew, all were currently on peaceable terms with the Normans. "Who then?"

"You, Cousin."

"*Me*?" Mara was astounded and bewildered. "But why?"

"Your reputation precedes you," Kharles explained. "In these past years, I have heard tale upon tale of your triumphs. They say there hasn't been a general in the field to match you since the days when our Grandfather Redlyon wielded his sword at the head of his armies. You never lose a battle. All enemies fall before you, one way or another. Who wouldn't fear such a fierce warrior-maid?"

He smiled as he spoke. Was this a jest? Mara would like to believe that Kharles was only joking, and yet she felt that her imperial cousin meant every word. "You feel me a threat to you because I've been more successful in battle?"

"Well," Kharles admitted, "I do grow weary of hearing your name cried up and down the streets of London, Paris, and even Edinburgh. The only thing the common folk of all my kingdoms can agree upon is their hatred of Spain and their love of you. You may think it petty of me, but it is no small matter. We Normans worship our valorous heroes, and you've given them a new hero. They might begin to think you'd make a better Emperor than I. It isn't wise to steal a sovereign's place in the hearts of his people, Cousin, especially when you are so close a kinswoman. Surely you realize how near you are? I have no brothers nor sisters living, and only one legitimate son, whom I confess I worry for. Now that your father is gone, one frail little boy is all that stands between you and the imperial throne."

"I've no ambition to become Emperor!" Mara protested, appalled at this accusation.

"No?" Kharles regarded her with his eyebrows upraised. "Well, perhaps the thought of it hasn't occurred to you... not yet, at any rate. In addition to your bravery in battle, the other quality everyone speaks of when I ask them of you is that you are a devout woman of the highest religious principles. It may take a great many cheers from adoring crowds and even more encouragement from interested advisors to convince you that God wills it so. From all the stories I've heard, Grandfather was just the same. You believe in Divine Will, don't you? I don't myself. I believe in power seized and wielded for its own ends. When I listened to the tales of your victories and saw where they might lead, I was greatly troubled about how I might maintain the power I now possess. I'm not so valiant a warrior, as my efforts to quash our rebellious Uncle Juan attest. I didn't see how I could succeed if you were to challenge me—and then an answer came from a quarter I didn't expect. I've recently made the acquaintance of an extraordinary young maiden." He smiled. "No doubt you've heard gossip about my penchant for pretty maidens, but she isn't one of *those*. Not pretty enough to my suit my tastes. I'm certain she must be a Seer of great gifts. She says not, but she did tell me a most astonishing tale. She promised that I'd see an end to all that troubled me. My fortunes would improve. My enemies would be vanquished. I might even have a glorious future to rival

Grandfather Redlyon's."

Mara had begun to tremble at these last words. "I am no enemy to you, sire."

"I hope you will never be. I've no wish to see harm befall you, dear Cousin. No sudden unfortunate and grotesque accidents. But I must protect my own position. That's why I hope we can come to an agreement between us that will preserve us both. I tried to suggest to that priggish brother of yours that he'd be a better Duke than you would, but he refused to hear it. Too damnably honest. He won't think of usurping you even with my blessings! At least, I have the comfort of knowing that Ambris's honor keeps him from acting against *me* as it prevents him from acting against you. But he's no use to me. I also considered your marriage. Old Ulaf of Iseland is a widower again, and our cousin Alexandre of Russe is in want of a bride. I had thought you might do well as Tsarina, thousands of miles away in Moskba, but now that I see you, I realize that that won't do. It seems to me now that the best solution to our difficulty is for to you remove yourself voluntarily."

"You mean, you want me to abdicate?"

"I want you safely out of my way, Cousin. What I propose will keep you safe from me, and I from you. Tomorrow morning when you meet with your Council, you will announce that you intend to go into religious retreat and contemplate taking holy orders. Some remote abbey, I think. You may choose whatever one suits your preferences, as long as it is far from Pendaunzel, on the outskirts of your dukedom. Keep your title if you wish. You may remain nominally Duke of the Northlands, since Ambris will refuse to take it himself. He will continue to serve as Regent in your stead. So long as he believes you've made this choice of your own will, he'll accept this duty. Neither of us need worry for the Northlands in his care. Once there are no more campaigns against the Spanish to increase your fame around the Empire, your past glories will slip from the memories of the common folk. You agree?"

"What if I refuse?" Mara responded desperately. "You can't force me into retirement. You can't depose me as Duke unless you mean to accuse me of treason—and I've done nothing to warrant it! Even an Emperor doesn't hold such power."

“Not an Emperor,” Kharles agreed. “Nevertheless, I do have such power. It was given me recently, with proofs that I cannot disbelieve. I’ve been told that if you do not comply with my wishes, then some horrible fate will befall you and I’ll have precisely what I want in the end regardless. It’s better that you not stand against me. You know what this strange magic can do.”

Mara could scarcely believe what she was hearing. Kharles’s demand that she leave her place as Duke was terrible enough, but now this conversation was taking on the unreal and horrific tones of a nightmare. Kharles seemed to be referring to things that only she knew. She, and one other. “How–?”

The door behind Kharles opened and a person entered the room without apologizing for the intrusion nor making any obsequies toward either Kharles or Mara. Why indeed should she bow to them? It was Alys, no longer dressed as a common guardswoman, but in the Emperor’s livery.

“You refused my gifts, Duke Margueryt,” she said, “but the Emperor Kharles has not.”

Kharles’s hand went to his throat. Mara saw that among the heavy chains and seals of office, another, slender golden chain hung about his neck. Suspended as a pendant from it was a streaked red stone like a flawed opal.

The End

www.ingramcontent.com/pod-product-compliance
Lightning Source LLC
Chambersburg PA
CBHW060141260626
47160CB00001B/78
* 9 7 8 0 9 8 4 8 3 2 5 1 4 *